KEYS TO THE "V" DOOR

CURT ORLOFF

ISBN: 978-1-963565-44-7(Paperback)
ISBN: 978-1-963565-45-4(E-book)

Library of Congress Control Number: 2025912392

Printed in the United States of America

Published by:

info@thequippyquill.com
(302) 295-2278

TABLE OF CONTENT

CHAPTER 1

"Waiter after, this rabbit is tough," I said with equal amounts of irritation and disappointment.

"I'm sorry, sir. I'll get another," assured the deferential youth.

"Ensure the replacement didn't also die from exhaustion at the dog track."

The apprentice chef remained expressionless.

Seeking approval from Father, I glanced across the table, but he seemed to be in deep communion with his fettuccini. I can't figure him out lately. He's the one who told me to be condescending to the help. It's not my nature to stick my nose in the air. Yet, when he explained how doing so helps promote the smooth functioning of society, I became a convert. Treat people like equals and they'll lose their desire to improve, like in China during Mao's Cultural Revolution. Let on you think they are inferior, and either they'll self-destruct, or try to prove you wrong. Some think Father is merely another beneficiary of the current oil boom. If Iraq hadn't attacked Iran and the price of oil had remained static, he still would have succeeded. All Cunninghams have relished challenges. Taller than average, with strong, broad features, exuding health and vigor we looked like people who relished challenges. Father vindicated the name besmirched by Huey Long's screeds and I intend to elevate it into one uttered alongside the pantheons of the oilfield service business. "Randall Cunningham" someday might be as famous as "Red Adair", if Hollywood can find another John Wayne to play me. Richard Gere might be good. People say I combine the same sensitivity and rugged good looks.

"You'll have a place of your own," Father said to the prompt waitress who refilled his water glass.

"Her?" I asked as the obese woman padded off. "She can barely make change." I reminded him of his derogatory comments about her when he helped establish the restaurant.

"I was under a lot of stress, already overextended," he confessed. "You know, for all of Chef Powell's talent, he had only come up with dry holes."

You know? I thought to myself. *When was the last time he said, 'You know?' Never. He'd cuff me if I talked like a teenager. And I am one!*

Something's wrong. He's not even smirking at the people standing outside, waiting to be let in. Not that I condone such behavior, snobbery without instructiveness is sheer self-indulgence. But it was his habit to be this way, a hold-over from his difficult youth. I accepted it. After all, without his skill and money, L-Powell's might not be the tourist attraction it is today.

Something's not right. He used to be as consistent as his wife, my fourth stepmother. He was as rock-solid as she, only he was that way because he had to be to run his business. She is because her brain cells had atrophied from lack of use.

Only when the sun finally mummifies her and she ceases to be desirable will she need to apply the mental power to run a boutique or serve as a house mother at a sorority.

"Ow, that's hot!" our little gold digger exclaimed.

"One doesn't drink a Cajun martini," I chastised. "One sip it."

"Thanks, heart; I forgot."

Noticing a spot on her wool gabardine pants, she let out a wail peculiar to the subspecies inhabiting eastern New Orleans, where industrial fumes have played so much havoc with the denizens' vocal cords they sound more retarded than they are.

Her Rolex banged furiously against the corona of gold bracelets manacling her wrists as she struggled with the offending stain.

"These stains ain't gonna come out. I need another outfit," she brayed in her peculiar dialect, the infamous "yat" (as in "where you at") which sounds more Bostonian than southern.

Neither her "cat-lick" rosary nor her gold-braided necklace obscured the cleavage that protruded as she bent over. Looking deep into her mane of blonde hair I could see a substratum of black roots. Our latter-day Mamie Van Doren knows what pays the bills. With little to do besides preening herself, Kimberly ought to arouse her libido. Got to give the devil his (or in this case, her) due. She's smart enough to capitalize on the fact men enter this world through a womb and spend the rest of their lives trying to get back in.

"I got to go to the bathroom," she whined. "Where's my purse?"

I and every other male except the enormous chef watched her wiggle down the narrow aisle. Instead of the pride and vanity, that usually brightened Father's face at such times, he appeared as disinterested as Chef Powell. The famous trencherman displayed more pride in the chicken jambalaya he was stirring than Father did in his voluptuous spouse. Something was wrong.

I contemplatively sipped my Cajun martini. My mouth instantly exploded with pain. To my chagrin, I noticed through the tears all eyes previously affixed on Kimberly's backside were now on me. Nevertheless, thanks to a boiled beer artichoke, a broiled eggplant, and preternatural control over my emotions, I was able to turn defeat into victory.

"We should give up selling tubulars, and start marketing this stuff to service stations," I said in a controlled voice. "The state should subsidize farmers to grow jalapeños and forget about ethanol."

Appreciative laughter replaced the disconcerting silence. So much for that gaffe.

"That would be no problem for me," claimed a broker wearing an Irish fisherman's sweater. "Instead of rounding up doctors and lawyers to buy rigs, I'd get them to pay for land and seeds. They couldn't care one way or another."

"As long as they think there's a fast dollar to be made on it," affirmed a landman wearing a button-down oxford shirt, khaki pants, and docksiders. "Could send them all on searches for keys to the 'V' door."

From the murmurs of agreement and smug looks, it was obvious every male knew what he was referring to. Most had experienced the rite of passage, it had been such a popular initiation in the days before the oilfield became so technical. The embarrassment of finding out a "V" door is the ramp between the drill floor and rig floor helped establish a bond with all who had fallen for what was analogous to a snipe hunt.

It's understandable that when a coterie of oilmen start talking, there's little that can be done to distract them. Kimberly failed to turn a fraction of the heads turned during her measured departure, and she resented it. How dare they talk shop instead of ogling her. A world-class pouter, she dejectedly returned to her gumbo.

Women are spoiled. Most of the female diners looked as put off as Kimberly by their meal tickets continuing discussion of business, oblivious to the fact they owed their comfortable lives to it. Women, you can't live with'em and you can't shoot'em.

I remember when Father's second wife refused to believe he wasn't able to afford a necklace she couldn't live without.

"All you have to do is write a check," she claimed with inscrutable logic.

I think it was the airhead's Father and Grandfather brought home who made me a misogynist. What type of woman would follow a "boomer" like my Grandfather or Father as they sold tools and scouted for oil companies throughout the boonies? The same kind who didn't mind them being away ninety percent of the time. They didn't have to be Jewish to be princesses. A woman of my class may spend money more wisely and purchase more tasteful goods, but she abides by the credo of "What's yours is mine, and what's mine is mine" just as tenaciously as the Kimberly of this world.

It doesn't matter if they're born at Charity or Touro, schooled at East Jefferson or Sacred Heart Academy. A princess of the Court of Rex and one from some shopping mall Krewe are superficially different. What did Ambrose Bierce say? "Oh, to fall into a woman's arms without falling into her hands."

"All I know is I want to put on the best party the Woman's League has ever seen," Kimberly injected into the money-oriented conversation the broker struck up with Father. Too beautiful to chastise, both ignored her non sequitur. No one who sops "da debris" from dressed po' boys at a company outing can hope to impress the old money in this town.

Father might have a crack at being King of Endymion, but he knows Rex, Comus, or Momus are out of the question. He knows his limitations. Not her, she thinks money is the key. Look at her, mushing dirty rice and crowder peas together, and shoving the mess onto the salad fork. Before her first cotillion, a debutante knows which spoon to use for shrimp andouille gumbo, and what fork should spear her catfish court bouillon.   A dessert fork is Kimberly's trident and a coffee spoon is her ladle. It's inexcusable to be so inept at such a place as Powell's, one of the few de rigor diners Father can take her. Why he has quit trying to turn her into a lady, I'll never know. He should know how to do it by now, after dealing with all his former wives. She could cost us business.

Donning a Brooks Brothers suit changes Father's personality. All Christian Dior or Oscar de la Rente originals do for our Eliza Doolittle is dress her up. At least Cinderella acted like royalty at the ball.

"This gumbo, it got okra in it," she informed us, once she quit making a pretense of following the conversation. "Real gumbo don't get okra in it."

"I agree," said Father.

I agree. What is this? Normally he'd indulge in a clever put-down, totally and deliciously above Kimberly's gorgeous head (especially with someone listening). One does not let one's guard down in front of these diners. The business can rend more friendships than it generates. Lest someone think Father is losing his grip, I brayed out my objection to the blaze' attitude the landman posited toward a recent case of official malfeasance.

"The D.A. has every right to indict anyone who misuses the public's trust," I declared. "I hope he does make political hay out of it."

"That's how business is done here," remarked the apologist in defense of the corrupt officeholder.

"He's lucky he wasn't killed. I know I'd want blood if someone shut my rig down because I didn't let a relative haul my wastes."

"Huey Long's deduct box isn't history it's a legacy," said another misguided soul.

"People think we don't have separation of power," rejoined the landman, trying to be funny. "We do. We've got Texaco, the Mafia, and the governor."

The broker, not Father, leaped to the defense of free enterprise. "That salesman of the company the governor owns, can you believe he's been made state conservation commissioner?"

"As much as I believe Edward's hunting buddy got his hauling permit reinstated," I said, gesturing with my fork. "Anyone caught rigging bids and making bribes had better be connected. It's more of a crime not to be well connected than it is to break the law."

Trying to get Father involved, I dove into the role of devil's advocate with a relish, really stirring things up, stripping away veneers of politeness, and uncovering unrepentant populists.

"Still get to keep more of what you make than what you used to," said a diner, while the landman (proving the stench of the Kingfish still permeated native thought) proclaimed: "At least you don't have to work for the governor to make a living."

The place scintillated with fiery rhetoric, the kind we thrived on at home when Grandfather was still alive. Yet Father kept quiet...until Mister Docksiders pricked a nerve. "Too bad Judge Perez has passed. Plaquemines Parish hasn't been the same since," he said.

"For the better," Father remarked.

"It hasn't been as organized since."

"Bribing the assessor to overestimate the value of my pipe yard was one way he paid for all that control. I'll wager I've paid half again what I should have in taxes."

Go, father, I thought. But rather than recite the tyrant's most egregious crimes against civil rights he merely grumbled about the I.D.'s our workers had to present to enter his fiefdom.

"Here's to clout!" chortled the landman with too much exuberance. Everybody knows since the judge died, his clan has been self-destructing, squabbling, and ratting on each other to the feds. With this being common knowledge, I determined the best response was no response.

By making a big deal of the tender rabbit the obsequious waiter returned with, I managed to defuse the situation.

"He'll go a long way," I affirmed. Turning to the landman, I asked if he also agreed, seeing how efficaciously the waiter swooped up his dirty dishes in passing. To disagree was to risk censure, and if there's anything a political animal like a Perez well-wisher wishes to avoid, it is censure.

"I wish the Saints' receivers had hands like that," he said.

"Couldn't hurt," said the broker. "What did they do last season? Won one in a row."

"But we still love them," I remarked. "They're all ours."

"Only in New Orleans," averred a fan.

Yes, only in New Orleans, I thought. *The Big Easy, as the saying goes, is "The city that cares forgot", but knows how fragile and fickle life is.*

"We've learned to embrace all we can," I remarked. "Ragheads make us rich by fighting among themselves, and a hurricane comes to take it all away."

This precipitated an expected flurry of horror stories that energized the never-say-die commentators as much as they bored their dinner companions. Their embellishments triggered a mass migration to the women's washroom. Their continued embellishments ended most of the dates. At Kimberly's insistence, we too joined the exodus, after impressing everyone with our platinum Visa card.

"Roger, you promised not to talk shop," my stepmother scolded.

"I get carried away sometimes," Father meekly apologized.

"Hey, quit shoving, we're next in line," complained someone in the queue to someone behind him as we squeezed out the door.

"People should learn to pay the price of not being in the inner circle," I remarked.

"You shouldn't be so rash," said Father, totally out of character.

"They got no class," said Kimberly, imitating an idiot.

She may be right, although not the way she had in mind. True aristocrats might not have snarled, then again, true aristocrats would not subject themselves to a two-hour wait. The upper crust knows only investors and friends are granted immediate entrance. Whoever didn't have the prescience or good nature to help a Cajun with a lot of talent but a bad track record deserves to be inconvenienced.

"These people will learn like we had to learn," I reflected aloud, trying to elicit a reply.

No response.

Trying harder, I volunteered how we, and those who still need polishing like they, are turning the town around. New blood has always kept this town alive. The Creoles laughed at the Englishman Caldwell when he turned a swamp into Saint Charles Avenue with his hotel and theatre. Social second-stringers built the Garden District. And who could forget how the most corrupt lottery in history financed the French Opera House? It's our turn now.

"You can bet on that, heart," replied Kimberly. Proving she entirely missed the point, she gushed like a can of soda pop about how we were on the threshold of being included among the city's elite. At least that's what I inferred she said. Interpreting her unique English is almost as daunting as interpreting Cajun French. I'm sure General Butler's occupational force had as hard a time understanding her argot during the Civil War as German wiretappers had trying to translate the French-Canadian signalmen the Allies used in World War One.

As an idiot savant, I'm sure she'll prevail upon Father to invite her betters to a party. Some will have to come for business purposes, others to get their name on the society pages. Getting written up in "Vivant" is the adult equivalent of appearing in one's high school yearbook.

"We're going to turn this town around," I averred as I picked up the pace. "Look at those carriage houses. Falling apart. Wasted. A little T.L.C. and they'd quintuple in value, and make Decatur look sharp, like it used to be."

"Takes money to make money," said our concubine; to whit, Father said nothing.

Without us what would New Orleans be? Strip joints, twenty-four-hour bars, the good time city of Carnival, and young blacks tap dancing on the recumbent body of a decaying national treasure. No wonder Tennessee Williams decried the modernization of Poydras Street. Like a fly, he feeds on carrion. To him, the bohemian antique shop and the Hellenic bar a coterie of Greek sailors were headed toward were perfect backdrops for another play about the decline of the South. To me, both cried for renovation (or salvation).

Poor Mister Williams, he can mourn the passing of the city that inspired him all he wants, and it won't change a thing. The times, they are a changin'.

Out of the shadows emerged three picanynnies.

"I betchya I know where you got them shoes," asked one, pointing to my wing tips.

"How much you wanna bet?" I asked.

"A dollar. How about a dollar?"

"A dollar? Why should we bet just a dollar? There's no way in the world you could know where I got them. Make it fifty dollars."

"Oo, you gots a deal there mister."

"Is that a cop?" I excitedly asked as I surreptitiously kicked off my shoes.

He looked over his shoulder. "I don't see no policeman."

"Maybe I was seeing things. Anyway...ugh...like I was saying, so where did I get my shoes?"

"On your feet. That's where you get your shoes. So give me my fifty dollars."

"You give me fifty," I said, pointing to my argyle socks.

"That ain't fair. You cheated."

"I didn't cheat. I just outsmarted you."

The three musketeers each uttered the same unimaginative curse and ran across the street.

"Don't think I took any pride in it," I yelled. "Too easy."

"It's a shame old Jax Brewery is home to rodents like them," I said as they disappeared into its gloomy shadow.

"Ought to tear it down," said Father. "Make the Quarter safer."

That's not very imaginative, for him. The only thing such a negative statement is consistent with is his newly developed depression.

"I disagree," I said, trying to lighten up the conversation. "The place is an opportunity crying to be exploited. Think about it. Name recognition, nostalgia, a view of the river, it's a sure thing."

"There's a height ordinance."

"There's no ordinance an extra campaign contribution couldn't repeal. Petrodollars can wipe away the grime and turn it into a first-class tourist attraction, maybe a French castle to compliment the Pontalba and Napoleon House, or a Spanish Monastery accenting Saint Louis Cathedral, the Cabildo, and the Presbytére. If promoted right, the historical society would preserve it regardless of what it had in it: a bowling alley, disco, flower shop, or bookstore.

"The entire riverfront is wasted," I said. "Instead of catching glimpses of the backside of wharves, tourists should see glinting storefronts separated by small parks, with benches for pedestrians to rest and watch river traffic."

"We've got the Moon Walk," said Father, thinking uncharacteristically small.

"You know what you can call the Moon Walk?"

"What?"

"A beginning."

The haunting sound of bagpipes rolled mournfully down the levee as we crossed into the deserted French Market, its ghostly silence a stark contrast to the vibrant activity during the day. A mist shrouded the grassy batture and partly hid the piper.

"Not that again," grumped Kimberly. "It's so scratchy."

She hated it when Father honed in on the apparition, like a sailor smitten by a siren. "He's so weird," she whined in a futile attempt to hold him back. The Scotch-Irish in him always prevailed.

It's uncanny how hypnotic the skirl can be. I can see why his ancestors could march into Old Hickory's Kentucky rifles, or Napoleon's Old Guard at Waterloo.

The chill, which habitually afflicts Saints fans during the usual late-season drubbings at open-air stadiums, afflicted our bored fans. Goose pimples marched up and down her legs, and progressed to her lips as she insisted we leave. Father's overly generous gratuity was in part due to the embarrassment her whining caused him. I, on the other hand, made sure her minuscule attention span didn't cut short our next stop, one I enjoyed immensely.

A cul-de-sac just off Jackson Square, hard by the Saint Louis Cathedral, afforded perfect acoustics for an ensemble I insisted we visit. The artistry involved in playing a dulcimer clavier, lira da gamba, and a Hardanger fiddle cast a spell superior to that wrought by the bag squeezer. The melodies composed a sense of well-being in me, calming and fortifying my connection with the past. That there are people who invest the time and effort to become virtuosos added to the enjoyment. I know from my piano lessons how hard it is to be proficient on an instrument, let alone an archaic one. I wouldn't do it, but I'm glad someone else did.

This time it was Father who wanted to leave. With the windbreak the buildings on Royal provided and the classic good looks of a musician, Kimberly felt no compunction to leave. I don't know what's behind Father's impatience. He had overcome a youth in such places of culture as El Dorado, Arkansas, Kilgore, Texas, and Dubach, Louisiana to cultivate an appreciation for the finer things of life. Like Sid Richardson, J. Paul Getty, Roy Cullen, and a host of other oil-rich Medici, he rewarded the arts with his largesse, at least he used to. I dropped twenty dollars into the musicians' velvet-lined case to make up for his failure to reward them. There's no denying he's been acting strangely for weeks.

"It's my pleasure," I said, in response to their "thank you.".

By the way, Father almost fled the scene, I could tell he felt bad about being so abrupt. His exit from the parking lot proved he was preoccupied. Not only was it jerky, but when he got onto Poydras, he drove right by the Saint Charles exit and pulled into Carondolet. Luckily, there was no on-coming traffic or cops. We hooked a left and stayed on Girod until making a right on the street we should have been on in the first place, where we progressed expeditiously as if nothing had happened.

Likewise wanting to pretend nothing had happened, I breathed deeply and dwelt on something diverting, such as the condition of the city, the former Jewel of the South whose luster I always intended to restore.

Too bad people without our insight have let downtown Saint Charles Avenue turn seedy. Slowing down behind one of those "Sane Chaws Streak Caws," as the trolleys are called locally, one can vividly see the neglect. Instead of being worthy of its place on the Monopoly board, it had deteriorated into a street as trashy as nearby Camp Street, with its Salvation Army shelter. Vagabonds appeared sporadically, infesting the steps of the old city hall, in the once gracious Lafayette Park, outside what was left of the Campbell House, and the theatre. The only place the flotsam couldn't be seen was outside the State Employment Center.

James Caldwell's world-class showplace was turning back into the hog wallow he had found it. It'd be more prosperous if the descendants of Pierre Percy replanted the pigsties and butter beans their ancestors raised here. If not for the local police's affinity for the Hummingbird Diner's ambiance and cuisine, the place would be crime-ridden. The only denizens with a modicum of respectability lingered outside the offices of jobbers, hoping to get hired as roustabouts in pipe yards like ours. Premier jobs for people like them.

It is fitting that the offices are close to the big YMCA building and Lee Circle. Both the brick edifice and gallant green general provided a demarcation between shame and pride, decay and prosperity. Maybe the World's Fair, which is being planned here, will spruce up Saint Charles--if it's not as botched as the Cotton Exposition was late in the last century. I'm sure no embezzler could ruin it like Major Burke ruined that endeavor. Business has become more moral and more sophisticated in a century.

Once past the ridiculous Jerusalem Temple and the fast food outlets, the street blossomed into a stunning avenue. Quaint and well-trafficked shops on both sides of the tracks give the first half mile of the Garden District the appearance of a small village, aesthetically pleasing and profitable. People of taste eschew department store fare and ordinary service for quality and personalized service. And the personalities! Where else could you find a Jewish tailor like mine, or the Russian émigré who fashions Kimberly's outfits? Further down stood famous hotels, four-star restaurants, and charming condominiums only the discerning live in.

Stretch limousines, valets, and trucks too big for the side streets blocked half the avenue, backing up traffic. Glamorous women wearing tight-fitting lamé originals helped me tolerate the inconvenience.

"Why didn't we go to the gallery openings?" asked my stepmother. "We never go, and now they're done with for tonight."

"I didn't know you cared."

"We went last year, up and down Magazine."

In and out of the bathroom she means. She spent more time looking at her reflection than at her artwork.

Stately Victorian mansions soon grinned at us from both sides of the street. With the requisite porches, gables, lawn urns, and as many rooms as a hotel, each was a monument to ostentation and big families, making honest women out of the Kimberly of their day.

"There it is," she said, referring to her favorite vegetable stand. "Let's make groceries."

Like the antebellum plantation, it stood in front of, the little portable business splashed more color on the scene. That's all it provided, as its prices were identical to those charged at the French Market, and a third more than at any supermarket. But it was quaint, as quaint as the street performers in Audubon Park and the frequently seen horse-drawn taffy cart.

Digging into the fruit baskets, our Betty Crocker fingered the mirliton and plantain with such ham fists, that she bruised them beyond repair. No matter how appetizingly our chef inserts seafood into the mirliton, or how much cosmetic cutting he employs on the starchy bananas, the blue hairs he'd invite over would still notice they're flawed.

"This fancy stuff'll impress them."

Fat chance. They can find fault with God.

Such fare is too exotic for me. Give me a tangerine any day. Tangerines are real; they're funky, like this town: tangy and succulent. In the time it took me to peel one, we passed by Doctor Squat's gym and the K and B Chris Kenner hung out. A Ph.D. who can squat nine hundred pounds, and a stevedore who reaps fame with songs like "The Land of a Thousand Dances" fit this place perfectly. Distorters of common perceptions. How can I not like it?

An appreciation for the slightly twisted can be financially rewarding. I don't have Father's spartan upbringing to overcome. There's enough personality in me to expand our empire into people-oriented businesses, like real estate.

Take those shotgun houses lining the side streets. Install inexpensive ductwork, apply a few coats of paint, hook up some brass ceiling fans, decorate with ficus plants, and--voila, a woman's dream house. Convince wifey the place is an irresistible love nest and her husband will have to buy it, regardless of the condition of the gutter, plumbing, wiring, and foundation. It's too easy.

The money you make selling junk to peasants can go into philanthropic pursuits. I intend to spend my own money to have the unsightly grit removed from the gothic Episcopal Cathedral we passed on our left. Passing the First Baptist Church on our right reminded me of my pledge to send Norman Traigle's famous choir on the road.

"Hey Kimberly," I mischievously bellowed, as we drove by the exclusive Sacred Heart Academy. "If you ever want your picture taken at your daughter's graduation over there, better apply now."

My stepmother glared at me.

Father remained mute throughout her outpouring of babble about having a lock on acceptance. He knows the real value of money, as exemplified by his telling glances at a Romanesque castle resembling the old Newman mansion. To him, its inevitable demolition will be a travesty. The palatial edifice was Thomas Sculley's masterpiece.

I've known all along he didn't buy all our Prudence Mollard and Chippendale furnishings as investments. No one who stalks auctions so assiduously, or who sits and stares at his purchases, can think of them as a stock or bond. He had looked more forward to the set of Jacobean Revival oak chairs that had been put on the block last year than children do to Christmas. Someone born to the oilfield should be partial to alligator hide recliners and deer head hat racks, not Renaissance sideboards and late Empire mahogany poster beds. Men with permanently gashed fingers and rawhide skin like Father's do not, as a rule, buy French bronze dore mantle clocks or Chippendale cherrywood chests of drawers. They are usually partial to oak and pine furnishings from Neiman Mark-ups.

Lacking his heightened sense of aesthetics, I find Uptown as intriguing as a citadel of Capitalism as it is a monument to good taste and refinement. The sandstone castle Harry Williams built, after helping fellow ace Eddie Rickenbacker establish TWA, stands as prominent today as a library as it did when his wife traded motion picture stardom for the role of socialite.

I care more about the acquisition than the spending of money, it requires so much more character and intelligence. Any fool can fork over bucks. The bank executives, the rabbis, accountants, and housewives don't deserve any credit for hiring Wiley to build the acclaimed bank building, synagogue, theatre, and classic homes lining the street. Those who founded the successful entities they worked for, who created the wealth they used to pay for the architect, deserved the credit.

Intrepid winners have forged another Park Lane, its flowering bushes and leafy trees suffusing the opulent residences with color and privacy. They also hid the traffic and prevented the Edwardian and Second Empire mansions as well as the Italian Villas and Swiss Chalets with their stained glass, curved windows, mansard roofs, Ionic and Corinthian columns, and gingerbread woodwork from assaulting the senses.

The only eyesore was the vulgar "For Sale" sign in front of Dukeman's Renaissance manse.

"His sensitivity is as poor as his business sense," I said. "He deserved to go bankrupt, thinking the name of his wharf would continue to attract business after what Mobile built."

The joke I made about Dukeman's petition to turn his Desire Street wharf into a national landmark did not go over very well. Father defended the banana importer.

"He understands the importance of tradition," he said.

Tradition? I could see tradition applied to one's school or family, not to where Chaquita unloads its product. What's with Father? He's a consummate businessman, not given to confusing commerce and art. Hadn't he paid top dollar for equipment for our pipe yard, while waiting for the former owner of our house to go bankrupt so he could buy it for next to nothing?

Further, he plowed what he saved on the price into renovations and landscaping, turning our Greek Revival into a genuine showpiece. It wasn't in original condition, either. The copper pipes and gutters he put in will last decades. Being made of stone, it'll outlast all those made of irreplaceable cypress. He didn't cut any corners, take on renters, or play the real estate game. Our house is no tax loophole or even an investment. It's a statement to taste, to elegance, a shrine where one can unabashedly worship the finer things in life.

It rejuvenated Father. He couldn't keep his eyes off it as he slowly drove up our crescent driveway. Neither our valet nor our butler managed to divert him. Both had to settle for polite courtesies. This was his refuge, the oasis where he could recharge himself in affluence and privacy.

Kimberly strolled into our lap of luxury with all the appreciation of a pampered house cat, heading straight for the liquor cabinets. I stopped to kibitz with Robert, our butler. And Father, what did he do? Did he escort his wife up our spiral staircase, so they could disturb the satin sheets on their Queen Anne bed? Did he flip on our projection television? No, he hit our Eighteen Seventy-Two Steinway (the first year they quit sounding like a harpsichord). The rich, noble sound he conjured contrasted sharply with the sprightly, even flippant, tones of the Yamaha I practiced on.

A somber Bach fugue reverberated throughout the house. The spacious rooms and vaulted ceilings performed like a sound stage, enriching and amplifying each note. Bach never sounded so good. Then again, Bach only echoed once before within the walls, when grandmother died. My Father usually celebrates life with Copeland, Gershwin, or, in moments of ecstasy, Jelly Roll Morton. Hearing anything else was cause for concern.

As Father continued his rueful playing, I couldn't help but wish he'd quit tickling the ivory and start tickling his wife. That's the one thing Kimberly's good at altering one's moods. That's all any woman is good at.

Planning the soiree Father reluctantly allowed Kimberly to put on a trip. Kimberly was a trip. I played private investigator, ferreting out names from "Woman's Wear Daily" and "Town and Country", as well as the roster of Twelfth Night Revelers, the Southern Yacht Club, the Louisiana Club, and several carnival organizations. I hired a real Sherlock Holmes to check the New York-based Social Register, fine arts contributors, and frequent guests at the Audubon Zoo-To-Do. The local Social Register Society proved useless, having been indicted for mail fraud.

All one had to do was look at the back issues of "Vivant" in the *Times-Picayune*. Aristocrats aren't camera shy, nor can they resist exhibiting their social coups. The names we ran into were hilarious. Mrs. Chadsworth Elkington, Donald Peabody, Ashton Worthington, the Third. Only the names of the help we hired were funnier: Quinnoya, Shwanda, Meshanda, Calandria, La Tasha, Jarmaine, and Shaymonique. How could we not hire someone named Shaymonique?

We did, however, manage to bag a few notables; not varsity like the Goodyears, Longs, or Slidells, but the class double "A" Farrars, Blums, Blakes, and triple "A" Knoxes and Montgomerys. The former had more money than status, and the latter had more status than money.

Father enjoys playing alchemist, trying to mix oil with water. And I must say the experiment perked his spirits. Come the day of the festivities he floated from guest to guest, cracking jokes, commenting on current affairs, and like a sheepdog, herded the two camps together, hoping oil patch folks would find the upper crust more down to earth than anticipated, and the upper crust would find those who make a hole for a living weren't all like H. L. Hunt or Glenn McCarthy. As for Kimberly, she was busily engaged in matching wits with the blue hairs of the Junior League and Ladies Auxiliary.

"Yeah, I'm going' to UNO," she said to a coven of the creatures. "Gonna be a computer programmer."

"Oh my," puffed a well-fed doyenne, fingering her pearl necklace. "That's quite a goal. Are you properly prepared?"

"Sure! Got my maths and takin' English."

"And what kind of math is that?"

"Algebra."

"As in high school algebra?"

"They teach it in college."

"Remedially. For those who didn't have it when most did. And that English. Is it remedial too?"

"Well...I guess."

"So you're there because of open admissions? I think Louisiana state schools are the only ones in the nation who let every high school graduate into college."

"You gotta start somewhere."

"But at your age?" asked a second wearing a royal blue Diane Dickinson outfit.

"I'm smart enough to know my limits."

"Indeed. That would be taxing."

"It sure is. What degree do you have?"

"Oh, none yet."

"How many credits do you have?" Kimberly asked.

"Dear me. I have so many."

"About."

"Over three hundred. I consider college an adventure for the mind."

"See, you're smart too," Kimberly told her.

An idiot savant, that's what she is. Sometimes I just don't appreciate Mom.

"I have a degree," stated Mini-Pearl.

"In what?"

"Psychology."

"That's great. What are you doing with it?" Kimberly asked.

"I use it in my work."

"Where?"

"As a librarian. Volunteer mostly."

"I bet it comes in real important with people with overdue books and things like that."

"It always comes in handy."

As if watching a tennis match rivaling a Wimbledon final, I chalked up the score. Thirty-love: Kimberly. Forty-love: Kimberly, when the dowagers withdrew to regroup. Game, set, match when they started grumbling about the attention her scooped-back silk gown attracted.

When she hit the buffet to gobble petrossian caviar and guzzle Dom Perignon she did not do so alone. A crowd gathered around her. Her cheap Jennifer George outfit and tacky Katie Voight jewelry won over more men than all the wearers of expensive Cathy Hardwick or Hanse Moi originals.

"Men are inscrutable," I said to jealous blue blood, whose Yahji Yamamoto dress and drop-dead jewelry nobody noticed.

"Don't get mad, get even," I said to another equally turned-out wallflower. "Find out what people like her wear and buy stock in the company that sells them."

Miss "I came to be seen" was seen to be very confused.

"Still," I continued, "There are a lot more people with her taste than yours. Wouldn't you rather own part of McDonald's than the Pavilion?"

"Why yes. That would be nice," she hesitantly replied. Her Rei Kowakibas gown billowed during her desperate retreat to the safety of her kind.

"Can't get a cat to bark," said Robert, acting very Jeevish, which is a neat trick, considering how unlike the mischievous butler he looked. Tall, blocky, but always nattily attired, his patrician face let him get away with resembling a gentleman of the Old South.

"You normally eavesdrop?" I asked.

"That's the fun part of this job."

"Well, I'm glad someone's having fun," I muttered.

"Your Father's a genius, gathering apples and oranges under the same roof. It's far out."

Far out? I thought. *What is that? Sixties, "Do your own thing", and "Peace and love" rhetoric. I didn't know we had hired Abby Hoffman.*

"Yeah," I said. "It's far out."

He was right. The party would have been an impenetrable bore had only Ralph Laurens and Anne Kleins attended. I'd hate to have to spend the night buttering them up, holding my martini glass at port arms, discussing such exciting topics as the weather with Mrs. Walmsley, or listening to another archetypical dowager go on about her archetypical trip abroad. I didn't have to feign interest when the vice president of an offshore drilling company asked where her money came from. The grand dame acted as if she had swallowed soap.

"It's nothing to be ashamed of," he remarked, lighting a particularly smelly Minado cigar. "I give lectures to my alma mater on how I made it big. It's easier to give my Aggies ten thousand today than it was to give them ten cents five years ago." He blew smoke in her direction.

"How interesting," she replied.

"Yes, ma'am. Now I can do the things I always wanted, like get on the symphony board. That's where the real prestige is."

"It does have its privileges."

"So, you're a member. Hot damn. How's about putting in a good word for me?"

Her affirmation sent him away smiling.

"Pigeons don't flock with doves and ducks don't fly with geese," said Robert, walking away.

"I'm sure hemlines will be lower sometime soon," I said to an aging debutante who wanted to know what the next fad in fashion was.

"Oh, maybe the experts' predictions of a new ice age might have something to do with it."

Rather than agree, I told her my opinion was based on the old stock market adage about how modest fashions follow market declines. "The last bull market was only cyclical. We're still in a secular bear market," I remarked.

Minus a few wrinkles, her face mimicked that of the matron. Finances weren't her favorite subject.

"There's Binkie," she squealed. "I've just got to talk to her." She hurried off.

"The fun occurs when peacocks associate with oil-stained seagulls," Robert said as he swooshed by with a platter of hors d'oeuvres.

"I like these paintings," said a wildcatter to the only Dillon present. He was referring to the pictures on the wall. "They're like drilling prospects. Who knows, one of these might catch on, and be worth something someday."

"I don't think a Drysdale or Heldner should be purchased in hopes for a profit," remarked the aristocrat.

"That's because there's no exchange to set prices for them. What do you think?"

"I think one should donate his collection to a museum."

"Where's the money in that?" asked the wildcatter.

There was carnage everywhere one turned. Men wearing Brooks Brothers diner jackets and Rolexes talked about golf, poker, and money and didn't listen to the talk about squash, bridge, and politics those wearing Alan Flussers and Lord Elgins favored. They drank martinis and bourbon, not scotch, and tolerated nothing liberal. Nothing.

An argument broke out between the painting connoisseurs, about where banks were loaning their depositors' money.

"Countries don't go bankrupt," claimed the Dillon.

"Banana republics do," insisted the oilman.

Another mismatched duo aired their differences concerning the Alliance for Progress Program Kennedy instituted to help our southern neighbors.

"You like it because you made money off the plants and factories that made the rich richer and the poor poorer," the third-generation millionaire said to the self-made millionaire.

I didn't hear the response.

Off in a corner, I heard a diatribe against prep school.

"Hard knocks. That's what makes a man," squawked one of those oil-stained seagulls. "Philosophers and writers, what good are they to you in the trenches?"

Another chest pounder pounded his chest about poverty in America, claiming it can't compare to that of India, where he, "Had to look inside every joint of forty-inch drive pipe for families. They lived in them."

Before injecting into the conversation my thesis on how Americans became spoiled, I noticed what happened between two guests Robert just finished serving. Both broke into an argument. Watching our butler, I'd say he worked the guests more than served them, acting like a catalyst, stirring them up.

"I see what you're doing. Are you trying to start something?" I accused.

"Absolutely. With a name like yours, I'd think you'd follow suit."

"Why?"

"Why not?" he asked.

"I don't know."

"I knew you'd say that."

So, I tried to be as "randy" as I could and took up the role of devil's advocate with abandon. It was wild, upsetting the status quo, challenging the older money and their preconceptions. First off, I gladdened the drive pipe realtor by making a point about how our Edison phonograph once cost half the price of a house. Adjusting the wooden grating muted the Connie Boswell record on the turntable.

"Volume control," I mentioned. "And listen to its internal horn. It was a genuine technical breakthrough in its time. A real luxury item," I added to ensure I got my point across.

Secondly, I broke convention by moving the Loyola string quartet to the middle of the room. "Why'd we hire you if no one can hear you?" I asked. I also gave them the go-ahead to hit the buffet if they wanted.

"Let me know if security gives you a hard time," I said.

That done, I continued to go for it, solidifying my position with the "with-its" at the expense of my and my family's place with the "not-with-its". The carnage was spectacular.

Citing she'd been under the weather, one of Kimberly's blue-haired guests decided she had enough and bade goodbye. She must have been the top hen as her ruffled feathers signaled the departure of most of the flock. Unexpected business prompted Matt Dillon to drive off into the sunset, taking a posse with him, each of who aired equally well-used bail-out lines, bidding adieu to all the boozy deals that might have been consummated later in the evening. As for Kimberly, this was her swan song. I'll bet the event will be the standard for insolence which others will be judged against. She'll never see these people again.

"I wonder if this will cure her ambition," I rhetorically asked Father after the last guest had left, and the impoverished music students had made off with the leftovers. "No matter what, Kimberly ought to be easier to live with."

Slouched in a plush Senorite chair, nursing a glass of wine, he remarked enigmatically "After what happened tonight, I don't know. I wonder if I will be easier to live with. I might need some of those people someday, maybe sooner than later."

"Those? They're dinosaurs," I said. "This city's been taken over by people like us. There hasn't been such a change in leadership since that bunch and their betters booted the Creoles off their perch. Their era is over. They were the only filler between King Cotton and Big Oil. It's all so symmetric."

"I wish I could be as sure as you."

Whatever was bothering him, it made him paranoid. His habits changed. Rather than visiting our pipe yard, he avoided it altogether and ordered his secretary to tell all callers he was in a meeting. As for participating in social functions, forget it. He RSVP'd every invitation into the waste can and took to spending inordinate amounts of time in his study with only his desk light on, doing what, I haven't a clue. He also began sleeping in, though, from the increased irritability Kimberly manifested, it wasn't because he was up late executing horizontal rumbles. Worst of all, he became jumpier than a squirrel, peering out the window and trading his afternoon jog around Audubon Park for magnums of Hennessy Cognac.

To cheer him up, I invited over several Chi Sigma actives, officers of the fraternity I wanted to pledge to.

"Youngblood, New Wave, that's what you need," I told him. "You'll see it won't take long for this bunch to start running things. They got what it takes."

"I don't know."

"Give them a chance. If they can't change your perspective no one can."

"Can't hurt, I guess. Bring them on."

On they came, arriving one Saturday evening wearing poplins and wide-wale corduroys, exuding confidence and superiority.

"So, this is the Randy Cunningham manse?" said the sharp-looking Chi Sigma president, extending a stiff hand Father pumped mechanically.

Robert adroitly took their coats and escorted them into the living room.

"A lot of heavy deal-making went into its purchase, I'm sure," proclaimed Michael King, the porcine vice president. "Serious scoots." I noticed he scanned the room.

"And taste to the max," the bespectacled treasurer remarked. "I'd wish you'd give me the name of your decorator. We need a genius like him for our house. Believe me."

I wanted to but didn't dare say they'd first need an Orkin man. Although I'd been in their house, I wasn't familiar enough with them. I'll tell them later. *Maybe after the special rush at the beginning of the spring semester, or during it, when we're blotto,* I thought.

"We knew which gay bar to scout," I said.

"And how did you know?" asked the president, like everyone else, congregating around the wet bar Robert attended.

"Ever since Father came out of the closet, I'm not afraid to admit I'm queer. Of course, he didn't become brave enough until Grandfather made the same admission. If the truth be known my ancestors died childless."

"I know what you mean," said the vice president. "My uncle's buried in the tomb of the unknown soldier."

"You must be proud," Kimberly remarked.

"You bet I am!" exclaimed Michael, losing his cool at the sight of our nymph in black nylons, a leather skirt, and a wicked teddy. I knew convincing her to stick around, not to "pass by her mother's" was a good idea. The tongue-tied officer failed to put three words together which made sense.

Aiding the breakdown of rationale, Robert manifested heretofore unrecognized talents mixing drinks.

"It's a good thing you work here," averred Stephen Boutin, the president and son of the famous furniture mogul. He watched Robert prepare the drinks. "Wouldn't last one night in a bar. Not a dilutionologist."

"It's a crime, sir, to pollute good spirits with water," parried our man. "If I ruled the world, I'd outlaw ice cubes."

Stephen put an arm around him and remarked, "Sounds like my kinda man."

The Singapore Slings and New York Teas he concocted ensured a successful evening. *Glad I hired him.* I thought. How could I turn down someone so confident? I like that in a person. He also was the only clean-shaven, healthy one to answer my ad. God, half were bums. I sure do have a gifted second sense. Proving it, I forewent idle chatter and homed in on what was important.

"What do you think are hotter wheels? A Lamborgini or Porsche?" I asked, ushering them into the far reaches of the living room.

"Me, I'm saving my money for a race boat. Want to give Al Copeland a run for his money," said Michael, punching the air to make his point, unaware he'd make better ballast than a driver.

"Don't need that much," I claimed, before divulging how a fuel-injected three hundred cubic inches engine outperformed a larger engine run on diesel, and that England made the most aerodynamic bodies...stuff I had picked up by having hung around marinas as a kid.

"Sounds like the voice of experience. Make any money?"

"Besides running drugs, no."

"Outrageous," said Stephen, no doubt daydreaming about flashy speedboats and sparkling tunas in bikinis as he led the pack deeper into the living room.

"Too much for me," asserted the treasurer, William Davis the Third, heir to Davis Consultants, one of the largest consulting firms in the oil patch. "I'd rather make money the old-fashioned way, representing injured workers. Having an uncle who is a partner in a law firm is a great eye-opener. I can thank a clumsy roughneck for our family's summer home. Got money from the drilling and oil company, as well as the manufacturers of every instrument on the drill floor, including the wire mats surrounding the thing that spins."

"Rotary bushing," I said, downing some poo.

"Money makers I'd call it," he remarked, firing up a 'rette. "An offshore rig is profit-city." He tried to discreetly look at Kimberly.

I quickly suppressed an urge to remind them the devices and tubulars my family rents out could cause injury. More points would be lost than won by remarking how we might be the defendants.

"A mashed finger can be worth fifty grand, a broken hand a hundred or more. Let someone wrench his back, and—pay dirt. You can retire or start your firm. That's where the real money is, and you don't have to deal with the unwashed. Know what one client did with a 200G settlement? Bought a Cadillac for each day of the month until he ran outta money. Typical."

"S.O.P. for a Coon Ass."

"Coon Ass?" asked Michael, showing an inexcusable lack of local knowledge.

"Acadians," Father answered, following behind us.

"Yeah, you know. Tossed from Canada. Evangeline and Jean Lafitte," I added.

"But Coon Ass?"

"It's not an insult," Father continued as he sat down on our Belter lounger. "It's a derivative of a French word, not the backside of a raccoon."

"So, it's not like calling someone a 'wop' or a 'pollock'?"

"Coon Asses want you to call them Coon Asses. I've been called a transplanted one because I moved down here from Arkansas," Father continued, stretching his arms out.

"How gauche," remarked Michael. Having had his fill of Kimberly he started to look around.

"Got to remember they've been inbreeding for centuries," said the young Boutin, finding our other lounger a good place to plant it.

"So have good ol' boys. Matched and detached, within miles of where they were hatched," said William.

"When did you learn all this?" I asked.

"I'm like Stephen. I'd rather make money off my brains than risk my back," said William. "Good businessmen know these things. Want to speculate in the pits, you better know all there is about commodities and crowd psychology."

"If you want to make a living off others, you've got to know the score," Michael pontificated.

"Got to know all about the Jones Act. Workers sure don't know about it," said Stephen. "The last thing a drilling company wants is a lost time accident, an LTA. Would rather see the whole crew counting bolts and convalescing in bed than admit they're waxed. Might lose the next contract. The oil companies, that hire contractors, are very sensitive about accidents. Fear lawsuits."

"Workers don't know they can sue," remarked William. Like Michael, he too started to check our things out. Instead of running his hand over the marble squares atop our rosewood specimen table, he found something fascinating with the china in our exergue. "Their ignorance will amaze you. That's why you got to protect their rights."

"Got to play spy to find out what's going on," Stephen said as he eased over to our McCraken sofa. I noticed they all moved around as if they were casing the joint. "My summer job was to monitor ship-to-shore microwave. I was the early bird who got the worm."

"My summer job included checking the numbers stenciled on tanker trucks," said Michael, the vice president. "Companies sometimes use water trucks to haul oil, to fool scouts."

The steady resupply of drinks lubricated my guests' tongues and wobbled them physically. All three either leaned against something or sat down.

"Got to talk their language," said Stephen. "Learn their lingo. Slap a lazy tongue around in your mouth for 'dem' rednecks and use inverted grammar for 'dem' Cajuns. That is how they say things, mostly."

"My uncle is head of internal medicine at Oschner Clinic," Michael bragged, "He couldn't make heads nor tails out of his black patients' medical histories 'til he learned to speak ghettoes. 'You splatter?' he'd ask the males. 'Your nature up?' he'd ask the females."

"He had to slum," I observed.

"Hey, Medicare doesn't differentiate."

"My brother made a killing filling their mouths with gold teeth," said William Davis. "That glow you see around Baton Rouge during a full moon isn't the Exxon refinery flaring gas. It's all my brother's brothers smiling."

"Brother," said our barkeep.

"Do I hear a contrary voice?" asked Stephen. "What is needed here is a deeper appreciation of what all this does for society. Our function is to make the work world fair. Companies fire employees before they retire, and corporate officers make radical salaries and bonuses while they lay people off. We transfer wealth, from the haves to the have-nots. Misused workers wouldn't get proper medical care otherwise and so might be lost to the workforce. Unemployment compensation drains public funds and doesn't provide the incentive for workers to upgrade their skills like a wad of cash might. Tort law keeps everybody on his toes better than OSHA."

"Check out the owners of the fanciest houses and most expensive cars in DeRidder, Leesburg, or Abbeville. Belong to the winners of lawsuits, the most common way rednecks become rich," said William.

"Real Robin Hoods," remarked our servant.

"Exactly," Stephen remarked, looking as relaxed as a cat when he finally started luxuriating on the McCraken.

"Or hyenas and vultures," Robert said.

"Depends how you look at it."

"Always considered scavengers underrated," continued our butler. "All that Bambi and Thumper, eagles and elephants' stuff is overrated. Give me maggots, ants, paramecium, and bacteria. Been around a lot longer than cute fuzzy creatures. All God's children got niches."

"What did Kaiser of Kaiser Aluminum say?" asked Michael, adjusting his designer glasses before taking a seat close to the dining room.

"Find a niche and fill it."

"We're all part of the gene pool." Our butler handed out refills.

I let the guests get woozy before I herded them through the dining room to check out the view from the balcony.

"Goes down like silk," remarked William, enjoying our overlook of the tree-lined avenue.

Robert and Kimberly joined us. Father stayed put.

"Ought to," Robert said. "It's a Between the Sheets."

"You my man," said the treasurer.

"So pimp me out like your ol' man pimps his stable," said Robert.

"How do you know what he does?" I asked mocking seriously.

"Used to work for one of his consultants. A company man on a phosphate rig. He made a grand a day ordering me around. I'm not complaining, make a lot less being ordered around here."

"So go back to dogging."

"Can't. No rigs running," said Robert. "Price got too high. Everybody drilled for it until there was a glut. With the recession, end of story."

"Who was he?" William asked.

"Went by the sobriquet of Sunshine."

"Oh, yeah. Good man. Drilled cheapest."

"Hard on his crew," Robert affirmed.

"A crew is replaceable; a spent dollar isn't."

"Hard words."

"It's a hard business," the heir to the consulting firm remarked. "That's why I got no intention to enter it."

"Have in mind something with a greater risk-reward ratio? Like hitting the professional poker tour?" our butler responded.

"How prescient of you. Actually, in the tradition of great Americans like Hamilton Fisk, Sam Insull, and Jesse Livermore, I intend to make money off other people's money, and maybe off no money at all."

"Selling ice cream to Eskimos?" I asked.

"Exactly. Athletes who haven't a clue what to do with their money; doctors, lawyers, and other professionals who aren't as smart as they think and can't admit to their mistakes, they'll be my clients. Mention oil and watch them salivate."

"Do I hear Colonel Ponzi?" asked Robert.

"Not at all," said William. "It's only good business to ensure those who join first make a return on their investment, while I wait for a good prospect."

"Limited partnerships are the way of the future," I inserted into the conversation. "They are the financial instrument of preference."

"So are blind pools," argued Stephen. "Managed money for...."

"The gullible," said our butler.

"Call them what you will. It's legal. Remember, drinking alcohol used to be illegal. So who's to say what's right or wrong?"

"You win. And may the wind be at your back," Robert said as he left to replenish the hors d' oeuvres.

"What, no more moralizing?" asked William Davis the Third.

"Moralizing? There's no need for me to moralize. I'm a passenger, not a pilot, on this flight," Robert replied loud enough to be heard from the kitchen.

"Be careful not to move too far too fast," Father remarked, cryptically. "You might get caught up by the mania which accompanies booms like the one we're in."

"I know about rising tides lifting all ships," said Stephen, the president.

"There's a lot of temptations on top of the crest."

The actives listened attentively.

"We've all seen our fathers weather business cycles," Michael, the vice president, finally said. He should know. His father is a big shot at GM, one of the most cyclical companies there is.

"Booms are different," Father said in a tired voice. "Especially once you've suffered through the inevitable bust. They're brutal. You have no idea what it's like to lose your patience and then hope. Bankers don't see you through the tough times like they used to. If you owe any money when the price collapses, the value of your collateral collapses and you're doomed. It's war."

The actives took in what he had to say with great interest. All had been trained to listen to successful people. I, on the other hand, didn't hang on every word. It wasn't because I had heard it before. I have, even from my Grandfather. It was Father's dispirited tone of voice. It sounded defeated. And why should he dampen the visit with the warning in the first place? Someone as shrewd as he would have kept the conversation light, and pleasant, like a good salesman should. After all, he was trying to sell me to them.

"Don't get me wrong. I'm not complaining. A little dog-eat-dog nihilism never hurts," he said.

"What did Nietzsche say? " I said. "Sympathy is only for the weak."

"What doesn't kill me makes me stronger," Stephen Boutin added, leading the stampede back inside.

"There are no moral phenomena at all, but only a moral interpretation of phenomena," said William Davis the Third, trailing behind Michael. Kimberly followed.

I wanted to add, "If we train our conscience it kisses us while it hurts us." But I didn't. Not to prove I took the same philosophy classes as my guests, but because it might strike too close to the truth. All my senses tell me Father has done something he regrets.

I think our butler sensed the same thing. While passing around some eat he said, "What goes around comes around", indicating to me he was toying with Father.

"Are you one of those?" asked Stephen, not getting the connection.

"One of us is better."

"Well, being rationale, all I can deal with is what immediately confronts me. The ever-present moment."

"And I salute you."

"Me too," said Father. "It's all we have."

"Here, here," said Michael King.

"But what he said about symmetry, believe it; there's a lot to it," Father remarked.

"Karma."

"Yes, karma I believe it's called," Father said dejectedly.

"If you believe all that," I said trying to change the subject.

"I do," Father reiterated.

God, he's got me afraid.

CHAPTER 2

Rush, what a concept. It's not humiliating, per se. It's more of a test, a rite of passage to see whether you have the character a particular house desires. Dogs sniffing each others' rear; tribal youths performing arduous tests of their manhood to weed out undesirables. It's in our mammalian genes, like a baby suckling on its mother's teats, or imprinting in a duckling.

To go to Tulane and not belong to the best frat is unthinkable, and stupid, considering the cost of attending the school. It would defeat the purpose of higher education.

"Contacts, that's what's important, not grades," Father had advised.

It's family lore how aggressively Grandfather mined investors. Then there was Dad Joiner's certificates, subleases, and personal scrip that turned the famous Daisy Bradford well into a communal effort for all of Rusk County, Texas.

What can you learn from school anyway? If you can judge the value a place puts on education by what it pays its teachers, I won't learn to squat there.

That there was a special, January, rush was an omen. Fate smiled at my surfeit of secondary education. Getting out of sync by taking those extra classes wasn't going to lead to the debacle most predicted.

The Chi Sigma place was rather unimpressive, as are all frat houses on Broadway, the road delineating "Jew Lane's" western boundary. Still, its bracketed, overhanging roof and the elaborate woodworking on its facade elevated it above the standard two-story fare. The absence of graffiti and no stupid fire engine on the lawn also helped project an image of sensibility and class.

Most frats are money-deep, and I have no qualms about that. However, one must possess an appreciation for the finer things, and have a cast of mind that encourages all noble pursuits. The actives may someday make a fortune in the pits, but they won't spend it foolishly. They'll contribute to the arts, provide venture capital, and improve the world.

Crossing Broadway, I was almost run over by a carload of loudmouth polo shirt types. On the sidewalk, I had to contend with a squad of rowdy alligators, a breed who'd turn the world into a football-crazed, trivial society if not limited by their mediocrity. Penguins, they're the best; that little design indicates self-assurance and taste. No one who wears the insignia is a slave to status or feels compelled to look down on others. Others look up to them as a matter of course. They know they are the best and that is that.

No alligator would kiss me on the cheeks, me a stranger who might not be accepted into the fold. But that's what one of two southern belles who graced the porch I ascended did. It was not mechanical like the artificial busses Kimberly plants. A plumber's helper could be more affectionate. The other enchantress remained seated, smiling at me over her mint julep, reflecting unimpeachable style. One look at her and you could tell she wasn't one of the goldfish bubble brains who floated around campus. Both were impeccably accoutered and coiffured and treated me with an interest I found beguiling.

Knowing how much women admire confidence, I told the foxy kisser she shouldn't worry about me being selected.

"You a legacy?"

"I have other attributes."

"I like a self-assured man. Find it quite alluring." Her angelic companion smiled radiantly. "I hope you do make it."

"So do I," cooed the stunning blonde, blushing.

Looking into her eyes, I could see the fathomless depths of intelligence, wonder, and fantasy. I could look into them forever, yet each second find something new and delightful.

"I hope you do get chosen. You seem nice," she said.

Nice! I seem nice! Not "sweet", "dear", "kind", or any other of the hollow adjectives the superficial fancy. That shows she's deep and different. Giving in to my romantic vein I honored Leslie (as she introduced herself) with the sobriquet "Beatrice", after Dante's divine companion. For her, I'd slay the dragons of social ridicule, throw myself into any den of iniquity, with a heart an ocean of alcohol could not demean. So, bring on the spiked Chambord, the Galliano, and the Cointreau, what are they to an inspired constitution? I know what I want, I want to be someone who can enjoy all the perks that go with lifetime affiliation. It's not being a crowd follower. It's being smart. There's a world of difference between prostrating yourself before a professor and playing the game the actives want you to play. Profs are good only for references if they remember you. Chi Sigmas can help your business. Hell, some of these guys might become McKinsey candidates.

The inside of the fraternity house was an enclave of well-wishers. In the dimly lit living room, surrounded by the clutter of a saturnalia in progress, I told an active who I cornered between a nondescript couch and a wall "Money is life's grade card." Judging from the brothel stompers he wore, it didn't surprise me he was receptive to the cliché.

"A savvy observation," he acknowledged.

Unleashing my gift for gab, I maneuvered the conversation into a discussion of success and how to achieve it, a tact he enjoyed so much he closed out by saying I could count on his vote.

He was typical. I shined so well that I soon felt as if I made an "A". My performance was excellent. And why not? I had done my homework and studied as if for a test. My final exam had come at the beginning of the spring semester. Whereas the final exams of future Arthur Anderson accountants, Colgate-Palmolive brand managers, and other corporate clones come at the end of schooling.

A glass of Golden Dreams and another of Sex on the Beaches cleared my mind and made me aware of what I was doing, exchanging ribald and scatological jokes, acting as if we were in a locker room. Boys will be boys. It's a male thing, no doubt bred in us to defend our homes and families. I remember being shocked hearing my prep school English teacher curse and ogle a waitress in a hamburger joint. Mister elocution and syntax rattled on like a sailor, not like

Shakespeare. Then there was potty-mouth Nixon on the Watergate tapes.

It's good to let your hair down and talk dirty. Look at the girls, they're getting into the swing of things. My Beatrice is giggling like a ditz. I don't mind. The most sophisticated women do that. When unleashed, men get rowdy, women get silly. To remain proper all the time is unnatural and unhealthy. That's why I have no qualms about being herded to and fro, from room to room, being blown out big time. Upstairs we sucked on some bones, dropped trou to coax a scream out of a hog who wandered in and took turns chug-a-lugging poo. We got wasted, and major disgusting. One ranger passed out, collapsing on the floor. Another bolted, puke oozing between his fingers as he tried to staunch the eruption. I too felt like praying to the porcelain goddess, but didn't, thanks to the resistance I had purposely built up for such an occasion. One can't have too many talents.

The scene got heavy. Good-looking women were brought in. Who, I couldn't tell, the room being so dark and swarming with humanity.

"Round up the wagons!" someone shouted. "Pledges in a circle."

A girl shrieked. A guy shouted. From behind me, I could hear the sound of a brief struggle, to my side a slurred protest. A crush of bodies pushed me into the center of the room where I prepared myself for anything.

Nauseated, I could feel bile curdle in my stomach and expand like yeast up my gullet, rising with each hiccup and falling with every swallow, leaving my throat raw and raked. I could handle it. The blurred vision, failing use of my extremities, and my headiness were manageable. I was aware of what I was doing. I had command of my faculties. I was still my person.

I chewed face with the fox who greeted me on the steps. It was inevitable I would, she being so fun-loving and intense. Swapping spit was probably her way of affectionately saying "hello". One dynamite Little Sister.

Zoned, but still under control, I continued to go with the flow. I mashed mouths with other Little Sisters and communicated with a smoky-voiced nymph in Braille. She loved it, her supple flesh flowing enticingly under my touch.

"They want it," I heard the actives say. "They pretend to be blown out so they can get all they can."

It took a while for my eyes to adjust, but when they did, I had to look twice to comprehend what I saw. Some geek was performing a horizontal rumble on my Beatrice, lying right on top of her. I wanted to "off" him and might have done just that had he not been hauled away, and I told him to take his place. At first, I protested and tried to shake off the hands that held me tight. But my strength deserted me. What could I do? My efforts to struggle free were ineffectual.

Then it occurred to me it might be wrong to protest, that I needed to be initiated into the realm of love before I could belong. Who wants, or needs a virgin? Though I'm sure nobody knew I was one, what's the harm in pretending I wasn't? Leslie was doing me a favor. Look at her. Irresistible in her defenselessness, her mane of blonde hair framed a luscious face, and those moist, full lips, beckoned with delight. She wanted it. And she wanted it done well, not like the last dude who just played "hide the salami."

I explored her with a gentleness only a person who loved her could possess. She moaned in what I'm sure was a delight.

"Ow!" She shrieked, probably in ecstasy. She then fell silent and relaxed, obviously enjoying herself as I began to perform to my maximum capability. With my tongue, I ravishingly probed the succulent interior behind her dewy lips, while my supple hands very gently rubbed her stomach before floating up to knead her firm breasts. Women don't like to be treated as if they are a piece of meat.

"She's out of it," someone said.

Looking at her glassy eyes I could tell he was right. She had passed out. I went limp and pulled out.

"Faggot. What's the matter? Gone queer on us?" asked an active.

Gay? Me? No way. How could they say that? My extremity kept retreating, but, come on. Whose wouldn't? It's illegal to screw someone who has gone Chinese. Damn her. She's going to wreck me. I forewent being delicate, driving my uncooperative member as far as it could go and feverishly feeling her up.

"Like shoving toothpaste back into the tube," I heard William Davis say.

"Bitch," I whispered. "I'll show you."

"Maybe you're a studmaster after all."

"Necrophile!"

"You?" Leslie murmured as she opened her eyes. "I never thought..." she drifted off again.

A nearby commotion took the spotlight off me. I quickly rolled off her and dressed myself.

"Get off, you're crushing my kidney," another female complained. Between the bodies, I could see the fox struggling to wiggle out from two overweight pledges. It was grotesque, sacrilegious, like drawing a mustache on the Mona Lisa. It turned my stomach. Her disheveled hair, smeared make-up, and wrinkled outfit had rendered her unfoxy, mediocre. I had to turn away lest I got ill, so repugnant was the scene. Noticing someone else crawl upon Beatrice added to the abashment. Feeling betrayed, I slunk off to the bathroom, only to find it crowded. Stumbling about, I eventually found refuge behind a sofa.

"Looks like we got us a refugee," shouted Michael King, the vice president, hours later, shattering the fragile equanimity I had managed to summon.

"Have mercy on a downed pilot," I pleaded from my sanctuary. Propping myself up, I could see the debris of a real blowout. Empty bottles, paper cups, cigarette butts, chips, pieces of brie, gingerbread, and other remains lay strewn across the battlefield. A bra and black panties tied the past with the present and cast a chill I didn't know how to take.

"Jetsam, utter jetsam, what should we do with him?" someone asked, referring to another pledge.

"Wheel him out," the voice said, pointing to one of the tubbies who almost had smothered the ex-fox.

"Get a crane," said Stephen Boutin, walking past me.

Who knew how much time had transpired since the orgy? My usually infallible internal clock had gone on the fritz. The sunlight that was shown through the window was indeterminate.

To quote Walter Lord "That was a night to remember," I said. No one responded.

"Look at this piece of trash," the vice president remarked, pointing decidedly at me. "What do we do with him?"

"Oh, that one," said President Boutin in a cold voice. "He's got to be told to clean up his act."

I pretended not to hear him, and I kept on pretending not to hear as he resumed giving light-hearted orders to his subordinates. What I couldn't pretend was the wrenching feeling that something was wrong. Most others were treated to friendly badinage. Those who weren't were unacceptable, second-raters who wore fake Rolexes and cheap imitations of last year's Yves Saint Laurents and Alan Flussers duds. Probably drove their Fathers' Mercedes. They didn't know the class was something you're born with. It's like someone with skinny legs wanting to become a running back. If you haven't got it, you haven't got it, and that's why I was completely perplexed about the present attitude toward me. As proven at the party I gave, I was among those who had "it".

I briefly considered drawing attention to myself by storming out, like Father did whenever stymied during a hard negotiation. But I bagged the idea. With several actives stacking the fallen like cordwood, others taking turns banging their heads against the wall, and the rest engaged in equally rowdy behavior, who would notice me?

"The best way to deal with a hangover is to stay drunk," I shouted to three polluted hopefuls.

Taking their cue from the president, none of them responded.

Being rational, the only conclusion I could come to was that they were testing me, seeing whether I wanted to be a Chi Sigma. For a second I wondered if Leslie complained about my performance, but wrought with conflicting emotions, I banished the thought.

"Maybe you ought to see what other houses have to offer," said the bartender as I ambled up for a little consolation.

"What did you say about no one leaving here sober?"

"That was last night. Today the bar is closed."

"Not even a Bloody Mary?"

"We wouldn't be doing you justice if we asked you to remain," said Stephen Boutin, injecting himself into the conversation.

"Stephen?"

A crowd began to gather.

"We look out for people. A pledge properly placed is a bonus to all Greeks," concurred William Davis the Third.

"We want what's best for you," remarked the president.

"You're more than kind," I muttered.

"Giving up a blue-chip prospect isn't being kind; it's stupid. Then again, no one's accused us of being geniuses." The treasurer used his handkerchief to clean his glasses.

"I'm sure it's a great sacrifice. Tell you what, I'll spare you the grief and stay."

"Wish we could, it would be so much easier on us," Stephen remarked. He decorously cleared his throat and crossed his arms.

"You're to be admired."

"With that attitude, you shouldn't find it hard to be placed."

"If you want you can try out for our squad," remarked a rugby player. "Judging from last night, you'd do well in a scrum." A teammate stood next to him chewing off the top of a beer can.

"Well, what's your answer?" asked the athlete.

An insidious grin spread across his buddy's face, warning me what would happen if I did try out.

Something had happened while I was two sheets to the wind, something that had turned their perceptions upside down. I was not dealing with rational people. They were right out of the Twilight Zone.

"Perhaps it would be better if I did see what's on the other side of the fence," I finally said. "Thanks for offering me the opportunity to find out more about myself."

"What are brothers for if not to help each other?" said William.

"Let us know how you do," said Stephen.

"I sure will."

Maintaining my composure, I picked up the articles of clothing I somehow had shed with all the dignity I could muster. If Father had bitched out all the irrational creeps he had dealt with, he might not be where he is today. Father never burned his bridges. And neither should I. I will not pass judgment.

Spotting Leslie slink off made me wonder if she had anything to do with it. A loathing so ferocious for her welled up inside me, I had a hard time refraining from calling her names. Someone as duplicitous as her is capable of anything. Only the fox was more suspect. Look at her, strutting out the door, staring straight ahead, as if she wore blinders, pretending I didn't exist. What a two-faced snob.

"Have a good one," said the active who escorted me out.

"You bet I will," I responded with assertion.

Thanks to the a.m. and p.m. dials on my Rolex, I was able to tell it was morning, not afternoon. Otherwise, there was no way to tell.

Broadway teemed with life and a vibrancy usually reserved for a rare "Greenie" victory.

Manifesting why they had won the reputation for being the bawdiest, most vivacious frat, the Dekes were out in force, two houses down, cavorting and raising hell. They were the intramural powerhouse all the other houses wished they could be. Alumni, sports writers, and Joe six-pack might cheer a Wautusi playing hoops for coach Fowler, a future high school coach who hits eighty-five mile-an-hour fastballs for homers, or a steroid behemoth who blows out his knees, but the real heroes are those who won't win their fifteen minutes of fame by being featured on the sports highlights of the local news.

"The crowd is always wrong," was a motto driven into me since childhood. All those who perform on the hardcourt, diamond, or gridiron eventually work for the captains of the rugby and soccer squads. Standouts only take longer to hire, after their pro career is over.

"What we got here? Been cut from one of them boy's clubs?" asked a luxuriating active sporting an alligator insignia on his shirt. "It's probably for the best," he told me. "Here you'll find that winning isn't everything, it's the only thing."

"So, who wants to lose?" I replied.

"Spoken like someone with potential."

"Potential? What's this potential? I've already arrived."

"A little cocky, aren't we? I like that."

"Shows confidence," said a colleague. "Confidence is the name of the game."

Several activities oozed out of the house to size me up.

"Oh, he's a cute one," cooed a redhead, planting a chipper peck on my forehead.

The combination of Chanel Number Five and beer breath did not repel me. It attracted me; the mixture of glamour and healthy earthiness, at the same time ethereal and approachable. Stunning in her sleeveless silk dress she exuded vitality, youth, and (with a daring décolleté) raw sex too. Giggling and blushing, she wrapped a caring arm around me and led me inside to hand me over to an equestrian in Jodhpurs. I was in Heaven. Her athletic wholesomeness was as exciting as the cheerleader's sheer carnality.

"You have strong arms," the horsewoman said. "I bet you're a fine horseman." Pulling up my trousers she exclaimed, "And look at those legs! Water polo material."

Thank you Soloflex. I thought. This enchantress had me. I didn't care if the cheerleader was now bubbling over the next recruit, or the actives wore quartz watches and clothes from the Gap. I felt comfortable here. The pain of the last few hours vanished. Physically and spiritually, the Dekes projected all the traits I could want and realized my high standards. However, I did notice a Chrysler Imperial parked outside.

My swollen tongue quit feeling fuzzy. I was able to swagger and mimic the way Father wooed both men and women, taking on aloof airs as if I could care less about their opinions. When let go by the horsewoman I was able to curse and brag, really flaunt the fact I was a prize catch. All without stepping on any toes or acting stuffy.

"Remember, presumed power is real power, aloofness is often confused for strength, vulgarity misconstrued for manliness, and always project the image of being tough, in control, dominate." These were Father's mandates.

"Nice guys finish last," I heard myself say in response to a generic sports question. Vince would have been proud when I unleashed his saw about operating on Lombardi time. It fits the occasion and sure beats "The early bird gets the worm." You'd think dilettantes would put a lid on the rhetoric. But what the hay? They were energetic and full of promise, and they wanted me.

A little imagination was all it took to appreciate cheese dip, chips, and peanuts as much as I did yellowtail, kiwi, and basil torta. Add a chameleon-like talent for figuring out what they wanted to hear plus the willpower to say it and, hey -- I was the life of the party.

"Of course, I exercise," I said over a flat beer. "I jump to conclusions, fly off the handle, push my luck, and avoid responsibility."

I was a hit--literally. Once I joined their rugby squad in a game of head-butts, followed by an equally diverting contest consisting of plowing what was left of our brains into a wall. But, alas, the idle wasn't meant to last, for the same disorder that afflicted the Chi Sigmas suddenly began afflicting the Dekes. Perhaps it was a phone call or some malicious Pheidippides. Whatever it was it caused the actives to suddenly start avoiding me. The entire frat, including the Little Sisters, acted weird, cutting off conversations, walking away as I approached, and turning their backs on me. The coup I managed to fashion by claiming the only thing worse than not being paid attention to was being paid attention to, proved to be pathetic. The few chuckles it elicited quickly turned into cackles as those too dense or too ignorant to appreciate my wit stared daggers at the handful who did.

"Oscar Wilde would have liked it," I said to the obstreperous crowd.

He also would have liked the way I cleverly parried their unsophisticated barbs. If you can't laugh at yourself, make fun of other people.

"Girls like you are always running through my mind," I said to Misses Jodhpur. "They don't dare linger."

She uttered a guttural epithet and retreated. Crude, but effective, far more effective than Miss Pom Pom's squeaky response to my comment about how women speak two languages, one of which is not verbal. I never accused her of being bright. What did Nietzsche say? "Women aren't so deep as to be unfathomable. They aren't even shallow."

"Stop harassing the girls," said one human battering ram.

"There are some things one cannot help. One can't stop a dog from barking, an armadillo from being run over, or me from blinding people with my sagacity."

"Screw you," ejaculated a pundit.

A brilliant riposte sent my detractors reeling.

"He's ugly," said the cheerleader.

My retreat will go down as a salient moment in history, comparable to the Desert Rats' withdrawal from Rommel, Russia's pullback from Napoleon, or MacArthur's departure from the Philippines, all of whom eventually defeated their foes.

"I shall return," I said.

"I doubt it."

Instead of hurling more epithets I changed my tactics and drove them mad with an eloquent use of silence.

"Got nothing to say?"

"It wouldn't be fair," I shouted. "You're unarmed opponents."

An outburst of monosyllabic obloquies immediately followed.

"Thanks for proving my point," I remarked. "And don't even think of someday asking me for a job."

"Ask you?" queried a soccer player. "What could we ask you for? The time of day?"

"Can't do that. He's gotta hock his watch if he wants to eat."

That modicum of wit worried me. Where there's wit there's truth, and the truth hurts. It was all I could do to depart with dignity.

"If life gives you lemons, make lemonade," was the operative saying here. I'll go elsewhere. What do I want with a frat so brain-dead, they think in clichés? The only thing Deke's got on his mind is his blow-dried hair. That they reach high places only testifies to the superficiality of the positions. Anyone can become a C.E.O. What does it take besides learning how to brown-nose? Practitioners of the art of ass-kissing, that's all they are. The yes-men of America. None of them could go it alone, start a business, and fight to keep it alive. Boring, brain-dead bureaucrats. No wonder they all turned against me without provocation. They're like the school of fry at a fish hatchery where I once panicked with my shadow. Mindless, instinctual behavior. No wonder the US economy is falling behind.

In the glaring noon-day light it occurred to me, that I had my values misconstrued. Both the Chi Sigma and the Deke's represent the outer fringe of life--the lunatic fringe--of privilege and ease. They were born with silver spoons in their mouths and an attitude; as if all they had to do was mark time until they received their just due.

I should have checked out the average houses first. A little humility wouldn't hurt. It wouldn't be so bad to be a Mu Phi or a Delta Nu. So they're not Price Waterhouse material. They're not Ralph Lauren poster boys, don't wear Cartiers or Louis Vuitton. Hickey Freeman, Kuppenheimer, and Hart suits are more their style, as are Levi's, not Guess jeans. For all their faults, they're real, I suppose, which is better than the fops who measure a person by what he wears. Deliver me from the trivial. Let me seethe in the depths of my being and roil in the heat of my belonging.

A carload of Mu Phis rumbled by shouting animal noises. I didn't mind. High spirits, the kind oil barons like J. Paul Getty, Roy Cullen, and Edward Doheny of Union Oil displayed in their lease hound days.

The same car returned. The middle finger one of the passengers hoisted stepped over the line separating high spirits and vulgarity. It's one thing to be uncouth. It's another thing to be disgusting. No dirt farmer's going to let a seismic crew on his land after being insulted.

Rather than be intimidated on the next pass, I heroically held my head high--and got crowned for it. The empty beer can rattle like a top on the pavement.

"Beware of Greeks bearing gifts," I shouted. What started as a measured retreat turned into a rout when a dog ambushed me.

Appearing from nowhere, the monster latched onto my ankle and wouldn't let go.

"Don't bite too deep. Might get blood poisoning," shouted a Delta Nu from a nearby porch.

Thoughts that Rin Tin Tin might merely be defending his territory were shattered by a chorus enjoining him to tear me apart.

Not until my Rolex flew off my wrist did the beast relinquish its grip. It dove for the piece as if trained by a jeweler to know value. Too proud to coax it out of its mouth, I instead matched my wits with it, turning my back and walking away, pretending I didn't care.

"Bring it here," the porch monkeys hollered. The confused creature didn't know what to do. It looked at its owners. It looked back at me, at its owners.

Like a flash, I struck. But warned by the mob, it leaped out of reach and raced away. Rather than pursue, I decided to let it go, let the cur advertise how well-to-do I was, and shame the dullards.

"Thanks for the watch," one said after extricating it from Fido's foaming mouth. "It better be waterproof."

"You'd better have a good bail bondsman," I responded.

"Why? You couldn't press your pants, let alone charges."

While summoning up a stunning reply I heard them say, "What's the problem? Didn't hear me? Or is it you're too poor to pay attention?"

I didn't hear what they subsequently said. I didn't hear anything, except the sound of my own two feet pounding the pavement, caution being the better part of valor.

My stomach ached from the torment I had put it through. And my limbs, they had congealed into lead. I needed to sleep. I needed to puke. I needed to get home to regroup, to put all that had happened behind me.

How I made it to my car off Willow, one street west of Broadway, I'll never know. Nor could I honestly say how I got into it.

Amazing how my resources rally in the most trying circumstances, proving I can tap the same instincts bears utilize to hibernate, birds to migrate, and marsupial fetuses to travel from the womb to their mother's pouch. I can perform almost any motor skill regardless of my emotional state, including driving a car, which had become as second nature as breathing. In my cells reside designer genes, invented to see below the surface of life, appreciate what others can't, and harness two hundred fifty c.c.s of the most horsepower money could buy.

Shoving the stick into reverse, I punched the peddle. I want outta here.

Shiiiit! Ugh! Oww! My head! I must have cracked the windshield. I certainly wrecked the transmission. Looking out the window, I saw a boot. A goddamn orange, balance-the-budget, screw-the-citizen, fascist abridgment of one's constitutional rights manacled my right front tire and prevented me from using my personal property. Just because of a few parking tickets? What do they want? What? I'm a good person, deep down. I never purposely hurt anyone, been fair to all I dealt with. It just wasn't fair. It just wasn't. It wasn't. I slid into the backseat to escape this fool's paradise called reality, this pernicious sheath of falsehoods and strife.

Sleep, that healer of wounds, progenitor of death, that is what I wanted, needed, to clear my mind, refresh my soul, douse the flames of insecurity with a renewed purity of vision.

It didn't happen. Reality didn't vanish with my awakening. Instead, I awoke worse off. Sticky with sweat from an unforgiving sun, the first thing I saw was a red "tow" sticker above my brake tag. My baby was going to be kidnapped. Why not give a ticket to a bag lady for jaywalking, or to a passed-out drunk for littering? What's the point? My luck may have turned for the worse, but that's no reason to side-swipe me. In this country, it's not the right to trod on people. Isn't that what the Declaration of Independence was all about?

As I walked home, I could not remember when I went so long in one set of clothes, without a bath, or bed rest. I felt like a grunt beating the bushes in 'Nam, fighting fatigue and fear. I can't deny my apprehensions about what's gone down. The only positive I can abstract from this situation is finding out how strong I am. Social ostracism destroys those with ordinary constitutions. I don't have an ordinary constitution. I'm no sheep, no crowd follower. I was brought up to be my own man. That was our family legacy, the second most important trait my Father taught. The first is family loyalty. In this cold competitive world, family is the only place of refuge and safety. One never loses his umbilical cord. It nourishes both mind and body and provides elegant communication among its members.

I didn't have to be told something wrong with my family was responsible for my abrupt change of fortune. Just as I could sense Father's good luck, I could sense a reversal of fortune. It isn't that hard. Our family was so influential. What affected it affected almost everyone else who mattered in this town. People react to what happens to us.

We elicit responses from people. I elicit responses from people. Like Leslie.

Sneaking down the backways and alleys I managed to get confused and found myself behind the Chi Sigma house, where my not-so-divine Beatrice had taken refuge to cry. Looking up from the stoop where she sat, she stared at me with animal terror, bristling with fear.

My first inclination was to sneak away. But, hey, what happened had been her fault. Like Yvette Mimieux in "Where the Boys Are" she was where she shouldn't have been. She had asked for it. She had wanted it. Her passing out might have been a ruse. I don't care how wide her eyes were, how frozen her face, devoid of anger in every detail. In the waning light of dusk, I still could tell all her anger was directed inward. Outward anger manifests itself with steely eyes and flinty expressions. She despised herself. Typical for women to do that, perhaps justifiably.

"All my troubles started with you," I shouted. "Good, run away. You'd better hide." She ducked into the house.

It had to be her fault. I thought as I resumed my return home.

It was too much a coincidence my problem began after my encounter with her. I thought as I neared my house in Saint Charles.

"It has to be her fault," I said as I came upon our gate.

"Au contraire, mon ami. In no way did your troubles start with that poor girl," I heard a recognizable voice say. "Your troubles started long ago."

Composing myself, I addressed Robert's comment with an urbane wit and undeniable sophistication.

"No, I'm not incredibly stupid," our butler said. "I'm incredibly on the money."

"Please, no philosophizing. My brain can't take anything complicated or weird," I said.

"Get used to it. Wiggle them lobes, redirect them synapses until you're completely comfortable with the law of Karma, 'cause without it you ain't gonna make it."

"Whatchya mean?" I asked in a tremulous voice.

To my mortification, I found out what he meant. A "No Trespassing" sign hung from an imposing shackle on my front gate. A notice announcing all our assets were confiscated dangled next to it.

My key jammed halfway into the locked gate. Turned upside down, it jammed a quarter of the way in. All hope vanished in the concentrated light of my pen knife. The serial numbers were different. The lock had been changed. Not since I found my dog poisoned had I gone so numb.

The sight of our belongings strewn in front of the darkened house looked like so much talus.

Only the sight of Kimberly curled forlornly on the curb lifted my spirits. There's something about retribution that makes me feel better. I patted her on the head and glibly said everything would be all right.

To Robert, I asked, "What happened, someone drops a neutron bomb?"

"Worse. IRS came down hard on your old man. Claimed he short-changed them."

"Never. Not Father. He's punctilious about money."

"Can't argue with that. Paid me on time. But I see no correlation between knowing where every cent goes and making sure the route it takes is legal. Feds think your old man wasn't all that honest about what he charged for a shipment to a rig."

"You mean they can ruin us on a hunch? Hitler would like that, or Stalin, or Mao."

"The IRS has overseeing your Father's pipe yard for some time now."

"That ain't fair!" exclaimed Kimberly, echoing my sentiments, and explaining a lot about Father's recent behavior.

"Oh, yes it is," said Robert.

"Please," I said. "No, what goes around comes around. I can't take it." Though, I must admit, Kimberly's pitiful condition showed there might be something to it.

"Who told them? Who lied to them? Who could be so vindictive?"

"Take your pick. All rich men have enemies."

"Not Father. He can tame a wildcat," I finished.

"Taming ain't transforming."

"It was that Mona Lambert. That's who it was. She got a hold of some stuff 'n showed people. That's what she did," Kimberly tearfully claimed. "She wanted to get even 'cause Robert wanted me more than her. That's why he divorced her to marry me."

"You talkin' about Father's previous wife?"

"I hope she burns in 'H', 'E', double toothpicks. That's what I hope she does."

"You see the evidence?"

"I heard what she said at a country club luncheon. Somethin' about loads of drill pipe she knew about."

"Knew something was brewing by the way the boss was acting. Started checking on his business, personal life," Robert said matter-of-factly.

"Prying?" I asked.

"What happens to him affects me."

"So what was happening?" I asked with a lump in my throat.

"Desperate men do desperate things."

"I don't want to know, though I'm glad you know."

An exchange of looks communicated an understanding fashioned from our many years together. Never before had I admitted to myself how much I respected him. His broad shoulders, shock of perpetually unkempt hair, and impish smile composed a persona that effervesced. No words of retribution followed my defeated glance downward.

"What can I do?" I asked.

"Buck up," he said, lighting up a fancy "Players" fag. "I can't say for sure your dad was cheating. That Caribbean company he sold some of his pipes to may not be a front to avoid paying taxes. Can't say for sure he charged Springer Oil fifty-five thousand more than what he reported to the tax man. Can't believe those IRS guys were so careless to admit I was right that was what they got on him."

"That's the drill pipe order Mona talked about," Kimberly said.

"What about the offshore company?"

"Didn't think they needed to know." He blew a lugubrious puff of smoke.

"Do they?"

"Only talked about the drill pipe."

"Father's not capable of cheating. He wasn't brought up that way. None of us were."

"Surprised me. So I looked closer at the invoice. A case could be made the original figure was erased and written over."

"Palimpsest?"

"Hundred-dollar words don't hide the fact it could be a forgery."

"If we could get our hands on it to analyze it."

"There are the 'Shipping' and 'Client' copies. They might report one twenty gs, instead of one seventy-five."

"Or they could be written over."

"It'd be easier to get your hands on them than getting the 'Office' copy from government lawyers. Might be the only way to convince authorities to check it out. Who knows, they may think it necessary to double check all their evidence, launch an investigation to see if someone was out to get him."

"Let me get this straight. So far that's all the Feds got on him. They are just assuming because he allegedly lied about one order he lied about others?" I asked.

"All I can say is the G-men were tight-lipped about anything else."

"So that gives them the right to steal our home, ruin our property, and confiscate our business? And Jimmy Carter is talking about reinstating the draft? Ask not what your country can do to you."

"Believe it. I had to quit my fifty large jobs as a crane man overseas 'cause the company accountant screwed up my taxes. With penalties, I'd had to go into dealing," said Robert.

"I don't remember any of that on your resume."

"Had to change my name and social security number. That's when I became a dogger on phosphate rigs until that line of work went tits up."

"Won't the Feds catch up with you?" I asked.

"Haven't yet. You'd be surprised how many numbers some dudes have."

"Then you hired on here, right?"

"Want to get wet, better go where it's raining. It was pouring in New Orleans."

"You get a look at the purchase order number?"

"No problem, 41552. The delivery ticket was BE 13137. Don't remember the date. Didn't have time to memorize everything. So, what you gonna do, track it down?"

"Got a better idea?"

"That ignorant yat. I knew she'd do somethin' like this. She ain't got no heart. I told Roger to watch out. That evil eye of hers," Kimberly continued to whine.

"How did she know?" I asked.

"What do you think? I'd be glad to wager her present last name can be found among the higher-ups of another supply company," Robert said. "It was a fatal mixture of serendipity and a grudge, my friend, that did us in."

"I'd never, ever, give her that much credit. A myna bird has a better chance of reciting Hamlet than she is conducting an intelligent act of revenge," I said.

"Underestimating people is dangerous," our wise employee said.

"But understandable."

"If I catch that woman, I'll rip her eyes out. Both of them, with both my bare hands," Kimberly viciously clawed the air.

"What would possess someone to be so hurtful?"

"What possessed the frat boys to run you off?"

"How do you know what they did?"

"A couple of pretty boys were among the crowd who watched the G-men loot us."

"Kind of like the fable James Thurber wrote, about what happened when a pig overheard a chicken call a goose a 'very proper gander.' The bird was run out of the barnyard."

"Let me guess, 'Very proper gander' became 'propaganda', which they took the wrong way."

"You got it."

"Once they got wind of what was going down you were toast."

"And to think I wanted to be one of those shallow pea brains."

"It ain't right. That's all it is. It ain't right," wailed Kimberly. "One stupid piece of paper shouldn't mean we get kicked out onto the street. Mona's well taken care of. Her prenuptial agreement was better than mine. Where's our lawyer? Where's the rightness in the world?" Tears carved rivulets in her make-up, ruining its sheen. Violent sobs shook loose her hairdo, rendering her grotesque and haggish.

"Why do you pass by ya mudders?" I asked in her hideous dialect. "You need to talk."

Like a rain-soaked dog called for dinner, her disconsolate face brightened with the suggestion. "But heart, how can I get there? I ain't got money, 'n I can't get to my car."

The butler handed her the keys to his car.

"Benefits of not being allowed to park in the driveway."

A quick bus, and a hearty, "Mudder will know what to do," and she was gone.

"Who was that masked woman?" Robert asked.

"She's the one that gonna go live in that cruddy neighborhood behind the projects on the East Bank. That's who she was," I said.

"To pay for the sin of not sharing the wealth with her family."

"You do have a way of proving your point. But why give her your car?" I asked.

"The repo man is gonna get it anyway. I'm not gonna make one more payment. Remember, your Father co-signed it."

"Father!"

"Wondered when you'd think of him. The Misses forgot him entirely."

"Where is he? Does he need bail?" I asked.

"No, that's been taken care of."

"How taken care of?"

"Best you don't know."

"Why?"

"Well, let's say you two shouldn't see each other."

"Why?"

"Complications." He flicked his cigarette butt onto the curb.

"What complications?" Another lump formed in my throat.

"Well, it's a matter of legalisms."

"Why legalisms?"

"Enough tautology. It was the presence of the fourth estate. The cats turned up at the bust quicker than tow truck drivers at an accident, and don't think they wouldn't stick to you like flies on stink. All of 'm want to be a Woodward or a Bernstein."

"So? I have nothing to hide. I'm worried about Father."

"Well, there you're wrong, my friend. You do have something to hide."

"Like what?"

"Promise not to kill the messenger?"

"Of course not," I said in total contradiction to my initial, adrenal flight-or-fight response.

"The boss, well, he put a lot of stuff in your name."

Out of my mouth poured an immediate rebuttal. "Father wouldn't have done that unless he had good reason," I said emphatically. "He'd never do anything to hurt me. Never."

"I'm touched; touched. It's rare to see loyalty like that. See why I worked for you. But, be that as it may, you'd best conduct yourself as a hunted man."

The lump in my throat descended to my stomach, where it hardened, not in a disabling knot, but in defiance. A lifetime of fealty does not unravel over hearsay. Though I don't dispute the butler's assertion, I refuse to jump to a simplistic conclusion, not after all the love and support Father had shown me. He made me. And he made me of firmer stuff than someone who succumbs to adversity. "Grace under pressure", that's the definition of manhood I was brought up to emulate.

"That's fine with me," I said. To seek trials, take the road less traveled; that is what life is about. As I've said before, what doesn't kill me makes me stronger.

"Follow me," Robert curtly ordered.

That was also fine with me. Following strangely appealed to me. Accepting help is a sign of maturity. And maturity is something I'd need in abundance, in Father's time of need.

"Don't mind if I call you Virgil?" It would be fitting, for my guide through the Netherlands.

"Don't care what anyone calls me, except late for dinner."

That felt good. I like designating authority. No one can do everything. Churchill couldn't fly the plane to Yalta, nor could MacArthur pilot the P.T. boat that evacuated him from Corregidor. One must know one's limitations, and gracefully hand his well-being to someone else, if only temporarily.

I was really surprised at how well I was taking this. Someone like my sweet stepmother might be crushed by what has happened. If I had only her talents to fall back on, I'd be crushed too. As for me, I'm not one-dimensional. I'm not in dire straits. I'm still enrolled in school (whatever good that is), have lodged in my bones a breeding in which employers would see value, and am dexterous enough to always land on my feet.

Robert also possessed smarts and an equanimity that rivaled mine. Rather than panic at the loss of his employment, he showed remarkable presence of mind. He knew, like I knew, that the best way to proceed was to take stock, take care, be cool, and find those "Shipping" and "Client" copies of the invoice. It's a long shot, but it's all we have.

We took to the sidewalk with a nonchalance befitting devil-may-care locals. It wasn't easy. We failed to negotiate all the cracks and fissures obscured by the shadows cast from the fronds and broadleaves overhead. Our nervous system betrayed us, like a lie detector, causing us to periodically trip.

"Build a city on mud," Robert said to ease the tension.

"And the city taxes your brains out to fix sewers and sidewalks," I responded. "Wished they still let convicts work on the streets. But they need to watch their soap operas."

"That's how a pessimist would look at it. An optimist would see all the money to be made jacking up sinking houses."

"Sounds more like an opportunist."

He explained how his ultimate goal was to be a craftsman capable of the delicate carpentry needed by the period mansions. "Only one old man can do the work right. Only one company in the Carolinas makes curved glass. Everyone wants to be a big shot developer on Poydras."

"Why don't you?" I asked.

"Need risk capital, a grub-stake."

Looking at him, I could tell more was at work than mere economics. Joe's butt-crack might be seduced by money. But, since you can tell a great deal about a person by the job he performs, our ex-butler marched to the beat of a different drum. It added to the allure of letting him guide me. It's far more comfortable to put myself in the hands of someone so worldly-wise, someone who I respect.

How could I turn down following someone who forsook more lucrative employment to luxuriate in Father's opulent surroundings? Look at how much he admired the Greek Revival mansion we came to and how effusive he was about its elliptical glass, fluted pillars, and towering vaults.

"All the parts blend like a beautiful face," he asserted. "It ought to be declared a historical landmark."

"So the owner will get to pay for all the work the historical commission decides it needs," I said to see how he would respond.

"There's always a fly in the soup. Way of the world."

Perfect, I thought.

A spot of bright light and a jangle of bells alerted us to an oncoming streetcar.

"Might as well go in style."

Might as well, since-- luckily--the car happened to be the one swarming with businessmen masked as Twelfth Night Revelers, clown princes of Epiphany. No cop would dare peep inside. They'd as soon run off second liners escorting their favorite marching band, outlaw Mardi Gras Indians, or disperse Jazz funerals.

"The Big Easy," I said as we joined the handful of regular passengers hanging on to the overhead railing.

"No, not really," claimed Robert.

"I already know about the hurricanes and epidemics."

"I was thinking more of the conquests and all the flags which flew over it and that it's okay to fail here."

"You can tell who the most desperate person is by how hard he laughs."

I received a purple, green, and gold "go-cup" from a purple, green, and gold costumed reveler.

"Tears of a clown?" I asked.

"Not here. Not with us," remarked a clown prince. "We stay too drunk to care."

"Sounds like my kind of people."

"We're everybody's kind of people."

"Has a certain *je ne sais quoi,*" I said, after a stiff quaff.

"That and a lot of Vermouth."

A celebrant wearing a tri-colored Harpo wig, and another in savage Medusa-hair of crinkled purple, green, and gold strands, kept the lubricants and *bon mots* coming, each wilder and more wanton than the last.

"So tell me," I said facetiously. "What colors will be used to decorate the ball you're going to?"

"By the time we get there, who'll care?" said Harpo.

"It's Kings' Day. We're kings, so we can do anything, though by the time we get there we'll have to be poured in," asserted the male Medusa.

"Build up tolerance for the season," said Harpo, fittingly, the captain of the rag-tag bunch. His silver whistle replaced the Marx brother's famous horn.

"Considering your present get-up, what do you do for an encore on Fat Tuesday?"

"Oh, we all go blackface and carry flambeaus in Zulu. Nobody ever catches on."

"Not here," chirped someone from the back. "It's plumes and feathers for me. A nimbus of fluffy Indian finery."

"Or here," vouchsafed a more distant voice. "I ride. Can't resist chunking coconuts at the crowd. I'll throw them something mister."

"Hope there's a cute baby in a giant King Cake waiting for us, a baby like Chris Owens," said another.

"I'd rather have a giant stripper in a cute little cake," said Harpo.

Perhaps to confuse pursuers, Robert insisted we get off at Lee Circle before the trolley swung around to Carondolet.

"You ever drive a getaway car?" I asked.

"Probably."

"Why did I expect you to say that?"

It was smart of me to realize how indispensable Robert was; I, a twelfth-nighter in mufti, an undercover knight of Proteus, Hellbound on a historic odyssey only a native "N'Awlian" can conduct. Given the absurdity of it all, I'd declare Saint Expedite as my patron saint, and make pilgrimages both to her statue in Our Lady of Guadalupe Church and to the wharf where the icon was found in a crate marked "Expedite".

The sight of three squad cars outside the Hummingbird Diner pleased my guide.

"The worst place to hide is often the best place," he said paraphrasing the sleuth of Baker Street.

"Elementary," I remarked.

This city would be safer if more donut shops were built, maybe five to a precinct with a Hummingbird as ad hoc headquarters, places to find cops in a hurry. I've waited an hour for the fuzz to respond to a mugging. Once, I was able to secure the services of a former sergeant only by interrupting his daily assignment at his girlfriend's apartment. But since his subsequent demotion, he wasn't around when I again needed him. Maybe I shouldn't have let anyone know he diddled with her when he was on duty.

In keeping with the spirit of King's Day, three Rastafarians offered us a couple of hits of their holy cannabis outside the unstylish little place. We politely declined. The Magi didn't wear dreadlocks or jeopardize the well-being of the recipient of their gifts. Cops may not have a clue what frankincense and myrrh are, but they have no problem identifying pot. Once inside, my eyes were drawn to the sparkle and sheen coruscating off several policemen in a far booth. Three were enough to hold a quorum, as they paid little heed to us. Which was fine with me. Their imposing size and weaponry were intimidating.

Unfortunately, the pungent smoke that had surrounded the druggies had clung to us, attracting the attention of other diners. Before it could attract unwanted attention another, more odious, scent obscured it. The owner stirred the air with his loose-fitting suit and jerky mannerisms, performing like a harlequin under the influence. Only he wasn't blotto, just tired and unwashed--street flotsam, but with a difference, with a dignity a typical bum sorely lacks. A Charlie Chaplin little tramp.

"You can turn your butt around and gallop outta here, Eddie Arcaro," growled the superannuated hippie behind the counter.

"Is that wise?" asked Robert.

"What are you, his mother?"

"No, not at all," I responded. "We find it incumbent upon us to remind you what bad business you're practicing. He represents profit for your employer and you represent overhead."

"He means you're outta line," said Robert.

The longhair uttered a very unloving expletive. The policemen looked at us.

"Please, I'm not worth the trouble," the little tramp said apologetically.

"Au contraire. What can be more important than reacquainting this Woodstock refugee with the precepts he had railed against in youth?" I flashed a peace sign.

"You can beat it too."

"My goodness, haven't we grown bitter with age."

"I have a job to do, 'n that guy's a deadbeat."

"It's not polite to refer to people in the third person," I scolded.

"Eddie, that's it isn't it?" The bedraggled little man nodded. "Okay, Eddie here is a deadbeat."

"May I remind you, you have to serve us. Thanks to Lyndon Johnson and his Great Society, it's the law."

"I don't gotta do a thing."

"Maybe the gentlemen in blue would think differently. It is the law to serve all customers, regardless of race, creed, or color."

"Is everything all right there?" asked a cop.

"Everything's fine," the clerk said loudly. Turning back to us he whispered, "The law doesn't say nothing about deadbeats."

"My friend and I are not deadbeats. We'll personally vouch for this maligned, misunderstood child of God."

"What does that mean to me? Who are you?"

"Oh, we have to be somebody? Not very groovy coming from an antiquated Aquarian."

"Times change. Ya gotta change with."

"Maybe you should reevaluate your position," I said, referring to his shabby attire, and less-than-glamorous profession.

"I don't see you checking into Commander's Palace."

"We're slumming."

"You're bumming."

"Semantics."

The police returned to their discussion as we, with Eddie in tow, slid into a booth. We stayed a long time, so long the next shift of New Orleans' finest served and protected from the same seats. Good thing there's only one murder a day in our fair city.

By the time we arose, the duo had become a troika, with each offering a unique talent to the mix. Eddie was a stopper, a member of the most eclectic fraternity there can be. What were the odds of meeting someone who cashes discarded track tickets? Someone who makes a living taking advantage of people's impatience and ignorance is someone I want to associate with. Like Father said, "The secret of success is to surround yourself with gifted people."

Pride kept us from asking for a room upstairs. We had the money, for a day or two, but balked at the thought of exposing our tenuous situation. Slumming does not include slumbering; and, besides, the geriatric flower children and outpatients who'd share our "space" might tell the pigs who I was. Times had changed.

The hour we spent luxuriating in Lafayette Park, several blocks toward the river, proved educational. In the open air, under the stars, our new companion revealed the business of living, much like Aristotle had for Alexander the Great. Like the great conqueror, I too could thank the simple stories and anecdotes of my mentor for better preparing me for my quest. The influence of a lifetime of judgmental thinking fell away with each word he spoke. Listening to how he employed an eagle eye, a photographic memory, and roamed from track to track, shamed all the exhibitionistic, Joe Namath, and Hugh Hefner exploits I was encouraged to daydream about.

With the stamina of a teenager, the frail-looking sexagenarian began each year at the Fairgrounds here in New Orleans, where he stayed until serious competition showed up. Then it was on to Oaklawn Park in Hot Springs, Churchill Downs before the Derby, and Pimlico in Maryland. Summer caught him in California at smaller parks from Del Mar to Golden Gate Fields, never in crowded Santa Anita or Hollywood Park. By fall, he was back in Louisiana at Delta Downs in Bossier City. Odd jobs filled the slack times.

"Don't like working for someone else," he stated.

An experienced free spirit, he knew how to live the telic life.

"I'm glad he knows," said Robert. "I don't want to learn. Fear of it keeps me employed."

"And I considered you my Virgil."

"Hey, Virgil had a job. A good one. Easy work and great retirement."

So Robert relinquished his position as my guide, stepping down to become a Sancho Panza. And? I took off my Renaissance cap and, instead of putting on a Spanish sombrero, put on the bonnet Alice must have worn through the Looking Glass. Condemned souls did not writhe in putrid vapors on Camp Street. Nor were there any windmills here. The tramps milling outside the nearby Ozanam Inn were not enemy soldiers. They were surprisingly well-behaved. They acknowledged our existence with polite nods. So did the volunteers who served us. Their smiles weren't condescending or smug. They received genuine satisfaction helping us. The fried chicken, stewed carrots, macaroni, and cream peas were palatable, and might have been tasty had I not already eaten.

"One must be a wolf in this business. Eat all you can, when you can," Eddie said.

The absence of any sermonizing prevented indigestion.

"Only place where you can eat in peace. Revival Center, Bethany Kitchen, and those Baptist places, oh boy, that's where you'll find the rowdies outside. All the lectures they got to listen to drive me crazy," continued Eddie.

The only allusion to the scripture I saw was a sign stating, "Jesus loves you".

The only sermon I was subjected to was an impromptu one conducted outside by a sidewalk prophet lubricating his lips with a fifth of Thunderbird. "Finger lickin' good," he claimed. His harangue about the impending Apocalypse proved too dull to tolerate.

"It's egotistical of you to think anything climatic is going to happen in your lifetime," I said.

"You'll roast in Hell."

"How can I? It's restricted."

Of course, he didn't get it. Pearls before swine. Then again, to be fair, who could tell my real mother was Jewish? I don't look Jewish. Another swig of his liquid sacrament emboldened the soap box Cassandra into bothering someone else.

"Losers need excuses," asserted Robert.

"Not always. What I've seen at the racetracks, you wouldn't believe," said Eddie.

"Winners want losers to make excuses. Keeps down the competition," Robert pronounced, ignoring Eddie.

"That's what Father and Grandfather used to say."

"And those they bested, how did they act?"

"We had to keep a law firm on retainer."

"And I don't want to relate what I overheard guests say about you."

"Don't have to. We know your adage about rich people having no friends. That's why family is so important," I said.

"It's no coincidence the family is the unit of preference. No communes or segregated herds," said Robert.

"Losing mine was hard," Eddie remarked.

"Judging from what you said, you don't seem the family man type," I rejoined.

"That's why I lost it."

It was hard to imagine Eddie domesticated. He was so at ease as a hobo. He looked like a hobo and acted like an experienced hobo would act. His ease with his surroundings reassured us. He was our white rabbit, able to inspire our confidence as he led us through this surrealistic veil, marched us down the gilded alleyways, across the rubble-strewn lots awaiting speculative builders, and into an unlocked Chrysler, where we could recline on seats of rich Corinthian leather and thick floor carpeting. Holding a conversation before sleep proved to be no problem. The insulation kept our discussion inside and the chill outside.

Before our collective body heat-induced sleep, I managed to convince my new companion not to take the dishwashing job he had been contemplating, to make up for a bad stretch at the track. What I wasn't able to do was dissuade him from conducting an odyssey of his own.

"Money's in the oil patch," I insisted. "It would be dumb not to take advantage of the boom. Family'd be living in a ranch house in Lakeview, running a furniture store had Grandfather not been a boomer. Make hay while the sun shines."

"I don't know. I'm getting on, and you know I haven't done much, much that matters, anyway," Eddie mentioned. "Being with you guys, and seeing how well you handle a brand-new experience has reminded me how stuck in the mud I've been. Don't be fooled into thinking I'm a free spirit. I got into the stopper business temporarily-- twenty-five years ago and am too lazy to change and too chicken to do what I know needs to be done. The world will still turn if I don't do it, but I always thought a person ought to do what he can; more than he is expected to do," mentioned our guide. He settled back to contemplate his statement.

Robert and I hoped our silence would entice him to state what he was referring to.

"You're taking on the whirlwind, if you're talking about what I think you're talking about," Robert finally said.

"I know what I'm getting into. It's just a darn shame the mob has to ruin the tracks. Trainers and hotwalkers, get hit upon. Don't know one rookie jockey who hasn't been asked to fix a race. Doping is as common as taping. Anytime a capo shows up I know somebody's been bought. What did it for me though was finding out what a bunch of wise guys did at my last high-priced claiming race. Boxed the only four jocks they couldn't reach. Bought four hundred bets at twenty-five each. I'm sure it would have made Guinness's, for the most anyone ever made on a perfect."

"I've seen the testicles of one snitch hung outside the gate of Delta Downs," said Robert, stroking his thick hair.

"I've seen worse than that. I know what I'm getting into. But, what the heck, I can't die young, and it's about time I did something useful."

Hearing a heroic call to arms compelled me to remember other virile pronouncements I have heard. None had involved anything more important than winning a prep football game. No one I could recall had risked personal harm just because it was the right thing to do.

"Kind of puts my little mission in perspective," I said.

"It shouldn't. Even if I clean up the entire industry, I'll still owe Saint Pete, big time." His tiny body was firmed with determination. It suddenly looked healthy. He looked like he could handle anything.

"Then it's settled," I said. "You will not accompany Robert and me in tracking down the invoices. But be assured you can call wherever we settle." Both my companions chuckled (*probably at my chutzpah,* I thought). They quickly forgave me and devoted themselves to prioritizing the best places to rendezvous.

When done, Eddie made a point of sparing my feelings. "Doubt if any company would hire an old foggy like me anyway...This is great. We each have our challenges, you two have your Holy Grail and me, the Golden Fleece."

"Sounds more romantic than climbing every mountain," I said.

"Or forging every stream," added Robert.

As I snuggled cat-like into a position comfortable enough for sleep I tried to put myself in Eddie's shoes. I wanted to because he was inspiring, not because Father taught me to look at other people's points of view. But I couldn't keep from dwelling on my situation, regardless of how much it palled compared to his. Visions of seeing the number "one hundred-twenty thousand" on the "Shipping" and "Client" copies of the invoice danced in my head. As sleep began to wash over me, I envisioned Father at the head of a convoy of flatbeds loaded with tubulars at Nuevo Laredo bribing a fat Mexican bureaucrat. "Only in Mexico," Father said as he drove away. "Only in Mexico," echoed a disembodied voice. "Not in America," I heard my voice say. "We don't bribe anyone to get business in the United States," continued my voice.

Instead of a fuzzy recollection of a town I've only seen once, memories of the pipe yard where the load had to originate came into focus. From the cab of the pickup Dick, the foreman used to cart me around in, all the sights, sounds, and smells returned with the thrills that had enveloped me years ago. The gleaming buildings, big bright signs, neatly arrayed equipment, a thick crunchy carpet of oyster shells, and the robust smells of the well-appointed warehouse all returned to make me anxious to reenter the yard which epitomized the way my family conducted business.

CHAPTER 3

Oh my god, they've all got tattoos! Harley-Davidson eagles, crosses, and bikini-clad women decorated both flabby and leathery forearms. A red heart with a woman's name underneath appeared like a birthmark on the tree trunk arms of a Chef Powell look alike. Another, in a muscleman t-shirt, was anything but muscular, his stick figures his punishment for a lifetime of abuse.

The Saint Charles employment office resembled central lockup, with mother-rapers, father-rapers, sister-rapers, and all the other kinds of rapers the filthy, sticky floor, dirty walls, and metal chairs were designed to accommodate.

Plumes of smoke rising from half a dozen cigarettes congealed in billowy, bluish-white clouds. The smell of urine was unmistakable. Litter abounded. What conversation there was, was guttural, incomprehensible, and so self-contained many were soliloquies. I'm sure compared to this the stands Eddie was clambering over were luxurious and replete with raconteurs. As it was Robert and I were free to suffer in private, if not for very long. Our obvious superiority did not go unnoticed.

The boss man motioned us to what looked like a racetrack betting window before our turn, as we were to be processed with all possible dispatch. Given the clerk's surliness, it was no surprise those who preceded us gave no lip. He knew how to handle them.

"Want a handout, go to Bethany House," he told the man ahead of us. "No advances."

He was more civil to us, readily handling the paperwork and informing us about our transportation. "One bag per person. No exceptions," he insisted.

"Enjoy reading our qualifications?" I asked.

Unable to bring himself to say "yes", he only grunted an affirmation. Typical for an inarticulate.

Posters on the peeling wall reinforced my growing assurance the situation was well in hand. The cartoons of laborers performing unsafe acts were simpleminded and childish, right out of the "Preventative Maintenance" comic books the army prints. Appealing to the same mentality, they showed unrealistically fit workers solving problems as adeptly as would Bozo the Clown, using a wrench for a hammer and spraying dirt off boots with a high-pressure hose.

"Don't gamble with safety," admonished one featuring a befuddled proletariat playing a slot machine. Another moralized about the work ethic. "If you only try to earn what you're being paid, you're already overpaid. You, trying to get by with the least possible effort, will be replaced." A third informed the reader that life is like lifting.

"One lifts his head off the pillow, his body out of bed, his hands to feed his body, and feet to make bread." Yes sir, that's what one does, lifts for life.

Its quaintness could only instill more confidence in me. What have I got to worry about? The horror stories those Pulitzer wannabes recently wrote about pipe yards, how they take advantage of workers, how truthful could they be? Exploiters do not post existential signs, or assemble a crew as efficiently as did an over-the-hill biker and the perambulating corpse who marshaled us out of the agency and into a van. So the building and the people in it had been seedy. They instilled a desire to better oneself, to climb the social ladder. As for me, I'd put in all the overtime necessary for showers and clean clothes.

How anyone could stand to be unclean was beyond me. Primitives, that's all you could call them, nothing but animals. No surer sign of sleaze or derangement exists than the wearing of soiled clothes. Hollywood heroes stayed clean under the most trying circumstances. John Wayne and James Bond do not sweat. Cagney's and Cooper's war scenes were more cosmetic than gritty. Only Bogey, the antihero, looked genuinely dirty, so dirty you could smell him.

With at least ten of us crowded inside the vehicle, we were whisked down narrow side streets toward the Mississippi River bridge.

Shotgun houses, grocery stores, taverns, and an occasional mansion hurled past the window in blurs of faded colors as we lurched through each curve and rattled over potholes. Once out of the old Irish Channel, up a curving ramp, and onto the Greater New Orleans bridge, we slowed to a steady crawl and remained that way until we turned south, onto Highway Twenty-Three, into Plaquemines Parish, Judge Perez's old fiefdom.

Rising like a "War of the Worlds" spaceship, a jack-up drilling rig lorded over the trees and levee to the left, standing in testimony to the might of the oil industry, celebrating man over nature.

Celebrating man over a fellow man or, more accurately, redneck overfed, the Dixie dumpster next to a Piggly Wiggly marked the infamous "Line of Spit" the Judge's stormtroopers laid down to protect their segregated parish.

From Father's description, I could recreate the scene. Olive-drab "deuce and a halves" filled with peach-faced olive-drab National Guardsmen faced a barricade of V-8 cop cars manned by craggy-faced, khaki-colored goons chewing Red Man. It was M-1 against Smith and Wesson, the gall of a warlord against the enforcers of a federal court order in an unheralded stare-down.

Maybe a statue is needed a pot-bellied monument to the day the Crackers seceded when the U.S. government backed down.

A modern Fort Sumter, die-hard rebels could make pilgrimages to it, maybe on Jefferson Davis' birthday. The Stars and Bars could be raised with a band playing Dixie each morning and lowered to the tune of Auralee each night. Segregationists could hold forth in its lee. And pigeons could shit on it.

We passed other neglected sites, the checkpoint where the judge's Brown Shirts inspected work permits everyone had to buy, and the abandoned separate-but-equal black schools that stayed separate-but-equal long after Uncle Sam abolished the practice. Subsidiaries of major service firms, the Gearharts, Schlumbergers, Dressers, and Bakers we passed may flaunt their company's colors and logo, but they undoubtedly were still subject to Leander's influence. Not even the F-4 in front of the naval air station convinced me the military was immune. What were sidewinder missiles and five-hundred-pound bombs to someone who had redeployed old Fort St. Philip from a historical landmark to a private prison? What failed to prevent Farrugut's

Yankees from sailing into New Orleans, succeeded at keeping the parish free from "uppity Niggers" during the mid-Sixties.

Give the devil his due. The judge didn't rise to power or turn parish residents into his subjects through coercion alone. Like his contemporary, Huey Long, he enticed his people into bondage. He did this by sharing the royalties he stole from government leases, by making the parish second only to Baton Rouge in importance, by raising everyone's standard of living, and by building up the infrastructure.

What did his subjects care when he fouled up the deal Huey's brother Earl struck with Truman to grant the state a majority of offshore royalties? That was 1948 and long since forgotten.

He was a perfect Machiavellian Prince, one who wanted his fiefdom to be a showpiece of his power.

The tunnel underneath the Intercoastal Canal we descended into was built with the money apportioned for a second bridge, one that another hurricane Betsy could have wiped out.

Further south, I noticed the towns were dirtier than I remembered them, blighted with litter and in disrepair. I seldom saw young bucks hanging out in small groups. They would have been in school, an all-black school, but one that kept them off the streets. The private academies built to avoid integration weren't as well kept now that they're public. The parish wasn't what it had been. Say what you will, even Mussolini kept the trains running on time, and both Hitler and his twin (according to Grandfather) F.D.R., lifted their countries out of The Depression.

The historical park on our right will continue to commemorate the judge's achievements until some ambitious politician makes headlines by closing it--after the family loses its influence, sometime in the next millennium.

The aura the family cast dictated their goons' conduct. Being stopped at a checkpoint didn't surprise me. "Relax," I told our driver, "These stormtroopers are just trying to relive old times."

"You sure?"

"Where have you been?" I asked.

"Outta touch," he remarked. "The joint does that to you."

How reassuring. I thought. *I'm sure whatever you did wasn't your fault. Too drunk.* Out loud, I confided to him how it doesn't take much to get in trouble.

"Got that right. Don't remember a thing the man said I did. Was so out of it drunk."

Perfect, I thought. These tattooed titans are easy to figure out, as easy as the "In the Heat of the Night" smokies who are shaking down those ahead. I can just see us being hauled in or fitted for ankle bracelets. I'm sure our chauffeur lacked some essential documents like the registration, proof of insurance, or some other form. I can just hear him run his mouth about how it wasn't his fault. I bet there's not enough money in this vehicle to grease one palm, let alone two pigs.

One by one the cars ahead suffered Boss Hog's and Barney Fife's inquisition. None were spared. And neither would we. As they motioned us forward, sunlight glinted off the duo's glasses, sparked their brass, and gleamed off their leather, turning them into radiant specters of doom, eager to send us to work on a prison farm after beating our brains out. Our cowering driver is going to lead them to suspect the van was stolen.

Considering how every thief in Louisiana hurries to the chop shops down here, the cretins would believe anything.

"Got a problem here buddy?" snarled the top cop, inspecting the paperwork the ex-con nervously handed him. You could feel the van shake with fear and sigh with relief when he pointed to the brake tag.

"Outta date."

"Oh, no problem. I'll buy a new one," said the driver.

"Could confiscate your license."

"I'll buy one right now if you want."

"No, that won't be necessary partner. Appreciate the offer. Just don't let me catch you down here without a new one."

"You won't. No sir, not from me."

"I like cooperative people," said his partner.

"Those who get with the program."

"Don't have to worry about me. I'm a get-with-the-program-Jessie. Mister Cooperation."

"Glad to hear it."

"Wouldn't want to hear anything else."

I'm sure they wouldn't. The hand that waved us on would have put a choke hold on the chauffeur had the expletives uttered after we pulled away escaped our rolled-up windows. Our driver's bravery increased with distance, and as it did, so did my resolve to right the wrong which befell Father and get the hell away from people such as him.

A cow in a nearby pasture shook off an egret feeding on its back. A sparrow hawk catapulted off a power line toward an unsuspecting wren. We miraculously avoided an opossum that bolted in front of us.

"These animals down here. They don't leave nobody alone," said a fellow passenger.

"Especially the pigs."

"Nothing wrong with strong leadership. What is there without it?" asked a biker-type.

A burst of acceleration knocked a rejoinder out of my mouth. No loss. My diatribe against absolute power was of the knee-jerk variety. It bored even me. Possessing the character to contain my urges is what sets me apart, and proves how blue my blood is. I guess it wouldn't be too off base to theorize that much of the color was a result
of holding one's animal instincts in check. Maybe that's the etymology of the phrase "blue balls".

The wealth of the parish became more and more evident. Tank farms, refineries, giant tresses, and conveyors moving mountains of commodities onto an awaiting freighter appeared by the river on the left. The upper peninsula of Pointe a la Hache was rich in industry.

Further south there was Point Sulphur and the wooden boom that arched across the road, feeding its foul-smelling cargo into a ship hard by the levee.

When industry played out, the soggy meadowland gave life to orange groves, cotton, and what looked like squash. Not buttercup or spaghetti squash, but the generic stuff that'll end up at the A. and P. or in one of many roadside stands. This is not ruby grapefruit or Adams avocado country. With flimsy buildings in *de facto* surrender to the next major hurricane, signs of fragility were everywhere.

The levees had starved the floodplain of silt. The river wanted to spread its load, change channels, move around the delta, and expressed its displeasure by dumping the soil of a million northern acres directly into its mouth.

The marsh spread out from both sides of the road and, past the smelly fish plant, thwarted the pavement. From there on only mineral rights mattered, as the land was more mush than solid and narrowed to resemble the fishing pole Mark Twain had likened the delta to.

From the bridge that rose above the stench, we could see the fishing fleet as well as signs of drilling, and iron towers rising from little compounds of metal buildings and trailers. Further out, in the brown water, submersibles stuck out like big, ugly beetles.

Rounding a turn, one of those barges suddenly loomed as gigantic as the Loch Ness monster, its superstructure and mast resembling the beast's massive body and long neck. The musty smell of drilling mud was primordial to the olfactory sense, and the screech of the drilling brake mimicked that which the legendary monster might make.

"Rabbit Rig Number One," the sign on the mast said.

A few miles down the road another sign attracted our attention to a board road reaching out into the distance. "Ace Number Seventeen" read the caption beneath a picture of a playing card, designating that somewhere in the distance stood a temporary steel Oz.

We passed a rickety sugarcane truck bearing a dozen blacks on top of a load of planks, looking to lay another board road to a rig.

"Why am I not surprised?" I asked.

The lack of response prompted me to wax prophetic about the future of uneducated Negroes, how they were a tinderbox of frustration because of the prosperity they were going to participate in only marginally.

Another round of silence proved everyone was absorbing what I said.

"Shit," proclaimed a cerebral colleague moments before Robert offered a predictable rejoinder about how those who miss the boat are either being punished for their failings in a former life or can look forward to a better time in the next.

"Shit," repeated the wit.

Shit, I thought.

A big belch of smoke heralded the appearance of yet another monster, its massiveness impressive with proximity. The exhaust pipes responsible groaned from the effort expended pulling the drill pipe out of the ground. I'm sure the derrick hand high above on the monkey boards also groaned as he wrestled it free from the elevators. A dozen ninety-foot stands already racked into the fingers testified to his competence. Pretty primitive. It's hard to think someone pitting his back against two thousand pounds of steel a hundred feet above ground is part of the manufacture of jet fuel and plastics. A holdover from the days of cable tools and steam boilers.

A flatbed tractor-trailer roared past us. It seemed everything was loud. Its chained load threatened to break loose at the next curve. A five-ton Blow Out Preventer would make a formidable roadway obstacle. So would the equally precarious flange and cementing head a hot shot driver transported.

Didn't know which was worse, watching the maniac swerve as if he wanted to lose his cargo, or listening to the biker-type's homily about what a profitable business the oilfield's version of UPS is. If he were so wise, why was he here instead of owning a company?

"Tried it," the tycoon said, reading my mind. "Woulda worked too."

That's what they all say, I thought.

"'Cept made the mistake of hirin' on my kin," he continued. "Got in so many wrecks, lost my insurance."

What is family for? I could see Kimberly's saucy bottom vibrating inside a cab-over-diesel. I could also see wifey numero two being shaken into an Estee Lauder, Liz Claiborne, Dansk, and Yves St. Laurent mess of pancake base, eyeliner, jewelry, lame', and fur, clashing for the first time in her life.

A parade of vehicles sped by, muscle cars packed with silhouettes in baseball caps and ten-gallon hats, as well as pickups with requisite gun racks. A light blue Schlumberger and a soft orange Dresser Atlas wireline truck raced by as if trying to beat each other to a well. A more lugubrious Halliburton cementer followed, knowing it had plenty of time. Wirelines are run before cementing. A grey tangle of pipes and valves clung like vines to the two big hoppers on its flatbed.

Behind the machines-on-wheels came the company cars with logos on the door and oilpatch humor on the bumpers. "Drive ninety, freeze a Yankee," said one. "Registered Coon Ass," said another under the picture of a raccoon's rear. The one proclaiming "I'm mad too Eddie" was exactly like the one on the back of my car.

I had put it there not so much to tell the world I was as mad as the owner of the Western Company of America, about the media's attacks on Reagan's pro-business bias. I had put it there and made sure to park where Father could see it, to remind Father about Eddie Chiles' offer to sell him a share of the Texas Rangers. I had all kinds of ideas on how to turn them into a contender.

Father's objection we should not expand into something we were not familiar with had been an early sign he was losing it. You diversify during booms. That way, you're sitting pretty during the burst, able to buy properties at fire sale prices. Just like J. Paul Getty did.

Flatbeds loaded with pallets of chemicals, drill pipe, and casing; truck-mounted workover units; and a convoy of trucks moving an entire drilling rig roared past us. An army of competitors was racing toward Venice to beat each other to the hydrocarbons that promised riches for all.

With a barrel of bottled water going for a couple of hundred bucks compared to thirty bucks for a barrel of oil, this boom has a long way to go. We have plenty of chances to make mistakes and enough time to clear up our present problems.

A tinge of excitement raced through me. What a place I was in; opened by Texaco and developed by untold speculators willing to risk their own (or if smart enough) other people's money, in an open-air casino, where the chips make the industrial world turn. Build too many rigs or over-leverage them and you go broke. Fail to drill commercial wells and it's sayonara. Go after elephants instead of the discards the majors stick their noses at, and you deserve what you get. The seismic and logs the majors spend millions to run are public property after three years. It's as easy as picking up sugarcane behind a lumbering harvest wagon.

"Best thing about all this is that it's mostly fair, now that the Perezes aren't what they used to be," I gushed.

"That's almost sweet," said the biker-type, former "hot shot" owner, who (if the name stitched on his leather jacket was his) was named "Bill".

"No," I insisted. "Nobody steals the minerals on public lands for themselves anymore. With Reagan coming into office, it's only going to get better."

"You almost make me want to hug you." With his muscular bulk and tree trunk arms, he'd crush me.

The appearance of a high school and a telephone company on concrete legs discolored by watermarks indicated an urge toward permanence. And the less permanent buildings, the tin warehouses and company trailers, looked as if they could be rebuilt before the water drained off the road. It was an outpost of progress.

A modern outpost of progress. Somerset Maugham did not account for an air force. A sleek blue and white Air Logistic helicopter churned above us. Descending rapidly, it came to an abrupt halt just above a power line before turning into the wind, to gingerly slide down to a heliport I wouldn't otherwise have seen.

Such could not be said of the next one. The Shell facility stared us head-on as we veered right, up an incline. The blades of a parked Sikorsky helicopter forced a dozen baggage-laden passengers to plow their way to the open luggage bay. The rotors of other crafts bobbed up and down from the wind. In a corner of the fenced lot, one small Bell set up a stir of its own, the whop-whop of its blades increasing in pitch as it moved laterally off its cement pad to an open field. Weeds bowed below its pontoons, forming a depression as it tilted forward and, like a giant bumblebee, lumbered forward, gathering speed to clear the fence by a couple of feet.

I always thought helicopters took off vertically.

A burst of speed threw us back into our seats. Smoke and the roar of a diesel engine obscured everything. I could feel us sliding off the road. With a second belch of smoke and a mighty roar, the tractor-trailer our driver didn't want to pass us, passed us. A car zipped by in the opposite direction at the same moment the truck pulled in front. We came to an abrupt halt.

"Sorry about that," our driver apologized. "Truck cut me off."

I didn't ask why he didn't want it to pass. I didn't want to find out he raced it out of sheer animal instinct, as the tattoo "Born to Raise Hell," might suggest.

"Must have driven for J. B. Hunt," remarked a dude so undistinguished he could, as I heard say, lose a tail in an elevator. But I somehow did remember him because I recalled someone at the employment office had referred to him as Sam. "Worst drivers on the road. Deserve to be picked upon."

Pulling into the yard shocked me. It's okay for the shell road we turned left on to be full of potholes. The big companies were responsible for their upkeep. The potholes in our yard's driveway, halfway down the road, were not okay. Neither was the shabby state of the fence, the empty guardhouse, or the litter. The last time I visited, the debris that washed up on our dock was picked up daily, and woe be it to the worker caught littering.

In the dimly lit yard, the van thumped over a stray board (one which might possess a nail) and pulled up to a sign with an equally pointed barb. "Don't even think of parking here," it said.

"Why park here with all the empty places?" asked Sam to the driver.

"I show them who they think they are."

Robert wagged a finger at me for wincing.

"Learn to accept; go with the flow, and be sure to be aware," he said.

"Let me tell you this, my friend," preambled Sam. "He's just a J. B. Hunter with an attitude."

Our first look at our accommodations exhorted one black Dixie Dumpster gourmand to complain "Migrants get better cribs than this." He had a point.

"Still beats living outta my car when I drilled phosphate," countered Robert.

If it did, his car must have been a lemon. The barracks weren't at all like I remembered them. The paint was peeling and faded. A patina of dust coated the interior. The bunks resembled bookshelves. The floor tiles were missing. And the kitchen, whoever named it a mess hall must have been inspired here. It would repel cockroaches.

"Old cookie would have had a heart attack," concurred Robert, removing all doubt as to why he and our fastidious, Paris-trained chef never got along.

Not that we were allowed to luxuriate in the surroundings, or even be fed. Once assigned a bunk and allowed to organize my locker (where I found a pair of coveralls) I was ordered to begin earning my good fortune. Any discussion with Robert on how to get into the office to look at the invoice had to wait.

Outside long enough for my eyesight to become accustomed to the dim light, and to realize the yard looked as if vandals had assaulted it, the obese straw boss snorted, "You work, then you eat." His fleshy face made him as fearsome as Ralph Cramden. The rage he flew into when Sam sniffed derisively was as fearsome as the Honeymooner threatening to punch his wife to the moon.

A slight drizzle drew our attention skyward. "It doesn't rain in the oil patch," the creature bellowed, ignoring the fact he was the only one protected by a slicker suit from the drizzle that came up.

"Even worms need protection," I remarked.

"You ain't worms, you's worse than worms; you are singles."

"Gingles?" I asked.

"Yeah, lower than worms."

"Hey, don't get him mad," whispered Sam. "Never have made a living if I didn't swallow people's loads sometimes."

The rain suits in the bin a colleague found contained the greasiest, slimiest slicker suit that had ever flattened against my body. My skin crawled.

"Quit playing with yourself," our boss said.

My skin crawled even more when I asked about our boots and hard hats. A reminder it's the law we should be protected wound up making me feel worse.

"Don't make enemies," Biker Bill reminded me.

"Being on his shit list is right there with a cat hissing at you," Robert said. "Won't come to anything."

The boots we jammed our feet into needed saddle soap and retreading. Red Wings they were not. The stamp under the brim of the plastic hard hats indicated mine was three years out of date. It couldn't stop a ball-pin hammer. What's happened to this place? Surely Father didn't know how shabbily things were run. He cared about his employees, even temporary ones. On several occasions, he mentioned he wouldn't be averse to the creation of unions--a seriously rad opinion, one that helped the local funeral homes prosper.

"Don't need this stuff no ways," said Bill, probably divulging one reason why his hot shot company failed. "When it's your time, it's your time."

"Sounds like you're not the only one who believes in karma," I said to Robert.

"I know. Though I doubt he knows it; he's like a cork on the water. He's like a guy I knew who wouldn't buckle up 'cause if he was gonna die, he was gonna die loose."

"What happened to him?"

"Thrown through the windshield."

"He lived?"

"Yeah. He became my boss, and ran the phosphate rig I worked on."

"Not much symmetry in that," I said.

"Who are we to say? Don't know what he did to earn his good fortune."

He was right. I let jealousy take precedence over logic. I just hope I don't have to wait until my next life before good things come to me. I'd rather overcome my travail in this life.

Within an hour from the time I rolled onto Father's former business, I found myself struggling with a pinch bar on top of a rack of pipe, with my skin suffocating in greasy plastic.

Maybe there's no such thing as karma. In school, I learned entropy will tear all sinners, all saints, and all raindrops into muons and quarks.

"Why are you so sure this Eastern belief isn't hooey?" I asked Robert during a break.

"Got to take it on faith," he answered. "Our biochemical brains aren't designed to contemplate things like that. First content yourself in finding the invoice."

"What makes you so smart?" I asked.

"Experience."

A poster on a dilapidated shed helped bring me back to earth. Beneath a picture of a wife and three urchins, a caption implored workers to be safe because "they need the money". The craneman's sense of humor continued the process. Jokes like telling me my face is sexy "all fucked up", and his claim a leaf bobbing over ripples in a pond resembled a clitoris ended all deep thoughts, replacing them with musings about how he could call the body part "the man in the boat."

It's hard to be existential in a facility for the bewildered.

As if to ensure deep thought remained impossible, the Wheel, as the crane man insisted we call him, worked my nerves with his steady stream of invectives. From behind his portable console, he bellowed "Get the fuckin' lead out", "you gingles don't know shit", and just plain "Get the fuckin' shit right." What a wit! A George Bernard Shaw. He wasn't dumber than a mule, but he wasn't any smarter.

Avoiding inclusion on his shit list merited no reprieve from his foul mouth. The man's belief in negative reinforcement bordered on the fanatical. On-the-job training by use of verbal cattle prods.

"Stupid shit, turn it the other way," was the motivating imperative he blared at me over the speaker as I tried to dislodge a thirty-foot drilling jar wedged inside a pile of models and collars. "Not that way," he reproved, without explaining the correct way the pinch bar should be utilized.

Two colleagues offered advice on how to manipulate the tools of my new trade. Being smart, I willingly listened, and graciously thanked them when the Wheel ordered us "fags to quit butt fucking each other."

Work did not stop for the night. Night does not fall in the oilfield. Trucks constantly rolled in and out, hectically loading and unloading in the surreal illumination of the few orange floodlights that worked. The shadow of the crane, the ball at its apex, and the spreader bar below the pivot distorted images. The dampness impaired footing. Only what was immediately in front of my face was recognizable. Nothing could be worked on safely.

Despite or because of the tattered work glove, I found my hands began to freeze when the wind picked up. The oil on them was no sealant. Handling slings, manipulating hooks, wrapping wire ropes, feeding pins through the eyelets of shackles--all that was involved in moving pipe from point A to B--grew arduous as my fingers curled into claws.

This didn't stop the Wheel from bawling out how lazy and slow I was. Each brain-dead word stung as badly as the pellets of sleet that replaced the rain. Ignoring him took character, although I noticed fellow workers took him in stride. They were used to such treatment. I wasn't. It's harder for a pedigree to eat offal than it is for mutts.

Not until I caused an accident did anyone do anything about my plight. I failed to ensure a "t" bar stayed parallel to the joint of the casing I was picking up. My hands were too numb to keep it steady, and my training too poor to know which hand signal to use. The resonant sound of steel banging against steel, then the smashing of steel into a two by four produced an equally discordant sound from my boss. By flashing the European equivalent of our middle finger salute I managed to end his tirade.

"What's that? Victory over usin' your brains?"

By throwing up my crippled paws I managed to win his sympathy.

"So, you want me to kiss them? Buy some real gloves."

"Take mine," said Bill. "These hands of mine, they're nothing but calluses anyhow."

I enthusiastically thanked him, knowing what a sacrifice it was.

"What's happened to this place?" I asked during the next break in a rickety shack. "The minute I get back I'm going to tell the bank or government agency (whoever the new owners are) what's going on, and if they try to slime their way out, I'll go to the newspapers." *Father doesn't deserve this as a legacy.* I thought.

"You might have only thought it was better," said Bill, airing the cynicism of someone who had lost his business.

"Shit flows downhill and collects at the bottom. There's no lower bottom than this. On the outside I mean," said Sam, exposing his seemingly commonplace background.

"Life is like a sewer. You get out of it what you put into it," remarked Bill. He leaned back in his wooden chair in self-congratulations and quickly lost his balance. He had to scramble to regain his equilibrium.

"Classy move," Sam said.

"Caught myself, didn't I?"

"Touchy, touchy."

"I guess not all of us can be so agile," I responded, winning his approbation. As a reward he signed for a cup of coffee for me...a well-meaning gesture which shouldn't be derided because the coffee was burnt. Whoever had brewed it for us must have done so last month.

A reluctant bunch had to be ordered back into the elements. Of the soggy sailors, I alone was burdened with more than a weak constitution. My rational brain struggled against my primal brain, trying to figure out how to sneak into the busy office to look for the invoice, without much success. Would Sherlock Holmes have been a match for Moriarity if subjected to the same tribulations? He needed an overstuffed chair, a pipe, a violin, and a pinch of snow to shut down the primitive ganglia of his forebrain. Imagine him loading a lorry on the foggy moors for twelve straight hours after being up all day, like us.

That's what I had to do, with only a half hour for the midnight meal, and the opportunity to sign for another cup of liquid tar. I also had to sign a ticket for my *haute* cuisine, leading me to suspect I also was going to have to pay for it. Inside the rustic little building, I forced as many field peas, lumpy mashed potatoes, and pork chops as I could get down my gullet. Nor could I be prevented from drinking all the curdled milk I could. As long as I promptly returned to work nobody seemed to care. My time was all anyone wanted. Twelve hours! Where else does a person work that much, playing with trucks, moving tubulars, equipment, and supplies in inclement weather, all under the ever-present eyes of a Dale Carnegie dropout?

To maintain sanity, I counted how often he insulted me for "not attacking the pipe" and how often my anal sphincter figured into his epithets. I also tried to count the times he uttered the "f" word but found it too tedious, and reverted to counting different manifestations of it, ultimately to conclude that it's as ubiquitous for male Neanderthals as the word "cute" is for female Neanderthals. Both are used for adjectives, adverbs, nouns, pronouns, injunctions, and for emphasis. Not bad for a drowsy deputy. Maybe I was the next Hegel or Kierkegaard. Only they could be as reflective under similar circumstances, so attuned were they to the world around them.

Nevertheless, the alliterative effect of the cretin's cursing was rhythmic, indicating he had honed a talent. Drill sergeants had nothing on him.

I'd be a liar if I said I didn't envy the forklift driver, being out of Mister Elocution's ken. For a sinful second, I even wished--God have mercy on my soul--for a union.

I didn't say anything. The person who did articulate the desire touched off a rash of cautionary tales, featuring violent reprisals suffered by former organizers. Seems whoever tried it regretted it.

Holding my tongue was easy, given what happened to Father when he got involved with unions in the North Sea. Like everyone else, he was forced to pay three weeks' salary for two weeks of work when Norway caved into its workers' demands.

As far as I know, it was his only foray into international business.

The debate raged as we were herded into the showers, where any desire to talk deserted me. A veteran of prep school locker rooms, I'm used to seeing well-toned muscles and athletic carriages, not these caricatures. My co-workers were hard to view, much harder than what I was subjected to entering the employment office. I heretofore hadn't paid attention to how important clothing was for preserving the scenery. It is far more than a fashion statement.

"It's my pride and joy," chortled a gargoyle, noticing my interest in his protruding stomach. "Spent a lot of money on her, beer money. The best kind."

Not to be outdone, a second monster remarked how his stomach habitually preceded the rest of him by ten minutes whenever he bellied up to a bar. The same couldn't be said of his male organ at a whorehouse. At fifty dollars an hour, he'd go broke before he could perform. I doubt he'd seen it in years.

The entire bunch could earn bucks being guinea pigs for experimental vaccines for scurvy, jaundice, tuberculosis, rickets, cirrhosis of the liver, encephalitis, anemia, and malaria. The four horsemen had nothing on them, except maybe physical attractiveness. I tried not to stare at them, as I did not want to be accused of being a fag.

The communal shower was like a sauna, swathing me in warmth as I waited for a vacated nozzle, each drop of sweat coursing down my skin until evaporating in the mist. The spray from the showerhead I soon stood under was uneven but still welcomed, massaging my weary muscles. Then I saw the floor. Bacteria shone like day-glo, matching the naturally occurring Lichenstein of rust and mineral deposits on the wall. Before athlete's foot could begin corroding my skin someone flushed a commode, and I was outta there, dripping with the other gas chamber refugees, nursing scalded skin, and coming to terms with the soap, which left us as refreshed as an oil slick.

I didn't return as most when the water cooled off, for it was then Sam felt it timely to accost me with one of his observations. I could feint interest in his remark "Everyone looks like the rats I sold alligator farmers back home". But I couldn't get by with just a nod when he launched into a narrative, he considered so momentous he showed every sign he was going to follow me back inside to relate it. Claiming I needed to wash my clothes I fled to the laundry room and wasn't surprised the threadbare towel I wore did not attract attention.

After signing for the use of the washer I put my slicker-suit and coveralls into I dressed, entered the tin mess hall, and chose the only seat left vacant at one table, thereby ensuring protection. Sam couldn't sit next to me.

From the reaction of my fellow diners, you'd have thought I was a Yankee. A fly doesn't alert a spider more than I alerted them. The tension was palpable. Several glowered at me, with a menace compounded by mashed potatoes that oozed between gaps in their teeth and patinas of grease on their feral lips.

Ignoring the bad vibrations, I feigned an interest in the condiments. They say Indian raiders balked at victims who acted crazy, and what could be crazier to these savages than someone who expresses intellectual curiosity?

Bottled locally, the condiments reinforced my sneaking suspicion about how self-contained this society was. New Iberia's McIlhenny Tobasco Sauce, Saint Martinville's Cajun Chef Hot Sauce, and Donaldsonville's Pure Honey were three of the more demurely labeled swamp products. Tony Chachere's Famous Creole Seasoning wasn't. The pride of Opelousas claimed to be better than salt or pepper and advised me to use it on everything.

Jalapeños and cayenne peppers, are the soul of this crawfish cuisine, camouflaging the bland and often overcooked entrees. My apologies to Paul Prudhomme and Justine Wilson, but the Dalton Prejeans and Francoise Charmais would eat sawdust if smothered in hot sauce.

I indulged in a little masquerade myself, by drowning the greasiest chops in history in Steen's "Sopping Good" Syrup. How could I resist, when the label on the yellow can promise nothing in it was extracted, nothing was added, and the ingredients contained no sulfur or lime? Work of an Olgivy and Mather copywriter no doubt.

The glare of many disapproving eyes spoiled my Epicurean repast. A shift in air pressure stood what body hair I had on end.

"What the fuck ya doing?" barked the Wheel from behind me.

"I'm inventing a new dish," I commented, trying to relieve the tenseness. "Maybe it'll catch on like blackened redfish."

"Get outta my chair!"

I turned to confront the personification of sheer malice. Rodan couldn't sculpt a more irate visage.

"No single can sit here."

"You mean may, may sit here."

His anger turned malicious. He was serious!

A sudden interest in saving my hide prevailed over saving face.

"You messed up, blood," said Sam as I retreated to the only seat left, the one next to him. "Shouldn't have sat in the bossman's seat. I figured that out the first time I worked at a yard."

It was all I could do to refrain from transforming my crooked fork from a utensil to a weapon and spear the critter. I could have used it for self-immolation, to redirect my thoughts as only physical pain could. Like Lucy said to Charlie Brown after she kicked him: "Gets your mind off your problems." But generous helpings of hot sauce performed the same function.

"Gotta watch yourself," repugned Bill, offering a look of condolence from across the table. "Don't know how much stroke he's got."

From the seat next to him Robert pontificated, "All in a day's work,", again proving himself to be my personal Zen master.

"With friends like you two to steer me, how can I help but learn the rules--after I've broken them," I said.

Quickly tiring of fending off the insults the Wheel's lackeys hurled at me, I engaged Sam in conversation. At first, I faked interest in an elaborate account of how he avoided sitting in a boss' seat. I didn't fake interest when he bragged about other aspects of "A life you have to say is 'above average'". I listened with interest. "Have you heard of anyone else stealing fifty cars? That's what I did in one year. Police said it was a record, and probably still is," he gloated. I stared at the twirp in disbelief. He must have misinterpreted my look, for he added, "Not bad for someone interested in just joy riding. Imagine what I could have done if I was serious."

"I could," said a coworker two seats over. "I was serious and did seven out of a thirty-year sentence."

Unfazed, Sam asked, "Where?"

"Angola."

"What cell block?"

"C"

"Did you know Warden Stewart?"

"Good man. So were his guards. Tough but fair."

"I agree," affirmed another. The table erupted with reminiscences and observations of a past that united all but a handful of diners.

They say only one gene separates apes from Homo Sapiens. I wondered how many separate me from them, or maybe there but for the grace of God go I. What a thought.

I have to admit they were a civil bunch. I heard that a good job and finding the Lord dramatically cuts down recidivism. Maybe they worship in private or their stints in the joint trained them like B.F. Skinner's pigeons to be good. Then again, since none of them are spring chickens, they might just be too old and worn to make trouble. As it's been said, the best way to get through the troublesome teenage years is to turn twenty. I know if I had wild hair I'd be pitching a fit about our bunks. They weren't bunks so much as giant bookshelves, boards nailed and glued together. The tattered mattresses placed on them, one behind the other, spoke volumes about management's respect for labor. Only in Alice's Wonderland would it be appropriate to sleep on torture racks, where my feet accidentally touched the head of the man behind me.

"We gonna make it!" bellowed Sam, as if he saw me pull my feet away. "Don't all of you pull your puds."

"Remember where you are," whispered Robert. "Can't get more Deliverance than this."

This place was designed to warehouse humanity, a real roach motel. Who else but the scum of the earth would tolerate the musty, stagnate, Quonset hut with its filthy window fans, naked light bulbs, moldy army blankets, and thin, yellow mattresses. Stretching out on it felt like lying on a mat of hardened oatmeal. Out of curiosity, I peeled the mattress back and immediately wished I hadn't. The underside was slathered with dried-out cockroaches, some over an inch long. Several lost adhesion and plopped like stale popcorn onto the beaverboard.

"Louisiana raisins," said the Mouth of the South. "Can't stop eatin' them." Jumping onto the floor he proclaimed to one and all, "You wanna see bugs? I'll show you the bugs. Take a look-see outside."

We followed him outside. He acted like the jovial friar who led Dante to the seventh bolgia, the one reserved for thieves. In a drainage ditch, what looked like the snakes slithering after doomed souls were in fact rats, fleeing from his flashlight, squealing in sheer panic, dozens of them, shiny-eyed and evil.

"What I could sell them for, I wouldn't need to work here," he said, gloating like an idiot.

"Too bad they, not nutria rats," remarked Bill. "Make good money at twenty dollars a skin. Encouraged by drivers to run over them, and trade for gas. Got so they could clip on the head as good as they could with a gun, so don't ruin the pelt."

The rats were on the outside, we were on the inside, and as long as that relationship held there probably was no reason to worry. If one or two did break in, they wouldn't last long. Someone among these primitives probably would skin them or eat them.

While ensuring I kept my feet from touching others, I tried to relax. Materializing from the fog of aborted thoughts, and incomplete thoughts, Leslie (the Chi Sigma's Little Sister) came to mind. She moved on a zephyr, heading west into a setting sun, holding at arm's length the invoice I was after. Upon waking I wondered which image was more important to me: the lady or the paper. Maybe my ego was trying to referee between my id and superego, between my primitive urges and my guilt-ridden conscious.

For one with a W.C. Fields rather than a Freudian outlook toward dreams, I failed to muster much enthusiasm. Random thoughts. Mind garbage. That's all they are. Leftovers wrapped in mixed-up, half-remembered plots. As I tossed and turned to get comfortable, the vision returned in complete focus, with Leslie as radiant as Beatrice or Dulcinea del Toboso, as Leander, the poor, misled damsel Don Quixote rescued from her lonely cave, and whose faith in men he restored.

I, the dandy who not only tricked Leander but also seduced her, writhed in pain below the abyss. Screams from my fellow despoilers reverberated in my head, growing louder with every lash cracked across their backs, growing hotter with the unrelenting approach of the beast in Dungeons and Dragons, roaring louder and louder, closer to the poor creature I put in harm's way, as I reached out to her, to the invoice, to push myself away from Room One Hundred One and the carnivorous rats, squealing ravenously inside the cage being fitted around my head. Oh Julia, my Julia, I'll fight Oceania. Hail to Julia, to Big Brother. Too....

Sitting up, staring wide-eyed into the void, my senses returned. As they did, I wish they hadn't. I deserved to be devoured. Oblivion is better than finding yourself capable of insipid behavior, performing a cliché found in cocaine-inspired soap opera scripts. "He awoke with a start, thankful it was only a bad dream." Gross.

Nevertheless, it was not as gross as finding out what a mistake it was to be awake when everyone else was asleep. Too bad I didn't have a recorder and put the cacophony of snoring on a tape I could play in stereo outside the Chi Sigma house.

A steady noise is more tolerable than the starts and stops inherent in sleep apnea and random flatulence. I could wake one or two and try to quickly fall asleep. I couldn't wake dozens. My only recourse was to accept my situation. I wonder how army recruits manage to sleep, then again, they're all young, and their bodies aren't decrepit and worn out from abuse.

Despite the conspiracy wrought by their noise-making and my aching muscles, I managed to sleep. I must have because the next thing I was aware of was the Wheel flipping on the lights and bidding us good morning.

I doubted he was human. Humans grant others of their species their privacy. They don't watch people conduct their morning constitutions. But that's what he did, stood by the bathroom door and made comments about our natural functions, telling us to "make room for breakfast."

It wasn't clear what he meant, it being four o'clock in the afternoon. The breakfast we signed for consisted of steak fingers, fried okra, pinto beans, and stewed carrots. If we weren't as hungry as Sam, who claimed he "could eat the ass end of a menstruating skunk," we'd have passed on it. All of us ate every morsel.

"Wife'd be patriotic black and blue if she screwed up this," Sam remarked before he cleaned his plate.

Our little thrown-together Ship of Fools expressed many universals of human nature and showed how similar all of us were. Sensing that, I also sensed the need to socialize. What little time we had for ourselves had to be spent becoming one of the group. I read <u>Lord of the Flies</u> and grew up observing how Father learned all he could about clients, so he could use the information to manipulate them.

Scouting the office for the invoice would have to wait.

In the idyll before work, I was careful about what I said. One takes tremendous chances expressing one's true opinions. Employing my training on how to be a politician, and how to talk a lot without saying anything, I dwelled on sports, women, schemes for making easy money, and other neutral topics.

"Can make a lot of money getting people to scalp for you on a clear day before a Saints game," I pronounced. "Or if it rains, you can make as much getting them to sell collapsible umbrellas you could buy in bulk if you joined a wholesale club."

I should consult on the side. Don Quixote may have remained maniacal, but not me.

It is a family axiom to spread one's luck.

Thinking about doing exactly that helped get me through the day or, more accurately, the night. More adept with slings, tag lines, spreader bars, pinch bars, clinches, and other implements of my trade, work proved less onerous than yesterday. Maybe the good weather helped, or the fact I found a decent pair of boots. I don't know, but playing with casing weighing a full ton, and joints of pipe weighing nearly as much lost its terror. Hand signals still gave me fits, though much of it was due to the Wheel's idiosyncratic interpretations. Lowering, stopping, and hoisting the block posed no problem. Not so with the boom. It required pantomimes worthy of Marcell Marceaux to raise, lower, extend, and retract. Maybe if grabbing your crotch, extending the finger, or spitting replaced hand waving there'd be less confusion. Maybe if he understood me when I resorted to shouting. Maybe if I gave him a book on phonetics. Only after Robert's mini-lesson in Delta Speak were we able to converse, human to redneck--a skill which helped me prevent the Wheel from sticking his crane in a mud puddle he didn't see. "Cut a chewie" registered quicker in his mind than "hurry up."

As before, work progressed at a feverish pace, keeping us too busy to do much complaining. Each time we started to complain we'd screw something up and have to redo it. Being wormy forced us to concentrate, to work as a team. The endless droves of flatbeds demanded all our attention, and when they didn't, the workboats did. Operating between the two, we were human functions, moving "x" amount of goods from point "A" to "B" to "C", from "C" to "B" to "A"; and any other combination, regardless how circuitous.

I wasn't so busy I couldn't keep an eye on the office or notice what was going on around me. The constant traffic in and out of the office, at first blush seemed sporadic and therefore impossible to predict. But I knew the salesmen and business types interested in deals came calling with a frequency, not unlike that of a comet. Everybody had a rhythm, a routine.

I don't know why there was so much traffic. The end of the fiscal year, when all unspent money needed to be spent to justify one's budget, was months ago. There had to be a time when activity slowed.

You can see a lot just by watching, and, taking care not to jeopardize my work, I watched as an apparatus used to cap wells rumbled onto the lot. Sneaking close to it I climbed onto the bay and inspected it. As I suspected, it was the same Christmas tree I had loaded yesterday. The valves were in the same open position, no screw had been scratched by a wrench, and the tags hadn't been broken.

"Boomerang tags," remarked Bill, the biker, startling me from behind. "Bet the sender's and receiver's initials are in the same handwriting. If you check the records, I bet you'll find we didn't sell it outright."

"Buyers pay for it with credit at a discount?" I said.

"And the yard buys it back full price, cash upfront."

"Not very well thought out," I said as I hopped down.

"Doesn't have to be. Nobody checks."

"They did when the previous owner ran the place."

He rolled his eyes, leading me to believe he either thinks I'm addled or that he knows something I don't about what happened here.

Ordered back to work, I held my opinions in abeyance until I again found myself close to the truck. Undoing the come-along, I noticed the driver looked and acted like someone I knew. The ruddy face, and close-set eyes (one of which looked at you, the other for you) were unmistakable. It had to be Dick, the foreman who drove me around the yard when I was a kid.

I was in no hurry and took care to guide the forklift into the reinforced palette the production device rested on. If the man was Dick he would sit on the truck's running board smoking his Swisher Sweets until he had to move. Dick was not to be hurried.

The same salesman in the same herringbone suit as yesterday appeared from the office, sporting the same leather briefcase. Instead of hurrying to his big Chevrolet pickup, he stopped to talk to my old friend.

I had plenty of time to load two bulbous pulsation dampeners onto another truck. Designed to fit onto a rig's mud pump, they were as small as large haystacks but solid iron and round. I bet we rattled them more than they rattled when they were working, controlling the vibrations of the pumps as the pumps circulated drilling mud to the bit and back.

After tightening the last shackle, I strolled over to Dick as he smoked on the running board. I had to look cool. Who knew what spies might be lurking? The operation was too smooth not to have safeguards built in. But I had to investigate, to find out what happened to this place since Father took his eyes off it (probably when he became so sullen). Maybe it can help his case, prove he had to have an iron hand to keep corruption at bay. It was so rampant.

"Dick!" I said louder than I intended, loud enough to draw unwanted attention, leading me to believe I was subconsciously begging him to tell me he wasn't an accomplice.

He took a nervous drag and reluctantly looked up.

"Who are you?"

"It's me, Randy Cunningham. You used to take me for rides."

"I didn't take nobody for rides." He snubbed out his cigar butt, languidly rose, and entered his cab. I noticed he wore alligator boots and had a Rolex on his wrist. "It would be against the rules," he said before rolling up his window and starting his engine.

Maybe I misidentified him. Then I noticed the ring on his wedding finger. Although bronze, it sparkled like gold. It did because he religiously shined it. A can of Brasso lay in the hollow atop his dashboard.

"It's also against the rules not to check your rigging before you leave," I shouted as he drove off.

"You don't get paid to think," growled the ever-vigilant crane man. "You get paid to work." He violently gestured me away.

Like an exorcist, he banished the ghosts of my past. His impersonation of Captain Quig exceeded his previous efforts. He used a microscope to oversee our next task, commenting on every little thing we did. I didn't want to dwell on my ex-friend anyway and hoped whatever happened to him wouldn't happen to me.

I needed to concentrate on getting the invoice. Judging from the Wheel's invigorated efforts to keep us busy, it soon proved to be vexatious. Should I glance at the office he'd appear like Cerberus, guarding access. It seemed fifteen feet was the closest we could come to the main building before he'd bare his fangs.

While guiding a truck back out of the way of another truck that needed to squeeze through a gap between two pipe racks, Sam inadvertently stepped into the restricted zone. Only a cornerback could have shoved him away with as much vigor as did our crane man. The trucker jammed on his airbrakes. Sam's helmet flew off his head and he had to take several giant steps to keep from falling. Once righting himself he charged, only to be stopped short by Wheel's menacing expression.

"Go ahead. Try it," our boss sneered.

Looking up at the imposing offender, the small guy reared back and told him, with all the bravado he could muster, "Don't let it happen again."

"I'll make a note of it," Wheel said, departing.

I noticed Bill looked away when I spotted him watching.

He and I seemed to be the only witnesses to the incident. No one believed the ex-car thief when he cornered a couple of hands and tried to win sympathy.

"You musta tripped," said the driver of the truck he was backing up. "Looked a little loopy."

"Better than what you look like," Sam retorted.

Like an avenging angel, Robert leaped on the running board and held the door shut. The driver looked big enough to knock him off. But despite his mighty efforts to get out, Robert kept him inside. Soon he became exhausted.

"Come on out chief," Robert said as he opened the door.

Out stepped a dwarf with an oversized head. His beady eyes seethed with malice.

"Hold it now, think if you can afford to get into a fight with everybody watching? Don't you think it'd be better to arrange a time when nobody is around?

"Fine," the guy snarled. He couldn't have been more than four feet something, one hundred pounds.

"Fine," Sam retorted. The two glowered at each other.

"I'm sure Sam was doing a fine job; has since I've known him," I said.

"Always will," Sam acknowledged, straightening with pride.

Looking at his watch, the dwarf remarked how he was getting behind schedule. "Don't think this is over," he said, retreating to his cab.

"You bet it isn't over." Sam looked as fearsome as an angry Pekinese, "Next time, you and me."

"Better get the best insurance you can," the diver said as the truck rumbled away.

"How did you know?" I asked Robert in private.

"Bet you never looked at a trucker behind a wheel in your life. You can tell. You can also tell Bill's in with the Wheel, and I bet you can find out how once you check out the office."

"Again, how?" I asked as I directed his attention to two strangers exiting the office.

"A good predator patiently watches its prey."

Like alert prey, the Wheel became extra sensitive to our whereabouts. He instituted new rules. We weren't supposed to interfere with work during our time off, meaning we were confined, like inmates, to the barracks, galley, makeshift TV room (where the television received only one channel clearly), and grounds in between. On Saturdays, a van drove to Buras, the closest town. I wanted to get away, but when the entire first group to go was fired for returning drunk I eschewed the service.

"Just as well," Robert said during a game of chess (where we used assorted replacements for missing pieces). "Need to know how everything works, how everything's related before we take any chances."

"Maybe the Mafia runs the place. They make examples of its rule breakers. And Bill, can he be a bagman or something? He has worked here before." I made what I thought was a clever move.

"Naw, they wouldn't run such a sloppy ship." He quickly made his move.

"Are the Wheel or Bill working for somebody then?" I pondered and pondered my next move.

"Certainly not the mob. They're too grubby looking. No associate would go around looking like a slob. Can't get any women. Whoever is running this joint doesn't know how to run a real business. Probably some receiver, like a bank. It certainly hasn't been Roger."

"So something had been going on with Father for some time?"

"For a while."

"What makes you so smart?"

"Being poor forces you to have a lot of experiences," he said after I finally made my move. He quickly made his.

"I'm beginning to see what you mean," I said, hesitantly taking my hand off the next piece I moved.

"Checkmate," Robert said without emotion. He reached out to shake my hand.

I certainly was beginning to see what he meant. If I wasn't reduced to such a lowly position, I'd probably never have known what it was like to be a laborer, never have learned what a laborer needed to know. My ignorance amazed me. Tools and equipment whose function and names I formerly didn't know existed had rolled in and out in profusion, providing me quite an education.

"That's a Bo Weevil test tool," said a driver whose truck I loaded. "Used to complete a hole, bring that oil to the surface."

"And that's a casing hanger tool," his swamper remarked, identifying a spring-loaded, spear-like device. "Used to hang a string of liner inside the casing that's already been set."

Both identified the Gemco float collars and Davis Lynch shoe and explained how the centralizers were "used to guide that iron wall cake into the hole." From them I learned about Howco swedges, and what a worn bushing, washover tool, mule shoe, pony collar, and butt tester were. I also picked up enough info about bits to realize I had a lot more to learn. There were so many different kinds! There were diamond bits, insert bits, rock bits, and newfangled PDC bits. Some possessed sealed bearings, different type journals, different-sized nozzles, and variable cutters. Sizes ranged from mere paperweights to forty-eight inches in diameter, manufactured by Smith, Security, Reed, Christensen, and Hughes.

"Drilling a well takes a lot of engineering smarts," I said, half out of conviction, half to score points with the Wheel.

"Don't need anything fancy. Wooden derricks and iron men. That's what makes a hole. Brought in the biggest field in history."

By mentioning the larger fields in Arabia, I managed to lose all the ground I gained.

"East Texas got us through World War Two."

I kept my mouth shut about how the Majors and H. L. Hunt swapped their hydrocarbons for yen before the war. Nor did I point out how poorly wood fares in the Gulf--the destination for most of this equipment.

An energetic conversation broke out within earshot upon the mention of easy money. I could see why the thought of wealth without risk or much effort is a universal lure. The fact Dick was the center of attention kept me from joining in.

I needed to hear how he acquired the big, new Ford pickup he stood beside as he flaunted his boots and watch. I needed to hear him hang himself with his tongue. "Easiest thing I ever done putting together my trucking company," he said, lighting up a Swisher Sweet. "Bankers threw money at me."

Up went the chorus of, "What am I doing here?" I noticed no one asked if he could hire on, and learn the ropes. All wanted to, as one said, "Take what I make here for a down payment on a Kenilworth diesel."

Bill again hung back, out of sight of most. This time he suppressed an anger that told me he was afraid Dick would expose their scheme. If there's anything I've learned lately is to be brutally honest about subtle signs.

As if on cue, Bill's covetous coterie turned its attention eyes right upon the emergence of a brunette from a Lincoln Town Car that rolled into the compound.

"I'd like to ride her," bellowed a biker-type, like Bill.

Upstaging them all, Sam uttered a cry horny tom-cats emit. I suddenly felt slimy, ashamed, wanting--but unable--to tell her not all men are so crass, that these creatures are from the bottom of the barrel.

I was immobilized and would have remained so, but Robert hustled over to a joint of pipe on the ground, wrapped his arms around its middle, and--unbelievably--lifted it. His thighs shook as they straightened, but the strain manifested itself in a smile, not a frown, as everyone's attention turned from the woman to him. Initially, it appeared he was showing off, but since he continued carrying it after the woman had fled inside the main office, I concluded otherwise.

"You getting it," cheered a low-life.

"Mine's bigger," said Sam.

"I could do that once," claimed Bill's look-alike. Other equally robust comments replaced the more derivative cat-calls. They soon gave way to unanimous praise, the kind you'd expect from yokels gawking at Evel Knievel or Mister Olympia.

Both ends of the pipe oscillated in quickening, unsustainable circles, ultimately forcing Robert to drop it, which he did with stirring bravado. The biceps he flexed unleashed a salvo of kudos, all southern fried, and so heart-felt they did not diminish when the sylph reappeared. Given how few even noticed the woman depart I concluded louts will take Hulk Hogan over Crystal Gayle, and (considering how they all also had turned their backs on Dick) over quick riches too.

They swarmed over Robert. I noticed Bill took advantage of Dick being alone to give him what for, up close and personal. And as I tried to read his lips I happened to notice, out of the corner of my eye, Robert jerking his head toward the office, signaling me to take advantage of the opportunity no one was around it.

I hurriedly strode into the forbidden zone and entered the dispatcher's office.

Only one person was inside. In sheer bulk, he equaled three normal people. In a reinforced chair the monster was grabbing a wink; his massive head bobbed forward and back. The paperwork in his giant paw wasn't there by accident. You have to give him credit. All he had to do was open an eye to look as if he was languidly reading it.

Gifted with a sixth sense which must have told him I was nobody important, he let the sandman rule as I checked out the place until we had company, someone whose appearance clogged all senses, including smell. The visitor's cologne assailed like ammonia. His iridescent gold chain, blow-dried hair, and leisure suit advertised a less than buttoned-down business attitude. No doubt the corvette I could see out the window had been the venue for romantic dalliances. I wouldn't doubt he had a hand ensuring the female rep who preceded him was so attractive.

The way Mister Smooth readily fell for the behemoth's faked perusal of the handy paperwork gave me the confidence to finish looking around before I left.

"Looks like no one's here," said the fop disappointedly. "Well, big guy, maybe you can be of service." He strode to the desk. The dispatcher lowered his feet and swiveled toward him. By staying as long as I dared, I don't think I missed out on much. Still, I hung around the door, should they reveal weaknesses I could exploit.

"Have a good one," oozed Leisure Suit Larry after a brief stay.

"Don't do nothing I wouldn't do," the monster replied.

The exchange gave me pause. After such a *cri de ceour* it was obvious I'd have to appeal to these people's basest impulse if I wanted to divert their attention long enough to go into the files I had noticed. Not able to hire Jesse Ventura or Mister "T", maybe the crew would create a commotion over a stripper. I'd attract the behemoth's attention if she'd pop out of a real cake. Maybe I could put on a party, which would require cash, and the will not to just get along with these people, but to befriend them.

I reapplied myself to work with a zeal and an attitude that made the Wheel suspicious.

"You trying to put something over on me?" he asked as I worked at half again the pace I had previously.

You have to give him credit. The suspicious eye he gave me at the start of my shift changed into one of caution, then surprise, when others picked up on my enthusiasm and became enthusiastic themselves.

Those I worked with at first grumbled when I leveled more than my share of dirt from a drainage ditch. When they saw I was not miserable, having made a game of trying to spread the dirt as fast as the backhoe could pile it up, they made a game out of it too. Further, they made it a mark of pride if they outdid one another. No one minded Sam out-shoveled us all or affected haughty airs by doing so.

We were the "Dirty Dozen" (as Sam called us) and prided ourselves on our eccentricities. Hearing the hyperkinetic guy refer to himself as "above average" ceased being so grating.

"I expect the same effort tomorrow," the Wheel grumbled at the end of the shift, as we stored away our gear.

But a surprising thing happened while we put on our boots, gloves, and hard hats the next day. Our boss said, "Keep up the good work" and, I swear, didn't utter an epithet.

The mystery was solved come the next shift change, when the other crane man gestured for him to "shove it" out of jealousy. All of us felt good about it and wanted to continue feeling good. Even when there was little to do we were so enthusiastic we found something to do without having to be told.

I started policing around the office, and when that was done, secured a can from the paint locker and started to make the parking lot more attractive. From the restricted zone I garnered a better idea of what was going on inside the office. Through the windows, I could see both shift dispatchers working the phones and frantically keeping records. The lack of activity in the yard did not warrant all the activity inside. None of the cars that did drive up bore company logos on the doors, meaning the drivers were bent on personal, not company business.

I'm sure if I looked hard enough, I'd find more than an incriminating invoice and bogus sales receipts in the file cabinet. I might find a bookie operation, maybe run by the mob, despite what Robert thought.

I remember the fear in Father's eyes and the tell-tale stiff body language he had affected after three men in expensively tailored suits invited themselves into our house. All the defiance Father had expressed before their visit evaporated after they left. The bodyguards he had to hire, the security system he implemented, and the indifference he had to deal with from the FBI, I bet they had something to do with his downfall.

Only the D.A. took the evidence his private investigators had amassed against the Mafia seriously. The case is still pending although more goons and more fake companies kept calling us, harassing us, filing suits, and trying to take us over.

One night a year ago, I was awakened by a phone call I knew from the saccharine voice the business the caller wanted to discuss was monkey business.

It was Mister Connack's office who arranged a sting at Fat Harry's when the caller later asked we get together. The bar's crowded, dark interior was a perfect place to stick a pistol in my belly and escort me out into the alley. I'm sure if the agents hadn't been so obvious, they wouldn't have scared away the potential kidnappers. I just stood at the corner of the bar and watched three well-dressed men enter, look around, notice three other men in suits and ties in a booth, and leave. The act of courage scared them, as I never feared being kidnapped again. Then again, I just could have been unaware. The second sense I assumed to be part of my make-up might be sheer self-delusion.

As the days coalesced into weeks, other concerns weighed on me. One day, my mind wandered as I wrapped lift hooks under and around heavyweight drill pipe that lay on the ground. Although the rusty chains and brittle canvas slings tore my gloves and grated my hands so badly, that I could peel skin, I couldn't help feel I deserved it. Reduced to an animal, hurt, cold, and more spent than I had been at anything I ever had done, I couldn't escape the torment of Furies who descended upon me. They were punishing me for the most grievous sin I ever had committed: for the way I had mistreated Leslie. No amount of rationalization excused my behavior. Made as dumb as an animal, I deserved to be cast into the whirlpool in the Second Circle of

Hell, with all the other carnal sinners, into the Sixth Bolgia with the rest of the hypocrites, wearing robes made of lead. I had made her a scapegoat. To pick a sweet, beautiful creature to blame for my ostracism proved how loathsome I could be.

The agony wouldn't go away.

My coworkers seemed to suffer no emotional duress as they worked. Like coolies they smiled while they worked. Nothing seemed to weigh on them. The prospect of payday superseded all other concerns.

"I don't know about you but I'm going to take my money to Hollywood," remarked Sam, sticking out his hairless chest in the shower room.

"Start a studio?" I asked.

"Star at one. What's the big deal? Anyone can do it if they have the courage. They say ninety percent of success is just showing up. And when the movie people get to meet me, I'll be in like Flynn."

"All anyone needs is a start," remarked Bill, also half-naked. His skin was a canvas of patriotic tattoos. "Everyone must take advantage of every situation that comes your way." His face brightened with enthusiasm. "It's the American way."

Others quickly joined in with their opinions and plans. But I wasn't listening. Bill's voice grated on me. It shoved aside my anguish over Leslie. I almost wanted to uncover all the evidence implicating him in the kickback schemes as much as I wanted to find the invoice. Almost.

Because payday would put everyone in a festive mood, I decided it would be best to ask if the entertainers could arrive immediately after we received our checks. Judging from the crew's revere as the day approached, the commotion would rock the house.

"What do you mean my credit card is no good?" I screamed into a pay phone the day before the big event. "I've paid off my balance every month." A brusque explanation so enraged me I slammed the phone onto the cradle.

"That amanuensis said my account had been frozen," I later explained to Robert.

He winced. "Sometimes I wonder if you could ever make it without your family's money," he said.

His chastisement made me think, which I believe was his intent. Because when I thought about what I had done I realized how incredibly dumb it was. Might as well have put a return address on an anonymous letter, and left a business card.

"Guess I shouldn't have," I said, demurely.

"It was stupid."

So was asking him, "How come you're not excited about payday?"

He stared at me as if I was a strange animal in a zoo.

Realizing what he was implying made me defensive. "Okay, okay. I'll admit I never earned a paycheck before. So does that make me a leper?"

A wry smile crinkled his face.

"That Socratic act of yours can get old."

"After two thousand plus years, it has proven itself."

A lot of thoughts tumbled through my head as I joined the pay line early the next day. Never again would I belittle or begrudge a working stiff. Getting paid for performing work was a new phenomenon. I've washed cars and mowed grass and got paid for it. But I've never received a paycheck. I liked it. I wasn't the only one.

"Gonna drink up my money," said a heretofore inconspicuous stump jumper a couple of people ahead of me. "Already am overdue at the Red House Lounge. Probably put out an A.P.B. for me."

From behind me, I heard, "Gonna raise Hell, kick ass, and take names," claimed Sam, not to be outdone.

"Better write in shorthand," said Bill, outdoing him.

"I'm going to take that money I saved missing meals and eat me a barrel of crawfish," a portly Cajun informed us. "Maybe eat another barrel for dessert. I guarantee."

"I bet you suck the heads," I said. "You folks will eat anything."

"That's very true. Woudda won in Vietnam had you done told us the V. C., they were good eating".

"Hollywood here I come," said Sam.

"A Greyhound ticket is all you're going to afford," remarked Bill.

"I'm not going right off. I can get a part as an extra here. Sign up for it at the employment office. Hey, I know it's not easy; takes a long time. I'm figuring on one or even two years once I get there."

The jovial mood soon evaporated. Waiting after twelve hours of work does that, especially if you're kept in the dark. Each passing minute augured something unpleasant. We could feel it. We could see it, the nearly empty office, the absence of bosses, and--finally--the appearance of a frail little man flanked by two big bodyguards.

"Look at their hands," observed Bill. "Never done a day's work in his life."

"He'd get thrown outta the places I go to," someone informed us.

Something told me such treatment would be justified. Anyone who dared jigger the first paycheck I had ever earned would deserve a redneck night out.

"I'm from a firm the yard hires to do the accounting," he said as he set up a little table. "I'm an employee like you."

Not since I was blackballed by the frats did my stomach churn with so much foreboding. The complaints of those ahead of me rattled me. I did not want to find coal in my stocking. I'd been a good boy, a very good boy, the best I've ever been, and I did not want to be denied.

Instead of elation, I received my envelope with trepidation, tantamount to last year's letter from the registrar of Harvard. I knew it would be disappointing, yet maintained the stiff upper lip bred into my bones. The inevitable rejection prompted me to proudly matriculate into Tulane, the Harvard of the South (for those who couldn't get into the Harvard of the North).

That I failed to immediately construct alternate plans upon the shock of seeing what I had earned proved how numb I was. Devoid of the thick hide Robert had developed and with no military service to draw from like others, I acted commendably, putting up a front every bit as brave as that formed by the guy who ate four meals a day and received a bill instead of a check. Refusing to cuss may have blunted a primitive urge. But it conserved my dignity.

I didn't care all that much about the money. It has little relevance to a person's worth. How could it? I knew how hard I had worked, and what I was worth to the company. I don't need any arbitrary confirmation from a few printed numbers on a piece of fancy stationery. It's ridiculous, absurd, a travesty, this third-party proof I'm a viable human being. That I had never earned a check before was immaterial, totally beside the point, and had no bearing on the matter.

Proving what little effect it had on me, I subordinated my personal feelings and showed my stripes by thinking about the others.

Swears like "I'm gonna tear a new asshole" and "They're cruisin' for a bruisin'" had an unexpected effect on me. They were particularly evocative, especially when compared to the wailings my boarding school classmates set up whenever they were short on cash. Acting as if God had it in for them only showed how thin-skinned they were. Experiencing the full brunt of reality was purgative. Let the privileged snicker at the misfortune of the meek. Not me. I'm above that. It takes maturity to empathize with the mouse who gives the owl the finger.

"What about motivation?" I complained loud enough for the accountant to hear. "Treating us this way. Who can live off what's left after the deductions? A hundred bucks for a month's work."

"Screw motivation," went the chorus behind me.

"It's insane of them to think we'd perform after this. They're cutting their throats, obliterating our loyalty," I said.

"Screw them."

"Maybe we should sue. A class action suit," I offered.

"Son, you do that 'n you'll never work in the oilfield again," someone remarked.

"He's right, you know," said Robert. "That Industrial Foundation of America in Odessa, it's going to get you some kinda way."

"Got that right," Bill continued. "Handles all onshore deals. Put the hex on you worse than a dishonorable discharge. And if they don't, that place on the West Bank in Gretna will. Got all offshore covered. Forget about even a galley hand job."

"That employment agency who hired us, you think they checked with them?" I asked.

"What do you think?" Bill asked rhetorically. He leaned against the wall of the office. "With the rest of the country doing so badly it ain't wise to bite the hand that feeds you. Steel mills, textile mills, Detroit, you name it, they're all shutting down."

"Even if that hand hits you?" asked someone, obviously as shaken as we with his tiny paycheck.

Bill lit a cigarette. "Cause my daddy used to whip me don't mean I stop being attached."

My passing comment about contacting the BBB failed to arouse much enthusiasm. Neither did my reaffirmation of a union. Then again it didn't engender all the warnings aired when I previously brought up the subject.

The idea of creating one provided the only solace for my crushed plans. I didn't make enough money to entice a bar maid to have a drink. Marshaling everyone's grievances would provide a distraction for going through the office and serve a useful function at the same time. The firebrand rhetoric and heroism inherent lifting hard working souls reduced to penury elevated the proposal to Promethean proportions. The idea was intoxicating. Better to be a rebel with a cause, a Knight Errant tilting windmills than a pawn of circumstances. The few warnings about rocking the boat that were aired sounded more pathetic than foreboding.

"It's stacked against us. We haven't a chance," moaned one defeatist.

"You guys just aren't imaginative enough," remarked Bill, blowing smoke rings.

The look I gave Robert must have conveyed my inner thoughts.

"Yes, he incriminated himself," he said in private. "Really blowing smoke."

"But we have no hard evidence, except if we found out he had worked here before. Probably would have to get a confession."

"Meaning any retribution will have to be off the record."

Entrapping Bill was an option. We could tell unbribed parish cops he was stealing from the yard. But before I could wallow in the thought of him swallowed by a penal system based on fiat and prejudice rather than due process I had more immediate problems to deal with.

The hurried departure of the accountant and his two bodyguards once the payments had been settled afforded a perfect opportunity to vent our frustrations. The absence of guards or observers was insulting. The yard's managers seemed to be daring us to do something. Sam kicked a chair and those who skipped meals to save money raided the galley. Others just grumbled or if they had to go back to work, they did so devoid of any vestige of their previous enthusiasm.

"This sucks!" I screamed as they withdrew.

"What are we supposed to do?" Sam whined.

"You're the actor...act."

"Might get into trouble."

"You're tight with all the wardens. Be like a reunion for you if you got into trouble."

His brow furrowed; his thin lips pursed with intense pressure. His entire face scrunched into a question mark. He scratched his head, shifted his weight, cleared his throat, and said, "It would be good for practice. But I need a script. I'm not trained to extemporize."

"So you're telling me you can't act," I said, waving my hand, pointing out all the workers who were throwing things and cursing.

With a whoop, he started shouting about the injustice. "You wouldn't be so brave if we were big shots!" he yelled at the departing car. "We're going to get a lawyer. File a suit. I bet Sixty Minutes would like to do a program here,"

The dispatcher peeped out the door. A foreman stepped outside his trailer. A growl from the on-duty craneman attracted everyone's attention.

"Get back to work. You don't deserve what you got!" exclaimed the Wheel's clone.

Seeing the recipients of the warning bristle inspired Sam. He began to imitate a real reformer.

"What we have here is a failure to communicate," he sneered with a bravado that stirred everyone who heard it. Workers on and off tour gravitated toward him. Bosses followed, uttering expletives that only reinforced the workers resolve to listen to Sam. Threats backfired. "So fire me. I'd be better off unemployed," retorted the Cajun who had eaten four meals a day.

"Fire us all," said Sam.

"Yeah, fire us all," several said in unison, before setting up a cacophony loud enough to drown out the opposition. Like an athletic cheer, the roister gave heart to the most cowed soul, and promised to create a riot if not contained,

The yard master, his assistants, the cranemen, the cook-- everyone of consequence converged on the protesters, shouting as loud as they, and brandishing either clenched fists or makeshift weapons which only incited the workers more. Farrah Fawcett Majors in the buff couldn't have provided a better diversion.

Totally unnoticed, I slipped into the dispatcher's office. The walrus's amazing disinterest in my entrance equaled his disinterest in the commotion outside. Lounging in his reinforced chair he looked at me resignedly, as if knowing he wasn't going to be spared becoming involved.

"Don't worry," I said pleasantly. "The Wheel just wants me to check some paperwork for him."

The failure of the creature to leap in defense of the files (at least to me) proved he wasn't privy to the scams.

"Wheel would do it himself, but he's busy." I pointed to a window that offered a perfect view of the craneman and Sam poking each other in the chest. The eyebrow the gargoyle lifted in response signaled his indifference to whatever I or anyone else did. Holding my breath, I yanked back the first drawer and bent the tabs of each folder to ensure I read them correctly.

I ought to be in pictures. I ought to be lots of places, least of all here. The urge of the moment was upon me, flaying me with emotions that threatened to expose me. Controlling them required more talent than I thought possible, leaving me wondering what other secrets I possessed.

Thumbing through the records, I tried to project the part crazy, part sane, part angry, part jovial, part frantic, part controlled, part careless, part meticulous persona of an All-American cracker; all the while studying the records with a weather eye out for a half-remembered P.O. and delivery ticket numbers. I kept the other eye out for information on the stolen equipment the yard bought back.

The widespread disorganization didn't help. The fat dispatcher was as gifted at his job as he was at keeping fit. The confusion of field transfers, vouchers, bills of lading, order tickets, weigh papers, drop tickets, transfer sheets, manifests, and inventories was daunting. The beast had to be alphabetically illiterate, with a faulty grasp on organizing dates sequentially. He was a real creature of a boom that accelerated Parkinson's Law, allowed people to advance to two or three levels above their level of incompetence.

Any added desire to uncover where our skimmed paychecks went dissipated in the hopeless disorganization. Father wouldn't have let the creature into the yard, let alone given him a key job.

"Know what you're after?" he asked, suddenly coming to life.

The two-minute warning.

I could only hope finding the numbers was like finding a pretty girl in a physics class, improbable, not impossible.

Numbers floated dream-like before my eyes, whirling in a congested maze of ill will. They taunted, teased me with perfidious hopes, proving the fundamentalists' contention that God hated the rich and loved the poor. He must, having strewn the path to riches with so many obstacles and crafted so many perils holding on to it. It was the easiest thing in the world to be poor.

"Don't make so much noise!" barked the sea lion. "There's enough noise outside. Can't hear myself think."

The one-minute warning.

Maybe God's a prankster, a joke-meister so proficient he can put it over on the dour Swaggarts and Oral Roberts of this world, make the holier-than-thou crowd think he had no sense of humor. He wouldn't even let me find paperwork on the Christmas tree or pulsation dampeners.

Then it appeared, without fanfare: P.O. number 41552, delivery ticket BE 131.... The last two numbers were hard to read. While trying to decipher them I noticed the dispatcher perk up at something he saw through the window.

"Let's see what you got," he said with chilly conviction.

I purposely dropped an adjacent folder. Documents scattered over the floor. A feral wail preceded a charge to clean up the mess.

"Beat it," he growled.

I did, with the invoice clutched tightly in my right hand. Had it been in my other hand the yard master certainly would have noticed it as we squeezed by each other in the doorway.

"What's he doing here?" the beefy man bellowed in my wake.

"What's it look like?" said the dispatcher. "Ran him out so fast I spilled all this."

I didn't hear anything else, but deduced from the absence of loud obliquities the lie went over well.

I also deduced from the smudges either the carbon between it and the "Office" copy smudged it or it was tampered with. The number "One hundred seventy-five thousand" was almost indecipherable, certainly open to interpretation. I opted to believe the latter, not the former explanation.

"Could be," Robert said when I showed the copy to him back in the barracks after everything had died down. "Never going to know for sure until you track down the "Client" copy.

The thought of having to expand my search scared me. I wasn't prepared. I always had considered rigs like poker chips, something to own, speculate with, but not work on. My family made its money selling shovels to gold miners, so to speak, not working the mines.

"You've been thrown across the Rubicon. You don't have a choice," Robert said.

The hesitancy I displayed surprised even me. It didn't make sense to backslide when the game's afoot. I noticed most others had ended up swallowing their pride and had gone back to work, either because they needed the money or because they'd rather deal with the devil they knew than one they didn't know.

"You're chickenshit," proclaimed Robert.

"I am not," I insisted.

"Then what's holding you back?".

Ultimately, after much soul searching, I had to admit it was my résumé. I couldn't believe it, but I couldn't deny I worried about what a month-long work stint would look like on paper.

"Those two agencies who keep track of employees' work record, they scare me."

"What do you care? Afraid of some paper shuffler a thousand miles away?" asked Robert.

"Won't get a job working for the company the order was shipped to unless I spent a decent time here."

"While your Father rots in jail."

"I'm only playing it smart." I sounded lame.

"You just don't want to see it through now that you've seen how far you have to go."

The criticism stung, which meant it rang true, stifling my knee-jerk retort about why he doesn't do it himself.

"Now don't go thinking you'll go to the Ninth Circle, what is it? The Cocytus, with all the other family traitors. You do enough self-flagellating in this life."

"How did you know?" I said in amazement.

"Don't ever play poker or bourey on a rig. And don't underestimate folks, especially me, Virgil. That's who you considered me from the beginning, isn't it?"

"Sounds kind of childish?"

"Don't sweat it. Adulthood only straps a person in a cultural straitjacket. Come on. Let's go get a beer."

"Shouldn't we submit our resignation?"

"You're right." We went outside and got within shouting distance of our craneman.

"Hey, you big fat jerk, we quit." Robert turned back to me. "That wasn't too hard."

"Don't be so sure," I said, pointing to the craneman as he charged toward us. A leg appeared from a group of workers he ran by. The big man sprawled ass over head into the ground, throwing up oyster shells and dirt as he tumbled into a parked forklift. Righting himself, bruised and bloody, he seethed and would have lashed at the closest breathing entity, if there were any. All the spectators were in hiding. The most likely suspect joined Robert and I jogging out of the yard.

"This running is going to make me thirsty," Sam said.
Yeah, let's drink a lot, I thought.

Heralded by "Just cause I vowed not to drink any more doesn't mean I'm gonna drink any less," we three burst into the sleaziest bar in Venice (or in the world; same difference).

Dark, dank, and dreary inside the only seats available were far from the jukebox. I couldn't handle cry in your beer music. The muted lighting complimented rather than obscured the dirt and grease. And if ever one were to cast a waitress to fit the surroundings, ours was it. A human pork rind, but with an angelic voice.

"Have you thought of telephone soliciting?" Robert asked, trying to be kind.

"Honey, I make my money entertaining on the phone. Call me if you like."

"What should we call you?"

"Candy, Sweet Candy. Pure sugar."

"Can't imagine what her advertisement looks like," I said as she padded off with our order.

"A real headliner," Sam admitted. "Called her twice."

"From the back of 'Hustler'?"

"'Velvet Lips', a local mag."

"You're that hard up?" I asked.

"A man can dream can't he?"

"What about truck stop queens," I asked.

"Road whores? Can't afford them."

"Are expensive," said Robert.

"Do I hear the voice of experience?" I asked.

"Spent most of my life either on the road or close to it. Learned nothing's free, especially with women. You ought to know better than me."

Considering what one vindictive woman did to us, I didn't argue. If Kimberly was right, Mona Lambert had turned one invoice into a document of staggering significance. It was Aladdin's magic lantern, the books of chivalry which transformed Alonso Quixano into the knight of La Mancha.

Fortunately, shedding Sam before he became privy to what we were up to proved to be no problem. His actor's ego compelled him to join a table of fellow escapees from the yard. Better he basks in their accolades than get to know us.

Besides the P.O. and delivery ticket numbers, the invoice sported a lease number, field number, well number, API number, company number, and a date in various states of legibility. It resembled a canceled check. The order numbers, contractor's name, rig number, and two signatures were, respectively, stamped, typed, posted, and written in ink. Father definitely had sent it, and a "R" "M" had delivered it. Robert agreed the price looked as if it was tampered with. Like looking at a
3-D picture, one could convince oneself the number one hundred twenty thousand originally existed, proving Father really did charge Springer Oil what he reported on his tax statement.

"Only the FBI's crime lab could tell for sure."

After knocking back a swig of Jax beer I asked what we should do next.

"Can't hand carry this. 'The Man' would hold me for questioning. Don't trust mailing, who knows where it would end up. A Xerox wouldn't be convincing. So, the most logical thing to do is hire on Marble Drilling, rig sixty-eight. What does it say there? The Marble Seabee," Robert stated.

"Then what are we doing here?" I asked, thankful we'd go together.

"Having a good time. Better enjoy it, don't know when you'll have another chance."

"He's right you know," cooed a painted lady who ambled up to our table. "Everybody needs some fun."

She looked as if her jeans were spray painted. Her make-up resembled layer cake.

"Would you like to buy me a drink?"

If you drink a pint of mouthwash, I thought. Her breath left a lot to be desired. "Of course," I chirped.

In the dim light the bottle the waitress brought appeared to be genuine champagne. The price certainly was above reproach.

My lady inserted a coffin nail between her luscious lips. Robert handed me a lighter and gave me a nudge. I smiled as she inhaled.

Her appreciation unleashed the envy in others.

From behind a pyramid of empty beer cans a table of spectators were constructing, several intellectuals implored me to kiss her, for an experience I'd never forget.

She rubbed her hand on my leg and flashed a gummy grin.

"Way she sucks she can jump start a Harley," said one of the architects.

"Can suck a baseball through fifty feet of garden hose," said his associate.

"You mean a football."

The insult hurt my "date". Pain transformed her. She took her hand off my knee and, with it, gripped her drink so tightly she rattled the ice.

"Don't listen to them," I implored. "Their spinal columns grow to the top of their cranium."

"What?"

"Their left brains were genetically stunted. Retrograde evolution."

"I guess."

A gentle injunction to keep her chin up kept my lady's chin up as I turned my attention to the ruffians. Launching into a narrative about a girl who wouldn't spread unless she was hot, I blew out a match and held it by its head. You'd have thought I was a magician when the stem splayed open. The audience howled with delight. Rewarded with the accolade, "You're all right" I won the right to be left alone, to charm my date, and impress her with my style.

While my former nemeses burned themselves trying to copy my trick, I suavely lit another ciggy for my lady and engaged her in small talk. Finding her receptive, I unleashed a salvo of pent-up intellectualism I was sure she never had heard before. Proving she was no simpleton, she followed my arguments with preternatural acumen, closer than had any coed. She absorbed my philosophies with the relish of an eager student, thrilled at the way I combined the best of Spinoza, Hume, Locke, and Aristotle into a symbiosis only a genuinely critical mind could follow.

"If I knew half what you do, I'd be rich and famous," she cooed.

"That can be taken both ways," Robert kidded.

"No, no," Miss Misunderstood pleaded. "I didn't mean it that way."

"I know you didn't," I said, petting her hand. "You're a rational creature."

She pulled her hand away.

"You are," I pleaded. "More than anyone else gives you credit."

"I've got to go," she snapped as she collected her things. "It's been good to know you."

Once freed, she fled into the ladies' room, like the dormouse hiding in the teapot.

"What did I do?"

"Don't know?" Robert asked rhetorically. "Maybe too much sophistry. It should be a snap for a creature like you," Robert said.

"You're kidding. That's all it took, calling her 'a creature'?"

"That's all it takes. Trust me,"

"Why should I trust you?" I asked.

His eyes narrowed in irritation. "Because if you don't you're gonna regret it."

I accepted my dressing down and moments later proved how repentant I could be. I didn't question him; I didn't doubt him. So when he unexpectedly ordered me to run, I ran, and I was glad I did. The sound of crashing beer cans and crashing bodies immediately followed in my wake. Someone had knocked over the pyramid of beer cans.

Curses rose from the din. "The sowers of discord," I announced to one and all outside.

"Redneck playtime you mean," said Robert. "Others nearby couldn't resist the temptation."

"Expecting these folks to act right when they're drunk is like expecting a thoroughbred to run straight without blinders," said Sam, using a racing metaphor Eddie might say.

Watching the tumult proved enlightening, if not entertaining. Like rooting for the Commies and Nazis to beat each other's brains out, with pool cues for weapons.

Watching my fellow evacuees proved equally intriguing. There was the oversensitive lady I called a "creature" swearing like a sailor and puffing away so vigorously on a 'rette, smoke-shrouded her charming face.

Arranged in cliques, most debriefed each other so enthusiastically that, taken together, one would think a war had been waged and each had barely escaped the grim reaper.

Along with the odor of stale beer and brilliantly rendered manifestations of the ubiquitous "f" word, the crowd became a mob. Character actors in an outdoor production, that's what they were, proving Sam's assertion that acting is nothing more than being natural. That being the case, it was easy to divine what would happen when one of them swatted the taillights of an escaping car.

Completely in character, the driver barreled out the door, gun in hand.

"Hey man, I'm sorry. I get wild sometimes," Robert pleaded to him. "I done wrong and wanna apologize." He extended his hand.

The perplexed gunman lowered his weapon and hesitantly reached for my sidekick's outstretched paw.

"I hope we can be friends. You good folks." Robert motioned toward a cop car that screamed into the lot. The short-circuited drunk quickly sheathed the pistol and greeted the constable with a smile. The real perpetrator hid behind a parked car.

So ended the dreadful Battle Betwixt Don Dingdong and Certain Wineskins before it had a chance to begin. Not exactly what Charles Bronson or Clint would have done, but it served its purpose, perplexing
the guy who swatted the car "Real good".

CHAPTER 4

The road north, rife with compelling sights on the way down, was stark and foreboding on the way up. The stars burned callously in the black sky, their cold light blowing a chill that cut to the bone.

Thumbing a ride proved futile. Nobody stopped. Nobody slowed down. We might as well have been invisible, and with a hundred miles to look forward to, felt the city was as far away as it was for General Butler's Yankees.

Not so Sam and Robert, my companions. You'd think we were strolling in the park, the way they carried on, jabbering about politics, of Cabbages and Kings--or, more precisely, of all the King's Men.

"Here we are," I said, "Jacked out and miserable, without means, without much in the way of prospects, in need of better clothing, transportation, and what are you doing? Paying allegiance to the demagogues who make it all possible, Huey, Earl, and Gillis Long."

"Just taking our minds off our situation. Why aren't you?" Robert asked.

His practicality knocked the complaints about our banana republic out of me. The populace's unabashed worship of corrupt officials suddenly ceased twisting my stomach.

"You got color down here," Robert explained, reading my mind better than I. "The sins of the past will fade. You'll someday enter the twentieth century, as will every third-world country. Your Longs, O.K. Allens, Jimmy Rogers, Blaze Stars, Dudley LeBlancs, the Louisiana

Hayride, and all the husbands Edwards had cuckolded will give you charisma."

"Not stigmatize?" I asked.

"Put it this way, who's more romantic, Louisiana or Ohio."

"You've got a point. Father remembers old Huey holding forth on the corner of Calhoun and Saint Charles for an entire afternoon. Killed off a fifth of Jim Beam before he was through."

"My kind of man," said Sam.

"We are different. The Napoleonic Code. Parishes. Pledging allegiance several times to the Tri-Color, to Spain, to the Stars and Bars, and Old Glory. With Jim Bowie, Jean Lafitte, Sachmo, Jelly Roll Morton, Chennault, and the pylon racers Wedell and Williams, this is a state of iconoclasts. The whole place started as a big land fraud in New Orleans. Bankrupted all of France," I said with budding glee.

"You should see what goes on at the tracks," Sam commented, again showing the same stripes as the member of the team he was replacing.

"Just carrying on the tradition," I said.

"One that doesn't need to be carried on," Sam said, proving how popular Eddie's sentiment was.

"All the riverboat gambling. Storyville. It all fits," I said, playing devil's advocate.

"It shouldn't. Somebody ought to do something."

"Why don't you?"

"Are you nuts? I like my life. Ironsides is the only actor in a wheelchair."

A car slowed. We moved toward it. It came to a stop. We jogged closer and were upon it when a cloud of luminescent ash arched outward, scattering us as it sped off.

My mood instantly soured.

"Peasants pummeling peasants, because we're not rich or famous," I said after we reassembled.

"And you never counted the stars on the cover of 'Playboy' to see if Hugh had slept with the playmate?" asked Robert as he brushed off the ash.

The barb worked deeper with every subsequent step, prying loose hidden secrets, and forcing me to come to grips with my failings. As we kept our council, I silently came to admit I was a little better than the litterbugs. Wasn't I as culpable, loathing virginity in males, thinking it a sign of weakness, all the while being a virgin myself until I was baptized second in line with Leslie?

"Pilgrims on the path of least resistance, that's all we are," I said aloud.

"Don't get on your case. You wouldn't be doing what you're doing if you were a wimp. Face it, you'd do anything to save your family, help your Father," Robert advised.

"I'm doing it for myself," I deferred.

"Think about it."

"It's hardly an act of nobility to try to save one's hide."

"Thought you said you didn't believe your old man put everything in your name."

"I don't."

He chuckled. I chuckled. "All right, you win. But you'd have to kill me before I'd admit being illogical," I said.

"Don't worry. I won't kill you. Wouldn't get my old job back. Just let me think."

He thought it best we split up. "Got to deal with human nature as well as mother nature," he said.

"Three's a crowd?" Sam asked.

"Two's too many."

One was just right. I jogged ahead and was picked up by the first car that came by.

"Couldn't turn me down, could you?" I asked the scruffy driver rhetorically.

"Couldn't drive another foot," he mumbled. "Might find some urine in my alcohol if I'm tested. Here, take the wheel." He slid over my lap to the passenger seat.

"What about the two guys behind?"

"What two guys?"

It didn't matter the gas gauge was nearing empty. We could run on his fumes. His snoring soon drowned out ominous noises coming from the engine.

Aurally insulated and driven into a semi-trance by the monotonous blacktop road and starry carapace, thoughts of Father and Leslie welled into my conscious, moving me with genuine, but uneven emotion.

Maybe I'm a male chauvinist, expecting men to be tough and women soft, or maybe I'm just a romantic. How else could I explain why thoughts of Leslie predominated? Whichever it is, I had been too long absent from her, my Dulcinea. But rather than do penance in the wild, when I get back, I'll make a point of seeing her, face to face. I have already spent my forty days in the wilderness.

As far as Leslie's herd-like behavior was concerned, "It does not matter what her background is...as to the use I make of her, she is equal to the greatest princess in the world."

After letting my Charon sleep it off at an empty lot hard by Old Man Acheron (the Mississippi), I marched lakeward through the warehouse district to the rendezvous Robert and I discussed with Eddie before we left. Maybe the Hummingbird would let us work for room and board until we tried to get on with the Marble drilling rig.

"What do you mean I can't work for room and board?" I asked the ersatz Richard Brautigan, being as hard-nosed as ever.

"Things changed."

I showed him my few remaining dollars, intimating I wanted a room.

"Not enough."

"It was enough last time."

"Price has gone up." Beaming, he showed me an article the *Times-Picayune* wrote, touting the joint as a repository of the Aquarian ethic.

"So how does being the place 'where real people can live and work in harmony' justify price gouging?" I asked.

"Read on."

I get it. Because it's now known throughout the land Roy Rogers orders out for your fried chicken when he hits town you're now a landmark.

"Business picked up two-fold."

"I'll make a good employee," I insisted.

"We've been turning away better people than you, now that the word's out the World's Fair coming. Snowbirds are coming down here to work it. Property values are going to go through the roof."

"Woodstock was free."

"Only after Yazgar sold all the tickets."

A few cups of coffee to settle down, a few more to kill time, and a final, lingering one in hopes my companions would arrive at the last minute and I had to relinquish my seat. Couldn't rent it forever. Two bucks only goes so far.

Four more bits didn't go much farther, a bland meal and a cot at the Ozanma Inn. That was all. As for a shower, Tulane's gym proved satisfactory, if unnerving. Who knew whom I might run into, especially after I stole a cotton shirt from an unlocked locker?

"We'll certainly keep you under consideration," said Marble's operations manager, scanning my impressive application the next morning. "This the right phone number and address?" His hard eyes and expressionless lips made him look disinterested. Judging from the clutter on his desk he had more important business to consider than hiring another hand.

"Or you can reach me at Dinwiddie Hall, the Geology Department at Tulane. Doing research under Doctor Marsh, the head of paleontology."

Yeah, I thought. *I'm going to research whether he'll honor the favor Father did him by donating big bucks to his department.*

"Interesting. Thank you for coming in." He offered a limp hand.

"I'll call every day," I said, shaking it vigorously like my wrestling coach had said to impress people.

"That would be fine," he said without enthusiasm.

The comely secretary smiled at me as I strolled past her equally cluttered desk to look at two pictures of company-owned jack-up rigs.

"I wouldn't want to go on one of those things," she remarked before pointing to a picture near a coat rack. "They're death traps." The photo featured a rig about to capsize in a giant vortex of froth.

"Everybody got off beforehand. But a lot of good people quit. One blowout was enough for them."

"I'll be careful," I said.

"I'd rather not have to be that careful."

The warning failed to worry me. The aspect of danger turned my experience into an adventure. Having never been in harm's way, I wondered how I'd handle an emergency.

I wondered how I'd handle the interim until I could get to the rig. As someone ready to tempt the Fates I didn't worry. The bright new buildings in the Central Business District gleamed with promises of plenty of employment opportunities.

It didn't bother me my first efforts proved futile. "It's like auditioning for a Broadway play," I told Eddie and Robert when we finally met at the Hummingbird. "Just got to keep trying."

The fact Robert had hiked more than me, knocked on more doors than me after experiencing the same put-off at Marble Drilling, and that Eddie had started figuring out how to deal with the corruption he had witnessed impressed me. "No, I won't tell you everything about it," the diminutive man said with a twinkle in his eyes. "In case somebody wants to know."

The character they showed stood in stark contrast to the nearby tramp who was heartbroken to have gotten turned down as a waiter at the Caribbean Room.

"It rained the day I was born 'and it's been raining ever since."

"I know what you mean," Eddie sympathized.

"I doubt you do. I doubt anyone does." His face fell with dejection as he went off to sulk.

"I doubt he could pronounce the entrées," I said.

"Maybe we should give it a shot," Eddie whispered. "It's slow at the Fairgrounds, and it'll be a while before the season gets going elsewhere."

"Why?" I asked, trying to diplomatically dissuade him. "They only want gays. Peach and cream toadies."

I refrained from telling him I probably could get hired there with no problem. That I had not applied could be explained by my need to maintain my anonymity. I'm Ralph Lauren's Polo, Lacoste's Izod, white wine spritzer, and Minosa, a perfect accouterment to gallery openings, catered galas, and opening nights. In the Timberland boots, chino pants, and chamois shirts I might somehow retrieve I can shine, and give the movers and shakers what they want. I'm wearing a Trafalgar suede belt and I own a watermelon pen for Christ's sake.

When it was time to relinquish our seats, we re-established the troika. To all my other attributes, I could add that of consensus maker. I ought to be a politician, a statesmanlike Eisenhower, allying De Gaulle and Montgomery.

We agreed Eddie should scout for a place where we could hang our hats. He needed a respite. Though he wouldn't be explicit about his recent experiences I could tell he had taken risks. The messianic look that he had acquired might have made him appear younger, healthier, more alive than when we first met but it also meant his mission was beginning to consume him.

"It's good for all of us to slow down for a while," said Robert. "We need a break."

Eddie certainly did. Although he didn't divulge everything, he was doing he let us know it had more to do with the mob than a bookie operation like I failed to prove at the pipe yard. The selflessness of his mission was inspirational. His heroic demeanor shamed my anxiety. Whereas I wanted to restore my family's prestige he wanted to keep an institution pure. What would I get if I succeeded? A return to the cushy life I now know I had enjoyed. What would he get? I'd hated to think.

Given his example, I didn't dare complain about the job I took while awaiting an opening at Marble Drilling. Selling Lucky Dogs, the foot-long sidewalk delicacy, was perfectly satisfactory. It and the mullet were the pinnacle of plebian fare, food that might not grace fine tables but whose economy of scale generated the profits gourmands needed to sell their gorgeous boards.

Knowing the value of what I was doing separated me from the less learned, less reflective. As Ayn Rand said, "There is no dishonorable work, if well done."

Entering the warehouse at Galvez Street was as startling to me as entering the Duchess' four-foot-high house was for Alice. Thanks to my nearsightedness, the wizened little man who met me looked like the frog-footman. He too looked into the sky when he talked to me. But rather than a consequence of having eyes on the top of his head, I figured it was because he was stupid.

"Can I come in?" I asked politely.

"Are you to get in at all?" I swear he said. "That's the question."

A great crash was heard from within.

"What am I to do?" I asked.

"Anything you like."

Just then the door opened. I ducked, fearing a flying projectile.

"I'm going to stay here. You're not right. We don't want anyone who's not right here."

"This is utterly idiotic," I said, quoting Alice. I marched in unopposed.

Rather than a cook, an ugly duchess, and an uglier baby immersed in hopeless clutter, two normal people stood in the middle of the spotless bay. Except for a pan which must have fallen off one of the vending carts, it also was in perfect order, the way a business ought to look.

The clean floors and shiny, well-organized wagons indicated a lot of pride and attention to detail.

Instead of crockery, a mechanic assailed me with verbal abuse.

"Hey buddy, you new meat?"

I diplomatically owned how I was recently hired over the phone.

"We don't need nobody new."

"Maybe you need somebody different."

"Not your kind of different."

"Don't mind him," said a nattily attired, good-natured gentleman. "He's part of a program I'm involved in with Charity Hospital."

"You must have a lot of patience," I said, sucking up to my boss.

"Got to in this business."

"I bet the profit margins make it all worthwhile."

"You're my kind of employee. You'll go far, I can see that." He put his arm around me and led me into his office.

"He's not the only one who's gonna like you," the outpatient said cryptically.

There was nothing cryptic or deranged about my orientation. The manager was like the Cheshire Cat. I couldn't recall a supervisor who smiled so much. By the enthusiasm he invested in explaining his business you'd think he was president of G M. From how to present the condiments to dealing with customers, he spared no detail.

"One customer is not just one sale; it is a hundred repeat sales. A good recommendation can generate who knows how many new sales." He moved to the edge of his chair, eager, aggressive, and with that enigmatic smile, he was exactly what you'd want your boss to be.

Concluding his pep talk with the injunction to "go out there and sell yourself" didn't disappoint me. It enlivened me. Witnessing sheer genius turn a cliché into a maxim was reminiscent of Beethoven transforming tired material into magic. Look at the magic Jim Henson put into mere puppets. I too should transcend the ordinary if I possess any talent at all.

So, come morning, I led the parade of vendors who marched out of the garage into the middle of the narrow, old-world street. In and out of the shadows we went, to the tune "Bridge Over the River Kwai" I whistled.

With paper hats and snappy paper vests, we impressed the winos and bag ladies as we wended toward the ocean of light on Canal, where we broke away to our assigned stations.

Mine was at the corner of Governor Nicholls and Royal by the Gallier house, where my predecessor failed to match the average of those who worked the spot before. This outside sales position may not be glamorous, but it is a tradition, more quirky than tacky, like Fat Tuesday's transvestite beauty pageant or the coronation of Zulu and Rex. The Quarter wouldn't be the same without us, its street performers, or art galleries. The removal of anyone would diminish this city as badly as when the Pelicans folded and Tulane Stadium came down.

The computer printout rating past performances at my location was very specific, from the number of condiments used to the number of products left at the end of the day. Weather and sales were cross-referenced, as was the time of day, time of year, and even the time of man. Day in and day out Scorpios did better at my location. That's probably one reason why I got the job. Hey, a businessman has to go for any edge he can, and if I get replaced by a musician who attracts crowds by playing goblets, so be it, if he increases sales. The same holds with a strumpet, though I doubt she'd do well among the residents.

"My, aren't you the cute one," intoned a Twinkie.

"I'm so glad we've got you instead of the usual wino. It's depressing to see some wasted old man whenever we look out our window."

The sandy-haired fruit I served first suggestively licked the end of his wiener. Not to be outdone, his peaches and cream buddy inserted his bun in and out his mouth and winked to make sure I got the message.

The duo was only a scouting party. I was a magnet, exceeding my quota before noon, finding I could easily double my commissions by teasing my customers. Come supper time, I possessed six phone numbers, three addresses, two personal notes, and a tempting offer to go out. I always wanted to see Les Cage Aux Folles. I could pretend my admirer did something wrong, offended me, and gave the same cold shoulder girls gave me when they wanted the date to end.

Lucky me, I soon developed a following. I think it was my humor. Using it as a shield, instead of warding off suitors, it attracted them. Witticisms like calling a fully dressed hot dog a Zen dog "one with everything" proved counter-productive.

The arrival of a gaggle of Chi Sigmas broke up a particularly persistent conclave of fans.

"Seems you're quite popular," asserted William Davis the Third, looking over his glasses.

"The fast food business," Stephen Boutin reflected. "Good idea. Sell sour dough to gold miners. Classic, classic."

"Receive quite an education," said William Davis with a smirk.

"As opposed to what you receive in school," I responded.

"One should slum. It's fun," remarked a voluptuous coed in a tight Norwegian sweater. *Sexual attraction must be as strong as gravity.* I thought as she prattled on. Some horny, latter-day, Newton should construct a formula, maybe something close to the angle of the dangle is inversely proportional to the distance from the object of desire. Suddenly, I saw her, my Beatrice, my Dulcinea, hiding demurely behind the actives, imprisoned by circumstances, the bird in a gilded cage.

I tried not to stare at her and redirected my attention to the bimbo, and her memorized send-up of entrepreneurs. Probably did a paper on it. Nodding my head at every pause, I deflected each Horatio Alger anecdote before it could bore me. Intuitively, I knew such tripe would contaminate the ecstasy my lady's proximity provided. Even the Copeland mantra, his donut to chicken success, his collection of water toys, of beauties, and his gaudy annual Christmas decorations, only nauseated me.

It was blasphemous to mention materialist pursuit in Leslie's presence. It insulted the sacrifice she underwent. How could I have violated this exquisite creature? This tribute to femininity?

That those present were responsible for turning her into a piece of meat, for placing her in harm's way, cut to the quick, turned my verbal parries into broad swatches. Their uncreative retorts infuriated me. I wanted to pour the scalding water at the bottom of my cart on the actives' blow-dried heads and, with my tongs, pull out the little sister's Fu Manchu fingernails.

"Maybe if you graduate at the top of your class I'll hire you," I pronounced. "Should own this racket by then."

"Going to interview us on visitor's day?" asked Stephen. He sniffed.

"Visitor's day?" I asked.

"Yeah, at San Quentin. Where you're going to end up before we graduate."

"The end of the millennium will be here before you own this racket; once we tell the police where you are," said William.

"What's that going to prove?" I asked.

"It'll clear my conscience," said the treasurer. "I couldn't live with myself if I didn't report the location of a fugitive from justice."

"The I.R.S. is very interested in your whereabouts," said the president.

"Whatever for?" I asked, knowing full well what he meant.

"Seems like your Father put his assets in your name. You're the man." Steven's smirk rivaled William's.

"Seems we're pretty nosy."

"We just read the papers," said Steven.

"May the power of attorney be with you," said the treasurer.

"What will people think if they see us talking to him?" Miss Jane Mansfield squealed with sudden insight. "They might think we have something to do with him."

"Wouldn't want to be thought of as classy," I remarked.

"I don't think we have to worry," said Steven, adjusting the sweater draped over his shoulders.

I glanced at Leslie, to see how she was taking the exchange.

Her sad eyes stopped me cold and aborted a rapier retort. She wasn't repugning me, not entirely, considering the confusion on her face. I could tell she wasn't judging and convicting me. By refusing to make eye contact with her group, by her slumped and narrowed shoulders, she sensed something wrong--not with me, with them.

"You're a loser," Stephen sneered.

Leslie winced, obviously repulsed by such crassness.

"That's for sure," I asserted. "If you continue to disrupt my business."

"You'll see who is going to disrupt it," William said for the rest, as he led them away.

"What is it about me that scares you?" I yelled at them.

"Better eat your products. It's the best food you're going to get for a long time," Stephen bellowed like a brat.

I noticed Leslie departed reluctantly. The several looks she cast back at me encouraged me, and gave me the wherewithal not to be intimidated. I continued hawking my wares, finding sales gradually picked up. Once, twice, the actives returned to check on me. The third time I blew them a kiss--and, the moment they turned their backs, I was out of there.

"Why so fast?" implored a hungry fag.

"The dogs will get cold if they don't get reheated."

"Doesn't your cart do that?"

"Not as well as it should. Don't want my hot dogs to be oxymorons."

"Hope you're not gone for long."

Only forever, I thought. I was in and out of the Cheshire Cat's den in a New York minute. After what I said it'll be a long time before his enigmatic smile revisits his slimy face.

"Get a Chi Sigma frat boy to take my place," I yelled in parting. "They're experienced cock-suckers."

With what I retained as fair wages, I hailed a cab and arrived at the Fairgrounds to plunk a Jackson on the favorite place. Over the dinner I paid for mostly with my winnings and drinks courtesy of Eddie's expert eyes, the troika mapped its strategy.

"Checked with Marble," Robert remarked offhandedly. "Said they were trying to contact me."

I gulped my wine down the wrong way.

"Already? I haven't even tried to see if they had contacted me."

"Me and the operations guy. We're connected. Don't worry, I'll see you get in."

"You got the stroke?"

"Like I said, we're connected."

I stared at him in horror.

"Not like that. I just happen to know a thing or two Marble is interested in."

"Like what?"

"Like what other drilling contractors are willing to bid for jobs."

"How do you know that?"

"If I didn't eavesdrop during the parties your old man put on, I wouldn't be doing my job."

"Your job?" I asked.

"Intelligence gathering. Don't want to pop your pretty balloon, but a lot of the parties were strictly predatory."

"Father only did what he had to do," I remarked.

"He only did what he could do at this stage of development."

"Think it would be a good idea to get in touch with him?" I asked.

"Not right now."

"Then when?"

"When things become clearer, more settled."

"You going to let me know when?"

"Between Pete and I, we'll keep you abreast of the developments."

"Pete?"

"That's my real name," said Eddie. "But I like aliases. I haven't paid taxes, ever. At my stage of development, I know how to remain anonymous." Over a third glass of wine, he assured us, "No one will know where we'll live after I find a place. Our official address will not be just a P. O. Box. It'll be that new place on Magazine, where each box is called a 'suite'."

"We'll pay for everything with cashier's checks. No bank accounts," added Robert.

"What will you do?" I asked Eddie (or Pete).

"Get that base for us, and check around. Don't worry about me. I've been on my own since I ran away from home."

"Be careful."

"Everything will be all right. I can feel it."

Fed, lubricated and refreshed from ten hours of sleep in an eleven-dollar motel, Robert and I set our sites for Morgan City, the Emerald City far out in the swamps, and the place the operations guy told him to go.

It seemed fitting we should begin our odyssey at the foot of the Huey P. Long bridge, finding it as hard to hitch a ride west, out of the city as we did north, into the city. The spirit of the Kingfish was mind-melding with passing drivers, telling them I was one of those enemies of the average man, an aristocrat in mufti. With "Every Man a King" the Big Lie of his day, anyone who didn't need a patronage job was *persona non grata.*

The fog that shrouded Governor O.K. Allen's tribute to the demagogue was cold, clammy, and too thick for anyone to see. This adversary of the common man eventually had to hoof it over the narrow span to Bridge City, all the while with Aaron Copeland's Overture playing in my head. Only when we passed out of the ghostly mist did it go away.

"Seems ol' Huey cast quite a spell," I said, referring to how tenaciously the miasma clung to the bridge.

"Neither Huey nor his stooges needed anything supernatural to be remembered. Their pyramids serve a function."

"Yeah, public works projects," I said.

"Like that low bridge in Baton Rouge which keeps ships from sailing upstream to Vicksburg or Natchez."

We aired other examples of their largesse, like the capitol building, which I claimed, "Was constructed in the shape representing every politician's favorite pastime."

Robert's rejoinder was cut short.

"You boys headed for work on a boat?" asked the native who pulled up in a Ford Fairlane. "Know a whole many of them captains who need deckhands. Can work up to engineer like nobody's business, ma Chaix."

Maintaining his status as resident ubiquitin, Robert owned how he had completed all but his exams for a z-card and two-hundred-ton mate ratings.

"In this life?" I asked as we got in the car.

"No better life than that on the water," volunteered our ride. "Started as a mate on a workboat and would still be there if the owners didn't forget to raise our salaries. I got ten years older, but you wouldn't know it from my paychecks,"

"I was so poor I couldn't pay attention to their excuses, so I sweet-talked the banks into lending money for a crew boat. Make ends meet once I put my family as crew."

The man's glib tongue added to the pleasantness of the trip. Alice couldn't have been more amazed at the Looking Glass House than I was at my old stomping grounds. Highway Ninety was crowded with drilling rigs, mimicking the chaos of Alice's animated chess pieces, and generating a wealth you could see in the improvement of the hamlets we passed. Boutte, Paradis, they weren't seedy anymore, and the grazing land and swamp between them also were seeing development.

"That rice field, t, there on the left, I'd take a lot more gravy to cover it than a few years ago," said Mister Guidry.

I must have had a quizzical look on my face, for he went on to explain all his kind were adept at such estimates. "It's in our blood, whenever food is involved."

Further on, I asked if he had any qualms about the strip mall we passed.

"Oh, no. Not me. It put my kin and them who owe me money to work. They kin too you know, some kinda way."

"Could do without those landfills I bet."

"They smell no worse than those who stay at the house so much I put them on my income tax."

"As in why are house guests like fish?"

"Everybody works down here. Got so many jobs, we have to hire transplanted Coon-Asses and maybe a Yankee or two."

"One or two?" asked Robert, playfully.

"Any more than a couple, one is bound to stay, become a damn Yankee."

To my dismay, we had to part ways at Bayou Lafourche, Bayou La lineage, where "Everybody in all the towns up and down the ditch got skiffs for the shrimp and blood from the same momma," said our new friend.

The next ride wasn't nearly as intriguing. It was torturous, like being stuck with a male Kimberly. Forever after, Highway One and the towns of Raceland and Thibodeaux will be Pavlovian linked to L.S.U. I anticipated trouble when our chauffeur claimed his surname was "as in Billy Cannon", the famous running back. His cocky gold and maroon beret and the copy of the "Tiger Rag" in the back seat confirmed my suspicions.

To be civil, I divulged my modest knowledge of the school's athletic fortunes. I should have played ignorant, as everything I said triggered so much school spirit the head of the pewter tiger behind the rear seat nodded with wild approbation. The miniature footballs hanging from the rear-view mirror banged together with glee. Robert picked up the slack whenever I stumbled, ultimately taking over the entire conversation when Billy Boy started waxing rhapsodic about the genius of Arnsbarger and Dale Brown. "Louisiana's Pride", he called them, "greater than Woody Hayes and Bobby Knight."

Where the swamps abutted Highway Twenty, west of Thibodeaux, I tuned him out entirely. The colossal McDermont yard interested me far more, crowded as it was with huge steel jackets that would soon become islands in the Gulf. Unlike mountains, which always seem to shrink with proximity, they loomed more gigantic the closer we crawled along the clogged artery toward them. Rush hour in the middle of a prehistoric swamp. The sight couldn't have been more impressive had the plant been a staging area for alien spacecraft, the towering structures, prefab separators, crew quarters, and innumerable add-ons massive cranes would attach like so many tinker toys composed the steel poetry Ayn Rand exulted.

McDermont was just an appetizer to the sprawling center at the other end of the swamp. Heralded by a big Parker rig, Amelia accosted us with its total devotion to one industry. From atop a bridge, a forest of giant cranes loomed to the left. A vast pipe yard sprawled to the right. Once on the downgrade, the world changed dramatically. A canal thick with tugboats, pushing barges loaded with drilling chemicals, wireline trucks, cement tanks--all kinds of oilfield equipment--paralleled the road. A blue-white light erupted from the superstructure of a tied-up drilling barge, showering the cutter with sparks. Above him, smoke from a welder's torch rose lugubriously into a cloud, filling the air with the acrid smell of acetylene. A seaplane set down like a duck in the water. Overhead, a helicopter chopped the air into bits.

Further on, in Morgan City, oilfield businesses crowded both sides of the road. Everywhere there were offices, warehouses, boat yards, machine shops, companies specializing in diving, tool rental, well servicing, mud additives, hydrogen sulfide containment, mudlogging, catering, and clothes. It was Venice magnified, with many small firms obscuring the big ones. For every Dresser, Hughes, or Baker Tool company, there were a dozen Reagan Industries, Louisiana Offshore Rentals, or Epco Manufacturers, each protected from the elements by sheet metal enclosures as flimsy as their counterparts in Plaquemines Parish to the east. Which didn't make a whole lot of sense. One hurricane isn't going to faze Schlumberger. The same couldn't be said of Piper Mudlogging.

Pedestrians were out in force, despite the absence of sidewalks. Most were scruffy transients, Camp Street types. In New Orleans, they were like cockroaches adding to the decay of their environment. Here, they blended into the surroundings, being as disposable as the cheap structures, ready to move or be moved should the boom go bust.

"Go Bengal Tigers go!" exclaimed our ride as he dropped us off at Marble Drilling. "You gotta believe!"

I failed to be as exuberant, uttering a meek "Later." Although Robert hasn't failed me, yet I couldn't help but worry that his alleged stroke was a tall tale, a figment of his imagination. What if I can't get on rig sixty-eight, where did the "Client" copy of the paperwork end up? What if I don't get hired at all? If they call the police? I'm not going to falsify my social security number.

A reassuring arm fell on my shoulder.

"It's okay to sweat it. Keeps you cautious," remarked my sidekick. "But look around. This isn't Manhattan. We're talking El Dorado here, the real Arkansas one. And Kilgore, you know, where rigs crowded next to each other."

I knew all about the Texan town, where a rig was erected in a bank lobby, right on the parquet.

"When times are good all you got to do is park yourself next to a rig and wait for someone to refuse to trip out of the hole, or get run off. That's what I did to become a dogger. See any lawyer types around here?"

"Looks more like their clients."

"Exactly. High school dropouts and geologists start companies, engineers run them, accountants manage them after they merge, and lawyers sell them."

He led me inside Marble's unadorned field office and didn't flinch when the supervisor claimed total ignorance of the deal he had arranged.

"What New Orleans says doesn't mean anything here," the tired-looking man snarled, obviously holding a grudge. "We're outta Lafayette. They once told me to process a pothead 'cause he was some main spring's kin. Would have lost my job if he hadn't gone out and got himself busted. Wasn't going to hire him for nothing."

Still, we did as he said, and were processed without incident, which was outrageous, considering how I filled out the application. The functionary didn't possess much in the way of general knowledge. He didn't utter a peep about the Post Office Box I substituted for an address, the phony biography, or the references I considered nothing less than an exposition of sheer genius: "Doctor D. H. Holmes, Ph.D., MD., ETC, 221 B. Baker Street, New London, Connecticut"; "Professor Thor, 123 Elysian Fields, New Orleans"; and "Winslow Churchill, Number Ten Downing Street, England Air Force Base, Alexandria, Louisiana."

He became perturbed only when I asked about benefits. Out of curiosity, I wanted to know how medium-sized outfits handled personnel costs in this boom. Their high cost was one of Father's pet peeves. An effort to commiserate about the onus of Workman's Compensation provoked him to a point where only the slickest apology tempered his anger.

"Just trying to show I'm interested in the big picture," I pleaded.

The not-so-grand inquisitor let me in on a not-so-grand secret. "Count yourself lucky we happen to need people now. Let us take care of all the other stuff." He stared straight at me. "We're a people company."

"Sure are," chirped a bandaged nonentity from behind a desk. "Pay their field roustabouts overtime after forty hours."

"Forty-four hours of overtime in a usual week," gloated the functionary.

"No matter how many rigs we work on during a hitch."

"Never jerked a crew off for anything but a straight-ahead reason. That game of pulling them off early so they won't get overtime is not for us."

"Pay top dollar, too."

"For your injury?" asked Robert.

"Hey, they do well by me. They know I love my job."

"Father wouldn't have hired either of them," I said outside to my ex-butler. Then again, I doubt Father would have hired someone like me; and I wouldn't want to work with someone he wouldn't have hired.

I then told him what I put on my application.

"Whatever rings your chimes. But don't forget, if they weren't hiring people like those two, they wouldn't be hiring us."

He was right, of course. A happenstance I was beginning to resent.

After a long wait in a company trailer (where Robert consistently beat me in checkers) our fellow worms arrived. Cut from the same cloth as those at the pipe yard they too were employable only because of the times.

Packed like illegal aliens in a van and whisked to the local clinic, we turned and coughed, were punctured, and said "aah". A visit to the Red Wing store for boots, then to a company warehouse for gloves, coveralls, underclothes, duffle bag, goggles, and a slicker suit convinced me Marble was not like the pipe yard. The promise of a knife as a Christmas gift confirmed it, it being so touching.

"Don't even think of gettin' on a rig without a rain suit or a knife," commented our guide. "Wouldn't go to your wedding in blue jeans, would you? You'd go in a tuxedo."

It didn't immediately occur to me how fortunate I was when we were handed our assignments. I panicked when Robert was assigned to rig seventy. Only later, on the crew boat, did I realize how lucky I was to be assigned to sixty-eight. Most weren't. For the first time in my life I begrudgingly admitted I was lucky. For the first time in my life I was totally on my own.

Taking a deep breath, I decided to go slowly, without fear, doing what made the most sense moment by moment.

I didn't expect it to be easy. I didn't expect crew boat etiquette to be straightforward. First, while loaded down with gear, I had to climb over the big tires protecting the stern, then thread my way around the tied-down loads on the bay. As for the water-tight door, I had as much trouble with it as Alice did with the fifteen-inch door. Instead of flaunting my dexterity, I was all thumbs, finding it difficult to turn the outside dogs, so the inside dogs slipped off their flange. My failure to resecure them once inside was cause for derision. Of course, no one would have noticed me had I not stumbled over the four-inch stoop.

Worms were relegated to the upper deck; the lower deck already was filled with recumbent bodies who refused to relinquish any of the four seats each couch was divided into. Besides we new hires;

service hands, galley workers, and itinerant roustabouts like the injured one at Marble's office crowded the upper level, their belongings piled in heaps in the main aisle. I had no choice but to squeeze in the only empty place on a couch facing a Formica table.

"We ain't goin' anywhere 'til we get this manifest right," complained a skinny deck hand, whose obvious familiarity with the crew was demonstrated by the swiftness he flicked on the lower lights and bawled out a name. Like those listed before him, a passenger had used ditto marks to indicate he worked for Marble Drilling. The trouble was, a Halliburton cementer had signed in immediately above him.

"I thought them marks stood for Marble," the genius replied in his defense.

A click preceded the whine of the engines and a jerk of motion. The boat vibrated with the sensation of speed, not much at first, but more as we entered the channel, only to almost come to a halt to let a small craft pass.

"Can get sued if we swamp it," explained the deckhand to the inquisitive among us.

The rumble of renewed movement settled into the background. The sheer red curtains muted the glare of a setting sun and imparted upon the interior the atmosphere of a cheap nightclub. Waves lapping into the aluminum hull acted like a sedative. The way I figured it, from what I overheard from a conversation from the pilothouse, we'd reach the rig early in the morning and, expecting the worst, we'd probably go straight to work. So, although I wasn't sleepy now, I knew I'd better get some rest.

An increase in speed and the onrush of choppier waters heralded our entrance into the Gulf. Immediately it became apparent we would be challenging a very rough sea. God wasn't about to make my quest easy. Waves began to slam into us, each one more ferocious than the last. One lifted the bow into the air and slammed us down. Another lifted my guts to my throat, lightened my head, and levitated me for what seemed an eternity before the boat plunged into the next trough, crushing my innards. It was a roller coaster without the fun, shattering my teeth and reacquainting me with my tailbone. Judging from the cursing and moaning, I was not alone in my misery. Copying others, I stretched out on the floor. Those left on the seats took advantage of the exodus, appropriating every vacancy so they could lie down.

I soon found out why most lay on their bellies rather than their backs. In addition to being able to stabilize yourself better, you are less nauseated. Had I stayed on my back, I know I'd have puked, like I had when I rode the bull at Gilley's on the number "three" setting. Suitcases, duffle bags, and seat cushions slid across the deck, as did a body or two. Several times the bottom of the boat felt as if it would crack, the hull seeming unequal to the pounding. Those with weak constitutions filled their barf bags.

That I couldn't envision anything worse only showed how poorly temporized I was. My bladder started to vie with my inner ear for attention. So did that of the others. A new malaise overcame us, triggered no doubt by the psychological impact of seeing spray viciously lash the windows. Cows defecate when you enter their fields and humans have to urinate when they see water.

A cacophony of complaints went up, demanding the boat slow for a pee break. Accommodating them, the captain eased back on the throttle, leaving the craft prey to the pitch, haw, sway, and swells that made footing precarious and aiming nearly impossible. I had to perform a hook shot, daring to take a hand off the bulkhead for the shortest time possible. Once finished, I prayed we'd get going again. Sitting dead in the water like a cork churned my stomach worse than plowing ahead.

Lacking sea legs, I rejected the idea of claiming a distant couch in favor of a five by six-foot floor space that became my refuge the rest of the way.

My entire body wept with joy when the engines slowed to an idle.

"Nobody's going anywhere until you dump your vomit bags in the trash," bellowed the captain as we backed up toward the rig. "I live here; you wouldn't let guests leave the mess at the house, would you?"

A very bummed-out brigade dragged itself outside. Looming above stood a metal city right out of the twenty-first century. Battleship grey, the brawny structure towered over the elements. The waves that had pummeled us lapped innocuously against its four cylindrical legs, alternately exposing and hiding a patina of barnacles while playfully washing in and out of a ring of rectangular holes.

Epitomizing the rugged spirit of adventure drilling entailed, I thought I saw John Wayne among the figures leaning over the handrail, watching us. It certainly would fit. He played the oil field fire fighter Red Adair in "Hellfighters."

Further underscoring the masculinity of the structure, a rubber hose hung from the underside like a big dick, disgorging a constant flow of white water.

Not everyone was as enthralled.

"What's the craneman doing?" questioned several when it was observed the operator had abandoned his post to join the other spectators.

The captain abandoned the rear throttle to answer a request heard over the radio in the wheelhouse.

"Are there any card players here?" he asked us upon his return.

No one responded.

"The companyman won't let anyone aboard until someone joins him in a game of bourey."

Still no one responded.

A plume of black smoke erupted from amidship simultaneously with the vibration of movement. Water around the stern turned from brownish-blue to frothy white and, further away, light green. The ubiquitous "f" word suddenly became popular, as did several time worn vulgarities as we began circling the rig.

"I've been informed that unless someone agrees to play, we are to spin our wheels indefinitely."

I noticed the deckhand removed the sports section from the newspapers before he handed them to the members of the first lift. *Cruel, but just revenge,* I thought.

Upon completion of the second tour, a chorus of voices demanded the obese Halliburton cementer volunteer.

"I don't know how to play."

"You can play hearts, can't you? You've got plenty of time to learn," said a hand.

"You don't do nothing but watch TV," scolded a roughneck. "Don't even get off the couch."

"Do to. Get up to piss, eat, and go to bed."

We had our human sacrifice.

Overhead, the yellow crane whirred into action, its long boom swinging over the water, spasmodically lowering a crew basket, swaying in and out of the rig lights, bobbing as we bobbed, and obscuring the identity of the hands clinging to the rope mesh. That there were only two of them depressed the sleepy horde and sent them back inside for an extra half wink. Two meant they were roustabouts, not departing crew members, of which there'd be the maximum four.

Only the first lift and the cementer were to go aboard. The iron cargo, not the rest of us, was next.

I stayed to watch a deckhand grab the tagline, only to surrender it to a big wave. The roustabouts lifted their feet as the rubber base ricocheted off a mud cleaner into a cargo locker. A second deckhand helped secure the line, guiding the basket down near an open space.

"That craneman, he ain't worth anything," a fellow spectator informed me. "Ought to charge him for all the dents he put in the rig."

"You're just jealous 'cause he got the job and you didn't," reproached a critic.

At first, I thought the whiner may be right. The wire rope the roustabouts had hooked to the grocery bin snapped taut. And the boom, it angled lower and lower as we drifted away, until it was as low as it could go. Something wasn't right, yet I didn't say anything. That's all I needed, to look foolish.

Nobody said anything even as the craneman started blowing his horn. I looked up at the skipper. He was arguing with a deckhand, oblivious to what was happening.

As I rushed up the steps, the cables started turning, causing the bin to slide, banging into, up, and scrapping over the stern railing. With a splash, it plunged into the water and rooster-tailed as it plowed toward the rig before arching up and swinging into a leg.

"See, I told you he's dangerous."

The former critic had no retort, instead commenting how he hoped the steaks didn't get wet.

Two apparent superiors rushed outside just in time to shout orders into the void.

"They know better than to say something to me," said the captain. "They know who they're dealing with."

I left that alone, climbed down to the deck, and enjoyed watching the rest of the equipment being off-loaded.

The return of the basket with the homeward bound precipitated a frenzy to get aboard. You'd have thought the boat was sinking the way the mob surged.

Of the four who snatched the work vests off the rope mesh, a Puerto Rican fumbled with the hooks, twisted the straps, and put it on wrong side out. He also decided to ride up sitting with the luggage on the canvas inside the donut. A proffered hand yanked the novice out. His bag followed. Someone who was identified as a barge engineer took his place.

"That Bull; what makes him so special?" complained the whiner. "He does a job like the rest of us."

Obviously, he, and someone who was identified as the toolpusher, were the chiefs, and this was not like the army Grandfather told me about, where leaders ensured their troops well-being before their own. These leaders believed in the modern all-volunteer army, where rank has its privileges. Hopefully, that doesn't mean another Delta One.

An odd sounding noise, a weird "hello", announced the basket's disappearance over the massive grey side.

More antics entertained us. The motorman who descended shouted "Oh baby, here I come." The motorman who went up lifted his feet off the donut, flaunted his bravery by hanging on with his hands.

The departing welder claimed he was going to perform a magic trick when he got ashore. "I am going to turn into a bar."

I hope he takes off that goofy hat of his. Another hand wore a t-shirt stenciled with the saying, "I may not go down in history, but I will go down on your sister."

Much to my enjoyment, the boat rose on a crest as the next returnees landed, jarring the yahoos. Had they not tried to anticipate contact by jumping, they wouldn't have suffered the embarrassment of having deckhands grab them to prevent them from losing their balance.

Another was grabbed as he attempted to board the basket.

"Service trash goes last," growled a hand identified to me as the assistant driller.

"I didn't know," the fresh-faced victim said, handing over the work vest.

"You'd better learn."

From behind me I heard someone ask the mud engineer what he was doing.

"Hear this companyman needs a lot of suckin' up," he said, applying vaseline to his lips. On his shirt was the message: "I Survived Jim Duhon." A Trilby to a Svengaili?

"I guess we're entering the Twilight Zone," I said to the chastised college boy. From the look on his face he didn't know what to make of me. Quietly telling him I had been to college temporarily won him over. Temporarily. To my dismay, a paunchy Don Juan in K-Mart polyester bellowed, "Yeah, I been to college too. I drive across Nichols State every time I go home. Got some kind of women there."

Another piece of work sporting alligator boots and a Stetson adorned with a big ostrich feather bragged how he was expelled from Southern Alabama, "For partying and raising Hell."

The mudlogger turned away from me. He retreated in earnest when someone watching from the rig aired over the intercom the tired invective about college breeding educated idiots..

"Don't mind Mister Bull," rasped the twin of Quasimodo. "He's tough but he's fair. He's just jealous he can't rise above barge engineer without a degree."

The apologist oozed irony and sweat. The pustules, pot marks, and scabs that ravaged his body, convinced me he was a cook. His being allowed on the same lift as the electrician, well before the galley crew, proved he was well regarded.

"Harvey's the only cook they've kept," said a co-worker who immediately started humming the Northwest Orient Airline jingle when the basket rose off the deck.

By the time the hummer joined two galley hands and I on the basket, he was treating us to the Tonight Show theme. Whether he continued serenading us, I don't know. My mind was elsewhere. No carnival would include one of these rides among their attractions. A crowbar couldn't have wrested my hands from the thick cord mesh I clung to. Neither the wave that collapsed the netting nor the one that banged us into a bollard loosened my grip. I held fast when we were yanked skyward and continued holding fast when we quit accelerating.

Below, I could see the little boat being ravaged by each wave, imparting a lasting appreciation of the skill involved loading and off-loading cargo and personnel. Further out, an army of white caps churned angrily, ripping the ribbon of moonlight to shreds.

Whirled around, the water suddenly disappeared. Replacing it was a confusion of stacked drill pipe, portable machines, iron boxes full of short tubulars and gadgets--the type of drilling equipment Father used to sell or lease. Commanding most attention, huge mushroom-like air vents roared with compressed air, deafening me as we passed by, squeezing onto a narrow walkway.

Only after we scrambled off did I notice it wasn't a walkway at all, but a serrated track, with the thick iron teeth pointing inward. I've heard of cantilevered drill floors but never saw one jacked out over the water before. Why it didn't topple over and take the rest of the rig with it I'll never know. It looked as unbalanced as one kid on a teeter totter. With the barge jacked up fifty feet above the water and the drill floor jacked twenty feet out, this oilfield needed college educated people.

Led away, the convex crew's quarters rose in front of me. Only two windows on the third floor broke the monotonous, cheap looking exterior. Vibrations underfoot shimmered my entire body. The bedlam of noise assaulted me, the cloppity-clop of compressors shoving air through the white pipes running along the circumference, the roar from the vents, and droning of engines as they supplied power to the entire rig. The puffs of black smoke belching from four horizontal smokestacks, the pungent odor of drying paint, and the musty smell of drilling mud threatened to do to me what the boat ride failed to do.

Further observations had to be suspended in favor of following the rush to the change room, where my first urge was to urinate in the stainless-steel basin in the small foyer. Fortunately, someone depressed the circular bar underfoot, releasing tiny sprays from a stainless-steel post. It was a sink.

Crisis averted, I then learned that the plastic container of go-jo on a nearby stand was for washing. Like a miracle, the slimy goo removed the grease I had picked up. It was like washing in silly putty with pebbles.

First herded to the galley where I signed in, I was then marshaled to the wheelhouse to receive a safety briefing. I didn't make it without incident.

"What are you doing with your boots on?" growled Bull.

"Walking," replied a Sladco casing hand.

The pear-shaped straw boss puffed himself up to auspicious proportions; his big belly inflating with redneck outrage. Unfortunately, that outrage failed to find articulate expression before we removed the offending foot gear. Frustrated, he ordered a galley hand with long hair off his rig.

"I don't care how many rigs let you on," he snarled in response to the boy's tremulous explanation. "You're on my rig now, you play by my rules."

Upstairs in the wheelhouse, we received a very peculiar briefing. Peculiar, because the safetyman--a Negro (Marble being an equal opportunity employer) talked without saying anything. The clever casing hand had to repeat his questions and paraphrase the mumbler's answers before it became clear that an intermittent alarm meant fire and a continuous ring meant abandon the rig. Which fire crew I was assigned I never did find out.

Apparently, I wasn't the only one who thought it odd when he pointed out the escape pods.

"This escape capsule on the starboard side (he pointed to the left) is the one you service peoples go to during a drill."

"What about the real thing?" asked the casing hand.

"Go to the same one I just said," he pointed to the port one on the wall schematic.

"You sure?"

"Sure I'm sure. It's my job to be sure."

"I'm not sure."

"Somebody has to be sure, 'n I'm that somebody."

"What about crewmembers?" asked a new roughneck. "Where do we go?"

"To the capsule on the port side." He motioned toward the one on the right on the diagram.

"Don't you mean this one?" The Sladco hand pointed outside to the one on our left.

"No indeed. The one to port."

"That is port."

"That's starboard."

"Starboard's right. Port is left."

"I know that." Mister Safety gestured toward a wall arrayed with what looked like a calliope of tubular bubble levels and pronounced that starboard. Both the Sladco hand and the roughneck disagreed. While they locked horns with the man, I grew infatuated with the control panel. The dials, bubble levels, and levers involved in raising and lowering the barge, as well as the wheel used for steering during towing forged a compelling impression.

I climbed into the pilot's leather chair and fantasized about young Sam Clemens on the Mississippi River. Looking out through the big pane of glass to the massive derrick and the iron phantasmagoria between, it dawned on me how subtly the rig resembled a paddle wheeler. Built specifically for its task, useless for anything else, it brought prosperity to those on shore by operating in a dangerous, ever changing, lonely environment. It too was functional art; the closest maritime engineers can come to creating a Starry Night. If it lacked the classy superstructure of a Natchez, that was all right. It had all its river-borne predecessors' attributes, including a display of fauna old Sam could relate to. I had the feeling, a vague intuition that whenever asked about a stranger, I too would say "I already know him; met him on the water."

"I'll tell you what to believe," said a tall, well-built electrician who entered the room. "Follow what's on the station bill and forget what this doe-doe says."

"It could be wrong," the safetyman whimpered.

Facing the helipad, with his back to the derrick, the electrician pointed straight ahead. "That's the bow and for the Einsteins among you I'll let you figure out which way's stern."

The safetyman's eyes brightened. Whirling around, so as to face the big man, he spread out his arms and reasserted that left was port, right starboard.

"Very good, excellent. Perfect. I take my hat off to you."

The black man beamed.

"You are exactly one hundred eighty degrees wrong. Totally incorrect."

"What you mean?"

"If I lay face down and pointed outward with my left would it still be 'left' I point to with that arm if I lay on my back?"

Thinking this through, the right side of the employee's brain became so overworked it enlisted the help of his left, leaving him little more than a vegetable. The feisty little guy allowed himself to be turned around, to face the bow.

"Now figure it out."

He eventually did and rallied well enough to inform us we must report all injuries to our supervisor then see him for treatment. "I be the medic," he said.

We swore never to get injured and rushed downstairs.

We didn't need to hurry past the toolpusher's office. Both Hammer, the toolpusher, and Bull, the barge engineer, were in the thrall of their own voices, holding court to two respective audiences. As for the companyman, we didn't have to worry about him either. We could have stared holes in Mister Duhon, so engrossed was he reading the paper. Or so we thought.

"You're not paid to stand around," the monster barked. "'N I don't want you here less you got genuine business. You got genuine business?"

We retreated with our tails tucked between our legs. After all, who would want to argue with someone who pours coffee on a newspaper so no one else can read it? Which is what he did as he growled at us.

"Where can I get an 'I survived Jim Duhon t-shirt'?" I asked.

"You ain't survived him yet," said the chunky Bedroom and Restroom hand from behind. "You're lucky Mister Duhon just won at cards. He's in a good mood."

"I'd hate to see him in a bad mood."

"You will. We don't always let him win. This way to your suite," the B. and R. hand snarled. "Don't need to be on this floor if you don't have to."

The first-floor room I was assigned to was a suite compared to the barracks at the pipe yard. Still, with bunk beds from the Paris Island collection, mattresses by De Sade, and lockers on loan from the Volunteers of America, it was designed to prevent oversleeping. Adding that special touch of elegance, a big iron hatch decorated the middle of the floor, perfect for tripping over. But it was home, and with a capacity of four, offered all the privacy I could hope for.

I flopped on a lower bunk, comfortable in the misery-loves-company I was in.

"You aren't thinking of sleeping there?" rhetorically asked a veteran.

"Just resting," I answered.

"Just rest on an upper bunk."

Maybe a fall from the ladder less structure or a rearranged spine thanks to the mattress' topography could result in a lucrative suit that could pay off the wolves besieging my family. Exposure to the safetyman's congenital incompetence would ensure a profitable verdict.

The mud pumps churned on directly beneath us, drenching us in noise, rattling our guts, and frying our stocking feet. We bolted for the beds.

"This is like back home when its so hot the flies won't go near garbage less it's in the shade," said my stocky bunk mate.

I turned in for a sumptuous four-hour nap before I had to go to work at noon. I kept my clothes on and stayed on top of the moldy army blanket. Didn't want my body to think it's getting the eight hours it desperately needs. And I was among the lucky. Half those who came aboard had to immediately go to work.

Anticipation, and insistent bowels awoke me before we were to be awakened. My descent from Olympus and traverse through the pitch-black Valley of Sin stirred nary a soul. It was a clear shot to the washroom, head, or whatever they call the bathroom offshore. I'd call it an onmi-toilet, where one could clean and dry everything on and in one's body in one room, in full view of each other. The tattered and stained shower curtains provided the only measure of privacy. Without partitions, the commodes were as exposed as the washer and dryer. Any squatter could reach out and touch a showerer, the showers being that close to the row of toilets.

Praying no one would come in, and nauseated by the smell of rotten eggs, I endeavored to execute my business post haste.

Somehow, God misunderstood my entreaty. He must have thought I wanted to hear a prayer, for half-way through my current project in came Elmer Gantry with his good book, intent upon releasing two loads, one on me, the other in the stool.

"All you need can be found in this book," the eager young man announced.

Instead of saying the pages would make better toilet paper than that on hand, I wimped out and politely asked if he was a preacher.

"Self ordained." He looked beatific.

"What do you do here? I mean your job?" I asked.

"Besides being an assistant electrician, you mean? I am here to see that others are ready for the afterlife," he said with chilling sincerity.

"They both pay, what, ten dollars an hour?"

"Have you made peace with the Lord?"

"Seen me on the boat did you?" I asked, trying to divert his attention from my wiping.

"Didn't have to lay eyes on you before. A holy messenger can tell a lost soul on sight."

"I'm not lost. I know where I am."

"God will smite all unbelievers on the Day of Judgment, when the righteous shall be blessed with eternal salvation." He paused to catch his breath.

"I'm Pentecostal," I pleaded. "I know what you're going to say." He unleashed a deluge of Bible banging rhetoric, assaulting my poor ears with all the clichés of his profession.

"Sinner repent; for Armageddon is nigh."

"Where? Here?"

"Not right here."

"Where, over there?" I pointed to the far shower.

"It's sacrilege to make fun of The Word." He puffed up for a renewed salvo.

A profusion of apologies deflated him before more effluvium could pollute the air.

"Bless you." He defecated.

As I stepped into the shower, I noticed a second victim innocently squat within hailing distance of the prophet. It tickled me to hear a reenactment of my experience, including the sinner's fake outburst of redemption. It assured me I wasn't the only one Anal Roberts could unnerve.

Their simultaneous flushing the toilets likewise tickled me pink. It scalded me. Had I not been forewarned by the fickleness of the "hot" and "cold" knobs I might be wearing first degree burns.

"Hell is hotter," sayeth the minister, hitching up his pants.

"You're getting water on the floor!" shouted Dennis, the B. and R. hand. "I told you to watch that." He started mopping the puddle the swiss cheese cloth curtains failed to contain.

Finding no clean towel at hand, and not wanting to disturb him, I pulled a soggy one from the "used" bin.

"What you think I clean towels for? They're on the sill."

Not knowing where the sill was, I thanked him for his concern, hoping he wouldn't pursue the matter.

"Suit yourself. Just don't complain if you get the crabs."

I was now certain the only way to learn the rules was by breaking them.

Upstairs in the galley, I found others also had failed to anticipate the rules. A little imagination was all that was necessary to reconstruct the events that led to the eager Puerto Rican's sullen demeanor. There was Bull, absorbing the adulation of his cronies until he positively glowed and there was the novice, nursing his wounds in solitude--a pariah who must have unknowingly sat in the pantheon's personal chair.

I'm glad I was present to see the college kid, the mudlogger, wear his gym shorts into the galley. Had I not been privy to the viciousness he endured, I wouldn't have believed it. You'd have thought he was a damn Yankee or a revenuer. Knowing me, I might have flouted such a stupid convention, performed a little civil disobedience if I had heard a watered down, second hand version of the incident. As it was, I'm glad he, not me, got chewed up and spat out.

Enveloped by smoke from the burnt shortening in the fryer, Harvey insisted Mister Bull was, "All right. He just has his ways." The burly cook dumped a basket of overcooked fried chicken into a tray. "Have some yard bird; nice and crisp," he said with pride.

It certainly beat the John Wayne pork chops. True Grit. In the other trays resided purple hull peas, blanched carrots, mustard greens, and lumpy mash potatoes. Only the salty biscuit was remotely tasty, though I ascribed that to mere luck.

"Would fall apart if I don't salt'm down," Harvey explained to a more discriminating Epicurean.

"Glad you made a lot of'm," said the mud engineer, now in blue coveralls. "Can use'm to supersaturate the mud, in case we hit salt."

"Salting them is what they do in prison," said a whiner, revealing Harvey's past.

"Makes sense," acknowledged Bull. "Learned how to cook in Angola, wasn't it?"

I tried not to look startled.

"What can I say?" Harvey admitted. "Got drunk'n did somethin' stupid. Paid my full ten years."

"No parole?" asked the whiner.

"Can see why he didn't get any, if he cooked like this," said Bull.

"Can't see why you didn't get better," remarked the jingle-meister, a welder, who like the one departed, wore the ridiculous hat of his trade at inappropriate times. "Five years at the woman's institute turned my wife into some kind of cook. Had to stop my brother-in-law from turning in my sister when she kept shoplifting. Quit having him over for dinner."

"Your wife cook chicken as much as Harvey?" asked Hammer, strolling in.

"We have it a lot."

"Makes sense. Birds of a feather. Jailbirds and yard birds, the only two birds that can't fly."

Still the food was palatable--and free, I think. The meal tickets we had to sign were just a formality. The ones the service hands signed were more suspicious, with spaces for company addresses Bull insisted be filled in. Still, if anyone was going to have to pay it was the company, not the individual, so each ate and ate, far more than any discerning trencherman would want to eat. Maybe that's why the food was so mediocre. A pain in the butt may come aboard and want to linger if the food was good. However, if that's so, then why was the dessert cabinet so inviting, filled with delectable, albeit conventional, sweets? Near the end of lunchtime, it needed restocking with my favorite, the pecan pie, long gone.

My aggrievement was quickly superseded by another dose of culture shock, as provided by another hapless victim, this time wearing a muscleman t-shirt. His retreat in the face of all the verbal abuse mimicked that of his scantily clad mudlogger.

Hammer, flapping his wings like a pugnacious toolpusher should, roared out to Harvey, "Why don't you tell your people what we expect of them?"

"He just got aboard."

"What's that got to do with anything?"

"You said you wanted a replacement for the hand Mister Bull ran off."

"That's the best you could do?"

"Had to hire him off the street."

"Lucky us, get rid of a hippie, get a bum."

I had thought the barge engineer was kidding, running that hand off for long hair. The equal opportunity policy on land apparently did not apply offshore.

Even the trim, Sigmund Freud beard another mudlogger wore didn't pass muster.

"Doesn't make no difference you can put a mask over it. H_2S can sneak into any mask what isn't sealed properly," growled Hammer,

"That's not what the Springer people told me at the spud meeting," the educated professional rejoined.

"You work for us out here now," bellowed Jim Duhon, marching in ahead of his retinue of lackeys.

"Yes, sir!" the mudlogger snapped in deference.

"Jim won't push it," the mud engineer whispered. "Mudloggers gave him coveralls."

"Tribute?" I asked.

"Part of the job. I wouldn't think of coming aboard without bags of blanched pistachios. Jim can't handle those dyed red, says they cause cancer."

"I assumed that kind of behavior ended long ago," I said.

"When you assume anything, you make an 'ass' out of 'you' and 'me'." Turtle, my aptly named bunkmate, leaned over and informed me.

"Want all card players in my office. I need more money," the companyman announced.

So much for checking out his files. It was beginning to appear his office would be as hard to investigate as that at the pipe yard, and require the same kind of subterfuge and patience to penetrate, maybe more, considering how crowded everything was. Again, I needed to find and exploit their weakness, which meant I was going to have to get to know these people. A good way to begin was to keep track of their names and nicknames (which seemed to be more popular). Memorizing them using the popular technique of associating them with an outlandish feature did not appear to be too difficult. For instance, Turtle certainly looked like an amphibian and the safetyman like a "Bones".

The beta males marched into the office with all the dignity of miffed Oliver Hardys.

"Buss them tables. This ain't the Waldorf," snapped the alpha male.

"A real work of art he is," commented Spud, my other roommate.

I'd better survive him, I thought.

"Mister Jim just has his ways," said Harvey as I scraped the "debris" from my plate into the trash. "His bark is worse than his bite."

"He's a good man," affirmed the rig preacher. "Goes to each of my Bible Studies."

"Needs to," angrily claimed a real live female (I think, she looked like a cross dressing troll). "Needs to spend years at them." She gnawed off a big chunk of meat from a pork chop.

"The Good Book doesn't tell you how to handle the fair sex," I whispered waggishly.

"Kathy ain't no fair sex," affirmed Spud. "She been rode hard and put up wet."

"Stayed unbroken," Turtle suggested.

He wasn't kidding. As my crane man, I quickly learned to defer to her every command. Tugboat Annie wasn't as abrasive, in possession of a pair of vocal chords the Valkyries would envy. I could hear her over the din of my needle gun as it chipped paint. I could hear her with rubber plugs in my ears. And I could hear her next to a roaring air vent. She'd blow the roof off the Mormon Tabernacle and probably cause the locusts to revisit with all her blasphemies, of which calling the token black roustabout "Nigeroon" was typical.

We wielded the jarring, high pressured, hand held needle guns instead of unloading drive pipe off the workboat because we were "lucky." High waves severely buffeted the big boat, banging the twenty-inch pipe in middle "c", treble clef, preventing their being offloaded.

Being suspended in a big iron bin high up the face of the crew's quarters proved to be fun. From it, I got to irritate the card players on the other side of the wall. I also could spy on others, watch the motorman, oil can in hand, chat first with the mud engineer, then the shaker hand as he changed out one of the wire screens on the shale shaker. I could see him enter the mudlogger's shack on the platform above the shaker and flowline that fed it. And I could see him exit it after a half hour. Other detours followed, each one taking at least as long, adding up to a sojourn that took up the better part of the afternoon.

Further entertainment could be gleaned from watching Harvey dump chum overboard. The hardtails boiled and jumped, turning the water white and attracting seagulls and gawky grey birds. Terns were more interested in the bread Dennis pitched. The dart-like birds dive-bombed and knocked morsels out of each other's mouths, either catching it in mid-air, or fighting over it on the water, displaying no class whatsoever.

What bit of business the B. and R. hand performed before he heaved the bread was anybody's guess. It looked as if he tampered with it, kneading it with another substance and rolling the two ingredients into a ball.

Before dinner, the Sladco hands boarded a helicopter, ostensibly to work another job instead of waiting for the casing to come aboard.

"Water must be calmer in West Delta than here. Can off load casing there," said Spud.

Bones, the safetyman, had a different idea, and pontificated it "has to do with the Gulf Stream and all."

"I can see leeward of Eugene Island being calmer," remarked Turtle, guilelessly.

"How's that? Pump jacks and Christmas trees tallest things on that island," said Kathy.

"That Gulf Stream does something to the wind."

"Gulf Stream doesn't go near West Delta. Main Pass and Viasco Knoll maybe," remarked Tar Baby, the assistant driller.

A siren blared, sending the motorman scurrying downstairs.

"That engine should never get low on oil," chastised Hammer upon Popcorn's return. The toolpusher removed a butterfly knife from his pocket and angrily flicked it. His already ample chest seemed to swell with indignation.

"That flow valve gets stuck. What am I supposed to do, stand next to it all day? I got work to do," responded the impish little guy. . His assertion that the part was on order mollified the toolpusher.

"Let me know when it comes in." He flicked the knife rhythmically, imparting a calm upon the scene. The top dog began to wag his tail, and we all relaxed.

I did, taking a last lingering sip of Harvey's excuse for coffee and strolled to the exit in the change room. I nimbly opened and closed the water tight door, letting everyone know how adroit I now was.

A blow stung me, knocked me woozy. Looking around, I saw only a dead tern, no doubt blown headfirst into the superstructure. A gummy substance oozed out its mouth. A second, just like it, lay on top the spooled hoses of fire station number twelve, its mouth also filled with tallow. The sight of a third and fourth in the same condition, and a fifth that fell out of the sky to writhe in agony until suffocating from the paste that emerged from its mouth led to the inescapable conclusion Dennis had something to do with it. Could it be yeast he was adding to the bread?

"Where's your hat?" shrieked Kathy, our resident Maritornes from her glass enclosed perch. I raced back inside, to receive the catcalls of all in the change room. A titter of secondary laughter accompanied the placement of my plastic helmet. I knew my helmet was prissy, virginal, snow-white and empty compared to the greasy, grimy, sticker-slathered helmets the veterans wore. If I was going to become Pavlovian about wearing the thing outside, I'd just as soon not want to stick out like an anorexic at a professional wrestlers' convention.

It was no tragedy it blew off in the wind tunnel formed between the cylindrical degasser and the shaker house. I didn't make much of an effort to retrieve it.

"I can pick it up on Padre Island," said the stout shaker hand as we watched it float away. "Should be there by the time I get back to the house. Can call my kin. They live in Corpus Christi.

"What you need is some customizing," Mamou remarked on the way to the mechanic's shop, where without my asking, a drill, a thong, and a flexible aluminum pin secured a headpiece he found for me.

I banged my head several times with it on, leaving me to believe I would have hurt myself if I hadn't worn it, though Spud claimed it was because I wasn't used to the extra height of the crown. I had no desire to test his theory.

Twice it blew off on the workboat Turtle and I labored on. Each time the thong kept it from blowing away, thank God. I had enough on my mind besides trying to retrieve that thing, as the vessel wasn't any more stable than the crew boat. Each move was a calculated risk, with treacherous footing and casing banging against each other. If I slipped amidships, there was no railing to prevent me from falling into the water. And I thought the pipe yard was difficult! Come night neither the boat's nor the crane's floodlights were much help.

Through it all, short, squat Turtle diligently performed his tasks, talking only whenever necessary to avoid mishaps, using the "f" word where it belonged, for emphasis, to get my attention.

A touchy deckhand wasn't as understanding when he strayed too close to a lift. The captain himself had to intervene to preserve the peace.

"I been working over my six-hour tower," the hand had whimpered.

Six hours! Turtle and I spent seven hours just on the boat. We were tired and increasingly careless, and nobody cared. I was glad, real blue collar, Budweiser, "Who Dat" Saints glad when my twelve hours were up. And I was a little peeved that we had unloaded all the casing. The other crew missed out of all the work.

I did not recoil at a roughneck impugning a mudlogger for how he earned his pay. Deep down, I felt he deserved to hear it.

"Easy money," the worker snarled. "I'd be ashamed to pick up my paycheck." The revilement followed the college kid inside the locker room. "Be like stealing."

"Maybe, maybe not," parried the clean-cut victim. "Would you want to work two weeks on, with only one week off like me?"

That shut'm up--and set me straight, like hearing the Overture to the Marriage of Figaro, completely altering my mood and outlook. God knows what would have happened had he flaunted his education rather than used it. Equal time is sacrosanct in the oilpatch, that much I know. To work more is unheard of, incomprehensible, like reading a book more advanced than Louis L'Amour or taking to the woods armed with a camera, not a rifle.

In deference to his sacrifice, the youth was allowed to shower with the rig hands. I had to wait my turn, which, thanks to the motorman and the Swisher Sweet he fired up on the commode, wasn't as bad as it might have been.

The lack of hot water abbreviated my shower and extended my stay at the sink (when I could get to it; the crew preened itself like cats). It was all I could do to just remove the grime, a skill not until now did I appreciate. Grit desperately clung to me. As for my fingernails, I yielded to the dirt encrusted underneath them.

Never again will I consider dirty fingernails a sign of impropriety.

Nor will I underestimate the wit of the tradesmen among my coworkers. Their banter was superior to that of my peers. The irony the electrician displayed when he complained it wasn't fair the scrotum should grow with age while one's teeth fell out surpassed any wry observation made by my prep school classmates. So did the motorman's lament about how unfair it was for hair to grow out the ears and nose while disappearing off the head.

Their practical jokes were more sophomoric than those practiced by my prep school classmates. The silver nitrate they dabbed on the towel the lanky derrick hand had used turned his privates as black as the paint sprayed on a preppie in gym. It was the Drispak the pranksters offered Hillbilly to remove it that set the prank apart. The compound swelled like yeast upon the application of water they also convinced him to apply.

"You've poured hundreds of sacks of Drispak in the mixing hopper," chided Penny, the driller. "You ought to know what it looks like."

The congregation that gathered to watch the safetyman peel away the hardened blob offered a perfect opportunity to sneak upstairs.

I barely made it to the third floor before Gordon, the clerk, appeared. Although nondescript, he still posed a threat. I knew he was too timid to stop me from entering the companyman's office but not timid enough to refrain from telling Jim Duhon about it. He struck me as the kind of employee employers dream about: company snitches.

I retreated and dove into the toolpusher's office. He followed.

"I want to look at the IADC report," I said.

"That's all right," he remarked.

I continued to hang around until I finished looking at the oversized pad on the surprisingly neat desk.

"Got what you need, chief?" he asked.

"Am lined out," I replied as I retreated downstairs to regroup and maybe catch a movie in the modestly appointed recreation room. A dozen plastic chairs, two recliners, and one tattered couch, all arranged in a half moon around a twenty-inch screen TV, was definitely inferior to the spare lounge in the Chi Sigma house.

Unfortunately, the film that was on failed to soothe my palpating breast. It irritated me. Porn flicks always irritated me. It wasn't the noises or banal comments the crew made, nor was it the terrible acting or pitiful production quality of the films. What depressed me was everyone's failure to see what they were looking at. Like all viewers of the genre, they did not realize the male actors' genitals received more air time than the females.

The fact their impressionability augured well for my mission helped relieve my frustration. Meanwhile, I could only suffer.

Not even the appearance of an apparition at the door claiming, with a thick Near Eastern accent: "This place must not be for the important people," cheered me. Neither did the geologist's huffy reply to Spud's subsequent insult.

"I am not an Arab. I am Persian," the doughty Iranian mudlogger said as he withdrew, shuffling his pointy slippers.

It took a woman, not a foreigner, to raise my spirits. Kathy, the craneman, showed I wasn't the only one who could see reality.

Her whooping and hollering subdued the prurient pack, actually embarrassed them.

"Look at the size of the hunk's thing. Hold me back. Yum," she said.

The crowd shuffled.

"It's Long John Holmes! My hero!"

Her stay so demoralized the pirates of Pensive they chose not to play another triple "x" tape after the conclusion of the one they were watching. Those who stayed watched a rerun of Starkey's Machine. The pack had shut up when the lady became a wolf.

Kathy was one to be reckoned with. It was no accident she was the only woman aboard. I couldn't imagine a more normal representative of the gender in her place. I didn't know how to take her.

Nor did I know how to take Spud come bedtime. He manifested the genius of his heritage by serenading us from his bed with an impromptu recital of Hillbilly's predicament that segued into a homily about his home. He banged on the walls to words he made up, a zydeco quasi French and English performance.

"But I got debris in the box, so I am happy," was the refrain which played in my mind when I finally fell asleep.

I woke to an altogether different sound. Someone kicked a bucket in front of Turtle's locker. The sound of liquid sloshing onto the floor was unmistakable.

"Goddamn piss," Turtle grumbled.

I had wanted to poke gentle fun at the renal recreant, threaten to tell I knew he had planted the bucket, so he didn't have to walk to the bathroom, and employ a little of the psychology I had studied to wield power over him. But Dennis ruined everything. Two seconds of him united all four of us in mutual enmity.

"Time to earn your money," he snarled, throwing on the lights. "This ain't no Caribbean cruise."

"You're cruisin' for a bruisin'," snapped our Turtle.

"Buckin' for a fuckin'," remarked Poncho our fourth roommate.

"Remember who washes your clothes. A cup of rig wash instead of detergent and you'll keep me in mind for a long time."

"Sometimes you forget you don't run the rig," countered Turtle.

"Sometimes you forget how long I've been here," he slammed the door shut.

"Watch yourself," warned Spud, sitting up in his bunk, worried. "He's got a stroke. Is buddy-buddy with the drilling superintendent."

"Don't care. No big shot can protect him from my Three Fifty-Seven." Turtle pulled from his duffle a heavy object wrapped in a towel. "Was going to use it shooting Johnny Mecom if the Saints have another one-in-thirteen season. But it needs some breaking in."

The pistol he waved became a magic wand that made the puddle of pee disappear. No one admitted seeing it. (I didn't; not even as I cleaned it up).

Dennis continued to blithely jeopardize his health. He angered or offended more than us; as his name was spat about in the general buzz of our eleven-a.m. breakfast conversation. Preventing any lapse of attention, he continued making enemies.

"Hey there. Stop that," grumbled Harvey to the troublemaker as he was interacting with the black galley hand.

"How do you know what I'm doing?"

"I seen that trick before. There ain't no heat coming from that butter."

Sambo started to pull his hand away from the stick Dennis held it over (ostensibly to let him feel the heat).

Dennis moved as to smash it into the butter.

"Don't even think about it."

Bowed, but unrepentant, the B. and R. hand sneered and performed more deviltry, splashing tobasco sauce on top of the ketchup the mud engineer had spread on his french fries.

Wanting to see how he would react kept the witnesses quiet when the Coon Ass returned with coffee.

"Ooh, I got that ol' channel fever," he asserted.

"But you just got here."

"Don't matter. Got to check on my wife, see how her frogging is doing."

Realizing he wasn't the center of attention, Popcorn, the motorman, informed us how, when he gets home, he'll be "so right I'll be left. Lie down like an old hound dog."

That said, attention returned to Sunny, the mud engineer.

"What's frogging?" asked Penny, the driller.

"Don't know, except she does a lot of it in the woods behind the house, especially on Saturday night. Comes home at sunrise sometimes." He swallowed a handful of fries.

"Ever eat the legs from the frogs she supposedly caught?" I asked.

"No, not really. But I tell you we buy some kind of meals with the money she made off them. So I know she was hard at work."

We watched in amazement as he shoveled in another mouthful.

"You think this extra spice means anything to this palate you wrong."

"No pain, no gain?"

"I'm on a seafood diet. What I see I eat. I see that tobacco goes on them potato sticks. Hey, nothing gets by me."

Not to be outdone, the motorman claimed how he too ate seafood. "From my wife's mouth. It's the only way she gets me to kiss her the way she wants. Knows that this Cajun tongue doesn't stretch out like a lesbian with a hard-on unless there's food at the other end."

"Don't know why she wants to kiss you," said Penny. "That Copenhagen you keep in your mouth; goddamn, I bet you got some of that worm dirt in there now."

"Keeps my mouth lubricated."

"Rots off your gum."

"This mouth. It's a steel trap. Bite heads off the little kittens we skin and sell to the blacks as baby rabbits."

The demure galley hand shook with mortification. He lost his ability to speak.

"Whadsamatter?" asked Dennis. "Cat got your tongue? You look catatonic."

Put on the spot, Sambo had to say something.

"I wouldn't eat no baby cat."

"What doesn't kill you makes you stronger," said another Nietzsche aficionado (they're everywhere, it seems).

"If that's so," the galley hand said, fishing for words. "Then why don't you clean up after yourself? My daddy would beat me like a redheaded stepchild if I was as messy as you." Judging from the bruises on his arms, he spoke from experience.

"If we'd clean, you'd be out of a job."

That confused the kid. "Some of the time I forget what my uncle preached," he finally said. "Don't know why. All I got to do is look at my arm to remember my place."

"I don't need to look to know my place. All of you better already know it," Jim bellowed as he staged a dramatic entrance.

I and several others used the smoke he exhaled as a screen to make our escape.

His non-sequesters about Edwin Edwards letting anti-Somozan rebels train north of Lake Pontchartrain echoed in our wake.

Five scintillating hours of work later (interrupted by a quorum of cars and women during our afternoon break) we returned for dinner to find Jim still elaborating on the governor's role in the invasion of Nicaragua. Having worried the subject to death, burial, and probably into Guinness's for the longest filibuster outside the halls of Congress, he avoided yielding the floor by launching into a diatribe of Jimmy Carter.

"If Carter had the guts to send marines in after the hostages were taken, we wouldn't be embarrassed today," he concluded.

"There were no marines to send in; they were too disorganized," claimed Hammer, exhaling his cloud of cigarette smoke.

"Don't need no marines," opined Bull, the big barge engineer. "All you needed to do was send some good 'coon hunters in pick-ups over there." He exhaled an even bigger puff.

"Yeah, the dogs would chase them rag heads into the Gulf," affirmed Hammer, the toolpusher. He sucked a drag so remarkable it burned half his cigarette.

Jim just grunted. With all the groceries he stuffed into his gaping maw, it was all he could do. If not for the sweet tea he imbibed, the chitlins, cornbread, red beans, rice, and turnips might have set up, to talk in the vernacular. His fork was a perpetual motion machine, disappearing in blurs of motion. That he was a bit noisier than the average diner was understandable, given the vast amount of food he masticated. If I were ever to canvass his office, I'd have to lure him away with food, as I figured I'd have to do with the walrus at the pipe yard.

He let loose a mighty belch at the same time Hammer let loose a cloud that fogged the entire table.

"A kick," Jim chortled, referring to his bit of business. He ignored Hammer's. "Could have been a blow-out hadn't I shut the rams. I better not lose circulation later, there cookie."

"Don't worry, Mister Jim. Bacteria wouldn't dare grow on my food."

"Bacteria wouldn't want to grow on his food," smugly said Hammer as he watched Bull put out his half-smoked cigarette in defeat.

"Blowfly will eat it," claimed Penny. "With them teeth of his he can eat anything."

The smile the black roughneck affected revealed several gold teeth.

"Turn to the left so we can get WWL. Charley Douglas' Road Gang might be on."

"If we're lucky we'll get to hear Red Sovine or Johnny Cash singing Harvey's song," said Bull.

We all turned to the ponderous cook.

The woolly mammoth admitted how he had written, "I walk the line."

"Make any money off it?" asked Hammer.

"Got thrown in jail for it."

"Thrown in jail?"

"Didn't hear a word from the producers I sent the song to. Forgot about it 'till I heard it on the radio. Wish I hadn't thrown the wrapper I wrote it on away. 'N wish I had been on the wagon."

"That's when you got in trouble?"

"It was a bad time for me."

"I've got the Fulsome Prison blues," sang the welder I had dubbed the "Hummer" on the crew boat.

Revealing his knowledge on the subject, Dennis turned to Blowfly and remarked how Harvey probably wasn't "messed with". "He's 'more crazy.' You blacks wouldn't dare come near him."

The well-built roughneck squared his shoulders.

"Did you undo your pants and dance around central lockup with your brothers, singing how you gonna overthrow whitey?"

"Never been to prison. Not like some folks that seem to know so much," Blowfly said, showing an unexpected backbone.

Dennis returned to his food and sulked in private. He was the only one who didn't notice the Iranian stride in. He was the only one who didn't bristle at the airs the dark-skinned foreigner oozed, airs the mudlogger should have learned last night a service hand best leave on the beach. But Dennis wasn't the only one oblivious to the stir. The object of everyone else's attention did not know what a disturbance he was creating, equal to that White Rabbit created at the Knave of Heart's trial. When the frail, tiny man deigned to sit next to me he proceeded to mimic the aloofness of the Tiger-Lily, choosing not to talk until someone worth talking to spoke to him first.

Like the rest, Jim looked at him as if he were a space alien rather than a terrestrial alien. As I leaned forward to prevent obstructing the companyman's view; Jim leaned forward. I leaned back; he leaned back. "Get out of my way," he eventually hissed.

With as much dignity as I could muster, I picked up my tray and moved to the other table; where I too wasn't above looking at the Iranian, albeit with some discretion.

Somebody had to say something. The tension was palpable. Through the pall of smoke that encircled his head, the Gizzard of Oz hit upon something to snarl about. "What are you doing in those coveralls? You're no Wilson's hand. Wear those fishing tool hand duds around 'and people will think we got a stuck pipe. Ruin morale." Snuffing out a butt, Jim's mouth stayed empty for the time it took to insert the spoils from the channel he carved in a nearby chocolate cake. When licked clean, he used the same finger to swab his ears and pick his nose. No one but me noticed. The rest were too fixated on the recipient of the criticism.

Watching someone so shaken he couldn't swallow wasn't entertaining to me.

"You didn't eat half your peas," an Algonquin raconteur told me as I got up to leave.

"May peas be with you," I said, hoping a little wit would stifle the hand.

His face screwed into a question mark that tied his tongue.

Arriving at the return window with my dirty dishes at the same time as the Muslim, I politely reminded him to scrape his garbage into the nearby can before placing it on the counter, thinking friendliness breeds alliances.

"Got to watch your p's and q's around these people," I whispered.

"What is a 'p' and what is a 'q'?" he asked, cleaning up as I advised.

"They stand for 'penis' and 'queers'," said Hammer, flipping his knife with self-approval. "Don't bend over to pick up the soap in the showers."

"Oh, I don't take showers with others," the Iranian declared, ensuring he'd remain beleaguered. The xenophobes babbled in his wake. Jim Duhon harrumphed.

The evening was given to slapping paint on the primer we had slapped on the metal we had stripped with our needle guns. Some time in the future we'll redeploy the torture devices and start all over; kind of like what Sisyphus had to go through in Hades.

Whoever determined the color scheme of our home away from home flunked art appreciation. The yellow that got on my skin and in my hair while painting the handrails clashed with the grey I had applied everywhere else. Only Turtle sported dollops of red, as he had helped the fat cementer Bull ordered to paint his unit, "So he could get off his butt."

Would it be too much to ask for a little color coordination, a frill or two to satisfy our deep-seated urge for refinement, to rise above the animal world? Auctioneers sold paintings, cotton, plantations, and slaves in the rotunda of the world-famous Saint Louis Hotel. So, the Deep South did set a precedent for civilized commerce.

Ensuring we didn't make ourselves miserable by thinking too much, Kathy saw to it we stayed industrious.

Towards the latter part of our tour (popularly pronounced "tower"), we set aside our palates, horsehairs, and berets to unload a helicopter. Landing on a corner of the helipad, its prop wash added a much-needed splash of surrealism to the corny company logo Spud just finished touching up.

In keeping with tradition, we assaulted the cargo bay as if it contained ammunition needed against attacking Viet Cong. Above the roar, I was chewed out for not unbuckling the straps securing cargo on the outward-facing seats fast enough. I was chewed out when I bumped into the pito tubes as I hugged the nose en route to the other side. I got chewed out for straying too close to the tail rotor unloading boxes from the main baggage compartment near the rear. The only time I didn't get chewed out I almost got killed. Lugging a survey kit, I was complaining about how everything in the oil patch was heavy and not paying attention to the main rotor until it brushed my helmet.

"Walk away at an angle," the pilot coolly stated over his intercom. "We're shutting down, wind plays hell with a decelerating blade."

Now he tells me.

"Pilot must have gotten the okay to eat," said Turtle as we hauled a box down the two flights of stairs to the wheelhouse.

"I've got to insist the safety strips be replaced. Both of us almost slipped," I said.

"Should we leave these bits here?" asked Poncho, the Puerto Rican, after we finished.

"Sure," replied Kathy, overseeing the operation. "We'll be drilling through the crews' quarters any minute now."

The bony Latin scratched his balding head. Spud explained what she meant.

"Women shouldn't make fun of men," he shouted for our crane person's edification.

"But men can make fun of women?" she replied bitterly.

"You don't belong here." Poncho's face turned red.

"I make my bread by keeping my buns in that cab. And I think it's about time you earn the right to keep your behind on this rig."

His protests about working hard enough weren't acknowledged. Worse, she considered it time Poncho and I needed a lesson in humility.

Kathy wanted us to find the keys to the "V" door she had "misplaced." Taken aback, I paused to reflect on my situation. Before my odyssey, I would have shown her how sophisticated I was by explaining the sociological meaning of the rite of passage snipe hunt. Now, glancing at Spud and Turtle, I knew I had to play along.

Their smirks were revealing. Rednecks are not known for their poker faces. Nor are they known to forgive someone who'll spoil their fun.

Maybe they had gone through it and sought vicarious revenge. I thought.

"Do I have to jerk you off?" Kathy said as she started to climb the ladder on the forward starboard crane.

The thought was so revolting, that I raced down the three remaining flights and across the rig floor, not worried I still had a little time left on my shift. I slowed only to stay out of the way of equipment being dragged from the cat-walk to the drill floor, up the "V" door. I pretended not to notice. By now word of our quest must have been spread, and to disappoint the sadists might invite ridicule.

To get along I had to go along, which didn't mean I had to act like an idiot. I could hide in the shadow of a real idiot. Realizing I was blowing an excellent opportunity to look for the invoice, I retreated to the crew's quarters to tag behind my fellow worm as he began his quest in Hammer's office.

Reclining in his overstuffed chair, the overstuffed overseer let us stand around like fools as he read a report. His usually pursed lips turned into a smirk when Poncho anxiously asked him if he knew where the keys were. Dragging out the joke, Hammer kept smirking when he made an elaborate show of searching for them, checking his metal file cabinet, metal desk, and metal shelves, showing me his lair was devoted to keeping records of what transpired on the rig, not what cargo was shipped to it.

"Nope, must have misplaced them. Ask that barge engineer," he said with muffled glee.

Bull was as believable as expected, which was to say, not believable at all. The only unbelievable aspect of his unbelievable performance was the way Poncho believed him.

"Don't get in nobody's way playing hide and go seek," the thespian warned as he scratched his crotch.

He wasn't finished. An inadvertent step toward Jim's office triggered a barrage of obloquies the Wheel would have been proud of.

"We find them quick and we are in like Flint," Poncho, our own Gullible, said as we scurried across the rig the minute our tour was over.

Starting in earnest at the shaker house, our Fernando Desoto plunged his protruding proboscis under the sink, behind the centrifugal pumps, and even lifted the grating to climb into the empty sand trap. He got sprayed by the seawater from the hose he kicked open and managed to bang his head after slipping on some mud left at the bottom of the possum's belly.

The call "Gumbo Attack" precipitated a meleè that diverted attention from us. Although it was a drill, to train workers for the inevitable top-hole problem, the floor hands and roustabouts acted like it was the real thing and raced to their stations, allowing us to snoop around the conical desanders and desilters unobserved. Or so I thought.

"Getting warm," said the driller on the other tour over the intercom.

Poncho slid over to the bright red Swaco degasser.

"Little warmer." The impishness in Pencil's voice did not slow Poncho down. He kept rooting around for the talisman, slithering in the muck underneath the tank, as eager as a kid on an Easter Egg hunt.

A casual stroll down to the Texas deck didn't fool a roustabout in mud-splattered coveralls. Red knew what I was doing and sympathized with me, claiming they had him "scoop for blue water with a bucket." That he was unable to do so "in deep blue water" was a mystery to him. "Can see if we were close to shore, where the water was brown, not way offshore."

Trying to get away, I tripped over a protrusion and would have slammed into a circulation hose had he not grabbed and whirled me away.

"Those two hoses, they're hot with all the mud the pumps move through them," said Pork Chop, another eponymously named hand who happened to be nearby.

Not to mention the rubber is as hard as iron, I thought as I touched them.

In the convivial tête-a-tête, we struck up, I learned the metal eyelet I stumbled over was for the Bureau of Shipping's benefit. "Hook what looks like a fish scale to the hole in the center; tests pulling power of crane."

The fact both cranes had failed the last test was included in a copy of the infractions he was assigned to help rectify.

"Jim pissed off the Coast Guard. Knew they had their pet peeves but didn't care. Got on their bad side real good," said the carrot-topped roustabout.

"Those guys," began Pork Chop, shaking his head. "They're like the U.S. Geological Society folks the other company man hacked off. Sunshine refused to monitor their radio reports when they're too busy to do it themselves." He paused for reflection. "What they want you to do you do. They can shut down a rig like that." He snapped his fingers. As he did I noticed that Jones, the electrician, and his holy-than-thou assistant, crawling over a filthy power rack, replacing plastic tie-wraps with metal ones. "Once shut down operations for two months 'til an eagle raised her family in the derrick, way up in the crown. It was on a land rig near Houma."

Spotting Poncho leaning on the rail, anxiously looking out to sea, I assumed he had figured out the ruse and was agonizing over having made an ass out of himself.

"I guess it was our turn to help reduce the stress everyone is under," I said, containing an urge to put a consoling hand on his shoulder. I just wasn't comfortable with such familiarity.

Ignoring my feeble attempt at empathy, he asked (referring to an approaching workboat) "Is that the Baskin-Robbins boat? Driller wants a vanilla ice cream cone. Hope I have enough money."

"I'm sure you have more than enough," I said.

"Hope you're right. I'm on his shit list for not finding the keys."

The boat did look familiar. It was the craft Turtle and I had unloaded, maybe returning from shore, though I didn't see any cargo.

"Didn't go nowhere," said Red, ambling up to my side. "Jim likes to keep the boat in the field, swapping crews with standby boats, or whatever."

"So they get to rattle around, doing nothing. Back at port, they could be loading up for the next trip." I thought of all the rush orders Father had to fill when available transportation was a must.

"Course, when he wants something. He wants it now."

"Of course," I said in departure, not wanting to be anywhere near Poncho when he asked the genial roustabout if the boat carried chocolate.

"I like chocolate; eat it all the time," I heard Red say.

"When it's time to relax, one beer stands clear," the scrawny welder sang as I entered the darkened rec. Room well after most of the rig crew had departed.

"Can you change channels?" asked Heavy Duty, the cementer, our recumbent couch incumbent.

The sign enjoining service hands "not to even think of touching this set" had kept the third-party personnel in their seats. Knowing how low on the totem pole service personnel were didn't prevent me from sucking up to them.

I'd suck up to anybody, I thought as I flicked from channel to channel asking for a consensus. I can suck up better than a Chi Sigma when need be. Who knew when I'd need the help of the second-class citizens? They did have access to the office, to hand in reports and logs. It's best I wheedle into everyone's confidence, can't have too many allies.

I sucked up to our driller as he burst in, a wolf among sheep, a Marble employee among "service trash." The interest I showered on Penny's claim that he was equal to the hunters on the hunting show caused him to glow. It deepened his already sonorous voice, giving it the timbre and texture I'm sure our resident apostle will hear come Rapture.

"Should have seen them picnickers when them ducks flew overhead last season," he said as he scratched himself. "Scattered like buckshot when the guns began going off. Sounded like 'Nam. Killed me a hundred before I was through."

"Isn't that illegal?" asked the Iranian, who felt a driller was high enough on the pecking order to talk to.

"Nothing's illegal if you don't get caught."

Collecting his thoughts, Abdul finally asked, "How'd you hide the bodies?"

"Hide'm? Why hide? Ate most of them. Not me alone. Family helped, 'n not right off; froze a bunch."

"You mean you still have them?"

"Some I stuffed. That's what I do on the side. Got a taxidermy business. Good one too. Do top work. Want to buy a specimen? The school's biology departments buy from me. Here, I'll go get some pictures.

"No, no. Please no. You're a crazy man." He scurried out of the room.

The levity only temporarily lifted me out of my funk. How could it be otherwise, with the thought of having to work for the driller should I get advanced to roughneck? I'm no "hail fucker, well meant."

"Always recommend mayonnaise jars, Hellman's mayonnaise jars. They make the best carbide bombs," he said, defending the fishing prowess he claimed superior to that shown on the Jimmy Houston program.

I hadn't felt so unclean since a homo once offered to pay for fellatio, claiming it would be better than what any girl could offer. I remember I wasn't outraged because of the offer, per se. It was my initial response to it. For a single sickening sabbatical of sanity, I had considered it, thinking how well-practiced he must be.

Why was I able to suppress the memory of my weakness until now? It has to be the circumstances. They say imprisonment makes a man reflective. The constant noise, vibrations, and total lack of privacy had forced me into my head. I couldn't escape myself.

Semiconscious before sleep, on a sagging mattress, I reviewed my situation, and let my new self-awareness hold sway. Having my life turned upside down so abruptly kept me from experiencing the normal stages of grief.   I had gone through denial, anger, bargaining, depression, and acceptance. No self-pity or remorse. Like a refugee, I didn't have time to wallow in my misfortune. I don't want to think how I would have made it without my companions. Just knowing they were there to catch me if I stumbled, was enough. To my credit, I knew I needed their help.

I still need help. Given the fact, I don't know what the score is. Is Father in jail; did he charge Springer Oil one hundred seventy-five thousand and reported only one hundred-twenty thousand revenue on his taxes? Why would he be so obvious? Who took the bribe? Was it whoever signed the "Client" copy of the invoice? Wouldn't it be some procurer in their office in Houston? And what about the offshore company he allegedly sold pipe to, to avoid taxes? Certainly, I would have had some hint of its existence. I was being groomed to take over the business. Though not privy to the details, Father made sure I knew about the strategy involved, usually over post-prandial drinks and games of poker with key employees or business associates. That's where I learned to read his "tells", and became as attuned to his moods and expressions as a faithful dog. I'm sure I picked up on his scary vibrations the moment they began emanating from him.

Grandfather didn't just leave us a business when he passed, he left us a heritage. The scrupulous honesty he employed to ward off the legal threats of the Longs, Perezes, and all their cronies was indispensable. Lawyer fees would have broken us had we something to hide. No, the acorn did not fall far from the tree. It remained in its shadow, completely in character, until just recently. Father's change in personality had been relatively sudden, certainly too sudden for the feds to build a case. Brilab took many months. And that was a sting operation. There were no infiltrators in our organization, no new faces in our house--except the ones I had invited.

Extrapolating from my experience at the pipe yard I realized I not only had to know the names and habits of the chiefs. I had to know the names and habits of the Indians. This rig is the home away from home for most of the crew. They know all about it, sociologically and from an engineering standpoint. Grandfather had to deal with rough customers. So did Father. I guess I'm going to have to if I hope to find the one who will help me enter the forbidden office. With a mighty effort, I climbed out of bed and didn't return until I had procured a pen and paper. I didn't go to sleep until, under a blanket draped over my night light, I had written down the names, positions, and everything I knew about each hand. When I later awoke to answer the call of nature I did not go back to sleep until I had drawn an organizational chart. Come breakfast I inconspicuously checked my work, or so I thought.

"Tar Baby, he's no driller. He's the assistant," said Turtle, craning his neck from two seats over.

"He's lucky to be that," said Penny, our driller. "Let me see." He hustled over and tried to yank the papers out of my hands. I made certain he only grabbed the one on top, the one depicting the organization chart. It only contained names, not opinions.

"Now get this, worms," he began as he glanced at it. "This hand here got the big dogs right. Hammer and Bull try to run the show, but it's me and Pencil who make holes. We share the assistant driller and even if he works both tours every day the only time he'll advance is when Hell freezes over. Only my floor hands will take longer. Got the sorriest roughnecks anywhere, the worst derrick, and the blindest shaker hands. Only Pencil's are sorrier. Kathy thinks she can operate a crane and babysit roustabouts at the same time. Jones and his goofball assistant, nick wires, and only the motors Popcorn is supposed to take care of make more noise than him. Then there's the service hands. Bones would be a good medic if he could ever get his head out of his ass. Nobody can screw up mud better than Sunny, Harvey and his chain gang will poison us, and last and very least there are the mudloggers."

"The least necessary evil out here," said Jim. "These college kids we got may know their rocks, but I never had to sneak looks into the units of the winos we used to get to see if they were asleep."

"If their unit was shaking, you'd know they were awake, with the dts," said Hammer. "Didn't have to worry about them not paying attention, being, and reading. Who'd want to listen to them? Can read only good enough to know what their dials and charts are saying, which they knew how to interpret."

"Give me experience and you can keep all the fancy computers, especially if you don't pay much attention to them anyway," said Jim, having the last word.

"Afraid of anything new. Pack animals." I wrote down next to the names of my bosses. "Afraid of anything new. Pack animals." I wrote it down about the frat boys. The similarity seemed obvious, so obvious I knew the only way I hadn't been able to see it was because I had been one of them. I had been as drunk with sycophancy as Harvey had been on beer when he also "did something stupid."

"Bully," I wrote next to Jim's name. As for Penny, I didn't know what to put, not after watching him and Kathy interact during a movie after dinner. I first thought Anne Haven's performance inspired my crane person. Throughout the first half of "High School Memories" she stroked and fondled the driller as ferociously as decorum would allow, not letting his resistance deter her. Only later, after Penny escaped did it come out, he was on his third consecutive hitch and, according to Kathy, should have been "as horny as a hoot owl."

"Crass and vulgar" is how I described Kathy, the complete antithesis of what a woman should be like, of what Leslie is like. My Marcella; the woman I'm as destined as Chrysostom to die from a broken heart for, couldn't be so crude. Leslie wouldn't stalk Penny, as Kathy did the next morning, sitting next to him at breakfast, staring at him. The pennies of the world stalk the Leslies. They're the ones who want to drag her through a rape trial, ruining her worse than the victim in "A Town Without Pity" because she wouldn't dare tell anyone what had happened. I can't imagine him dragging Kathy to court. She'd drag him.

Pinching his butt as he got up from the table and blowing him kisses, she kept up her harassment, much to his chagrin and our delight. In court, she'd probably brag about raping him and give lurid details. The embarrassment Leslie would suffer would prey upon her like lupus. She'd be like the beautiful doe whose liquid eyes hid the pain of blowflies and parasites.

As Kathy pursued her prey in and out the rec. Room, the store room, and downstairs in the pump room, I pursued mine in my head, letting my Dulcinea's entire being consume me. The silken hair that framed a classic face, and her lithe features, remained imbued in my mind, protected from the coarse environment I was in by a will as steely as the quixotic hidalgo's armor.

"Shark. We got ourselves a shark on the line," Hammer bellowed over the P.A. Shouting "fire" couldn't have cleaned out the rec. Room quicker. I almost got trampled, being the only one to show class. No one even cared I was the only one wearing a hard hat and completely tied steel-toed boots. Hammer exemplified the norm, with his exposed shock of greying hair and untied sneakers. Rules were suspended for special events.

Peering over two rows of shoulders, I caught glimpses of a demon churning the grey water white.

Appearing out of nowhere, Bull ordered the iron basket lowered.

"Like Hell," growled Jim from an above balcony. "Springer Oil doesn't pay you to play with the equipment it's renting. Break it 'n we gotta pay for a new one."

"Yes sir," Bull abjured. "Pull on that line!" he bellowed to us.

"I do a lot of things, but that ain't one of them," said Penny.

"You people earn your keep."

"I don't work that cheap," Sunny stated.

The rush to the crew's quarters to find work gloves did not last long. No one wanted to stay away from the action.

"If they were this excited working we'd finish the well in a week," Bull observed.

"Sooner if there was a twelve-point buck at T.D.," chirped Sunny.

A bunch of us grabbed the nylon line and, when we realized what we got ourselves into, threw our backs into it.

The fish spasmodically flashed silver near the surface and turned dark and shapeless as it sounded.

"Tiger shark," Spud grunted.

"Bull shark," Blowfly, the black roughneck, said with authority,

"Has to be a Bonnet Head," claimed Penny, with even more authority.

All speculation ended when the tug of war began in earnest. Fourteen hands and seven backs strained with one mighty effort to first set the hook then yank it up, one excruciating tug after another.

Bones, the safety man, fluttered in our way, uttering banalities nobody listened to. Jim shouted imprecations that infuriated us. Hammer gave the orders we listened to. He'd say pull, and we pulled until our knuckles whitened and back about broke. He was our conscious, our brains, the Old Man and the Sea for all of us as we struggled to raise our Moby Dick to the surface.

"Hammerhead!" several shouted as it launched itself out of the water.

"Let go!" Hammer screamed. "Let go!"

I let go without question and watched in awe. The rope snapped taut as the prehistoric beast arched backward, momentarily and forever freezing itself in my mind in mid-air. The rope hissed as it plunged back into the water, to run out the line in milliseconds.

"Thwack." The iron railing bent backward, and I'd swear could have broken had the line not broken first. Nylon line.

The crowd hushed in reverence. The Gulf quickly repaired itself. Lazy crosscurrents erased all signs of struggle. More interest deserved to be lavished on Blowfly and Bones, both of whom got hurt; the former suffered a serious fall and broke an arm, and the latter only banged his head.

"Too bad Blowfly instead of Bones has to go in," complained Heavy Duty, the cementer during the post-mortem. "Don't like what that safety man watches on television."

"Too bad the rope didn't knot around his ankle," said Dennis with a sneer. "A water skiing Moulie, that'd be a sight."

"A Captain Ahab," I instantly regretted saying. (No one knew what I was talking about).

As for the black floor hand, no one felt sorry for him. He had held on too long. "Can't follow orders," claimed Dennis. "See that half ear of his? Got it shot off in 'Nam. Told to 'get down' in a firefight, he got up and danced around."

The crowd dispersed to conduct postmortems, the gist of which I didn't find out until the air ambulance arrived. "God help him get well," said Reverent David Prejan solemnly as the helicopter flew off. "May the doctors at Our Lady of Lourdes work their magic."

"If he prays for his one arm to look like his other, he'd better be careful which one he chooses. Both are gonna be messed up bad if he gives us a Lost Time Accident," threatened Bull, who had a big stake in maintaining a clean safety record. I've known since I could remember how vital good safety records were. Father had made a point of dealing only with those enjoying excellent reputations and would recall an order should the client come under a cloud. Of course, it wouldn't hurt if Bull went in with Blowfly, to ensure he was properly treated and didn't wander off.

As for who would replace the injured hand, everyone breathed a sigh of relief when Hammer gave Turtle the nod.

"Now you don't have to punch anyone out to get ahead," observed Spud.

"I don't hurt nobody who doesn't deserve it."

"What about Dick Nolan?" asked my roommate, impishly.

"He's still gonna get it. Worst coach in history. Wastes a first-round draft pick on a Bush league kicker, Russel Erxleben," he sneered.

Turtle waxed so much wroth it infected others, turning the floor crew into a sour bunch before the end of the next tour. It was as if he had a vendetta, wanting to ensure everyone suffered from the burr up his ass.

"I don't have to live here now that I'm on the floor," he told Spud when in our room. "No offense, but I'm gonna take Blowfly's bunk."

"No offense taken. Here, don't forget this." Spud threw the pee can at Turtle.

"You did that on purpose."

"It just slipped out of my hand. I wouldn't dream of harming a superior."

Turtle was the center of interest the next morning. Rumor had it Bull had come down hard on him. Somebody had punctured his piss can and it was said the dried urine stank up the room.

"So you got chewed on," sneered Spud.

"I'm still working on the drill floor."

Thus were sown the seeds of a practical joke war. Mamou, the shaker hand, pointed out the pipe dope on Spud's forehead when we broke for dinner. The sticky, oil-based goo had been smeared on his helmet liner.

"Circumstantial evidence," countered Turtle. He went into an elaboration as convoluted as the Mock Turtle's story. When he finished explaining the impossibility of transporting the sealant undetected from the floor to the locker room, we were too glad he shut up to punch holes in his story. The same held at the midnight meal when he was accused of filling Spud's boots with sand. A surfeit of salt on his greens courtesy of his ex-roommate "lessened the lesson."

Their quadrille moved to the rec. Room, where he choked on the water Spud poured into his mouth when he fell asleep on the couch. A boot hidden behind a locker and a lemon fish under a pillow turned out to be the parting shots of the war. "Turtles don't forget" was the swan song as interest soon waned, replaced by the ongoing Sade Hawkins race between Kathy and Penny as well as a growing fascination with Poncho, the token Latino, who was blossoming into the rig's chief foil. His antics bemused even the two combatants. How could they maintain an audience when the dolt began holding vigils for the "pussy boat" once he learned the Baskin Robin's boat had been detained by the Coast Guard for lying about the amount of fat in its product.

"Bitches can't lie," he professed. "What you see is what you get."

It was genuinely precious to listen to what he'd do with the women when he got his hands on them.

"Don't laugh," Sunny advised me. "Scouts kept a close eye on the whores down in South America. When they break camp, they know the well is coming to an end."

Hammer owned how when he was a worm, a cathouse on a barge plied the swamps south of Lake Arthur. "Still can see it rotting away at Castle's Landing."

Poncho ensured I wouldn't enter my dotage devoid of stories. No one would accuse me of lying when I tell them the Don Juan swaggered out to work the next day garbed in alligator boots, tight denim, and semi-metallic polyester, all crowned by a spit-shined helmet with a "Cat" decal. Nor could they dispute my claim he fended off Kathy's tirade by insisting he works best in his "sex suit". It was too stupid.

"Me and Freddy Prince." He pulled out a ring of knives, carefully selected one, and used it to par his fingernails.

"Backtalk is a run-off offense," barked the rig sex symbol, obviously unimpressed.

Slow to respond, the novice selected another knife (a puma) to spear a grasshopper that had ridden swamp grass offshore.

"Forty-eight hours, that's how long I can go," he said as he reluctantly left to change into coveralls. So Poncho became Poncho of Forty-Eight Hours; and coincidentally was given that much time to justify his new title. For, instead of a Love Boat, a helicopter arrived with a hammer crew (who would bang the drive pipe into the seabed) and one hoyden who would grace our humble abode with her charms.

A beached blonde, a whale of a woman, with a center of gravity a hurricane couldn't dislodge, she descended from the pad to the scrutiny athletes receive entering a playing field.

"Need to pour flour on her so you can find the wet spot," said Spud, betraying a little excitement in his voice.

"The crew wouldn't look twice at her if they worked four weeks on four weeks off like they do overseas," remarked Sunny. "One wonders about these 'two and two' heroes. You'd think they were more deprived than depraved."

Well put, I thought. *A pundit among pinheads--a resurrected Euripides providence sent offshore to protect my mental health.*

We had a new sex symbol and, with it, a resultant catfight. The rig shook twice, once from Penny momentarily letting go of the brake to gape at her and again from Kathy's angst. Each wolf whistle and comment arched her back.

At first, it was entertaining to watch Kathy turn green as Penny later proclaimed, "Everybody is going to have to wait his turn behind me." Kathy even was jealous when Turtle disclosed how he was going to have his way with her inside a preload tank.

If she distracted Jim as much as she distracted Kathy I'd be able to camp out in his office.

Poor Kathy seemed to lose her libido. She became sullen as if she lacked the will to compete. I heard of quitters but never saw one in action. It was sad to see Penny lose his fear, and regain his sassiness. Others weren't so compassionate and took advantage of our craneman's depressed state of mind.

Two of my coworkers thought the time to break out some bones under the cantilever deck but within direct line of sight of the starboard crane.

"I'm not worried about her," said Poncho of Forty-Eight Hours, hinting he and she had some sort of relationship going on.

"Nothing's come of it so far," said Spud, receiving the joint.

"When she doesn't see her hands where we belong she's gonna come looking."

"She's not going to do anything," Poncho reaffirmed.

Unable to control myself I asked why.

"Because she's a woman, and no woman is gonna do nothing to hurt 'The Man', 'Mister Lucky', the 'Sultan of Seeds'."

"The wind will blow the smell out to sea," Spud insisted.

Maybe so, but the one part per million the eddies swirled back toward the crews' quarters was enough to attract Dennis.

We must have made him feel comfortable because one toke was all it took for him to regale us with his life as a dealer. Leaning against the Blow Out Preventers we'd install later in the well, the burly bedroom and restroom hand described how he dumped his excrement in his trash when he found out the feds were looking for evidence. "Ammonia works good against the dogs," he said, taking a serious hit.

That he spent three years in the joint didn't dampen his advocacy of Hunter Thompson's chemically dependent philosophy. "Have me a real good time ashore."

Taking a big drag of his own, Poncho proclaimed, "This job's all right. There's thirty-foot joints, buckets of dope, and a pusher."

And a big sister to watch over you. I thought as I noticed Kathy in the crane's cabin. I fled to a hiding place. She kept staring at Timothy Leary and their friends, her glare the intensity of helos; focused and potentially lethal. Nothing came of it. Nothing at all, and it scared me. Antipathy, not reproach, rearranged the topography of her craggy face as she sat across the dinner table from the druggies. No sign of an ulterior motive was discernible when she engaged Turtle's replacement in small talk, nothing like the transparent scorn she projected when she mentioned the newly arrived competition.

"Know why men like big tits and tight pussy?" she asked the admirers of Miss Voluptuous. "Because they have small dicks and a big mouth."

She momentarily beamed with contentment at the laughter the comment engendered before resuming her sullen demeanor.

Poncho then became the center of attention. The adroitness he manifested with his arsenal of knives spearing his food garnered everyone's mumbled accolades, everyone's except Hammer's. His hands were fast, like a magician's. His deftness sure, like a surgeon's. He was as familiar with each blade as a juggler is with each prop. And if he had possessed a double-digit I.Q., I'd credit him with a psychiatrist's ability at manipulation. Hammer stewed and sweated growled, and fretted until he finally accepted the challenge. Out came his butterfly knife, glinting and savage. He flipped it up and down, with meaning, heart, with unbridled provocation.

Poncho heated his performance, cutting and paring with the alacrity of a skilled butcher. Both clanged away, eyeing each other malevolently, two aspirants vying for our admiration, saber-rattling under the fluorescent noonday lights.

"Got chickens, fightin' chickens," brayed Popcorn, craving his share of the limelight. "Give'm a little water, run, shave, 'n they can't be beaten."

Having usurped center stage, the motorman continued unabetted, broadcasting how his favorite fighter won seven straight matches. "Now, this ain' no shit, them Cubans changed the odds when my Popeye, he got stuck in the eye. Scrambled all over the place, makin' new bets. People watched the stands more than the arena, so they missed my Popeye dodge the *coup de gras* 'n stick that big red rooster right in the belly. The fight that broke out! Ooowee!"

"There's two kinds of lies," proclaimed Jim as he strutted in with Christine, his blonde girlfriend. "Fairy tales which start, 'Once upon a time' and an oil patch tale which starts, 'Now this ain't no shit'."

Behind the couple trooped Bull and Penny. "His puppies," Spud asserted. "Look at the bird-fed smiles on those two alley cats. Think they're going to get a shot at her."

I looked at Kathy. Sheer hate enveloped her face. She squeezed her fork. Knowing what I do about women, revenge had to be on her mind.

Bull didn't seem to think that playing pocket pool would tip off anyone of his intentions. Nor did Penny, as he swaggered behind her, his usually muddy eyes bright with anticipation. Jim was full of himself, beaming with satisfaction, and as gross as ever, picking at an alligator-shaped fruit cake Harvey had whipped up to "make Misse Jim feel she's appreciated." He removed the cherry that represented the head of a man caught in the animal's jaws and popped it into his mouth.

"Oh, this is wonderful food. I couldn't possibly cook something this good," she cooed after one bite.

I doubt Harvey could again. The prime rib, green beans almandine, stuffed peppers, and cara-peanuts we enjoyed were a first, and probably a last.

"I don't have to worry about you all being well taken care of," vouchsafed the new center of attention.

To her credit, she did maintain a queenly disposition, absorbing the stares of her admirers and the glare of her lone detractor with a grace Kimberly could only dream of. If only there wasn't so much of her. If only the trench she inadvertently wiped in her acrylic face hadn't dashed the illusion of perfect skin. If only she hadn't smeared her lipstick removing more stray food. If only she was a little more discriminating with her tableware. I didn't need to see her shove stray beans onto her fork or eat french fries with her fingers.

Her failings prompted Dennis to depart. I didn't know he possessed such refined sensibilities.

"Gonna break open his magazines," whispered Turtle. A reproving look from Jim silenced the chuckle before the strumpet could figure out Dennis left to masturbate. Crisis averted, she finished her meal and inserted a post-prandial Virginia Slim between her ruby lips. Immediately, three matches and one lighter appeared, masking her behind a wall of flames.

"Ooo, what gentlemen," she chirped.

Kathy started to break out a cigarette of her own, but quickly put it away. The absence of any offer to ignite it would be too embarrassing. I kind of felt sorry for her. Kind of, in the same way, I felt sorry for Blowfly, who just back from the hospital with his arm in a cast.

I knew he'd be assigned "light duty". A country black, he somehow possessed an urban edge, one that would prevent him from becoming a Step and Fetch It. Unlike Gordon, he could be of some use.

Nevertheless, our bosses wasted no time in enlisting him in their ongoing card game.

"If you can play secretary, you can play cards," Jim stated with a finality that prevented any objections, even about his being one-handed.

Decorating the far wall were several teak and oaken plaques congratulating the crew on one- and two-year periods without a "Lost Time Accident". Panoramic portraits of the entire crew wearing new coveralls and baseball caps with field-grade ribbons on the beak accompanied each award.

"With my wife here, I feel lucky," said the head m..f.. in charge. "Who else wants to join us?"

Heavy Duty melted under his patent stare. The safety man didn't.

"Card playing isn't my job,"

"Have you ever thought you may be in the wrong job?"

"I just do my job. That's all I can do." He crossed his arms to make his point.

"You know you're not coming back after your hitch," Turtle later told Bones.

"I don't care," the skinny man remarked. "I gotta stand up for my rights."

"You'll find out your rights soon enough. I'd give ya the 'classified' if I ever find a copy of the paper."

Most sniffed at Bone's temerity. I didn't. Despite his incompetence, I was impressed with his strength of will. He wasn't a diamond in the rough. Maybe a common garnet would be more fitting.

That rough got pretty thick. While later watching an obscure fight between two black boxers, the safety man provided more color than the commentator. "He's got some right hand," he said of one. "A chin that can take a brick," he said of the other. Oxymorons and clichés popped out his mouth like scat. "This is the worst fight of the century I've seen in months," he complained. "Look at them, they don't know strategy."

Once the nonviolent Iranian led the exodus of mudloggers, only Spud protested Bone's inane patter. He dubbed him a "frigging expert", as in "Who made you a 'frigging expert?'". And when the pool game in the expatriate's galley threatened to get good, only I and Sambo were left to find out he was an "F.E." in other areas, areas as disparate as autos and local politicians. He regaled us with factoids gleaned from the supermarket tabloids and added to our knowledge of astrophysics when a newsman mentioned the space probe Voyager had accelerated past Neptune, heading for Uranus.

"Hundreds of millions of miles, three years away!" Bones exclaimed. "You have any idea how much gasoline that's going to take?"

Sambo shook his head in amazement. "I didn't know it had such a big tank."

"If our excuse for a safety hand can pull himself away from the TV his presence is requested on the drill floor," enjoined a voice over the intercom.

A metallic clang shook the rig and explained why he was wanted.

"I ought to teach them respect," the little guy snarled as he stomped out.

Subsequent bangs of the pneumatic pile driver interrupted my explanation of the law of inertia to Sambo.

"I don't believe nothin's out there anyway," he confided, comprehending but not agreeing with what I said. "Outer space is Heaven, 'n only God 'n the Righteous can be there."

Countering with evidence the Apollo missions provided proved futile.

"They were all done in Arizona to fool people. It's too hot to land on the moon. It shines, doesn't it?"

He had a point.

"What do you think Heaven's like?" he asked.

Not wanting to alienate him, I responded as evasively as I could, concluding with my affirmation of the Biblical account.

"Me, I think that's where you sit on a gold throne, watching a TV made of diamonds."

"So that's why you put up with the beatings at home?"

He squirmed in his chair. "It's not for long. God uses my uncle to test me. My wounds will disappear on the Day of Judgment."

"Most will disappear on the Day of Judgment, to tumble forever into the fires of perdition," said David Prejan as he entered the room. "One must earn entrance through the Pearly Gates."

"I have," claimed the galley hand.

"Not through punishments incurred during life, but through faith in The Word, through the love of Christ."

"So who says I haven't accepted Jesus as my savior, don't have faith in The Word?" Sambo asked.

"I didn't say you didn't. I was just makin' a statement," our minor league Jimmy Swaggart responded.

"Maybe you don't know as much as you think you do." Sambo was mad.

"Me? I didn't once when I ran around on my wife; didn't pay my boy's much mind. Now I'm a Bible-thumping, pew-jumping, soul-redeeming, shouting, screaming, overcoming child of God."

"Amen," I enthused.

"Amen," the two answered simultaneously. The pile driver again rattled the room.

The giant piston banged relentlessly through my sleep and even caused me to jab a fork into the roof of my mouth during breakfast. But whatever irritation it proved to be while inside the crew's quarters, it was far worse outside. The decibels certainly equaled those of jet engines. Handling such huge joints of casing taxed all my skills. I had to pull with all my might on the tag lines to guide them to the catwalk, where the air hoist would lift them to the "V": door to the rig floor. Unscrewing the thread protectors proved even more onerous. I strained muscles I didn't know I had, tugging on them with thirty-six-inch pipe wrenches. Because each joint had to be welded onto the previous before they were pounded into the seabed the process was slow, which proved a blessing as it continued into the next tour, forcing the midnight to noon crew to do most of the nippling up. We didn't have to tighten any bolts on the bell nipple or install the diverters, piece together what looked like an iron Buddha with its hands outstretched. All we did was help lower the riser and connect it with the diverters and the drill floor.

"Dodged a bullet," remarked Spud after we got off work. He said what we all thought, explaining why we were a happy bunch. Our crane man wasn't. She still harbored a grudge. She was easy to figure out. Jim wasn't. Telling us we were "below standard" as we entered the changing room was only a fraction of the ill will he spread. He growled and sneered, stomped, and spread as much gloom as he could. Most ascribed his behavior to worry. After the insides of the drive pipe were drilled out, and the well officially began ("spudded", I learned it was called), a critical point in the operation was reached. We were about to "kick off", and drill at a specific angle and direction to a target that was thousands of feet to the northwest, using the newest technology.

"It's real tricky," said Mamou over our midnight meal. "Screw up here, and we might not ever get the well going the right way."

"I'd be out of sorts too," affirmed Tar Baby, the assistant driller. "Miss the target, what have you got?" His oversized head shook with compassion.

"No one's ever made money from a hole in the ground," added Spud,

"Most of you been here long enough," thundered Jim as he stomped in chewing on his cigarette. "Fifteen minutes is all anyone needs to eat." He strode directly to the ledger on a stand by the kitchen door and instantly exploded. Being furious about service hands not signing for meals was only a precursor to a tirade that found fault with everything and everybody. Salvos of abuse would either slow or halt all who attempted escape. Some received it without making a move for the exits. The Iranian mudlogger heaved with tears from the insults about his eating habits. "Peas shouldn't be eaten with your fingers," Sunny remarked, to deflect the geologist's embarrassment. "Fingers should be eaten separately." It didn't work. The mud engineer immediately was blasted for a mistake his absent subordinate already had been blasted for. By now everybody knew Hillbilly, the derrick hand, had left the equalizer on in the mud room, draining mud from the suction pit while filling up the return pit. Hearing it again was intolerably boring.

"So you can see why we mud men are stooped-shouldered and flat-headed," the mud engineer remarked, shrugging his shoulders and banging his forehead.

"He should grease their shoulders, make slick so he can crawl up Jim's ass," Spud whispered.

Like hostages the crew stayed put, patiently waiting for the companyman to calm down. Spud again whispered how the overbearing boss "must not be keeping his woman satisfied" and met all but one approving nod. Poncho of Forty-Eight Hours ignored the remark as he casually fiddled with his knife, appearing to know something nobody else knew, and feeling completely at ease about it.

With so many held captive the time was ripe to rush to the office. Nobody of any consequence was upstairs to stop me. All I had to do was take off and expose myself to Jim's ridicule. The risk of censure was minute. He wouldn't remember me, a lowly hand. But I sat, as still as the rest, afraid of what the inscrutable tyrant might do.

Having overstayed our allotted fifteen minutes before he entered, we compounded our guilt by remaining. But he already proved he'd get mad should we try to leave. A sneer creased his lips once he sensed our predicament. It hardened with each minute and might have turned into something sinister had Heavy Duty not gotten up and commented, "I don't know about you, but the more I eat the more I get paid." He ambled to the serving counter.

"You ought to be a millionaire," said Spud.

Anxious as he was to say something, Jim was more anxious to eat. He tried doing both. His fork was faster than his thoughts. He choked on half-formed sentences until, swallowing hard, he managed to say, "I don't want anyone working for me who isn't fit."

I got ready to leave my chair.

"This isn't a third helping," claimed Heavy Duty as he returned to the counter. "I'm getting stuff I didn't get the other times."

I got up.

"Then how come you're so stout?" Jim asked.

I reached the trash can by the door.

"Big boned," I heard the cementer reply as I escaped into the hallway. I was in the stairwell, taking two steps at a time before I heard Jim's retort--barely. He gagged on some food in mid-expletive. So much for my "galley time". Hopefully some "office time" would prove at least saner.

The presence of the clerk absorbed in paperwork did not upset me. By now I knew I had to expect obstacles.

"Don't mind me, I like work. I can watch it for hours."

"Do you have permission to be here?" Gordon craned his neck and squinted at me.

"Just want to see what's happening," I said, referring to the remote monitor featuring a display of real-time drilling variables.

"Toolpusher has one in his room," he said throwing out his chest.

"I know. I am interested in learning this end of the operation."

"Workers advance to toolpusher."

I reined in my urge to intellectually humiliate him. "Not my forte," I said in the calmest voice I could muster. "Like to use my brain."

"It was a long hard road. Ever do anything hard?" He leaned back in his chair and looked at me as if I was retarded.

Yeah, I thought. *And I'm doing it right now.*

"Maybe not hard that way. But I need to push myself," I managed to reply.

"We all do, some push themselves harder than others."

God he's making this tough.

"Could you help me then?" I scanned the room.

He ignored my wandering eyes. "Later, I'm pretty busy. Catch me another time," he said, obviously bored with me.

"Can count on that. I'm ambitious, want to get ahead."

So I can fire you someday, I thought.

I had to go outside, and inhale fresh air before I started to believe my b.s. A mighty tug on a rusty dog on the nearest watertight door and I was outside, breathing robust sea air.

A light mist caressed my face. Under a full moon, a silver band stretched to the horizon, illuminating playful white caps tumbling atop the inexorable current. The sounds of the engines, mud pumps, cranes, air compressors, and draw works coalesced into a background hum as vibrant as any noisy forest glade.

Two nearby fishermen added a human touch to the setting. Leaning over the railing, working their lines, they appeared intent to add to the suspended amberjacks and the silvery mackerel bleeding into a bucket. The contented way they engaged in their hobby spoke volumes about their ability to handle stress. I envied them. Before I realized what I was doing I found myself also leaning on the rail, within earshot of them.

"This job is okay," said Jones, his tall, gaunt, Scotch-Irish frame limned in the moonlight. "Where else can you get free food, paid well, and bring home food?"

"Good thing my family loves filets," said Hillbilly, the white-skinned derrick hand. "Couldn't eat it all by myself."

"Couldn't get it on a helicopter even if you could, with those weight requirements. Sometimes I ask to take a boat in," said Jones. "Wife doesn't mind if I'm late if it means more food. With four younguns, she has her priorities."

I now was so close to them that I had to enter the conversation. "Looks like you're doing okay," I brilliantly said.

"Can't catch as many fish as my wife catches back home, in freshwater," said Hillbilly for my benefit. "Can't help but get jealous. Bass and trout come running to the bait she'd rub between her legs."

The crassness destroyed the Disneyesque idle. I retreated and would have withdrawn had I not remembered where I was. Julie Ward Howe didn't take umbrage at Union soldiers when she heard their vulgar marching songs. She thought they deserved better and composed the "Battle Hymn of the Republic." People with character can see through the surface. Although my bunch isn't going to face bullets and cannonballs there's a lot to be said for what they do. The dirty, dangerous, lonely work they perform has to be done competently. A little allowance for their testosterone would be only fair.

A glance downward further chilled me out. In the glow of rig lights, a school of needlefish put on an esthetic show. The Rockettes couldn't have been more synchronized, flashing silver in the surreal light, turning, twisting, diving, each animated stick keeping perfect formation. Several slow yellow tails glided by, indifferent to their display. So was a nearby Portuguese Man of War, resembling Heavy Duty in shape and deportment. A half dozen hard tails pecked doggedly at its tentacles, maybe nibbling on tiny crustaceans or the flesh itself, its touted poison not being effective at all.

Moving on, I didn't pay much attention to where I was going and almost ran into two figures draining their lizards over the side. Seeing me, one remarked, "Water's cold."

"Deep too," asserted the other.

I just had to get used to the idea I live in a locker room. Slipping out of their sight, I made sure I didn't again stumble into an equally embarrassing situation. The extra care I took paid off. Without being detected I ran across Poncho of Forty-Eight Hours by a leg, between a coiled-up hawser and a barrel of thread protectors.

Although I couldn't believe what he was doing someone else could. "We got someone choking his chicken by the barite tanks," I heard over the P.A.

Both Poncho and I flew outta there, he a bit slower than me, as he had some business to take care of.

"Hide that thing," announced the ethereal voice.

The alarm had been sounded. From his perch on the monkey boards, the derrick hand on the opposite tour had seen what I saw and wasn't shy about broadcasting the news. I wasn't the only one who thought he was satisfying Jim's girlfriend. Only I certainly didn't care enough to humiliate him. Poncho was a marked man.

"Pick up there Poncho, if you can spare a hand," Spud said as we later prepared to unload a boat.

"Use both hands to secure that shackle," Kathy insisted when we prepared to unload a boat.

There was no reprieve.

"Think your right hand will get jealous if you use your left to hold on to the rail?" asked Bull, enforcing the safety rules concerning stairways.

Hammer loved it. He flipped his butterfly knife with abandon. The tide in the battle for top critter turned in his favor, and he relished it, proclaiming at supper: "Look, he also uses his right to eat."

The toolpusher took no prisoners, seeing to it a nude from "Hustler's Beaver Hunt was taped inside Poncho's locker with a note that asked. "Can Rosey Palm go forty-eight hours too?"

The crew proved it had no mercy. I'm sure everybody masturbated. Nobody wanted to be reminded they did; and I'm sure everybody was envious of his suspected relationship with Christine, though nobody would admit it.

I didn't hear Jim's voice over the intercom or see him at all. I couldn't believe he was reticent to join the chorus seeking retribution because it was beneath him. Only when word of a new arrival reached us did things make sense. The ego that prevented him from believing a lowly worker was behind his problem with his girlfriend flared upon the arrival of a directional driller.

The oilfield equivalent of a master sergeant often irritated the oilfield equivalent of a company commander. They generally made more money and were given as much clout as a pilot. Having to defer to a long-time adversary had to be particularly grating.

Neither said a civil word about the other.

"About gagged when I heard Jim was on this rig," said Charles Fontenot, the directional driller. Another of obvious Scotch Irish descent, his rough face, and raw features indicated a hard constitution, one which commanded respect (at least to me). Over coffee, he regaled us with the admission he ran himself off the last time he had worked with Jim. "If I didn't, I'd have thrown his fat ass overboard. He's proof this boom won't last. When people like him rise to the top, watch out below."

No puppy rallied to his boss' defense.

"Heard you break weight came aboard," Jim thundered upon reentering the galley. The length of ash on his cigarette defied gravity. He had to have taken a mighty drag for courage before entering.

"Better than a paperweight," said Mister Fontenot, looking up from the plate with repulsion.

"Do I detect a little animosity?" asked Spud.

The two hissed and spat and might have exchanged fighting words had My Fair Lady not momentarily brought them together when the contents of the hard-boiled egg she cracked spilled. Jim wiped her dress. Mister Fontenot wiped her place setting.

"I'll be damned," said Dennis loud enough for everyone in the kitchen to hear. "She got the soft-boiled one."

"Don't bother to help me again," growled Harvey.

"Be that way 'n I won't tell you which muffins were made of baking powder."

Harvey's outcry was animalistic. "I try so hard, 'n all I get is shot down."

"I don't need to hear this," whined the hoyden, still distraught over the mess both heroes were wiping up.

"Tell Harvey to be quiet," Jim said to his puppies.

"Something I can do to help?" asked the galley hand who came aboard with the directional driller. "There's such a rumpus going on."

"Who are you?" Jim bellowed. He puffed up like a beached puffer fish.

"I don't know if I can stand more of this," complained the lady. "The bickering, screaming, the practical jokes, it's giving me a headache." She got up to leave.

"Oh, now dear," Jim pleaded, putting his hand on her shoulder. A titter of laughter turned his face red. "This is a new crew. The trouble with the oilfield today is it's full of worms and weevils."

"And deadwood," responded the directional driller, insouciantly.

"I've had it!" My lady squirmed away from Jim and marched out of the room.

Distraught, Jim commanded loud enough for her to hear, "Now listen up, From now on, bothering my wife is a run-off offense." The lady whirled around expectantly.

"Your wife?" Mister Fontenot was incredulous.

"Wife to be." The lady glowed.

"How many wives-to-be have you got? One per rig?"

The woman fled in tears. Kathy seethed as Penny hurried after her, probably hoping to console her. I left before Jim spent his ire on us innocents.

"That company man, he has a lot to learn about dealing with people," remarked the new galley hand. "He's not nice at all. A real stinker."

Uh, oh.

"A blade," Dennis warned me. "I can smell."

So could I, after my Lucky Dog experience. As much as I wanted to deny it, I knew a little of the French Quarter had followed me offshore.

"I'm so glad to get a real job," David said as he settled into Turtle's vacated bunk. "Tending bar was such a bore." He cast an affectionate look at me. "Oh, don't get me wrong. I love people; the more people there are the merrier. But dealing with customers just wore me out."

I remarked how I too was acquainted with the feeling. By doing so, I got him going about the failings of the work world.

"So many are like that Dennis. I can tell he's as lazy as sin." Without asking, he ripped the sheet off my bed. "This should be replaced daily. Mind if I get you a clean one?"

I hesitantly agreed.

A cynical glance over my shoulder, as I peered into my locker, verified my suspicions. Davey was sniffing it.

The doughy little guy clung to me like a duckling, asking questions, offering help, and making a nuisance of himself, a nuisance too dangerous to even consider enlisting his help...something I did think about, considering how successful I was with his kind.

"Looks like you've got a friend," said Dennis entering the room. Dave immediately fluffed the sheet.

"Birds of a feather," Turtle commented as he followed Dennis inside.

"That kind of stuff puts a foul taste in my mouth," Penny later snarled. (Word must have gotten around).

"You know, that alligator reminds me of a joke," said Dennis, referring to the remains of the fruit cake. "A guy walked in with a gator and told the patrons he has his pet so well trained it would not bite him if he stuck his dick in his mouth. After making the bets he dropped the trowel, slapped the gator so it'd open its mouth, and stuck it in long enough to convince everyone he was in no danger of losing his manhood." Turning to Sweetpea (as Dave was called), he continued. "After he left, the bartender asked a Twinkie if he thought he'd want to do that. 'I don't know,' the blade said. 'I don't want to be slapped.'"

Sweetpea blushed and pretended to ignore the burst of laughter.

Dennis kept after him, never missing a chance to make a double entendre or performing an insulting act like wiping the untouchable's chair after he vacated it or reaching into the shower to turn the hot water on full. However, Spud pulled the cruelest trick.

Sweetpea had a habit of sealing off his bed by hanging blankets from the upper bunk. What went on inside was anyone's guess, until the smell of rotten eggs seeped out of the enclosure at the same time Spud was more flatulent than usual.

"Jesus fucking Christ!" screamed the homosexual, throwing on the nightlight and sticking his head out. In the muted light I could see a length of poly flow line being hauled up the wall.

"You think I'm an asshole, don't you?" Dennis asked me a few days before we departed.

"I don't know," I lied.

"Well, don't worry. It's official." He began reading the contents of a letter he produced.

"My roommate is so cute. I could die and go to Heaven with him. But there's a B. and R. hand who is a total asshole who gives me a hard time every chance he can." It closed, "Affectionately yours, the Pooter Scooter."

It occurred to me Dennis must have stolen the letter from the rig mailbox, a federal offense. I didn't dare attempt to do anything about it. I didn't mind much. Like Bones and Poncho, the Pooter Scooter was destined not to return. Rumor control passed word along that Jim threatened to run the catering service off "for sending such trash."

Jim remained pissed, now that the directional driller and his wireline unit became fixtures.

"Wouldn't want to leave, seeing what my presence does to his big fat ass," pronounced Mister Fontenot.

Had Jim left I would have missed a seminal experience, one I'll remember as long as I have to deal with bimbos and hypocrites, which is to say, until I die.

It became more obvious than ever that Christine, his "wife-to-be" was being serviced by someone else. Even Jim noticed it, though I doubt he figured it out by himself. She probably told him, as punishment. Who it was consumed him as if the culprit was the cause of his problems. No one believed Dennis when he claimed it was he. And no one believed Poncho was still servicing her if he had serviced her in the first place. He was too humiliated. The rest of us enjoyed the show, particularly the part when Kathy threatened Penny with a blowtorch. The survey she took to find out who had been circumcised was nothing more than a way to embarrass him after he failed to confess. How did she know he was the only one who hadn't been, no one wanted to think about it. I doubt anyone would believe me if I told them who did get lucky (if picking a pig can be considered lucky), even one who knew how to enhance her modest attributes with makeup.

My search for the towel Dennis should have left on my bed netted me a century note. That was what David Prejan, our pew jumping, shouting, screaming, overcoming child of God paid me to keep quiet about the tryst I interrupted. From now on I'll be sure to knock before I open closet doors.

CHAPTER 5

"The 'A' team's going home!" shouted Spud amid the clutter of duffel bags in the crowded rec. Room minutes before our boat was due. "Hurricane Sally, here I come."

"Who's that?" asked Hillbilly, the derrick hand.

"She's my woman. Nobody but me can handle her. She farts and pees on you when you eat her."

Sambo and Bones winced. Kathy glowered.

"Hey, what's a hurricane without wind or rain? I can take the weather."

"When I get home, the first thing I'm gonna tell my ol' lady is to blow me. 'I'm used to it,' is what I'll say," remarked Popcorn, as vulgar as ever.

"Me, I got my balloon doll when my wife's off working," said Sunny.

"What's the fun in that?" asked Bull.

"What do you mean? There's all kinds of fun. Bite her, she lets go, runs crazy around the room, and then takes a flying leap out the window. Patch her up, 'n she'll do it all over again."

"It takes a lickin' and keeps on tickin'," the welder remarked.

Channel Fever spread like a contagion.

"A few more hours I'll be home drinking beer, pissing foam," said Red, the opposite tour roustabout.

"There are many good reasons for drinking; one just came to mind," remarked his colleague, Pork Chop. "If you can't drink while living how can you drink when you're dead?"

I was thinking of contacting Father. Which I kept private. The same went for the sentimental urgings that washed over me concerning Leslie, my Beatrice, whose superiority over the "wife-to-be" was accentuated by her mediocrity.

"My wife, she bitches all the time because I go drinking and chase the women," Penny said. "I asked her what was her problem. She doesn't drink and has all the pussy she could want."

"Half the money too," interjected Kathy.

Ignoring her he held up a coke and offered a toast, "So here's to creatures divine. They bloom once a month and bear fruit in nine. They're the only things on earth that can draw meat from nuts without cracking the shell."

Not to be outdone, Spud offered a toast of his own. "Here's to the crack that never heals. The more you rub it the better it feels. But there is no soap this side of Hell that can wash away that fishy smell."

Turtle's contribution to the cultural exchange was little more than a dreary documentary on family violence. "Gotta let's know who's in charge," he stated. "I punched my woman in the stomach last time I was in."

"She called the police?" I asked.

"She kicked me." Everyone stared at him. "Didn't come to nothing. She's been in line ever since."

"Had the same problem with my last wife," Popcorn claimed.

"Which last wife?" asked Turtle.

"The last last wife. Those before her died of mushroom poisoning. Not her. She died of contusions, and wouldn't eat the mushrooms."

"I'm gonna lay around like an old opossum," affirmed Tar Baby, the assistant driller.

"So you gonna do pretty much what you do at work?" rejoined the Bull.

"Won't find me goofing off at the house," said Mamou, the shaker hand. "You find me in my skiff if you find me at all. Fish, crab, shoot poule d'eau, you name it, I do it."

"I shrimp," Hillbilly responded.

"Not for long, if you keep cutting in front of them big commercial boats," Red observed.

"No one owns the channels. No one owns the currents, and if the shrimp float out only at night when I can maneuver well, then that's the way it is. It's a free country."

"I trap," Penny remarked.

"Yeah, I followed behind you when you were trapped," said Spud. "Never seen so many three-legged critters in my life. When do you check your traps, once a month?"

"What animal would be so dumb to get caught by you anyway?" asked Hillbilly. "Probably leave beer cans all over the place, and trails of spit."

"I heard about one muskrat dumb enough," claimed Sunny. "Must have been a Coon Ass, 'cause he needed to be told that biting off a foot was a good way to get free. I'm sure he was a Coon Ass 'cause he needed to be told which one to gnaw on. But he wasn't told. So the story goes he had only one more to go when the trapper got to him. The story also goes that the trapper turned the three free paws into good luck charms. Would have done so with the one left, but it was all mashed in from the trap."

We wound up doing a little paw gnawing ourselves. The boat was late for some undetermined reason, leaving the "A" team with unwanted time on its hands.

The amorous adventures of Blaze Storm and Annie Sprinkle helped raise our spirits. But it was Seka, the blonde goddess, who lifted us out of our funk, who precipitated a crotch-clawing fit as she dove into Angel Cash's muff. For most of us, that is. The only thing she raised for Dennis was his ire (probably because he knew he wasn't going to get any onshore). I noticed Kathy remained pissed.

"Hey Bones, why don't you and Sambo dip?" asked Penny.

The safety man sniffed. I winced. Why can't they give the topic a rest?

"You Moulies don't make sense. All of you would love a white woman. And white women love to be eaten." He looked at Kathy. Kathy stared daggers at him. He turned from her and continued. "Tell me the truth, wouldn't you love to pull that curly blonde hair from your teeth?"

"Once you get past the smell, you got it licked," said Spud.

The galley hand blushed.

"All you people ought to be the last to worry about something stinking," said Dennis, showing he had an agrarian past. "Nothing stinks worse than a van full of your kind returning from a day in the fields."

The ill feelings ended with word of the boat's arrival. Whereas after, everyone focused strictly on leaving. Crying "fire" couldn't have cleaned out the room quicker. Reassembling outside the crew's quarters, banter gave way to impatience. Tucking their Wrangler jeans inside their church boots, they assaulted the personnel basket as if the rig was sinking. The top dogs went first, four to a lift. The mudloggers went last, after the galley hands.

The boat taking us home was not the same one that brought us out. Springer Oil had "changed colors".

"That other boat captain, he tells that company man off," said the skipper, the same Mister Guidry I rode with on Highway Ninety. "Me, I can swallow a little pride if it means I get my belly full of money. This boom isn't going to last forever; 'n I want more than my share of money before I have to make do with less than my share." His squinty eyes beamed with intelligence.

Rather than watch the raucous card players, I stayed in the stainless-steel wheelhouse to chat with the cherubic captain.

"Why so slow and careful?" I asked after we got underway. He nursed us through each wave.

"Hey, these here folks are like me. I wear the pants in my family but my wife, she holds them up." He went on to say the card game was the only fun the p-whipped gang would have all week. "Deer season is months away, so they will be hanging around the house, seeing more work performing honey-dos than they ever dreamed of working on the rig. Most aren't looking forward to wine, women, and song. Beer, TV, and the old lady is more like it."

An angry voice crackled over the radio.

"That must be Jim. He's mad as Hell. I gave him unbleached pistachio nuts and diet cokes. Who does he think he is, telling me to bring blanched pistachios and regular cokes? I may know which side of my bread is buttered on, but it does not mean I have to eat the crust."

"Don't believe a word the old bugger says," said what I assumed to be his wife. She was as stout and as genial as he. "He'll do anything for a dollar." She handed him a cup of coffee. "Even marry into it."

"If not for that dowry I would have passed you by, toot-suite." He wrapped an arm around her and pulled her close.

"Then why did you keep me after it was all gone?" She kissed him.

"Because you work cheap. Know what a cook costs? Besides, I always thought marriage was good. That's why I did it so much. Keep more of your money and get more sleep at night.

"I tell you wives are like cars," he told me after she left. "If they need a tune-up, fine. I spend the money. But if they need an overhaul, that's something else all over again. Got to let them go."

As the grey water turned brown, the ocean became crowded with box-like production facilities, with occasional backups whose derricks rose like spires into the sky.

"These platforms are where you'll find us Cajuns nowadays, t." Mister Guidry said while sipping coffee in his swivel chair. "Jobs on them drilling rigs is work, and since no one ever lazied himself to death, we moved right over to them. That old saying about it never raining in the oilfield is only half right. It never rains on a drilling rig. But on a platform, that's a different story. And, ma chaix, not one of us strained a back changing a chart."

Commercial shrimpers with their outriggers up, waiting to put them in at night, and fishing boats swarmed by noisy seagulls limned the horizon. Two terns mistook us for food gatherers and peeled off a flock to follow, keeping up with amazing ease.

"Watch. They gonna stay with us 'til we dock. They are as spoiled as us. The rigs spoiled us all. Couldn't make a living fishing 'til Kerr-McGee showed how to drill offshore. Their barnacles and itty bitty fishes don't have any reefs to grow on so they grow on steel legs and hulls. Ma la, when all God's creatures got plenty to eat they reproduce like Cajuns."

The few dials and gauges on the console indicated no problems. The Loran navigation equipment indicated we were on course. A child could operate the wheel; it was so responsive. Both of us lapsed into our thoughts. But as one who respects culture, I soon renewed the conversation, asking him what I had asked him on Highway Ninety: if he was afraid of losing his heritage.

"Like I said to you before, there's nothing good in being poor. We may be slow, but we're not that slow, would rather crab and trap because we like to rather than because we have to. I went out all day last Saturday to catch shrimp for a boil I had with my neighbor, not to pay a house note." He elaborated with humorous anecdotes featuring two characters named Boudreau and Thibodeaux.

We soon roared past buoys marking a shipping fairway and slowed down when levees appeared on either side of us. Moving at a crawl, our wake lapped upon wooden pilings and the remains of an abandoned pumping station. On the backside of the levee, an entire world had been flooded. Partially submerged trees, grass islands, and an occasional ruin attested to the erosion.

Mister Guidry tooted his horn as we turned into the main channel.

"Makes my wife madder than a trapped nutria rat when I still do it."

He told me how he used to blow the horn before docking his tug upriver from his house.

"That way, she has time to shoo out any gentlemen caller before I arrive home. Surprises can wreck a marriage."

In addition to the nautical courtesy of tooting twice when passing a vessel on the right, his horn saluted the tug we waited to cross at the intersection of the Intercoastal Waterway. It saluted fishermen, boaters, and an alligator sunning itself on a log.

A prolonged blast heralded our arrival at the wharf. To my horror, a herd of pinstripes anxiously awaited us on the quay. Like vultures, they edged forward and jockeyed for position as we cut the engines. They had to be restrained as Mister Guidry's son tied a hawser around a bollard and all passengers *sans moi* swarmed over the gunwale.

"What are you doing there, t?" asked Mister Guidry, finding me on a couch, half under a table. "Trying to stowaway? I already got all the cheap hands I need."

"Thought I'd grab an extra wink."

"You afraid of them suits out there?"

Who, me? I thought. *Why should I? I've only falsified everything about myself and am wanted by the Feds. Maybe I'm on the "Ten Most Wanted" list.*

"Come to think of it, I'd be shook too if I saw a mob of salesmen; kinda like running into a black bear family. You know they're supposed to be tame. But you never know."

Salesmen!

I emerged into the sunlight to witness a sight worth waiting for. Worker ants aren't as attentive to a queen as they were to Hammer and

Bull. The two top puppies glowed like top dogs. The toolpusher and barge engineer respectively flicked his knife and clawed his groin with equal abandon, each thrilled to see the sophisticates grovel and beg.

If the products were as good as claimed, a well could be drilled trouble-free in the one-bit run. Which has never happened. The charts, graphs, and promotional material the businessmen promoted were as inventive as anything Madison Avenue could produce, real All-American puffery, ready-made to influence Tweedle Dee and Tweedle Dum-Dum.

Logos stenciled on the sides of mid-sized cars identified the companies the puppies' puppies worked for. So did the colors, to the trained eye, which mine were becoming. How else could I have distinguished between Reed Rock Bit's dull red Lincoln Town Car and Smith International's bright red Oldsmobile 88?"

Now, how to get home. I could intercept the stampede before it mounted its vehicles, or I could thumb down a stranger.

"Hey look, Turtle drives a Dodge!" shouted Spud as he climbed into his Chevy truck. "A Dodge!"

"A Dodge?" chortled Penny from the cab of his Ford pickup. "Why not a squint-eyed Jap truck. A Toy-o-ta."

On second thought, maybe I could hit up one of the mudloggers. I didn't want to. Being educated, they might read the business section of the paper and put two and two together. Father's story must have been news for weeks.

"Do all you Yankees drive little ol' lady cars?" shouted Hillbilly to a mudlogger from the passenger seat of a pick-up that sported a confederate flag on its antennae and a gun rack in the back.

"Don't you ever have anything in your window besides a rifle?" I asked when I drew near.

"Sure do!" exclaimed the driver. "Shotgun goes there come duck season."

The vehicle threw up gravel as it roared off in a futile effort to beat the rush to the gate.

"They're sad, really," I told the mudlogger. "They may have the oil down here, but we Yankees make the rules."

"We?" Screwing his face into a question mark brought color to his pale skin.

"Yeah. I was born north of I-10, like you."

That bit of wit earned me a ride. I proved myself of a like mind as he.

Together we commented on bumper stickers like "Oil Field Trash and Proud of It", and "Drillers Do It Better" vied with NRA logos, chewing tobacco ads, and political messages such as those which purposed to "Keep America Pure".

The hands that rushed from the next boat that tied up added to the congestion. Blacks stuffed four to a seat in ancient Coup de Villes, scruffy galley hands and standby boat crews in old Buicks, post-adolescent drill crews in Cameros and GTOs, and recently graduated service hands in subcompacts created massive gridlock.

Horns blared, and tempers flared, but no one was going anywhere. Kathy had sideswiped Penny and rather than move out of the way, argued who was at fault.

"They won't fight for two reasons," said Mitch. His enthusiasm kept his face ruddy. "They are still under Coast Guard jurisdiction and aren't drunk."

A second dispute erupted when two rubberneckers collided.

"And they won't fight because there's no woman to impress."

I kind of felt sorry for Kathy. But rather than risk showing allegiance to the drill crew by expressing my sympathy I remarked how "if this was Mexico, they'd be history." An interested look encouraged me to continue. "Down there anyone who hangs around after an accident is considered guilty by default."

Smile lines radiated out from Mitch's close-set eyes and almost connected with the smile lines from his thin lips. His muscular body relaxed with familiarity. Stroking his thinning hair with one hand, he pointed to an empty beer can in a ditch with the other, and remarked, "Know what's the difference between a redneck and a good ol' boy?"

I admitted I didn't.

"Good ol' boys throw empty beer cans in the bed of their pick-ups. Rednecks throw it on the street." He then buoyantly launched into a recitation about the local fauna, and how they drive their vehicles for "First Fidelity Yahoo" and "The Bank of the Swamp."

He went on, divulging the local's passion for buying on credit, collecting ex-wives, and making babies. By reciting what I thought nobody my age knew, he proved himself to be an intellectual and spiritual equal, like me, a fox in sheep's clothing. We both were like

Nero's Petruchio, like Zorro around the Mexican police, or Batman when he played socialite Bruce Wayne.

Soon we were out, sandwiched between two huge pick-ups (the regional version of low riders?). A flatbed trailer ferrying a portable Schlumberger wireline unit squeezed past on our left. Hard behind it, a midnight black Trans-Am honked with impatience. Laying on the horn was my well-built ex-butler and, beside him, the unmistakably pointy-featured Eddie.

"Old friends," I explained. Despite the temporary bottleneck it caused, I switched rides to shake Eddie's hand in greeting with the same enthusiasm I shook Mitch's in parting. Only too late did I realize how blue-collar jumping in with them must have appeared.

Both my companions immediately asked if I got the invoice. As I failed to respond positively, they let the subject go. "Am doing great," Eddie suddenly enthused as he pulled me inside. His pungent cologne assaulted my senses. It almost obscured the new car smell and Robert's expensive fragrance. Dapper in his off-the-rack suit, the little guy bubbled. After some hurried pleasantries, he blurted out what was on his mind. "That guy who had my money horse killed 'cause I wouldn't pay off a jock I knew, he got his." He paused to scratch his balding head. "Maybe he got it a little late. But, better late than never."

I tried not to look stunned. Judging from the gentle hand he placed on my shoulder I apparently failed.

"Don't worry. I'm not some wolf in sheep's clothing. I've always been a sheep in sheep's clothing. I'm just starting to act ornery."

"How ornery?" I couldn't help but ask.

"Enough to interest the I.R.S. in his winnings. Don't worry, they don't tell who snitches." I must have the worst poker face in the world because he felt he needed to continue his explanation. "Better I get ten percent of what they collect. What good would it do anybody if the Genovese found out he fixed the races at their track?" His chuckle grew into a laugh. "That lob always bragged how he got along with the Feds; all his crew bragged. 'Like horses dealing with flies,' he'd say. He doesn't know they know all the names he bet under. I'd like to be there when those flies bite."

I hoped I wasn't watching a mobster emerge (or reemerge) from the chrysalis of a mild-mannered hobo.

"I wouldn't fool with G-men," said Robert. "Wherever they are I isn't. Maybe you could have more fun letting him think you told his family instead of the feds. You said he didn't share his winnings with his underboss."

Maybe Robert was Mister Hyde.

Eddie sparkled with the idea of tricking his enemy into confessing and asking forgiveness. "His hands would look good nailed to the paddock." He rubbed his hands with delight.

"We're here if you need us," Robert assured him. "Consider us the Sackets, looking out for each other." He turned to us and beamed with satisfaction.

Knowing little about Louis L'Amour's characters I risked being thought of as a high brow and remarked how we resembled the Three Musketeers more.

"Athos, Porthos, and Aramis!" Eddie slapped my shoulder. "Duty bound to fight the evil Cardinal Richelieu, or any suitcase who does us wrong."

The convoy thinned out. Robert punched the accelerator, jerking Eddie and me back into our seats. "The Dumas' were geniuses, pere and fis," said Eddie.

We stayed pinned to our seats until we caught up with the car ahead. We catapulted forward when he slammed on his brakes. The ride then smoothed until we came upon a patrolman writing a speeding ticket.

"Watch this," Robert warned as we crept by in second gear before he jammed the clutch into fifth. A backfire exploded out the tail pipe. The cop drew his revolver and dove for cover, his ticket book splashed in a puddle.

I never laughed so hard in my life. The look on the swamp Fascist's face froze in my brain. He was petrified. Tears clogged my sight. Robert must have been in the same condition because we ran an oncoming car onto the shoulder and skidded through a sharp curve, coming to rest on top a little levee. Recovering, we spun back onto the road and rushed to the first house with a driveway.

"Watch the fun," my ex-butler advised.

A cruiser screamed by with its lights flashing and siren blaring. Another pig followed, earnestly prosecuting his public mandate, protecting the populace from what he thought was a gun toting menace.

With a jarring yell, Robert gunned the car backwards, swung it around, and jammed in into an opening in the passing parade.

"Love it," he said. "They call where you park a 'driveway' and a road a 'parkway' and people wonder why I'm crazy." He then serenaded us, singing a cappella to the tunes on a classical rock station. "Eight Miles High...man, there's nothing like it." He unveiled a joint and offered us a hit.

Knowing what I did of doper etiquette, I didn't dare turn him down. Anyway, how could I resist sucking a bone through the most reactionary land in the U.S? It'd be like waving Old Glory in Red Square or wearing docksiders at a formal.

Thanks to the tinted windows the storm troopers couldn't tell what we were doing when we pulled up to a blockade. Then again, they wouldn't really care. Thanks to the movie "Smokey and the Bandit", by the time we rolled by they must have been sick of midnight black Trans-Ams. We could be shooting smack and they wouldn't have noticed.

In the two weeks I was gone my partners must have found themselves. "Everything came together," Robert proclaimed, reading my mind. "'Synergy' I think it's called." He banged on the padded steering wheel to the tune "Born to be Wild" that bawled from the stereo. "I'm being paid back!" he bellowed. "Paid back."

Eddie slouched in his seat, equally satisfied. "Synergy with energy, near Tulane, where we rented a hooch that needs breaking in." He glowed.

Robert looked at us. "To chase college chicks. Hey, we're going to need some R. and R."

"I didn't think you matriculated," I said.

"Got all the time in the world to study Plato's <u>Apology</u> or Hobbes' <u>The Leviathan</u> on my own and can do it whether I'm on the job or not."

I didn't say anything when he explained he had been run off the Marble number Seventy rig.

"Craneman and I had a minor disagreement. He wanted me to work harder than I wanted to." I held my tongue when he explained he had become a surveyor, with a salary, and a bonus whenever he was called out to a job. "Even if I worked half the time, I'd make twice the money I'd have made on the rig." And I kept quiet as he segued into a narrative about when he lived next to Texas A. and M., about there being so few coeds the gyms were full on Saturday night. "And those few were so ugly, know what they put behind their ears to attract men?"

I refused to guess. I refused to think about anything but the fact he abnegated his responsibility. There's no way he now could get on my rig, help me get my hands on the invoice. And over what? A spat!

"Didn't you hear? Their ankles. They put their ankles behind their ears. Isn't that funny?"

I confronted his broad grin with a stony stare.

"Looks like you flunked," Eddie said dejectedly. "Maybe it wasn't fair, you only known Robert here for how many years?"

Panic seized me. I couldn't think of anything intelligent to say.

Robert again turned around. "No worries mate; we're just taking the piss out of you. I'd have done the same if I were in your shoes. And I am, almost."

They left me to figure out what he did was in everyone's best interest. No doubt he found it hard to transfer rigs. Nagging might have raised suspicions. "So, you're going to take care of the home front?" I asked.

"Why not? Can't work on a rig with all those mean crane operators."

First, the beer. Always the beer. We followed my crew to a rustic little place aptly named the "Shrimpers Lounge." Hard by a seafood processing plant, the fishy odor that permeated the air outside also permeated the air inside, lending the interior the proper olfactory ambiance. Recollecting the swamp parties of my prep school days wrought an unexpected appreciation for the real thing. I found myself reveling in the cheap decor and boisterous patrons. No preppy could be as entertaining as was Penny as he tried to impress a woman who looked like a fisherman's wife.

"Haven't I seen you someplace before?" he asked confidently.

"Maybe. That's why I don't go there any more." The earth mother flashed a gummy grin.

Confused, the driller retreated to mull over her response.

Instead of a James Taylor wanna-be, a genuine fiddler enveloped us with the vibrant rhythms of the fishing port. The woman eyed Robert and honed-in, attracting everyone's attention as she ambled over. "Is this seat empty?" she asked.

"And this one also will be if you sit down," he said.

She stood, stunned. Penny hoisted a beer in salute to my guardian. My status among the crew soared from mere association.

"This Bud's for you," said the welder from an adjacent table. Next to him, Spud popped up to attract her attention and intoned, "Maybe you didn't pick the right guy."

Penny stood up and threw out his chest. "I'm a driller."

Before anyone knew how to respond (least of all the woman) a shrimper with more money than brains burst through the rickety door and took the nearest seat.

"Two hitches on a fifty-footer," the stocky, colorfully dressed man announced without prompting as he flaunted a wad of big bills. "Stayed out until we couldn't hold one more of them whites."

Like radar, the lady homed in on the scratch, leaving the cash poorer suitors behind.

"Mind if I sit here?" She cooed. "Anyone tell you have sensuous eyes?"

Robert laughed. So did I. The driller sat down in high dudgeon.

After a little small talk, the female pried her prey from the chair and escorted him through a door marked "office".

"Bet she'll have the place stunk up in no time," Spud bellowed loud enough for those in the parking lot to hear.

Flush with confidence my association with the hero of the moment afforded me I countered Spud's sour grapes with a chuckle. His narrow face pinched with anger. "What do you know? You ought to sneak inside, learn something. Bet you don't even know what's written on the end of a rubber."

The crowd hushed, making my admission that I don't all the more embarrassing.

Strike one.

"I bet you also don't even know what a satisfied female says?" he asked after the laughter died down.

"No," I answered, rekindling the laughter.

Strike two.

"Know what bad pussy smells like?" asked Penny, joining in the inquisition.

With only one sordid experience under my belt (literally), I had to lie to regain what stature I once possessed.

"Sure do. It's God awful." I scrunched up my face to emphasize my repulsion.

"I don't. Never had a bad piece in my life."

"There's no such thing as a bad piece," concurred Penny.

Strike three. I had used up all the good will I had amassed being Robert's friend.

I slid into the shadows until the aldehyde in my critics' drinks obscured all memory of the incident. Watching them drink I'd gladly put money on any one of them against a champion frat imbiber. It amazed me how any of them could find the door, let alone drive home.

That they did further convinced me the Scotch-Irish's reputation for holding their liquor was more than justified. Real native talent. We were among the few who didn't drink as much as fast as they could, who were around to hear the mating call of the Southern Vixen.

"I'm so drunk," warbled a female in a dimly lit booth.

Being the only bachelors, guilt (as in the fear of being caught) did not hold us back. We harkened to the cry, to find the brunette attractive, interested, available, and totally nuts, rowing madly with only one oar in the water.

"Where's my joints?" the trim maiden wailed. "I left my joints in my cigarette pack, but they're not there." She forlornly thumbed through the pack. "I know they were in here."

Robert winked as she lifted a Virginia Slim to her lips. I managed to singe her eyebrows with the lighter he slipped me. No matter; she barely noticed.

The cronies she called from an adjacent booth turned ours into the Mad Hatter's table. All rationality evaporated in a dizzying round of nonsense. Her friends seized the moment to twist English as viciously as had the March Hare, saying what they meant without meaning what they said, dumbfounding we mere mortals. A somnambulist among them drifted off like the Dormouse. All were oblivious to the time. For them, time stood still and would have remained still had Miss Glassy Eyes not remembered that her birthday was in the offing. From then on, time was measured by the number of drafts all but I, who volunteered to be the driver, guzzled celebrating her unbirthday, trying to get her drunker and drunker, to no avail.

Out of the corner of my unfocused eye I thought I saw Penny smooching with a woman who looked a lot like Kathy. If she was, I'd feel sorry for her, having to exploit the oldest ruse in the mating game, making herself available at closing time.

Before I could make positive identification, our moveable feast moved outside, into our respective cars, and somehow wobbled all the way to one of those apartment complexes spawned by the boom, the kind faddish real estate trusts buy and sell to each other on flimsier and flimsier credit. A sheetrock firetrap, that was Alice's place, its temporary nature reflecting her personality. With her friends gone, in her tiny second story efficiency, she flitted from thought to thought, action to action, to wind up in the kitchen heating a gruel of corn and barbeque beans, thinking she was entertaining us with her prattle. What we were concentrating on from the couch in the living room were her tapered legs, athletic glutes, and copious hair.

Both Robert and Eddie winked at me and relinquished their seats when she handed out her concoction. With their encouragement I maneuvered her to my side, where I slipped my hand inside her blouse. Upon Robert's nod, I moved it under her bra. Her head jerked up, then she relaxed, enjoyed my massage. Eddie turned on the radio and I found myself being helped out of my seat and lead into the middle of the floor to dance, where she led me in a slow shuffle. The mellow sound of light jazz drew us closer, closer than I had danced with anyone else. We moved synchronously, as if we've been together forever, deftly avoiding the furniture, in rhythm with the music.

Robert abruptly intervened, not to cut in, but to offer a cigarette. She readily accepted. Eddie turned off the radio.

"You don't think I smoke too much?" she plaintively asked as she shoved the fag into her mouth and learned toward Robert's lighter, so as not to delay her first puff.

"No. Not at all," I said. "Don't be so hard on yourself."

She started coughing, ejecting plumes of smoke as she did. With an armed wrapped around her I steered her outside to the balcony. A night breeze tinkled the glass chimes suspended from the roof and ruffled the leaves of her potted plants. "You're a very special...woman and a really good cook," I managed to say. She smiled faintly and leaned over the railing. I tightened my grip. She drew closer, popped the cigarette into her mouth, and just as quickly snatched it out..

"The wind blows your hair back in diaphanous waves," I whispered, running my free hand through her curls. Her lips puckered with expectation. They were moist, full, eager. I reveled in sensate desire and slipped my tongue behind them. Her tongue met mine half way and flitted with the tip before plunging clear to my esophagus. A vibration alerted me to pull out. A cough erupted so violently had Robert not caught her she might have lost her balance.

"You need to take it easy." He snuffed out her cigarette on the table he passed leading her to bed. Busying myself with a damp towel, trying to wipe off the mark it made, I didn't pay attention to them until I heard the bedsprings creak.

"That's private," Alice protested as he pulled her undies off. She did not say anything else. She could not say anything else, having passed out. Lying on the bed she looked so innocent and helpless Robert couldn't have been more reprehensible crawling on top of her.

"At least you should try to kiss her," I objected.

"A kiss is not a kiss unless it's reciprocated."

Eddie grabbed my arm as I retreated. "What's with you?"

Before I could think of an appropriate reply Robert moaned, "I can't get it up." The bed again creaked as he rolled off. "You try," he said to me.

A lump congealed in my throat. Handed the mantle of manhood put me in a similar position as I had been at Chi Sigma, only more so. Then it was peer pressure, the fear of social ostracism that pushed me over the edge. Not until now did I realize that I wasn't really forced to do what I did. I had options. I could have said "no". I was still under the impression my family was prestigious, and there were other organizations who would want me. I wasn't trapped at all; not like I was presently trapped. Now my safety net is my inquisitor. Without Robert, where would I be? Homeless, that's where. What can a fugitive do? It took the devastating reality of real dependence for me to see the errors of my ways. I was a fool, a weenie to do what I had done at rush.

"You gonna do it or not?" my own compare asked as I staggered closer.

I closed my eyes and set upon her with all the alacrity of Maynard G Krebs. Reluctantly, I kissed her, growing more enthusiastic as I did. I again fondled her boyish nipples.

Robert rolled her rear over. "Look at this ass; ain't it great?" He lifted her perfectly shaped orbs for me to view. "Look at it."

I looked at it. Keeping my eyes open, I also looked at her face, her delicate features. With her eyes closed she looked like a baby. Taking advantage of her smacked of all the heinousness responsible for violating Leslie, my Beatrice, my Dulcinea. She didn't deserve this, regardless of the fact she led us to her home. To say she did was sheer rationalization.

I dismounted, ready for any and all reprisals.

"Your turn, Eddie," I said.

Feeling little pain, Eddie backed out, claiming the all-purpose cop-out about being too blotto.

"I bet it's considered rape to have sex with someone who has passed out," I told Robert as he tried to remount.

"You think?"

"In a state that makes it illegal to shoot a burglar in your own home?"

"You may be right...don't need more complication." He backed off. "Better leave well enough alone," he demurely said, leading me to believe he had a physical problem and some ego to protect.

We left Alice alone, to sleep it off and repaired to our new den of iniquity, a house converted into apartments. Eddie and Robert let me rest on the hide-a-bed in the living room while they took the double beds in the lone bedroom, their heads propped up on frilly pillows and their bodies wrapped in embroidered comforters no real bachelor would own.

These feminine items were the reason we received a wake-up call later that morning. Robert had lied to Alice about his name and phone number, Eddie and I hadn't, so we were the objects of her scorn.

I must say I did a fine job of calming her; almost as fine as what I did to drag the thief back to the scene of his crime.

Already into her drinking and smoking, the gravel-voiced victim had settled down.

"I just want them back," she said to us at the door. Motioning us inside she led the way to her kitchen. "Care for a drink?"

The mad tea party started anew, replete with all the diversions enjoyed yesterday, with the addition of a pinch of snow. No amount of teasing could entice me to stay.

"Why are you leaving?" Alice inquired forlornly.

"Yeah, why are you leaving?" Eddie asked. My companions looked at me scornfully.

"Temporary business," I lied. "I'll be right back."

It wasn't a complete fabrication, although I doubt anyone would consider sneaking out to find a woman a pressing need. How could I explain my feelings to anyone? I barely could articulate them to myself. Perhaps I craved to prove a Dulcinea del Toboso could exist among the gold-diggers, sirens, Medusas, teases, and whores of this world.

As I walked atop the levee, keeping pace with the Mississippi's current I realized I needed to apologize to Leslie and rescue her from her environment. *What good is it to be a Little Sister?* I thought. *Where does it lead one?* Only a Kimberly could envy a daughter of Penelope or want to belong to the Metairie Garden Club. Even Kimberly would balk at being gang raped. Some flicker of conscience would induce discomfort regardless how much it was expected of her. It would have to.

When I arrived astride Carrollton I rushed across the battue by the river, then up and down the levee in front of it, followed the trolley tracks, and turned into the subdivision I once dismissed as being full of lower middle class tracts. The tumult of pot holes, shifted concrete, and sparse lawns at first rendered the neighborhood unsightly. But, upon closer inspection, the sturdy, neatly arranged houses looked well kempt and better built than those in the suburbs, which was remarkable considering many were a century old. Each was unique, as unique as the mansions on Saint Charles.

Then I chickened out, vetoed any desire to enter fraternity row to look for Leslie. Too many loiterers were about with nothing to do but scan their turf.

A sentimental detour to my padlocked manse reminded me of my mission. The notice declaring the property confiscated by the I.R.S. chaffed my ass. As if the government could have built a business as successful as ours.

Through the wrought iron gate, I could see in the bright mid-morning light how deteriorated the grounds had become. It was a crime to let the genius of our former gardener go to pot. Weeds were starting to choke the paths garden clubs strolled down when they visited. Fungus discolored the silent fountain. An international outcry would attend the comparable neglect of Versailles.

A blue hair stopped with her husband to remark what "nasty crooks" we were. "Trying to cheat the government is cheating us all."

"They gave people jobs, real jobs, no bullshit jobs the Feds create," I snarled.

Rather than debate me, the pampered, man-protected dowager stared at me. "You don't have anything to do with these people, do you?"

"What would that have to do with anything?"

"They say the son is still loose."

"So?"

She looked at me up and down, contemptibly. "He's about your age."

"So are a lot of others." I affected a solid pose. She grabbed her husband's arm and marched off.

A more obnoxious socialite replaced Miss Marple, one I shouldn't have tangled with. If only the battle-ax hadn't been so sanctimonious, so pretentious. Father would have defended himself. So would have Grandfather. Though I'm not so sure either would have fled like I ended up doing. It was so undignified, sprinting down Nashville to Freret, then through a yard like a common thief.

A cop car cruised by. A second set up a blockade at State and Willow. Whether it was just to check brake tags I don't know. Nor was I about to find out. I slipped between two Victorian cottages, raced down a narrow ally, leaped over the hedges delineating another yard, ran down the driveway, and entered Tulane via a hole in a partition put up more to define campus than keep anyone out. Settling down, I tried to blend in with the crowd, tried to slow my breathing, my pace, act like I belonged. Which I didn't. Not any more, not since I've learned what life really could be like.

As I slowed to a stroll, I remembered how envious I once was of outlaws, how I invested their exploits with romance and daring-do. I also remembered how I once considered the swamp parties and rouge idles I attended proof of my scandalous nature. The extent of my callowness was embarrassing, leading me to wonder what other opinions of myself were pure chimera, established because I didn't have a clue how spoiled I was.

They say extraordinary times make extraordinary people. I say one rises to the occasion in direct proportion to his training, and though I might have enjoyed a lot more advantages and privilege than I realized, I was trained to be a Cunningham, if only by example. Seeing Father sometime stay up for days without once losing his cool during all the crises he had to deal with was inspirational. He charged up everyone, and with his never-say-die panache, always prevailed. I was told Grandfather did the same.

Not to do likewise would be sacrilegious, proof I wasn't worthy of my heritage. With as much nonchalance as I could muster, I eased up to a telephone stand outside the University Center and adroitly leaned as far as I could inside, hiding my head.

Good thing I did. From behind me I could hear my nemeses shouting and screaming as they charged from a car, bent on proving what a rough bunch Chi Sigmas were. Caught up trying to impress the milling crowd they blew right past me, just as an operator was giving me the number to Angola federal prison, the place Father more than likely now resided. The din was receding as the secretary at the East Feliciana Parish facility started to object about taking a collect call.

"I need to talk to Roger Cunningham," I said with desperation.

"Who is this?"

The operator repeated the fake name I gave her.

"It's not our policy to...."

"I'm Randy Cunningham. His son!" I blurted out. There was silence on the other end, as if she held her hand over the speaker to consult with someone.

"All right, we'll accept the charges," she eventually said with an exquisitely even voice.

Judging from the movies I've seen, I probably have a couple minutes before they traced the call.

"It won't be too long," said the operator. "How have you been? Your Father repeatedly has been asking about you."

From behind I heard a second wave Chi Sigma actives, probably returning from some tepid saturnalia, shouting and screaming as they charged from their cars to their house.

"The 'A' team has returned!" yelled the sergeant-at-arms.

"We're gonna make it!" big, fat Michael King, the vice-president shrieked.

"Patience is a virtue. Sex is a sin. Sins are forgiven. So, sex is in!" whooped the treasurer, William Davis the Third, obviously drunk.

Thirty seconds went by. Then a minute.

"Is he coming?" I asked.

The operator assured me he was.

Two minutes passed by.

"What about now?"

"Don't worry," she remarked.

I finally confronted her saying, I was about to hang up.

"Don't do that, he's almost here."

"How can I be sure?"

"I've just been informed to tell you he has divorced his wife, Kimberly, I think he said her name is."

"Why can't he tell me himself or are you stalling?"

"No, I am not. It's just that he's having second thoughts about talking to you."

Three minutes went by. That was all I could risk.

"Tell him I love him and am doing all I can for him."

"What does that mean?"

"It means good-bye." I hung up.

Not sure whether the Sigmas were still nearby I stayed in the booth.

"You going to use it or what?" I heard a male voice ask. I could feel people staring at me.

"Got to make a call." I reached into my pocket for change. Not finding any, I panicked. "You got a quarter?" I asked without looking back.

"Use your calling card."

"I haven't got a calling card." My voice broke with desperation.

"No change, no card. You got any I.D. Or are you trespassing?"

Grandfather was a big contributor to the school and I'm a trespasser! I thought. Pissed, I wheeled around and confronted my accuser.

"Shit, just seeing how the other side lives."

As I hoped I suddenly became invisible, like someone who's handicapped. And like someone who's handicapped I was expected to be decorous enough to go away, so as not to be an embarrassment. Again using the thespian training I learned in prep school I became exactly what everyone expected me to be, a lower class hick.

"We need a security gate," someone said as I ambled off.

I spent the fifteen minutes behind the planetarium across the street contemplating revenge. I didn't worry about the phone call being traced. After all, this is Louisiana, struggling to enter the twentieth century. I thought about letting the air out of the Sigma's tires, burning their house down, or maybe ask the geology department for a little marker dye to drop in their swimming pool.

However delicious those alternatives may be, I had to veto them. It didn't feel right to lower myself to their level. I had to protect my integrity. It's all I had.

Circling around, I reentered campus south of Freret, which I paralleled until crossing a block from Broadway, not believing I, despite all else, felt sad I no longer had a mother. It's happened before, for almost six months one time. I remember I didn't like it and was glad when Father remarried. Guess I am used to hearing the patter of little feet and Gracie Allen-like prattle around the house.

Given all the diverse activity, it looked like I could safely enter campus. Strolling nonchalantly into the bustle I felt like one of Ned Fowler's cinder men. No fourth semester Watusi freshman could have been more out of place than I among the yuppies, debutantes, and Long Island Jews. My Shoe Town outfit clashed with their L.L. Bean khakis, Guess jeans, Banana Republic linen jackets, and Sharper Image over blouses. My hat stood out among their blow-dried coiffures. The stubble I let grow to hide my facial features contrasted with their clean-shaven faces.

Two thick-hipped debs in designer fatigue slacks regarded me malevolently, as if they knew who I was. So did the Exeter, Hotchkiss, and Concord Academy crowd, one of whom sported a sweatshirt advertising Tulane's "Coed naked Lacrosse team/Huff, puff, in the buff." Another wore one exalting "Spring Break '79/Wasted in the Caribbean."

But they proved to be the exception rather than the rule. Most ignored me, like those in hot pink polo shirts playing porch monkeys outside the library. The same held true with their camp followers Miss Jacquard pull-over, Miss Tropical print camp shirt, and Miss Christian Dior side-wrap. Which was as it should be. Who'd want to have anything to do with people so clothes conscious?

Moving on to the square outside the University Center was an excursion into oblivion. The cotillion princesses I passed didn't glance at me. They continued holding court, yakking about parties they had attended or will attend.

Off in a corner Miss Anne Klein and Miss Bergdorf Goodman exchanged intelligence on which quaint French Quarter shop sold the most "exquisite antiques". Their bemoaning the fact that fifty dollar an hour jobs were hard to find compelled me to claim a space on the bench next to them. There's something intriguing about irritating personalities.

"It'd work just right for my schedule," said the White Queen on my immediate right.

To think I'd been trying to win the affections of women like her! To think I'd be like the stud trying to impress a clone of hers about his prowess at L'coste Tennis Camp, someone totally engrossed in his own self-importance, totally unaware of the people on the fringe: the lesser-lights playing hackesack, the guitar player, and two eggheads discussing Aristotle. Other formerly invisible obscurities drifted in and out of sight the longer I watched, soon outnumbering the upwardly mobile three to one. K-Mart ultimately overwhelmed Yves St. Laurent, as did Cooter Brown's over Audubon Tavern II.

How blind I had been! How deaf too! Overhearing two girls eagerly discussing organic chemistry suddenly was ambrosia to me. Not so long ago I'd have dismissed them as professional virgins and unworthy of my attention, unless they were perfect "elevens", "tens" with a hysterectomy. Then I'd lament the waste of good bodies.

The two scholars held the thick textbooks with the unmistakable affection good ol' boys display when they've wrapped their hands around a cold one. They couldn't have raised my spirits more had they propositioned me.

I must be growing up, or becoming a better person, because I was smitten with the urge to hug them for being so enthusiastic about their studies, not to get an "A" to help procure monetary and socially rewarding careers, but for it's own sake. It was so pure, so noble, so delicious, so different.

The idea of instant gratification was now an emetic to me. Maybe I heard one too many "I'd like to do her." I don't know. I only know hearing those two talk about benzene rings and gauche positions made me glad all over, like I feel when hearing "Mister Tambourine Man" by the Byrds after a long hiatus.

"Watch out, little boy," snarled Ms. Anne Klein as I inadvertently stumbled into her as she got up.

It was the hospitality hostess from rush; the elegant fox who lured us horny hopefuls into Chi Sigma's lair. Initially elegant and desirable, her features changed before my eyes.

"Stop staring at me you little mole."

Her impeccable smile and fathomless eyes turned duchess' ugly. She didn't recognize me! Out of uniform, I must be as unrecognizable as the Prince and the Pauper. Without an alligator, polo player, or Penguin on my shirt, I was a non-person; I didn't exist.

"I thought you were someone I knew," I said.

"Not likely."

I needed a double take to identify her companion. Ms. Bergdorf Goodman was Leslie. It's amazing what a change of hairstyle and make-up will do. But underneath the perm and behind the Elizabeth Arden cosmetics was the woman I befouled, kittenish and beguiling. Whether her choice of associates was voluntary or beyond her control, how could I tell? How could I tell if she was really into the conversation? Who was I to judge, anyway? Me, the roustabout, a bird killing, tobacco chewing, ball scratching, ignorant, clam dipping fisherman with younguns. That she didn't recognize me attested to the metamorphosis I must have undergone working so hard.

I followed Leslie up the terra cotta steps, repulsed at the urge to take advantage of the angle of observation to check her attributes like I had done many times in the past, devoted as I was with righting the wrong I had committed. Once inside the cavernous interior she blew off the Maid to the Court of Midas at the class ring booth. Luckily, she didn't disappear into the cafeteria on the right or the bookstore on the left. Ignoring the American Express, jewelry, and travel agent booths she came to a halt to scrutinize the all but ignored literature the Sierra Club had on display.

I thought only biology students in bib overalls spend time on out-of-vogue groups like the Sierra Club. The radical chic causes were South African apartheid and the homeless, causes that were getting national coverage. Earth Day was over a decade ago.

I saw her sign a roster, put several pamphlets in her purse, and listen appreciatively to the attendant.

Her dainty script stood out among the masculine and angry signatures on the petition to end toxic dumping. With all the curlicues, it was barely legible. In the time it took for me to decipher it another customer arrived to receive the bearded attendant's spiel, letting me escape before being asked to join a march to Baton Rouge to protest dredging in Lake Pontchartrain. Thank goodness.   I was more interested in searching through the campus registration book at the information desk.

"I'm auditing your English class, and I'd like to know if you'd like to get together for coffee," I asked her over the phone.

"I'm pretty busy." I heard her fumble with the phone.

Thinking fast, I claimed to be a member of the Public Interest Research Group.

"Really!" she exclaimed.

Bingo! Arranging a date was academic, far more academic than the date I tried to set up with Father.

Against Robert's better judgment he agreed to drive me to the correctional institute on the eastern bank of the Mississippi River. "Not because you'll do any good but because you need to see what the score is."

The "score" proved to be as disappointing as he predicted. The disguise Eddie created for me was elaborate, exhibiting an expertise which must have taken a long time to learn. If there was a brother of my third stepmother, I looked like he. A superannuated himbo, complete with pot-belly, greying hairdo, teetering atop platform shoes, and (for insurance) a mustache, I fooled everybody. With a fake I.D. my partners procured I easily got inside. Because I used Grandfather's unusual middle name, I'm sure Father knew it was me. Why he refused to see me I ascribed to his being cautious. The cryptic message he told a guard to convey proved it. What else could he have meant by, "Tell him I'm not familiar enough with him, and he's not familiar enough with me."

Without knowing it Leslie helped me get over the disappointment. In one of the avant-garde coffee houses that are proliferating across the city, she was surprisingly open and forthright, totally unlike the person I "assumed" she was. That she still didn't recognize me I could thank Eddie's cosmetic touches (I particularly liked the false ear lobs) and the coaching he offered on how to inflect my voice. Her candidness might also indicate she had buried the incident deep within her subconscious. If she hadn't why was she still hanging out with the actives?

She readily took to me. The rabid libido offshore must have made me appreciate a woman's intelligence more than any other attribute. I genuinely ravished having a thoughtful conversation, and it showed.

"I want to make a difference, but I'm trapped." Worry lines marred her perfect complexion.

Sipping my Viennese blend, I told her I knew how she felt.

"I knew you did. My first impressions are always right."

I refrained from explaining myself, from informing her I was more concerned about solving my personal problems than those afflicting the planet.

"Mom and Dad would take me out of school if they knew my real interests." With tears in her eyes, she ruefully mentioned how everything she did was for her parents. "I don't do anything for myself, until recently."

Her classic face contorted in despair. "Romance literature, what is that? I wanted to study something real, something that would make a difference, like biology; but mother said it's unladylike. She wants me to be like the rest of the women in our family. She doesn't respect what I do. Like it doesn't matter. 'If you must study biology, you can be a nurse until the children come and go back to it when they're older.' I want to do something that makes a difference." Shaking the rickety table, she spilled some of her Brazil Oro.

I asked what brought on this attitude, then immediately regretted doing so, fearing the ordeal I helped perpetrate was behind her epiphany. But it wasn't. It came during a more mundane experience, when she was chastised for receiving a "C" in math.

"I learned something. I didn't fail like they said."

"Rebellion is dangerous," I said.

She started to cry. I wish women wouldn't do that. Father's ex's all used tears to get their way. Still, I chivalrously wiped them off with a napkin, and consoled her with words I didn't know I had in me. I certainly didn't pick them up from the distaff side of my family. They had all the compassion of a Barbie doll. As for the men, they were career builders; Bismarcks, not Donahues.

I got her to trust me without letting her know much about me. By mentioning the few teachers I happened to know I was able to convince her I was still enrolled. Then I went too far. I gossiped about an English prof we both knew, foolishly telling her I was attending his class.

"So I'll see you in English class," she burbled in parting.

Jesus, I thought. *I only knew him because he wrote a Chamber of Commerce speech for Father.*

So I audited her eight a.m. English class. Luckily a teaching assistant performed the duties, using her underpaid post as a bully pulpit to promote woman's literature, the more modern the better. I've barely heard of Alice Walker, Gail Godwin, and the local Ellen Guilgrist. At least I'm familiar with Mary McCarthy, Catherine Anne Porter, and Joyce Carol Oats (from her articles in "Playboy").

From there, I was Leslie's guest at an Ecology class, where the underpaid, overworked lecturer played Paul Erlich, belaboring the hazards of overpopulation.

Claiming urgent business, I managed to avoid her other classes. God knows what I'd have been subjected to. Acid rain Spanish, Amazon rain forest algebra, and Jimmy Carter oil taxation techniques. Who are these teachers? Woodstock refugees who never got out of college? At least the clerk at the Hummingbird breathed real air, not the rarefied stuff in ivory towers.

I did put on quite an act at the Louisiana Public Interest Group meeting that night, being more eager than the salesmen who had set upon Bull and Hammer at the dock. I had to, to overcome the fact I had lied about them knowing me. Since I didn't dare lock horns, I agreed with all they said, not mindlessly, but in order to listen so attentively I could figure out their behavior and their methods.

To curry their favor, I volunteered to compare car insurance rates for a twenty-one-year-old bachelor. That excited them. Returning from my assignment with all sorts of damaging evidence the next day excited them more. And having it published in the "Hullabaloo" as well as being aired on the school's radio excited them most of all. Who else but me would even think of checking the agencies Moody's bond rating in order to look at the shakiest of the lot?

Actually, it was a toss-up between the thrill of debunking advertised claims and winning Leslie's favor. It also lent me the credibility I needed to wheedle into their confidence, maybe lend them a balanced view.

Robert also was zealous. While I was out serving the interest of consumers, he was hogging his share of women, good-looking women who dated him for his car only to wind up under his spell. Pretty, intelligent women, not the gap-toothed cows I'm sure the rig crew bed down with.

"He's so interesting," cooed one coed (the third he had in three days). "He's bad, not like the goody-goody boys I date. They're so boring."

"Women want fantasy, not predictability," my personal Sancho Panza counseled. "They want stubble on their hero's cheeks. They want rouges."

"You have a point," I concurred. "All famous lovers were cads, from Don Juan to Warren Beatty."

"Yeah, they were real millionaires. Not nickel millionaires like us," remarked Eddie.

"Don't matter. Not if you tell them you're rich."

"How can you tell them we're rich?" Eddie swept his arm across our ordinary living room, with its cheap furniture.

"Easy, lie. Tell them you're working on an impending big deal. Have fun with them. Lie out your ass, they'll believe anything, so long as it's outrageous."

That night I was serenaded by the sound of two couples engaged in horizontal tangos.

"Couldn't be more right," Eddie affirmed after seeing his partner off late the next morning. "Told my lady I had three money horses and was only pretending to look for tickets to overhear the line in the crowd." He gulped his coffee.

Then Robert stumbled out of the bedroom with his date. I about gulped my own coffee. I'd swear it was her again, the Chi Sigma fox, Ms. Anne Klein. Sans make-up it was hard to tell for sure. But the inescapable snootiness in her voice gave her away. I doubt she could sound sincere at a funeral. Her plastic "hellos" and small talk were not convincing. No matter what she did, what she said, she couldn't escape the fact she was Robert's lay. No more, no less and it was great. Miss Stuck-Up, stuck by an ex-seaman, ex-phosphate dogger, ex-servant, cockswain extraordinaire.

"All women are the same," he said after running her off. "They just wear different brands of perfume."

Later, while sitting on our tiny front porch, drinking iced tea, I thought about what he said, and found it too hard to accept. It was impossible to accept. I couldn't do it. The man of La Mancha held all women in high, not low esteem. Jack London once lifted himself out of depression by reminding himself the world couldn't be a bad place if there were women in it. The great misogynist, H. L. Mencken eventually married, as did his sidekick: George Nathan. How much of my sidekick's animosity was born of unresolved anger, jealousy, and a failed childhood, I don't know, and I don't care. I'm just not going to regard Leslie that way. I resolved to prove him wrong. I had to and damn the consequences.

Over Espresso Con Panna, in what was becoming our little hideaway, I cleverly orchestrated the conversation so as to blunt the effect of the admission I worked offshore. "While I attend school part-time," I lied before quickly volunteering to be a double agent, to uncover the waste, graft, and whether my industry complied with environmental regulations.

"You'd do that for us!" Leslie squealed. "That would be wonderful!" she kissed me on the right cheek.

Making mad, passionate love might be fair compensation for what I intended to do. For a woman, I was going to risk all, descend into the maelstrom, tilt windmills, and become a man, not an Alan Alda, but the real McCoy, a b.s. slashing, shouting, screaming, overcoming tower of strength and versatility. Like Gor-Tex, I was going to be strong and supple. Imperturbable, that's me.

"I'm not that special," I demurely said.

"You'll go down in history. Like Ida Tarbell, Upton Sinclair, and Rachel Carson," she enthused.

I'll go down about six feet if my body can be found. Employee Information Service will put my picture on cans of Budweiser. The caption will read, "Have you seen this man?" I'd be as marked as an earnest game warden.

I did have to admit, I would feel good going public with the dirt I'd uncover. I'd do for my industry what <u>Unsafe at any Speed</u> did for the car industry, only it wouldn't be as vindictive.

Do-gooding can open doors. For instance, it opened the palatial double doors of the Sigma Sigma house. The doorbell chimed the first few notes of Laura's theme before an oriental houseboy came to our assistance. With my Beatrice leading the way, I was escorted into the recesses of the mansion, where the furnishings lent the impression of pampered security, a regal womb decorated by Mary Kay.

Sorority sisters floated by like goldfish in a bowl, as if on valium. Two greeted Leslie with kisses on the cheek and soft handshakes for me. The ghost of Christmas Future held my hand and made me visible.

The fat housemother smiled at me, as did a dashiki-clad Venus David Prejean or Poncho of Forty-Eight Hours would have assaulted on sight. Not me, I held my libido in check, all the while wondering how civilized I'd remain if forced offshore for an extended length of time.

I complimented Leslie on the house.

"It's neoclassic, exactly what Mrs. Newcomb wanted."

I complimented her on the display case full of trophies.

"We've got a proud heritage. We're one of the first chapters she and her husband founded at Tulane."

Her attitude changed once we stepped inside the ornate study. "I've got to get out of here," she confessed. "It's killing me staying here. It's purgatory."

"Bad memories?"

"The worst; you can't imagine."

The Jungian "anima, animus" I had read about, where a woman resides inside every man and a man resides inside every woman, came to the fore in the hope I could form a bridge of "collective unconsciousness".

"I know exactly what you're talking about," I said.

"How could you?"

"I was there."

She stared through my disguise. "You! I thought I recognized you!"

She leaped out of the chair and pointed at me. "Get out. Get out of here!"

The room suddenly filled with angry sisters and one mean Red Queen. "Off with his head!" I swear I heard the housemother bellow. "Off with his head!"

A "complex" of emotionally packed ideas and images charged me with the urge for self-preservation.

I cut a swathe through the lovely "archetypes," body slammed the houseboy, and experienced "synchronicity" with the pewter statue on the lawn. The muscles I hadn't used since prep track remembered how to sprint well enough to achieve an insurmountable lead.

"What's that?" asked Robert as I limped inside our apartment.

"A reminder," I said, setting the groom's arm on the kitchen table. "It's black, it's broken, and it's stolen. And I'm not going to rest until it's restored."

"A symbolic mission?"

"A holy mission; to restore my 'center', find my 'self' so I can prove myself to Dulcinea I'm her knight in shining armor."

Robert did not look up from the carrots he was peeling over the sink. "Jung was a cool dude. Spiritual and optimistic, makes a good argument we're all linked. But you aren't even close."

I didn't dare dispute him. He might have been Carl Jung.

CHAPTER 6

I needed Robert's dose of reality come time to go back to work. I needed a level head. Being torqued up would have hindered my ability to drive the car Robert bought for me to take to the dock. Al Unser would have had a hard time driving it, it being as road-worthy as a donkey cart. The hundred he paid for it was a swindle.

The fog obscured the road. The bald tires, burned-out headlight, cracked windshield, and noisy transmission, initially troubled me. That they didn't daunt me I could attribute to my recent competence at what others would dismiss as blue-collar labor. My confidence level never had been higher. My problems kept me more aware than worried and allowed my mind to wander. The eerie morning setting spawned loose associations, each eerier than the last until the eeriest of all emerged predominant. The fact the Sigma Sigma house was to Leslie what the Bates house was to Anthony Perkins became apparent. Each was infested with pernicious memories. Leslie had to be kept away. To do that I had to win back her faith in me and make good on the pledges I had made. I couldn't undo the past, but I could convince her of a promising future.

So I had two missions to think about as I crept down the gravel road to the port, found a piece of high ground to park, and struggled to get comfortable in the dilapidated waiting room. If McDonald's installed chairs as uncomfortable as those available to us, customers would finish their meals and be out the door in half the time. They certainly didn't help me handle the return of my co-workers with much patience. I have to admit, though, there's artistry in being as simpleminded and mule-headed as they. It makes life so much easier. Like one guy, Tiny, Bones replacement. The evil empire is flexing its muscles in Afghanistan, all industries but oil are in recession, a population bomb might be threatening the planet, and all the lanky Yahoo in an Alabama football jersey could talk about was the merits of Bear Bryant.

"Greatest coach of all time," he announced with little provocation. "I'll match him against Landry and Shula, any coach who ever lived, college or pro."

I wanted to but was too sleepy to bring up Chicago's George Halas. Watching the six feet ten-inch human pear pontificate was too entertaining.

"The years I spent wearing the Crimson Tide were the best of my life."

Did we have a scholar-athlete here? I wondered.

"I left a mark on the glee club that'll never go away."

His continued discourse helped keep me awake. It was an antidote to the tedious replies every arrival had to how their two weeks off went. No derivation of hearing "It wasn't long enough" alleviated the sheer boredom of it. Spirits rose when word went out that we were to take a helicopter. I didn't care. My spirits rose when the crew started to compare notes about the new company. I already knew how mutual enemies unite people.

It appeared he was as bad as Jim.

"Wouldn't sign a work ticket 'cause the casing hands didn't work hard enough, or so he said," remarked Spud.

"His drills, they're something else," remarked Mitch, the mudlogger. "Changes the routine all the time. Sometimes woke us up in the middle of sleep. Said we needed to learn emergencies can happen at any time."

The shared experience forged a common bond that might help my new, expanded plan. I could end up with a rig full of spies at my disposal, all eager to cleanse whatever rot there was, like white blood cells.

The banter they exchanged likewise encouraged me. Now somewhat familiar with them, I could relax in their presence.

Spud and Penny renewed their Crosby-Hope debate on hunting.

"You're so lazy only skins you got are from the opossums that hide in your garage," said the driller.

"Least they don't stink. That tuna you put in the bottom of the goofy stove pipe traps of yours wrecks pelts," replied the roustabout.

"Wife gets to wear great fox stoles."

"And get mobbed by dogs."

The turtle was surprisingly demure. Getting up to get a cup of coffee, I could see why. He limped.

"Showed the wife who was boss?" asked Spud.

"Put out a peace bond on me."

"That's good. Maybe that'll teach you. Don't want any violent sort on my floor," reaffirmed the driller.

"What about all the doves and coots you said you wanted to shoot?" asked Spud.

"What about them? Worked my dogs to death retrieving all those I killed. Am sure I left a good-sized flock out on the paddies." His solemn tone of voice was disquieting.

"Some blood spilled on the barrel of my rifle."

Everyone became quiet and still. It was uncanny.

Finally, Heavy Duty, the cementer let those as ignorant as I in on the superstition. "My daddy died when woodcocks dripped on the end of his carbine."

"Your daddy had been on Saint Pete's wish list for years," said Pencil. "Was as big as a barn."

Breaking the tension, Popcorn called my attention to another characterization of the group I could exploit. It wasn't the cruelty the crew exhibited by laughing at him for shooting poule d'eau swimming on a pond (I guess everyone just knew fish-fed poule d'eau were nowhere near as tasty as grain-fed poule d'eau). It was their reaction to his admission he had refrained from seeding a nearby field that perked my interest.

"Ain't worth it. Already lost a bunch in fines.

"Nothing's worth it if you get caught all the time," said Tar Baby, the assistant driller.

"Don't make sense to do it if you can't get away with it," said Turtle.

"You're doing something wrong if you always get caught at it," said Red. Hammer interrupted the roustabout's attempt to cite what he would have done differently by bursting through the double glass door, throwing his bags on the tile floor, and blurting out what he knew about the fate of Hillbilly, the derrick hand.

"Just like I said, mess with the big fish and you get eaten." The toolpusher twirled his butterfly knife like a pinwheel. Others let out gasps of concern. "Vietnamese fishermen will kamikaze your ass if you cross them," he said, glowing in the dual acclaim of messenger and seer, standing tall and erect, looking so much like a leader Bull had to do something to diminish him.

Biding his time, letting Hammer explain several times how serious Hillbilly's bullet wounds were, where he was treated, and how to get in touch with him, he ensured interest had waned before unleashing his secret weapon.

With the smugness of someone exposing an unbeatable hand, he remarked how he spent one of his two weeks off hauling bulls on a Western Star.

The crew again fell silent. The RPMs of Hammer's knife slowed appreciably.

"All Hammer ever done was move steel in a Peterbilt," Pencil explained in a whisper. "Cab over diesel."

The two circled each other, eyeing each other malevolently. To their credit, they held their tongues until the strain drained from their faces.

"Too bad Hillbilly didn't take up driving instead of fishing," Hammer said. His evil eye softened. "Pays a lot more."

"Maybe what happened was supposed to happen, to show him."

David Prejan, the rig's spiritual guide, looked at me and said, "Judge not lest ye be judged."

"Judge all you want as long as you're ready to be judged yourself," said Sunny, himself bursting inside. "And as long as you aren't my creditors, I don't care."

His breezy familiarity with the crew bespoke an intelligence I wanted on my side. He lit up the room.

"How's those bedsores?" asked Dennis.

"I told you to flip me over when you changed sheets." The mud engineer playfully punched the bedroom and restroom worker's potbelly.

"No wonder you're sore, considering how often that happens," snorted Bull. Something more than mere displeasure at the scruffy hand's bad work habits added menace to his glower. Dennis held something on him he could do nothing about.

Affecting a fake somber tone, Sunny segued into a tale about how proud he was his wife had given up for the more lucrative profession of counseling troops in a motel across from Fort Polk. "She has a degree in social work you know."

The killing he made in Silver Futures was behind his good mood. Speaking his language, I pushed a couple of buttons and won his friendship. Like all investors, he hungered to divulge his system, to find someone who understood the charts and grafts he showed me and appreciated the technique he used to predict the outlook for commodities.

I didn't dare tell him I considered technicians the psychics of the investment world. Both Father and Grandfather railed against them. If I was going to marshal his good nature, I had better do it quickly. People who are dead certain about the direction of a market are notorious losers.

It was going to be difficult to do much with him. As a service hand, he was assigned the last flight. I was among those on the second flight. With a front moving in, odds were he and the other "nonessential personnel" would leave on the workboat that had yet to be put into service.

I wanted to inquire whether he thought someone took a kickback for the unused vessel. His sense of morality might be so great he'd agree to find out who was involved. With his easy access to the companyman's office he'd be indispensable, should I convince him to expand his search. But before I could ask, I had to "cut a chogie", and leave. The dispatcher wanted to get another flight off before the storm hit.

Heavy Duty, the Halliburton cementer, joined us on the nearby concrete pad, as we watched the arriving helicopter cut in front of the blackened sky in the west. Word was the human monstrosity had bribed the dispatcher with a baseball cap.

No one appreciated having to hurriedly stuff his luggage into the compartment in the tail only to have to stand around as the rotors thrashed us with the incipient rain until it was decided which two hands had to be bumped to make room for him. Unfortunately, I wasn't among them. They had to be two big men.

Despite coming equipped with his own stoop, we still had to haul him in. We had to tuck his girth into two seat belts. We did balk at rigging two life vests around him.

"It's against regulations not to provide me with a flotation device," he complained.

"Use the life raft," the pilot retorted.

"That's stupid."

"Just don't pull the chord until it's outside."

"There are no earplugs."

"Use the headsets."

"I'm too cramped."

"Lose weight. Most of you need to shed some meat. The manifest's got more lies on it than a Weight Watchers convention."

Looking at his clipboard I noticed Heavy Duty was the only one to admit being over two hundred fifty pounds on the manifest.

So we stayed put, burning fuel rather than expelling a huge heavyweight who listed himself as a middleweight.

The pilot used the extra time to go over safety. Good thing he did. When we lunged into the air, I had to contort myself to keep from lunging into a window. If I hadn't, the pressure I'd have to put on it would have far exceeded the fifteen pounds it took to push it out.

We beat the front by seconds. A wall of water hid the field we took off from. My ears popped from the decreasing pressure. The decreasing temperature chilled me. A frantic egret popped out of the gloom and straight into our path. How we missed it I'll never know. I'd have hated to see such an exotic bird be torn apart. I'd also hate to see how our craft would withstand the impact. The shaft attached to the blades had looked as flimsy as a pipe cleaner. The array of dials on the front panel blinked on and off with each bolt of lightning. All buttons and levers looked fragile. All interior instruments appeared to be designed for easy removal. Exposed wiring was bundled together with plastic tie-wraps. A pen knife could knock us out of the sky.

Only the radar instilled a semblance of confidence. Yet, it failed when we flew into a squall. Static obscured all images. To add to my paranoia, it occurred to me how dangerous having only one pilot was. He was not exactly the epitome of physical fitness.

"Don't worry," he shouted over the ratty sounds of the rotor after we recovered from a vicious downdraft. "I was shot down three times in Vietnam."

"Yeah, but what happened to your passengers?" asked Spud.

The pilot had no reply.

Despite the tumult and nauseous vapors, the cementer lit up a fag. The match he flicked at the ashtray missed. It lay smoldering on the floor. Spud kicked me when I went for it. He kicked me again when I went after a pinch of hot ash. I wasn't kicked going for the still hot butt which likewise ended up on the floor. I let it burn, let it threaten to ignite the J.P.4 fumes and blow us out of the sky. I was going to grab a nap.

I must have, because when I next looked out the window, the clouds had dispersed enough to offer a view of the offshore oilfield below. A brave Otis work barge struggled against the waves, its legs waving like twigs in the wind. A shrimper heroically proceeded with its boom tucked in and nets tied down. More forlorn than either, a poor standby boat rode out the seas anchored near a small jack-up. The legs of a much larger, deep water jack-up rose as high as its derrick, showing how shallow the water was.

Far outnumbering the drilling rigs, production platforms appeared everywhere, individually and in two and three, connected by walkways into huge complexes. They were like metal mushrooms, all having sprouted above salt domes, sucking up oil and gas trapped between faults and fractures. They were the two-hundred-foot-high marvels turning a substance miles beneath the surface into a commodity, creating wealth, and providing jobs. A platform reminiscent of those I've seen in pictures of the North Sea suddenly loomed gigantic with its exposed separators and pumps. Banking toward it, it looked as huge as the Norco Refinery on the Mississippi.

The deep, resonant chops that replaced the blade's raggedy whir as we neared the platform awakened my fellow passengers just in time to witness our entrance into another squall. The cabin instantly turned black. Rain bashed against the window. The radar screen turned green. The entire craft shook. One passenger managed a brief curse, but that was all. We were terrified. The rotors felt as if they were about to break off. All the power the engine commanded fought against the weather. Downwind, seagulls arrowed by the window. Upwind, they struggled as we struggled, barely making headway. Then the platform reappeared, filling the window with yellow pipes, compressors, turbines, absorbers, dehydration units, and a yellow sign: Shell Oil Platform 14, marred by a poor wren that had smashed into it.

The rig alternately disappeared and reappeared at crazy angles as we tilted toward and away from it.

Ripples on a puddle distorted the pectin painted on the helipad that materialized beneath us. The windsock on top of the radio room stuck out so straight I could see through it. The roustabout manning the water cannon fought to remain upright. It didn't surprise me to see the cap blow off the head of the galley hand who met us. It did surprise me the only cargo he received was a manila envelope, which immediately ripped open in the wind, exposing the contents. Quick reflexes prevented all of the newspaper from being soaked or blown overboard. I couldn't believe it. All this to deliver a newspaper!

Things got worse. Heavy Duty had thought he was on Marble sixty-eight and was out the door. Fat must have clogged his ear canal because he couldn't hear us shouting. A water spout then appeared over his shoulder and was closing fast.

"We leave!" shouted the pilot.

A forest of arms gaffed the cementer.

"Now!" Backs popped yanking him inside.

Away we went with our human ballast still not buckled in.

We plunged off the platform, jerked upwards when we neared the water, banked left, and right, and then rose like a rocket. He flopped around like a fish, at times slamming into us, into the backs of the front row of seats until coming to rest on the floor.

"Stay," ordered Spud, stepping on him.

"Who are you to give me orders?"

"I'm above you, that's who."

An updraft rattled us. The monster grabbed a chair leg and remained on the floor, whimpering like a dog.

"I need help," he cried as the safety man hauled him up to his seat.

"What an offensive lineman you'd make," said the pride of the Tide.

When we finally arrived at work, six were needed to lug him and his gear down to the crew's quarters. Six who would gladly volunteer to be his pallbearers. Six who didn't receive so much as a "thank you" after negotiating the treacherous steps and who had to return to the craft to retrieve their gear. The air gap to the deck was daunting. So was the steep, narrow stairway inside the crew's quarters. Out of frustration, I kicked the monstrosity's duffle down one flight.

"I saw that, hand," growled Hammer. "We don't need nobody going around sabotaging other people's belongings." He started flicking his knife. "People that got no respect for other's property don't belong here." He paused for my response. An incorrect one would be disastrous.

"I guess I'm just pissed 'cause my time off was too short," I said.

He harrumphed and marched off, flipping his knife with a calm, methodical rhythm, like a contented Keystone Cop.

I only casually watched the goings on in the galley as I ate one of the sandwiches laid out in the traditional crew change day spread. By now sick of him, I wouldn't have given the cementer a second thought when he came in had Harvey, the cook, not congratulated him on his quick recovery from surgery. "It must have gone real good."

"Didn't need no surgery. Doc says half my artery is clean. Only need a third. With the drugs he gave me, I'm ahead of the game." He piled two B.L.T.s on top of each other and added cheese. He also raided the cooler, extracting a piece of pie and a piece of cake. He washed the snack down with coke from the soft drink machine.

"He says I'll be fine if I take it easy."

"If you took it any easier, you'd have to be dead," remarked Spud.

"That's the truth," declared who I assumed was Sunshine, our new boss. As imposing as Jim, affecting the same omnipotent airs, he differed only superficially, as in the amount of hair he sported. It was everywhere, out his ears, his nose, jutting like shrubbery from both temples and the back of his neck and down his shoulders, leading me to believe his entire backside was fur-lined. His eyebrows looked like bushy caterpillars, like Brezhnev's. They diverted attention from the jutting jaw that made his face resemble a half-moon (which was appropriate, considering how cratered his complexion was).

Amazing how these guys look like caricatures, I thought.

"You're not going to set cement on your hitch." He also stacked two sandwiches for himself. "No chance of reaching the next casing point in two weeks. Drilling mud is so screwed up it'll take days to circulate and condition. I told the office they should have kept adding rehydrated gel before they changed systems. Either Jim don't know shit or he wasn't paying attention. I'd bet he didn't know shit. He once kept the pH so low the mud caked up like cow pies.

"I bet the mud man had a hand in switching the polymer," he said as Sunny walked in.

"It doesn't flocculate," the mud engineer replied in a professional tone of voice. "Company spent years on R. and D. before they put it on the market."

"There are five McComber Chemical people who are in jail for falsifying lab reports."

"I do not represent that company. Bell mud has an unimpeachable record." Sunny stood resolute.

"That maybe true. One thing is for sure, though. You been trained to push chemicals. Admit you get a percentage of whatever we buy."

"Sure, I get a percentage. It's standard practice."

"That's why we're no longer going to use special treatments. A barrel or two of anything is worthless in a four-hundred-barrel annulus."

"You're the boss."

Sunshine took a massive bite out of the sandwich. "And that's why I should ask for a consultant," he said with the food in his mouth. "Using a representative of the same company that supplies the chemicals is just asking for a million-dollar mud bill."

Spotting the Iranian mudlogger, he gruffly asked how much his company charged for its services. A particle of food flew out his mouth as he did so.

"I don't handle pricing," the swarthy alien stammered as he wiped off his coveralls.

"Then you'd better call those who do; 'cause I'm sure there's a mess of companies that do what you do cheaper." He took another bite out of the sandwich.

The geologist stood tip-toe on his pointy slippers. "That may be true, but everyone in my company, except the sample catchers, have college degrees."

"How long you been in the oilfield?"

"Six months."

"Which means when everything's going good, you're fine. But when things aren't, you don't know what to do. When things are fine, I don't need you. When they aren't you're useless."

"We have state-of-the-art computers. Mini computers."

"I'd rather have someone who can tell what we're drilling in by tasting it, who can feel trouble coming on. You don't drink do you?"

"No, never. It's against my religion."

"Probably why I never heard of a Muslim mud dabber before." After a monumental swallow, he launched into the same spiel Jim and Hammer recited the last hitch about how he liked seeing his mudloggers suffer d.t.s. "Don't trust nobody who don't smoke and drink. Never had."

He finished off his sandwich and inserted a pinch of Skoal long cut into his mouth. The smokeless tobacco seemed to calm him. He got up and left without making anyone else miserable.

"Don't know what Mister Sunshine's problem is," Harvey said during dinner. "He gets a cut of almost everything he orders. Only orders stuff from his own yard."

"He just doesn't want to see anyone else do well," Sunny responded. "I know his kind."

He certainly did. After some prodding he admitted to ticking off the companyman by winning big at a late afternoon game of bourey. "He hated it. I enjoyed it."

A clash between Sunny and Sunshine boded ill. I needed the mud engineer to win the companyman's good graces, so I could take advantage of his access to the office.

Sunshine was vindictive. It wasn't Sunny's job to stand by the shakers whenever drilling mud was being circulated through the system. Nobody can stay up for days on end. That's why there's two shaker hands, each working twelve-hour shifts.

Sunny's attempt to stand up for himself may have won kudos from Tiny who compared his courage to that showed by Joe Namath when "he threw a pass instead of falling on the ball in the closing seconds of a national championship." But it put him on Sunshine's "shit" list.

The sarcasm Sunny resorted to when he said he'd call his office to send out a "shale shaker watcher" didn't sit well.

"I don't like being made fun of," Sunshine said.

He did finally give in, showing how one had to stand up to him. In lieu of exhausting his only mud engineer, he told the shaker hands to call out mud weight and funnel viscosity every fifteen minutes.

His insistence the mudlogger call out gas after the shaker hand stirred up more bad blood. Blame the Iranian's lack of imagination.

Flatly stating he was not going to do such a commonplace thing threatened his tenure on the rig.

Lucky for him he complained only to the hands. Once word reached Sunshine it was so diluted and garbled the despot couldn't come down hard on the professional. Only a warning sufficed, one that he fancied so well he leveled it on others.

"Not doing what I say is a run-off offense," he proclaimed to Hammer, Bull, Tiny, and--of all people--Heavy Duty, who I can't imagine complained about anything, with his get-over job. Being a puppy merited no reprieve against someone who managed by intimidation.

"Best way to deal with Mister Sunshine is to avoid him," observed Harvey. One foray to his office was all I needed to find out how right the cook was. Not since I was caught when I was a kid by a K. and B. employee stashing a Snickers bar in my pocket was I chastised as much. I was lucky he didn't run me off.

Following the cook's advice really posed no problem for us roustabouts. We've become experts at being where the boss wasn't. The skill was a necessity, as Kathy was more obstreperous than two weeks ago. Apparently true love must have hit a road bump (Penny wasn't admitting anything). However, when it came time to unload a boat, we couldn't escape her scrutiny. She worked the intercom overtime, as if it was essential to bring aboard in record time wireline logging equipment we won't need, if Sunshine was right, for weeks. Electric logs are run immediately prior to running casing.

Our diligence entertained the rig crew. With all the circulating that had gone on in the past several days, most had nothing to do but "operate brushes".

Entertaining all of us, both the craneperson and our shaker hand expressed an interest in the radioactive formation porosity tool. She, because "It might fit the entire way", and he, by volunteering to use his body to help calibrate it. The kit that accompanied the thirty-foot collar didn't contain the usual calibrator skirt.

"What I can't see can't hurt me," Mamou said as he mounted it directly on top the port the Amerylium Berylium source would be inserted before going down hole. Whether there was lingering radiation from the last time the source was screwed inside, we didn't know. No one asked for a Geiger counter.

The radiation his body generated enabled the grateful engineer to check the precision of his tool.

From then on Mamou was awarded the moniker, "Mamou, the Weenie Washer." Since the crew was at it, they named Hillbilly's replacement Dirty Dan. To be present at a christening was an event, to go down in history as the first time I vomited, the first time a stepmother divorced Father, and the first time I was suspended from boarding school. Indelible experiences all.

I can't wait until I'm assigned a nickname. I'm going to have to watch my step to avoid being stuck with something I couldn't live with. Whatever it was, the mere fact I had one would prove I was accepted.

To be accepted became more than an expedience. I couldn't deny the urge to be considered "one of them", a valued worker, one who's competent and genial.

Appreciation for the difficulties my lower-class job involved reshaped my opinion of the caste.

Only the hardy could hold up under the pressure. Offloading that night's cargo proved how dangerous my work could be. Crosscurrents buffeted us. Water sloshed over the deck with every trough, soaking the warped planks. Each crest jacked up the rear, like the hindquarters of an excited cat. Each assault threatened to pop the shackles on the equipment and squish me against the railing.

The wind died down when we finished. From then on it was our turn to engage in make-work until the end of the tour.

"There's nothing more dangerous than a Coon Ass with a hose," I heard several say to Mamou the Weenie Washer when I meandered over to the flowline.

Instead of hosing down the critics, the newly named shaker hand affirmed, "You're not working hard enough if you're full of talk." An evil outcry from the crane echoed his sentiments and sent the hecklers scurrying. One earns his money when one is on duty.

Rather than rush to the showers when I was done, thankful my work was over, I leaned over the railing. Dawn at sea can inspire the meanest soul. The streaks of yellow and orange that materialized on the horizon grew bolder and more pronounced as the sky changed from black to blue. Clouds took on colored fringes, and where the sun emerged, turned bright pink. While the grey water below warmed to a bright green, the few basic colors above exploded into countless hues and shades. The once commanding moon faded into oblivion.

"Want a lounge chair?" yelled Kathy. "Maybe I should serve you a Bloody Mary, want a radio, a lap dance?"

"I'm off tour."

"Should work over to make up for all the gold bricking you've done." She strutted off. I wished she'd go back to chasing Penny.

Holding my ground, I was soon joined by a slew of unaesthetic types, there not to enjoy the view but to fish. To them, the water's glassy sheen wasn't something to rhapsodize about. It was a sign mackerel might be running.

Handing me a rod and reel tall, affable Dirty Dan advised, "You'll have all the fun you can stand." He broke open a frozen case of cigar minnows.

As if to proving him right, blues and hard tails broke surface. "Running scared," announced Spud. "Something's getting to them."

That something was king mackerel, swimming on the quietest current.

They were surface feeders who fed only in the morning. They also swallowed the hooks, starting the fight to bring them in without delay. Which was what happened to all but two lines, mine, because I lowered my reel upside down and fouled it and Turtle's, whose bait was only nibbled upon. He yanked back the tip of his rod, reeled in some line, lowered it, then let out a yip of surprise. Line whizzed out of his reel and threatened to completely unspool as the fish raced under the rig. With but one wrap left, it inexplicably reversed directions. Turtle cranked as fast as he could. The fish broke surface in an eruption of water. Those not working their own catches quit what they were doing to lend a hand. For thirty minutes they fought, passing the rod from hand to hand until it ended up in my hands.

My wrists ached; my chest heaved; and I was a little dizzy, but nothing could have thrilled me more than seeing the thing float dead-tired on the surface.

"It's a Wahoo!" exclaimed Tiny in a high squeal. It looked like a monster minnow. Its big head, blue strips, and long dorsal fin were as impressive as its sheer size. It was at least eighty pounds.

Dirty Dan slid his agile body into the crew basket and held on to the supports as he was lowered to the water. He continued holding on to a support with one hand while he pulled on the line with the other.

"Grab it by the gills!" shouted Hammer. The line snapped near the leader.

With complete guilelessness the derrick hand held up the broken line. "Lookee at this." It almost was sweet. The exhausted fish drifted out of reach, toward a shadowy form.

"Barracuda," whispered Penny.

It commanded awe, like a Mafioso hit man, ready to attack upon the slightest provocation, each muscle primed for violent use.

We expected it to bolt, became anxious when it didn't, and jumped out of our skins when it did, almost at a right angle to the wahoo. Zero to sixty in a bat of an eye.

At the same time two inquisitive lemon fish dove out of sight. Why they did became obvious when another form arrived to claim the meal.

Hammerhead, the same one we had previously hooked; the barb protruding out its mouth, the line it broke trailing behind. The same surge of fear that had swept through me last time swept through me again. Looking down at it was like looking back to the Jurassic Period. It's terrifying to realize you're not on top of the food chain, that you're nothing more than a source of protein. *Thank God for the comet that wiped out the dinosaurs and gave us mammals a chance,* I thought.

"It don't want to attack," the reed thin derrick hand shouted. The beast rammed into the floating meal. "He's just playing with it." It turned to swim over the wahoo's dorsal fin. The shark then convulsed, splashing the forlorn hand.

"Raise me up. I got to go to the bathroom."

"Jerk that ignorant bastard up," commanded Hammer.

The craneman obeyed verbatim. The jerk knocked Dirty Dan off balance and for a moment he looked as if he'd lose his grip. A frantic grasp with his free hand saved him.

"Guess I don't have to go to the bathroom now. Just done my business," he stated as he was hoisted aboard.

On its next pass, the shark wrestled a chunk of meat from the fish, disappeared underwater, then hit the bait on a neglected line by the seawater intact tube.

We didn't make the same mistake we made last time. The fire alarm sounded, rousing all other off-duty personnel. Some wearing coveralls, some clad only in their underwear, in boots or wearing flip-flops, the sleepy-eyed bunch stumbled to either the port or starboard lifeboat. While rummaging through the bins for life vests Sunshine accosted them with a verbal barrage that validated his reputation.

"I don't care if Tiny posted the new station bill yesterday," he shouted to someone who had the temerity to explain he had mustered at his usual station. "Checking it daily is one of your jobs. If you don't want to make it one of your jobs I don't want you on my rig."

Mass confusion resulted as people were herded back inside to check the new station bills to find out where they now should muster. Hammer, Tiny, and Bull yakked incessantly over their portable radios trying to account for people, all the while eyeing the line to see if the shark still thrashed below.

Apoplectic at the chaos, Sunshine stormed and stomped around, cursed under his breath. Only when some semblance of order prevailed did he corral his anger into one thought.

"I don't want to see anyone not knowing what to do," he growled to those assembled by my boat. Among the things he expected everyone to know, lowering and operating a capsule were by far what he considered most important, and demanded a show of hands of those who didn't know how to do them. No hand went up. "That's what I like to see." He turned to Hammer. "Everybody knows what to do when they get inside?"

"They'd better. Gone over it enough."

"I'm holding you responsible."

"As well you should."

The intermittent alarm changed to a continuous ring. The crew queued up alongside the chain in front of the capsule.

"What you waiting for? You're dismissed," the companyman shouted.

Tiny didn't look up from his clipboard. "That's the abandon rig signal. The all clear is alternating short and long blasts." The fire team arrived wearing protective clothing, helmets with face shields, and oxygen tanks strapped to their backs.

"From now on announce what drill it is. And make sure everyone puts on their life vests correctly." Sunshine motioned to Tiny to turn one hand's vest the other way, so the stenciled brand name of "Billy Pugh" faced outward. "Check to see everyone has a whistle and light that works."

"What about a safety meeting?" asked Tiny.

Sunshine glanced at the taut nylon line. "Learning that anything can happen at any time, that's something for now." Tiny's miniscule face scrunched up in perplexity.

"We need to keep reminding them drilling is a twenty-four-hour operation," Hammer asserted. He turned to the gawky safetyman. "How about turning on that all clear signal?"

The jumbo-sized medic hesitated before lurching toward the crew's quarters. Looking at his bosses instead of where he was going, he knocked his helmet off his head passing through the door. It bounced off the grating onto the lower deck, spun around, and tumbled off the rig into the water.

Alternatively, short and long blasts rang over the intercom.

The vibrating nylon line attracted everyone's attention.

"Anyone who lends a hand is exempt from the safety meeting," Hammer announced. Everyone looked at the ponderous companyman. He remained immutable.

"The deal with that fish is that it's got nothing to do with the drill," he finally said. "But it will teach you about teamwork and discipline."

What a handful of men couldn't do a pack could. The shark had worked the hook deeper, enabling us to haul it up. Through it all the companyman maintained a steady stream of instruction, acting like a coxswain, telling us when to pull and when to hold back, instilling the rhythm and coordination we needed to eventually succeed in hanging the thirteen-foot monster upside down on the deck.

I wonder if Bull will send the gag picture Turtle took to "Field and Stream" or "Mississippi Outdoors". It wasn't the barge engineer's idea to hook a six-pound test line to the shark, but thanks to a fortuitous coin flip, he was going to get credit for the miracle.

"Maybe the Tenn Reel Company will give me a contract, be a company spokesman." The big barge engineer smiled beatifically, exposing a tangle of crooked teeth.

"Yeah, but you gotta live with the truth. You didn't earn the right to be famous," Hammer remarked, squeezing his knife sheath so hard his knuckles turned white.

"As if you did," Bull said cryptically.

"What can I say? I confess, I'm a member of the lucky sperm club." The toolpusher relaxed his grip on his sheath.

What roman a clef is he about to share? I wondered.

"Have to admit," asserted Blowfly, the injured roughneck, his arm in a cast (and heard to be enjoying his new job as assistant clerk). "You're the only white man I seen that can jump."

Hammer actually shuffled his foot Gary Cooper-like, and said--I swear--" Aw shucks".

Badgered to perform, he acquiesced after sharing a homily. "I was brought up to be modest about the gifts the Almighty gave me." His rock-like body softened. "I gave up performing 'til the reverend that baptized me sermonized how talents should be used to glorify the boss upstairs, not oneself. So when I do what I do, I do it for Him."

What he did he did for Him, certainly not me. Only Jehovah at his most inscrutable could find glory in a cracker who jumps into and out of a forty-two-gallon drum from an upright position. After all, He's got a champion leaper in the flea.

"Why don't you go pro?" asked Turtle--sincerely.

"For the same reason I don't brag about it. Wouldn't be right."

The sparkle disappeared from Bull's eyes. He momentarily sagged, then rallied, throwing his shoulders back as he rushed inside. Leaving two volunteers to clean the fish, the rest followed, to interrupt Tiny's safety meeting in the rec. room. Any hope of including the intruders in the discussion ended when Bull produced a rope.

"Watch this," he announced, scanning the room, ensuring he had everyone's attention. With aplomb, he tied a knot in the middle, yanked the ends to show it was tight, and somehow untied it without letting go. He further amazed us by undoing the double knots Spud eagerly tied taut around each of his wrists.

"Didn't even use his fingers," Turtle said in amazement.

After his final trick, snapping a weighted rope in two, the rig pantheon regained his status as top critter.

"God dog; if that ain't one hell of a deal," said Dirty Dan.

"I'll bet cash money no one else can do all that," he challenged.

All eyes turned to the ex-carnie Dennis.

"Give me several weeks, 'n I might be able to duplicate his tricks."

"Give me a couple days," murmured Hammer.

Bull sniffed. His eyes blazed with pride, and I would swear under oath his bald head glowed.

"I know it takes time to get good," injected Popcorn, the motorman. "Had me a guitar three weeks before I dared put together a group and perform gigs."

"It took seven years for me to obtain my Master's," said the Iranian mudlogger.

"And look where you are," snarled Penny, mirroring the general sentiment. "Some people just slow."

"Give it up," whispered Mitch, his colleague. "It isn't worth it."

Sitting back, obviously bored with the banality of the boasting, the scruffy B. and R. hand offered a challenge. "How about a contest where neither Bull nor Hammer have an advantage?"

The crew stared at the two and agreed what a good idea it was, to test their natural abilities, ones they haven't practiced.

So the safety meeting was officially adjourned and the barge engineer pinched a nickel between the handles of two sledgehammers. He pinioned it as long a Hammer did, as it turned out.

"Longer, if you use my watch. I was cheated," Bull insisted.

"Then let's try one more thing," said the electrician, equally bored. "Let's see if you can kick a broom out from behind your kneecap without falling."

"I may have been born at night, but it wasn't last night," Bull announced as Jones strode to the closet.

I'm sure I wasn't the only one who thought he had reservations about going first, thinking it might be a trick.

"I go first; that way I know if you cheat."

Guided by the tradesman, he crossed his legs, squatted down, slid the broom between his legs, and with his trailing foot kicked it. He toppled like a tree.

All the years of bodily neglect and abuse were exposed in the pitiful way he tried to break his fall. Nobody laughed.

Wordlessly, the crowed dispersed. Sunshine sniffed and, with Gordon and Blowfly in tow, marched back to his office. As he did, it occurred to me I wasted a perfect opportunity to go through the files. Great move.

Bull suddenly became a beast. All the discrepancies the USGS. wrote up on the rig had to be fixed immediately. Jones and his assistant found themselves slithering along grimier, harder-to-get-to power racks than last hitch. They sorted out the wiring in the frigid

S.C.R. room and battled frozen bolts on junction boxes. Equally put upon, the mudloggers got to rerun wires, install E.Y.S. fittings on sensors, and insert an audio alarm on the driller's explosion proof remote, all the while still having to monitor the well. In lieu of protracted coffee breaks, the rig's mechanic and motorman found themselves in the pump room with the derrick hand, drenched in sweat changing the check valve, mandrel, and swab of a malfunctioning mud pump.

Although he infringed upon the toolpusher's territory, Hammer didn't mind. "Got to be fixed sometime," he said. "Driller did say his gauge was showing a loss of pressure he couldn't otherwise account for."

Sunshine minded, and not because shutting down one pump prevented drilling. He minded because the welder suspended construction of a barbecue for him in order to make the rig contamination
proof, to contain spills. "To keep one step ahead of them environmentalists," said Bull.

I wrote down his activities, even drew a little diagram to show how extensive they were, for the sake of the PIRG people.

The shit continued to flow downhill. Bull had Harvey enclosed all desserts in saran wrap, put the salad dressings in the refrigerator, and ordered him to ensure all who ate signed tickets for each meal. All of this would have been no big deal if he hadn't been such a jerk about it. Who else but a caveman would have thrown a gritty pork chop against a wall in a nighttime display of culinary dissatisfaction?

"Night cooks don't last long with him," said Mitch, the mudlogger.

"Neither do lippy loggers," remarked Dennis.

He did have a point. Bull acted as if he had a vendetta against them. He flew into a rage when the Iranian picked up carrots from the fruit and vegetable tray at supper.

"These are meant to be used!" Bull bellowed, holding up a pair of tongs.

The alien shook with delirium.

He also shook when told, from then on, Petrograph personnel were to eat after the rig crew. "Gets too crowded," was Bull's reason why.

The geologist's spasms continued when he wrote a letter in the rec. room.

"No paperwork in the rec. room," our Argus commanded. His eyes blazed with the intensity of the monster Dante described in his book <u>Purgatorio</u>.

Playing Mercury I tried to trick the cretin with a little mental gymnastics.

"Only 'recing' is allowed," I said trying to show him how stupid he sounded. To no avail, as it turned out. Reality doesn't necessarily imitate art.

The barge engineer "Puffed up faster than a Jew fish being reeled in," Mister Fontenot, the directional driller, remarked afterwards.

"But I am not bothering anybody," the Iranian whined. He was right. But neither were Joseph, the Armenians, nor the Afghanistan's bothering anyone before they were attacked.

Bull turned crimson. His veins stuck out. He looked ready to explode. The mudlogger slung his belongings under his arm and hurried out.

Bull wasn't the only one with a vendetta. Sunshine decided spreading a little anxiety and fear of his own was a good idea. Picking on anyone "who stood out any kind of way" (as Spud said) satisfied a primal need.

Threatening Sunny and Heavy Duty over imagined offenses might have made him feel better about himself. But it bred animosity. Insisting the mud engineer inventory every bag of chemicals and the cementer work on his cement unit all day long only created enemies. He made a mistake harassing Mitch. Seems despite the catcalls the mudlogger had to put up with when he jumped rope, he had more admirers than detractors. He was a celebrity, being able to cross over, speed jump, and skip on alternate feet for an hour at a time. He impressed me. He impressed most others, enough that they objected when Sunshine decided he should pick on him too.

"Don't need anyone outside without boots or a hard hat," the companyman said during an evening break in the galley.

"He's just jealous," Turtle whispered to widespread acknowledgment.

"What about the drill?" asked Spud, referring to the flip-flops and unprotected pate the nearly bald companyman preferred to a helmet only a few hours before.

Sunshine reared back. His stomach protruded like a threatening weapon. "That's different. Don't need no jump rope or towel sucked up in a rotor," he declared with a finality that did not brook objections.

Mitch looked traumatized. "I can hear a chopper two miles off," he pleaded.

"Heard where a fella fell off the helipad, over the chain link and all. Never found the body," said Hammer.

"Been on rigs before that forbade sunbathing," said Dennis, alienating the handful of sun worshippers.

Hammer winked at Sunshine. "Glad to see there are those that got enough sense to follow the rules."

Both the toolpusher and companyman were deaf to the rumblings of insurrection. From the satisfied look on his face, Dennis seemed to relish it. So did I, though I hoped it didn't show. A subtle push may be all I need to instigate a mutiny or maybe a disturbance distracting enough to allow me unfettered access to the office.

Seeing Hammer leave with Sunshine's arm wrapped around his shoulder traumatized Bull. The envy in his eyes boded ill for all of us. Craving an arm around his shoulder he issued a breathtaking series of edicts, the worst of which was ordering the air conditioning to the bottom two floors shut off. "To save money. Day rates haven't gone up nearly as much as diesel," he explained.

"What about us?" pleaded Tiny, sticking his head into Bull's office. "What about our safety?"

"You ain't gonna melt." Bull motioned him inside and shut the door. The barge engineer's voice attained enough decibels to awaken sleepers down the hall. The safetyman did not again brooch the subject. Only Sunshine brought it up--to *compliment* Bull for his good idea. He remained deaf to our complaints, no matter how vocal we became. My much hoped for rebellion looked as if it might materialize. Turtle loaded his pistol, Spud readied a truncheon. Even Mamou swore a couple of times. Unfortunately, it didn't take long for the heat to melt all hot tempers. It's hard to be a revolutionary when you swelter in bed.

"I got these upper two floors the way I want," Sunshine stated in the galley. You actually could see his breath. The cooler was warmer. "Anyone touching the vents or thermostat, well, they better not."

Nobody dared. Nor did anyone repeat Gordon's admission the cost of diesel remained the same. As rig accountant, he certainly would know. "It's all for show," he admitted to me. The rolling of his beady eyes and the curling of his thin lips gave me hope, not much, but more than before, when I just considered him to be nothing more than a character in Rice's play "The Adding Machine".

"Then why is Sunshine purposely making us miserable? The floor of my room is right above the pumps and can be too hot to walk on," I complained.

"*Quod licet Jovi, non licet bovi*--the gods can get away with conceits we mortals can't," he said. He left me to ponder my place in the two hundred fifty by three-hundred-foot universe.

With a wad of Skoal in his mouth and a Camel between his lips, our god gave orders incessantly. He overloaded the rig with rented tools we wouldn't need until much later, costing Springer a fortune. He refused to wire up the logger's resistivity probe even though it could inform us whether we were dangerously close to drilling into the salt dome (said the fifty dollars a day charge was too costly). And he had Hammer buy for him on Marble's expense account goods purchased on shore from a Wal-Mart. I bet he didn't even know the lower decks were saunas. I bet he didn't care. I never saw him anywhere but in the galley,, in his office, or playing pool. It was an event when he trekked all the way to the drill floor.

"He's a work of art," Harvey commented.

From his perch behind his desk, looking out the window, he lorded over his domain. Omnipotent and omniscient. Or so he thought.

No one would dare tell him about the two posters which appeared in the locker room, the ones marked "Our HMFIC" (which I translated as "head MF in charge"). Rumor had it Bull and Hammer had chuckled over them, not in their wildest dreams thinking they also might apply to them.

Below a caricature of an infant were these words of wisdom, "A boss is like a diaper. He's always on your ass and is full of shit." Another drafted by someone more talented at calligraphy than grammar defined "stress" thusly, "That confusion created when one's mind overrides your bodies desire to choke the living hell out of some asshole that desperately needs it."

Later modifications did not tip Bull off he had become the primary brunt of our enmity. The sweat drawn pouring off all characters may not have been obvious enough. Neither were the evil eyes we sweltering wretches cast upon him. Nothing we did seemed capable of penetrating his conscious. He even took more interest in a pigeon that blew aboard than he did about us.

"Rig needs a mascot," he declared. "Good for morale."

The way he doted over it turned us even more against him. Making a production of its welfare, he assigned "hawk spotters", set out feeders, and told Tiny to care for its medical needs. Other birds, more exotic birds from passing freighters meant nothing to him.

"Let it live in a hot box," grumbled Spud as he and I washed away droppings that coated the balcony outside the galley.

"It's worse than a wife, eating, sleeping, going to the bathroom all the time," said Penny.

"Let it get fat on one of Dennis' rolls," snarled Spud to everybody at dinner, revealing his knowledge of the B. and R.'s crime.

"Screw the yeast. Let'm use some carbide them logger's got," advised Tar Baby, the assistant driller. "Blow it out of the water."

Sunshine pushed away the mountainous plate of food he had just started devouring. "Got something better than that. Got some peppers you won't believe."

"Jalapeños?" I asked, remembering Chef Powell's martinis.

"Cayenne peppers?" asked Blowfly.

"My ass. What I got will burn your nose hairs." He lumbered off to his room, to return clutching a bottle of what looked like jelly. "Was going to make any mudlogger caught sleeping on tour eat a spoonful." He planted the jar on the table.

The toolpusher leaped up to volunteer. With a flourish he spread the goop on a slice of bread. Holding it to his mouth he paused to acknowledge Bull's stormy entrance. The barge engineer sniffed, too perturbed about the repairs he had been supervising to be interested in a bit of extraneous business.

"Kelly patina peppers, they're called. Found them hunting along the Brazos and Colorado. Look like china balls."

Hammer scrutinized his snack. "Reminds me of when I was a youngun'. We were so poor we had cornbread for breakfast, water for lunch, and swelled up for dinner."

"Know how I found where they were?"

Hammer took a bite.

"I'd see mockingbirds dive into the water."

If Hammer were a mockingbird he too would have dove into the water. His eyes popped open in horror. His face scrunched up in pain. I expected to see smoke billow out his ears and fire roar out his mouth. He sweated. With lightning speed, he stuffed a salty biscuit in his mouth and chased that with a pint of water.

"That was pretty tasty," the toolpusher painfully uttered.

Bull's howls drowned out our considerable laughter.

"You look worse than my uncle after he came in from a night out," Sambo, the galley hand, remarked as he handed the toolpusher a glass of milk.

Sunshine lit a cigarette. "Didn't mention how the fruit explodes soon after turning red. Goes up like a claymore mine."

As if by divine intervention the on duty craneman called over the intercom. "We got us a pigeon sandwich."

We rushed to the stairs outside the rear door. A shower of feathers drifted from the pulley at the end of the boom.

"I'll be a sonnavabitch," murmured Penny.

An unrecognizable slab of meat gently slid off the crane and fell into a school of hungry bait fish. It disappeared in a froth of white.

The figure by the remote console, under the crane, shrugged his shoulders and extended his arms. "What could I do?" the craneman pleaded. "Damn thing wouldn't get off the line. Blew my horn and everything."

Too overcome with grief Bull did not lash out. He became stoic and aloof. Hammer's strained laughter did not faze him. He even turned his back when the toolpusher swallowed wrong and started to gag. He wished to be left alone and remained so for the rest of the day.

Early the next morning a strange "coo-coo" was heard over the intercom. The third time it was heard the barge engineer got on the phone and let everyone know his funk had ended. "Whatever weevil is making that noise is gonna get kicked into next week."

I had to contain my laughter until I was out of sight behind a cargo bin. So did others, including Kathy. If she hadn't, she would have been ordering us to return to work. None of us could keep a straight face when Bull recovered, returned to form, stomped around, and issued heretofore unheard of (if not particularly imaginative) curses. All in all, I'd give him a "nine" for sincerity and a "two" for creativity, which is quite high for out here.

"Cooing" replaced the odd ball "hello" as the sound of choice over the P.A. Penny did it. Tar Baby did it. Spud did it. Even Kathy did it. She was the only one caught.

Nobody witnessed how she defused Bull. The venom he initially spat at her over the intercom had simmered to a decent tone of voice after he had confronted her. "She has her ways," Penny said without elaborating. Whatever she did the rest of us appreciated it. Not being punished for having fun at someone else's expense seemed too good to be true.

"I suggest you keep your life vest by your head and sleep in your clothes," Dennis told me.

He knew what he was talking about. Three days after the shark drill a "Whoop whoop" over the intercom rattled everyone's sheets. We stumbled out of bed and fumbled with the plastic Scotty gas containers. I ripped one fingernail in half trying to unsnap one latch. When I finally did open it and removed the oxygen tank and webbing I instantly realized I hadn't a clue how to put it on. I tried slinging a strap over my right shoulder only to find I couldn't buckle the belt. Same thing happened when I slung it over my left shoulder.

"Need your life vests," said Spud, having a much easier time than me with his gear. I tried watching him put on his gear but quit when I became conspicuous. Besides, he did it so fast I barely could follow. Giving up I just carried it and the life vest outside to join the biggest group next to the port lifeboat, where I renewed the effort copying how others did it. I might have gotten it if Bull hadn't stormed among us, pointing to a small group on the helideck, shouting for us to "Get up there!"

It made sense, as the cascade hook-ups for us to plug into were there.

"But the wind socket shows gas will be blown there," said someone.

"This is a drill. You're not supposed to think. You're supposed to learn how to react."

Tiny appeared and for an instant looked like he might disagree. He leaned into the barge engineer's personal space as if to argue face to face.   A stern look of reproach sent him reeling. "That's a good idea," he deferred.

I made my way upstairs dragging a train of webbing and straps behind me.   The renewed berating, we encountered afforded me enough time to get straightened out.   Once I hooked up and had air blowing into my mask, I couldn't hear a thing the big shots said. But I could tell from the reaction of those who could hear, Hammer approved of the H_2S drill coming when we were asleep. Their disbelief was manifest in their slumped shoulders and, after Sunshine apparently concurred, through the frustrated expressions observable through their glass faceplates. I'm sure he made some remark about being tired is part of the job. The cold-blooded smile he affected almost assured me that's what he said.

Then came the inspection of the troops and the berating of each who wasn't hooked up correctly. The berating continued after the continuous abandon rig alarm sounded. Thankfully I now was adroit at putting on my life vest. After placing my air pack neatly in a row with the others I followed those who knew what they were doing down the steps and into the escape capsule. I took a far seat and buckled up correctly.

"Won't right itself in the water if you're not buckled in or if the lower seats not filled first," Hammer proclaimed.

He chewed out Sambo for sitting too close to the red lever marked "danger". "Pull that, 'n we free fall."

Deciding we were less than honest last time, when we let Sunshine believe we knew how to operate the capsule, the three chiefs agreed we needed a refresher. Problem was, all they did was bitch. The real instruction came from Tiny. The lumbering giant showed us how to lower the craft and jettison it. He taught us about the sprinkler system, the oxygen tank, the radio, the supplies, how to steer the thing, how to start it, and how to trouble-shoot it if it didn't start. He even suggested we swim cross current if we ended up in the water. "Burning debris will follow you down current like an All-American defensive back." Other athletic references helped us remember other words of wisdom. Without them I doubt I would have listened to a thing he said, the interior of the capsule being so dank, damp, and cramped. We all were grateful to hear the all clear signal and celebrated being released by either tripping on the steps below the exit or banging our heads on the hatch above it, stumbling like drunks onto the landing.

Greeting us was Bull, standing with his hands on his hips, regarding us with derision. He let the overbearing companyman have the final say. "Fold your vests right, get with the safety man about the air you got left, and, if it's okay, put your packs in the cases the way you found them. No telling when you're gonna need them again."

We didn't hear anymore "cooing".

An hour later I purposely lingered outside the main office pretending to be reading the posted company newsletter. Although able to understand very little of the mangled English of those inside I did hear quite clearly Sunshine brag how he wanted "People to worry about me. Don't want them to figure me out."

Knowing the intentions of one's enemy is invaluable intelligence. It gave me an edge and an insight. It allowed me to regard the b.s. session I attended among the lesser-lights in a lower floor bedroom with more empathy than I otherwise would.

When Penny lamented how all he wanted to do was earn his check he spoke for all the other practical jokers. When Turtle concurred by stating "I got bills to pay" I couldn't help but think of their personal histories, and how they must have been browbeaten all their lives. Like Sunshine (whose Father must have been a "wheel") they had been taught to keep the social order since birth.

So much for the insurrection, for enlisting them to help me rifle through the files in the main office. They weren't Russian serfs ready to drown their masters with alcohol. They were too afraid, didn't have the urgency to change things I had. I couldn't even ask them to divulge a little dirt I could use to impress the Public Interest Research Group.

As for Sunny, the mud engineer, he was absent from the goings-on. Demure during the drill, he kept to himself, staying in his mud lab, on the pits, and maybe in his room. He avoided contact, didn't linger over meals, and stayed in the third-floor offices only long enough to hand in his report and inform the bosses about his business. I didn't ask, as I was afraid, he was distracted by the futures contracts he had boasted about buying. The deep antipathy I had acquired about technical analysis and following charts probably was once again proving right. I remember Father once challenged a friend to predict the latter half of a pattern he had slyly copied from an electrocardiogram. The so-called expert's prediction couldn't have been more wrong. Besides, pork bellies are too thinly traded, too easy for a big player to manipulate. I think he got a little too confident after his luck with silver. Pork bellies, what is that?

Refusing to abandon my quest, I begrudgingly turned to Dennis, the rig maverick.

Not wanting to be obvious, I waited until he changed my sheets before talking to him. Asking the usual questions about how long he intended to spend on this hitch, where he came from, how long he has been in the oilfield only elicited grunts. Only when I asked how long he thought the well would last did he speak coherently.

"What do you want?" he glared at me.

"Just making conversation," I said. His frown and his dead eyes indicated a boredom that might have been daunting had I not spied a forlorn turn of his shoulders, a vulnerable tilt of his head.

"You're the only person worth getting to know out here," I said with as much conviction as I could muster.

"You're quite knowledgeable," His eyes came alive. His sloppy-looking body showed life. He let down his guard, a little.

"Gotta be, out here, everywhere, all the time. Knowing what's what and who's who is what sets me apart." He finished tucking in a blanket, took one haughty look at me, and left. It was as if he wanted to be disliked.

Got to admit, though, he wasn't blowing smoke. Should anyone think he just had a swelled head, the arrival of Marble's drilling supervisor set everyone straight.

Mister Roger Otis may have gone directly to Hammer's office to pour over reports upon his arrival but that did not stop him from jumping out of his chair to greet the B. and R. hand the moment Dennis lumbered inside to clean.

Reading the safety newsletter on the bulletin board across the hall put me at an angle to see inside. I could see the stocky man wrap an arm around the lanky lowlife and proclaim "He's my boy. Bet he'd know how to get us drilling faster."

I wish I could have taken a picture. Two green rednecks is a sight to behold. Hammer and Bull each craved to smack the smirk off the underling's face, and "get him a window seat."

"Would rather take his advice than that of any engineer graduate. Dennis' street smarts are going to make him someone we're going to report to someday."

The animosity the two had leveled at each other now focused on Dennis. And Dennis loved it. He put his arm around Mister Otis and claimed the supervisor was only being kind. "Not inaccurate, just kind."

"Ain't he something." The stocky man beamed, then as if overcome with a sense of purpose, donned his engraved metal helmet, put on his Tony Lama boots, and headed out. "Alone," he insisted. "Want to get the skinny from the hands, not gold-plated poop from their bosses. Been reading your reports every day. Great works of fiction." He strode off, leaving Dennis alone with his nemeses and me, acting obvious by quickly turning away from him. Luckily, he didn't even look at me.

"If you excuse me, I've got work to do," Dennis said as he dragged his mop and bucket into the middle of the linoleum floor. There was a long silence. "You done your reports." The big wigs looked incredulous. "Somebody's got to do something constructive."

I split before the duo could take their frustration out on me. I wondered if they knew I had been eavesdropping as I tried to walk away as casually as possible. One thing I was sure of, Dennis knew.

"Always perform better to an audience," he later admitted as I peeked into his little room.

"You're something else," I said.

Looking up from the "Penthouse Forum" he acknowledged I was right. "Only next time wipe rather than lick my boots. It's more sanitary."

Respecting him, I got right to the point.

"What would it take for you to do me a favor?"

"Depends."

"On what?"

"On what's in it for me?" He fondled the glossy cover of the magazine.

"You read "Forum" often?"

"It's almost all I read."

Feeling out his personality, I offered to provide him recent back issues of the rag. His sunken eyes lit up. They remained lit up when I agreed to bring Nineteen Seventy-Eight "Hustlers", "Velvets", and "Cherrys" in exchange for him helping me.

"Why that year?" I asked.

"Let's just say I was out of touch with the general population."

I entered his room, his sanctum sextorium. Decorated in centerfolds, it was a shrine to adolescent hormones, something you'd expect in a teenager's lair, not an over-the-hill doper's.

"This is my home."

"You mean home away from home."

"I mean home. Stay in motels on shore."

I noticed the bed wasn't made, the trash needed emptying, the floor hadn't been swept, and the smell of unwashed clothes lingered in the air.

"You must have had an interesting life," I said, looking at the paraphernalia on the metal desk. Beside Grateful Dead concert tickets and Spiro Agnew watch, well worn copies of <u>The Tropic of Cancer</u>, <u>The Story of O</u>, <u>Lady Chatterly's Lover</u>, and <u>Fear of Flying</u> lay strewn on top. No adult bookstore fare was visible. Holding a prominent place and thread-bare through extended use, sat an arcane tome titled, <u>The History of the Masons</u>.

I pushed the right button asking him about it. Completely out of character, he launched into a recitation of the mystic order, educating me on an aspect of history I had known nothing about. He was well versed, taking me from its inception among the Hebraic craftsmen in Ramses' Egypt to the modern symbolic masons. He told me how, from Hyrem Hibif on, they invented geometry, built Jewish temples and European cathedrals, built the Temple of the Mount, and hid the Ark of the Covenant (with its staff of Aren and Ten Commandments). Asides about renegades like the lodge P2 that controlled Italy, the prince who paid Jack the Ripper to kill prostitutes he impregnated, and how a pope stole its secrets to create the Knights of Columbus may or may not have been true. But they made good stories.

I wanted to, but didn't, ask where he fit into an organization dedicated to preserving morality, obeying the laws of the members respective countries, and who believed in God.

"Wondering how I can be so loosely screwed together to think I can join them?" he asked, reading my mind. "Let me offer you a drink."

"You can't have alcohol on board."

"That's the trouble with you worms. No imagination." He removed several slices of bread from a loaf. "It's time for some aftershave. What's your fancy? Old Spice, Brute, or Aqua Velva?"

Humoring him, I opted for the smell of the ocean.

"Not me. I'm an Aqua Velva man." He strained the colognes through the bread and caught the filtrate in shot glasses. "Bottoms up."

No fan of hard liquor, I was an old hand at secretly spitting out the swill. Dennis knocked back his concoction with gusto and insisted I share a bump. The Dr. Trischner mouthwash he handed me stung on the way down.

"I'm a thoroughly honest man. That's my trouble. I know how the world works. Made a fortune as a carnie betting people they couldn't beat me at the game in my booth. Not one person was smart enough to realize I spent months perfecting my craft. That's why I can't get along with anybody." He took another swig. "People aren't rational, can't stand reality."

As diplomatically as I could, I asked how long he had been this way.

"Since I found out Jack Kerouac spent more time writing his book than he did on the road. Lived with his mother mostly. That put me on a bullshit watch."

I winced when he next brought up Vietnam. I knew all about the invasion of Cambodia and Laos and familiar with all the latest conspiracies.

"Thought you heard it all in spades? Did you know of the ugly Americans who sacked the Saigon treasury; that the C.I.A. is still raping the place? Didn't get any better, with the Trilateral Commission. And didn't you think it was a little suspicious the Iranian hostages came home the same day Reagan was inaugurated? Bush secretly met with diplomats in Paris."

I thumbed through a magazine called "Jugs", hoping he'd change subjects.

He did. "All so-called literature is prick-tease and bullshit adventure. All entertainment is. Look at how popular "Three's Company" is. So why not go whole hog about it?"

"This is whole hog? What about real women?"

"What about them? More bullshit. Ever notice how they put on make-up before they piss in the morning?"

I had to pretend I did.

"They use your urge to screw them to fleece you."

"Can't argue with that," I said.

"These women in these magazines don't want your money. They don't bleed or get yeast infections; they don't bitch, whine, fart, pick their nose, belch, smell, have stubble, a mustache, or dandruff. And they don't have boyfriends. Add the pros and cons and you're not right if you choose a real woman over pictures of Candy Samples. Look at them serious hooters. I bet in real life she's a saggy hog. It's all bullshit."

Capitalizing on his frankness I asked him about the business practices of Marble drilling and Springer Oil. I hit a nerve. He launched into a recitation that, if true, depressed me. Hearing genuine dirt did not set my reformer's wings flapping like I thought it would. Sure, I'd use it to impress Leslie and her muckraking buddies. But I wasn't excited about it. Guess I'm more Horatio Alger than Upton Sinclair. I didn't care as much as I thought I would that he had enough on Sunshine, the drilling supervisor, the dispatcher, expeditor, and most of Springer's accounting department to send them to jail. Corruption sounded more pandemic than endemic. I just hoped his anecdotal evidence wasn't representative of the industry.

"Think we need a workboat as a standby boat? The extra money it costs goes into Sunshine's and the dispatcher's pocket. Sunshine signed a ticket for a six man hammer crew. I only saw four men. He signed an invoice for thousands of dollars worth of blue paint. Seen any blue paint on the rig?"

The only colors I saw were grey, white, yellow, and red.

"What about that workboat?" I asked, referring to the one that hadn't moved from the dock.

He told me who made money keeping it on the payroll and furthered my education with a story about oil company accountants who wanted to know why they were receiving bills for helicopter flights when the drilling rig had moved off location months before. "They didn't know a platform had been set. Ignorance and stupidity are handmaidens of booms. Where's too much money floating around there's going to be all kinds of graft. Look at me. I was a choir boy until I found out dealing paid the bills quicker than anything else I could do. It's the free enterprise system at work. You'll see the oilfield get self-righteous and police itself when the price of oil or--worse--gas dumps. You'll see the drug problem end when it's cheaper to buy a joint than a cigarette. Economics." He strained all three colognes through two slices. "A Long Island Tea."

"What about Jim?"

"He's just an oaf. So is Hammer and Bull."

To ensure he'd help provide the hard evidence I needed to prove Father was not involved in these kickbacks, I promised I'd also bring him the Nineteen Seventy-Eight issues of "High Society", "Cavalier", "Genesis", "Oui", and "Swank", among others.

"Add "Monster Jugs" and I'll doctor any evidence. Throw in "Foot Fetishes" and I'll see to it no incriminating evidence exists."

The offer was tempting, if unnecessary. Father didn't leave incriminating evidence. No innocent person does.

Fired up, I went to bed thinking of the scavenger hunt I would conduct when I returned home. I woke up thinking about it and in between, in my dreams, had come up with a reasonable way to do it. The fine points had to wait until after work. For in addition to performing my own duties I had to break in Poncho of Forty-Eight Hours' replacement, Brother-in-law, an ordinary guy who needed nepotism to land the job.

It was amazing how someone so unassuming could work our nerves so badly. His weak chin, thin face, receding hairline, and nasal voice made him look and sound stupid. And if first impressions did not invite ridicule then a little exposure did. It didn't take long before he would subject any listener to his creed, one summarized in a ditty he'd repeat upon the slightest provocation, "We the willing led by the knowing are doing the impossible for the ungrateful. We've done so much with so little for so long we are qualified to do anything but nothing." Its surreal nature gave me the creeps. I didn't know what to make of him and, not knowing, assumed the worst, assumed he was a gingle put in my life by a malevolent god. That is, until I spent more time with him.

"I came here to work," he said as we shackled a big container box. "Teach me."

"Teach me?" I couldn't believe it. I stood stunned. Me, the worm as veteran. Water collected in my eyes, preventing me from focusing on his guileless features. I never had seen unassailable honesty before. I suddenly knew how people must feel when they are smitten by the holy spirit, are reborn. I stared unabashedly at him.

"When can we begin?"

I showed him why you shouldn't shackle a dead horse. I screwed a pin through a link in a chain we were picking up, making sure the horseshoe curve of the shackle was attached to the cable. I showed him how to unsnap a boom without it springing into his face, how to latch a sling around the casing we brought aboard without tangling the lines, and how to keep the spreader bar level. I imparted tips concerning safety, like watching out for pinch points. I didn't know I knew so much. It was fun.

During slack moments I explained to him what an expansion joint, float baffle, thruster jack, sea water check valve, and a drawwork break were...stuff I had seen while at the pipe yard. I also showed him how to use a mud buckle and a deadman clamp. We went over the handling of a pinch bar until I, not he, tired. Back to work, I continued showing him the tricks of the trade, like waiting for the crane to tighten the slings instead of doing it manually and, conversely, to wait until the wire rope is slack before fooling with the shackles. He was an eager student. What took me days to learn took him hours. I had no qualms about letting him signal Kathy after I went over the signs. He even rubbed his hands together when a small load was about to be caught on an overhang on the grocery bin. I hadn't gone over that.

He watched with interest when I spread out the sling he had wrapped around the middle of a five-foot sub and said "thanks" when it was obvious, I hadn't balanced the load, It would have slipped out when it was lifted by the crane. He caught on to skills we learned together quicker. He removed twice as many thread protectors on the casing. And I had a bigger wrench.

He was proud of the sweat that soaked his clothes. "Showed I earned my money."

Showed I shouldn't be so quick to judge, I thought.

The swarthy little guy "recreated" properly in the rec. room, and displayed just the right amount of sassiness, taking advantage of the fact he was related to craneman opposite Kathy, all the while knowing he had to earn respect. He also instituted a contest that brought the crew together. Who would have thought Penny, Spud, Hammer, and Bull would have enjoyed themselves comparing notes, reciting everything on a rig named after an animal.

Those with the least experience blurted out the ones most commonly referred to in daily operations, such as the catwalk (where drill pipe and tools were laid before being winched up the "V" door to the drill floor) and the possum belly (where drilling mud pools below the flowline before flowing onto the shakers). Pony collars, pup joints, mule shoes were so common several mentioned them. The same held true with the driller's dog house, catlines, and junk left in the hole (called fish). It was their knowledge of the more exotic items on a rig that identified those with the most experience and explained why they were on top of the totem pole. Since the bosses recited an equal number of butterfly valves and donkey dicks it also became obvious they knew as much as each other, were equals...a situation which didn't unite them. It grated on them, caused each to set off to prove his superiority; Hammer, by perusing the big, fat IADC reports with an accountant's eye for detail, looking for mistakes and Bull, by breaking out his T.I. 80 to figure out the absolute best way to distribute the weight of all the equipment to make room for the casing coming aboard.

Unfortunately for everyone, Sunshine took over the job of supervising the job of measuring and positioning them sequentially, for easy access to the drill floor.

Brother-in-law looked out the only porthole in the rec. room, frowned, and put his hands on his hips. "It isn't his job to be a deck foreman. That's Hammer's job."

Word reached us the companyman managed to confuse everything. My crew got to unscramble the mess he created when we came on tour. We had to make sure each twenty-seven to thirty-foot joint would be lifted to the drill floor in proper sequence.

"No way would we know where the shoe would be set it if we just stuck them in," I said to anyone within earshot, trying to sound profound. My protégé's quizzical look compelled me to explain why the end of the first joint of casing--the shoe--looked like a steel condom. Before I could articulate an easy-to-understand answer he remarked, almost off-handedly, "It's probably for buoyancy." I hadn't thought of that. He probably was right. Gathering myself, I remarked, "Like the rubber that's been in my wallet for years. It's got a hole in it."

His eyebrows furrowed. His lips pursed. "To circulate cement and drilling mud I bet."

I shut up in the face of such precociousness. I would have remained silent if he hadn't exploded at the sight of Sunshine returning to the main deck. But I couldn't resist shushing him as I slapped one hand over his mouth and restrained him with the other. Thoughts of having to break in a replacement kept my grip taut long enough for the bantamweight to calm down. Going limp, he thanked me, then just as quickly fired up with renewed indignation when we both witnessed Kathy suffer a dressing down for refusing to obey Sunshine's renewed commands.

"That's no way to talk to a woman," he said before stiffening with resolve. Smacking his fist into his palm he announced the philosophy he decided was applicable to the situation. "Obstacles separate the men from the boys." He scowled with conviction.

Luckily, he wasn't put to the test. Totally confused, the companyman quickly threw up his thick arms trying to fix what he had fouled and stormed inside the crews' quarters.

We joined him when dinner time rolled around. As frustrated as we were, he was more so, by a power of two. There was no steak. Yesterday was Friday and we had our seafood. Saturday traditionally was steak day. Not to serve it was a serious infraction. After uttering surprisingly fitting imprecations he stormed out the galley, kicking the door jam as he left so he could leave us with the lasting impression of the door slamming behind him. Or what we thought was a lasting impression. Returning with two small canisters he lit and lobbed them over the serving counter, into the kitchen near Harvey. Each went off with a pop and a puff of smoke. Two Vietnam vets dove under a table. I jumped. The giant cook leaped, screamed, and danced as if he had a hot foot. The "Nigger Chasers" followed the gyrating hulk around the kitchen. Wherever he went they went, in a billow of smoke and whiz of motion. His spastic movements were unnerving, frightening. Equally frightening was Sunshine's laughter. Banshees couldn't have been worse. That the bulky companyman kept guffawing until Harvey settled down made him all the more diabolical.

The perambulating gargoyle did not calm down easily. Amid the lingering smoke and stale gunpowder smell Harvey developed a twitch and a moan that made him harder to look at and listen to.

"I try to do my job," he muttered after Sunshine's withdrawal. His raspy voice was more grating than usual. "I try to stay out of people's way. No one will let me." He started to sob. "What I should do is get back at him. I'm not in jail. If I get run-off, I'll be sent to another rig."

I poured two cups of coffee and invited him to join me at a table. "You're right about not having to put up with abuse," I said.

The man's basset hound eyes began to clear up. His face quit looking so hideous. "I don't know why I do it. Habit, I guess," he said.

He knocked back a big swig. Coffee dribbled down his jutting chin and stained his white uniform.

"We're all conditioned," I replied.

"You have to go along to get along." He finished his cup with another messy gulp. "But sometimes going along turns you into an accomplice." He grabbed my forearm and looked imploringly at me. I gulped. The onus of being an ex con's confessor was a lot to ask. Messaging the soul that writhed inside the morbid exterior was a job for a trained professional. Still, I must have handled my responsibility well, said the right things, conveyed genuine sympathy, because he came to trust me so much he broke a sacred covenant. He ratted on Jim.

"I learned to keep my word; had to. It's all I had going for me in the joint. But if someone does me wrong, then it's hard to keep." With tears welling in his eyes, he confessed he was an accessory to a crime.

"Mister Jim didn't make me do it. He didn't come out and say I had better help him or be fired. I wasn't drunk like I was the last time I did wrong."

What he did was agree to do a favor for the now departed companyman. "I didn't know how many steaks he'd take. Should have. Them burlap bags he got from the mudloggers were full."

He didn't know whether to tell his office what had happened or order replacements and pray the chief steward wasn't paying close attention.

"But if Sunshine complains I got to tell. What if they don't believe me. How can I explain the theft, or even losing my job, to my parole officer?"

With an air of certainty, I advised him to be as candid with his people as he was with me.

"Honesty gets you in less trouble," I said with a straight face.

"Yeah...it'd be better if Jim takes the heat. He deserves to." He began to perk up.

I perked up. "Then go for it. I'm sure you can find all kinds of incriminating evidence on him, so much he can't do or say anything against you."

The idea transformed Harvey. He became less hideous to look at. His pustules and scaly skin quit commanding attention. Instead, I was drawn to the totality of his being, his big, lumpy, never-hurt-a-fly (when sober) presence. It was nice to see someone so blighted by luck be happy. The thought of buttering him up so I could use him was repugnant to me. I had to leave before I did something that would spoil the good feeling I enjoyed by helping him (and it wasn't because he didn't have access to the companyman's office, I think).

Any attempt to add to my good feeling by helping another distressed soul wasn't in the cards. Running into Sunny in the hallway he volunteered how he had to fork over thirty grand for a margin call. The glee in his voice would have led one to believe he had made a killing. "Charts say it's a double bottom. With higher lows, the price can only go up." He winked. "It's all coming together."

At least there's one guy who's his own man out here. I thought. *One, out of what? forty?*

Over the P.A. Sunshine's still irritated voice irritated us all with a complaint about how much rig time was wasted by running the casing slowly.

"I'm going as fast as I can," Penny retorted with conviction.

"If you can't go faster I'll get someone who will."

"So go get the mother fucker."

I gulped. I couldn't believe my ears. I never could have said that, regardless my situation. *Who else was I wrong about?* I thought. I've never witness such a display of backbone. Apparently neither had Sunshine, considering how he babbled over the P.A.

That nothing immediately happened to Penny, that he kept on running casing, showed me what a little moxie could do.   Sunshine wasn't invincible after all. Maybe I can manipulate him. I just needed a little courage, not to march inside his office and shoulder aside Gordon and Blowfly and rifle through the files, but to wheedle into the big fat ass's confidence, fool him into thinking he could trust me.

"You need to see me after tour," he finally articulated over the P.A. There was no need to identify who he was referring to.

Sunshine's ego was a weakness that cried out to be exploited. It was the key to his files.

Showing some guts I visited the companyman after my tour. His quiet demeanor gave me pause. He must have resolved his tiff with Penny. I was as clueless about how it went as I was at how Penny and Kathy resolved their affair. There must be a good-ole-boy code of conduct I'm not privy to. Sunshine actually was in a good mood.

"There's nothing I like better than someone who thinks poker is a game of luck," he said after I volunteered to sit in for the driller. "But, there's a better way to help me, other than giving me your money."

So, during my next tour I played look-out. I didn't dare take my eyes off the porthole he sat behind. Paul Revere couldn't have concentrated more on the Old North Church, squinting as I did in the twilight to see if he fired up a cigarette.

The chore would have been easier had Kathy not ordered me to clean up the mess by the shakers. Both shaker hands had forgotten to turn it on during the casing run. Mud that should have vibrated through the screens, to be recycled, either dropped into the Gulf, or sloshed onto the deck. Neither the drillers nor the mudloggers detected the loss, meaning they weren't doing their job, meaning Sunshine lost his good mood, became pissed when he found out, meaning he wasn't about to brook any backsliding by me.

One of the four legs supporting the rig partially blocked my view of the porthole he sat behind. A mist descended. Watching for the signal while wielding a shovel taxed my ingenuity, and ultimately taxed it too much. I had to sneak over to the Texas deck, where I was afforded a clear view.

A red glow briefly appeared, followed by a wisp of smoke. I rushed to a phone, only to be wracked by second thoughts. What if it was Tiny or the puppies who lit up? A quick review of their habits led to the conclusion only Bull smoked, and that was to irritate Hammer.

Praying I wasn't making a *faux pas*, I called out, "Pick up Springer companyman." The silhouette closest to the porthole got up and did not return to the table.

"What are you, a peeping Tom?" bellowed Kathy. "Got that mud cleaned up?"

Admitting I hadn't ticked her off. "You roustabouts are a dime a dozen," she bitched. Seeing me later, she corrected herself. "All men are a dime a dozen."

By the way she fidgeted at supper I could tell she wanted to elaborate but was afraid of making a spectacle of herself. Instead, she stared daggers at Penny, making him more uneasy than he was when Sunshine glowered at him, indicating he really must have done her wrong. Nobody knew how to take Sunshine's favoritism toward me.

After upbraiding Penny for continuing to reset the pit alarm each time it went off, and for not changing the circular chart, he slapped my back and pronounced what a good hand I was. He was up a couple hundred when I called him away from the game.

Being the boss' pal extracted a price. It meant I could engage in such robust activities as watching him play cards because I "Was a good luck charm", compete with the pantheons in pool (which cost me all my pocket change), and be the brunt of practical jokes.

While I was bent over, shining a light and talking to Spud as he cleaned out a preload tank, monitoring his safety, I felt something on top my helmet. Turning around, there was Sunshine, gyrating his hips, wearing a big stupid grin. From the strands hanging over my eyes I knew the foreign object was a mop. He was "breeding me", which I instantly thought odd because he was doing so without an audience to impress. I smiled knowingly, guffawed, and pretended to be thrilled by his attention. I grinned and grinned and grinned until he finally left, satisfied I was sufficiently impressed with his wit, leaving me shaken but unbowed.

That was the downside. The upside included getting to hear oilfield stories, such as the one when he escaped Iran after the Ayatollah took over. I found it best to let him initiate and direct the conversations. He wasn't very good at answering questions. Thinking vexed him. Most of his thoughts were stillborn.

Sucking up to him I asked why he thinks the oil patch will eventually fall off. He enlightened me and the puppies who happened to be nearby with the claim that "Companies been giving roustabouts cars. None of them can keep'm going for more than a year." He punctuated his statement with a huge stream of spit, a Jim-sized exhalation of smoke, and a hacking cough.

His introducing me to his favorite dip was touching. Now we could share the same waste-can, be comrades in expectoration. Make a three hundred dollar a day man a few bucks and you get to learn what nausea is all about. The Jenny Craig crowd should try it. It'd cut down their caloric intact, I "garontee."

Having a dip under my lip was like having a fifth of whiskey in my belly. It gave me bed spin. I viewed the world as if through a prism, barely aware of what was happening. There I was cleaning up the mess Heavy Duty made of the Halliburton unit (after he cemented the casing Sunshine said he probably wouldn't set during his hitch).

There I was cleaning the mud pits to prepare them for the change-over of mud systems. There I was in the flowline trying to fix the rig's flow-show paddle. And there I always was, outside the office. My status as plaything did not include access. Sunshine was too territorial to let just anyone inside. He bristled when Blowfly breezed past me as I stood outside, rereading posted company newsletters and memos. If the injured roughneck hadn't hopped into a chair and immediately gone to work I bet he would have been yelled at. Of course, Sunshine just could be a bigot.

If he was, Blowfly didn't mind. The rig scribe had his face buried in paperwork every time I saw him. Whenever I wanted to talk to him I had to lie in wait, corner him when he emerged from his self-imposed sweatshop.

"Checking service hands' tickets, checking memos for spelling and grammar, making sure all forms are filled out right, stuff like that," he enthused, answering my emphatically worded question about what kind of work he did.

"What about Gordon?" I asked.

His masculine features tightened with reproach. He looked as fearsome as Mohammed Ali when asked if he could beat Leon Spinks in a rematch. "All he can do is type; you should see the records, they're a mess. Me getting hurt didn't help me much but it was the best thing to happen to this rig."

But not to me. His conscientiousness kept him in the office, working diligently. When he shared it with Gordon the tension was so palpable I could feel it. It was suffocating when I did tentatively enter. My presence raised both their hackles. They stared daggers at me and, in unison, asked, "What do you want?"

"Just seeing how the intelligentsia work," I said. They allowed me to leave without a scolding.

Having failed so miserably to get anywhere near the files, I did not share everyone else's excitement about the advent of crew change day. I moped around, not even trying to make a final, desperate effort. Mostly I collected material the PIRG people might be interested in: drawing diagrams of pollution curbs on the deck and where drain holes and collection tubs were. A jarring brief attracted my attention. I resisted looking up at the drill floor where the sound originated. I didn't want to be like everyone else. I noticed the door to the paint locker was open. Closing it, a commotion on the floor inadvertently caused me to look up. The kelly had been run to the crown and was pinioned in place by the slips which hugged the tool joint of a collar at the rotary table. I could see Sunshine gesturing wildly at Penny, who just stood his ground, his arm folded, appearing bored.

"You bet I'm not coming back. I run myself off. You know what you can do with your screwed-up hole." I heard the driller say after I joined a few others on the floor. Sunshine was crimson. His eyes bulged. His veins stuck out. He started to move toward Penny but stopped when the much more fit driller clenched both fists.

"Go, Penny!" Kathy shouted from the crane.

The lumbering company man grabbed the telephone. "I won't have anyone getting on his side."

"So run me off, too."

Sunshine stared at the roughnecks. They raced to the slips, to begin a futile struggle. Sunshine then looked at us spectators. We scattered.

I was not surprised when Penny's replacement stepped off the crew basket hours later uttering a steady stream of curses. Having to free the kelly would turn a saint into a sinner.

The browbeaten bunch didn't sound so browbeaten once they got on the crew boat. The driller was hailed as a hero. Nobody liked Sunshine and any act of insubordination was a sign of manhood.

Propped up over the top of his chair, turning his head back toward the rest of us, Turtle couldn't resist pontificating, "A body can be pushed only so far. You can only do your best."

It came out Sunshine had stuck his family jewels in Penny's pocket when the two argued about how to drill.

From the back of the boat, Kathy shouted, "You can do that to me."

Penny whirled around to look at her, longingly. "Thanks for the support. Appreciate it."

"You deserve it." They maintained eye contact as he got up to occupy an adjoining seat. Those in the same row moved over to give them space. The rest of us left them alone, to devote ourselves to post-mortems of the event.

From the middle of the rows, Hammer stood up and surveyed the scene. "That Fontenot had gone to bed ordering Penny to put less weight on the bit and to speed up the rotary. Said that is the way to slow down on how fast we increased the angle the hole was making."

He fondled his knife sheath. "Well was building close to two degrees from vertical every hundred feet."

Although drilling wasn't his department Bull stood up from across the aisle to add his two cents. "Plan on the wall chart called for one and a half degrees of build."

"Putting more weight on the bit and slowing up the rotary like Sunshine wanted makes for more too much build. Have to put some big doglegs in it to get it going in the right direction. The hole would look like a roller coaster. Great way to get the pipe stuck."

Hammer couldn't resist having what he thought was the last say. "Can miss the target."

"Nothing more worthless than a hole in the ground," grumbled Sunny, scrunched up, with his arms crossed in a seat in the back. He had not taken his second margin call as well as he had the first.

Without getting up, Jones spoke loud enough to attract everyone's ear. "Sunshine likes to drill West Texas style. Blowing and going." The electrician then won everyone's respect by prefacing a point he wanted to make by claiming he was a former driller who "had gotten into one too many pissing contests with company men" and changed careers. "Got tired of worrying about my hide. Kicks don't stop people like Sunshine. Just will flare it off as they ram that pipe down. He was a toolpusher, an old-fashioned toolpusher weaned on turnkey jobs." Lighting up a cigarette he kept the floor. "Got paid by the foot, not by whether he did things safely. People like him think safety only costs them money."

"Entire oilfield is on day-rate now. So it doesn't make sense to drill that way," remarked Bull.

Brother-in-law grimaced. "Still isn't right to foul up drilling."

"That extra stabilizer he told Mister Fontenot to run makes it too hard to keep the bit going in the direction you want it to. Blades are too big," said Hammer.

I didn't mention the tool came from Sunshine's yard. And it is policy that if we have one in the hole we have to have a second as a backup.

Near the bow, Heavy Duty tentatively remarked, in his slow monotone, how Sunshine had shoved him off his machine while he was testing the integrity of the casing shoe. "Told me to go home and stay at home until my piss cleared up. He said I didn't know what I was doing. He's the one who didn't know what he was doing. He pressured up all right, but after it broke over it bled way down. Too far down, below what minimum pressure should be., way down."

"Went to zero?" asked Bull. He looked at Hammer. "How could you have let him? You should have demanded we squeeze."

The big toolpusher boyishly shrugged his shoulders. "He's the boss."

"You know that isn't the way to do it," remarked Bull. "Should shut it down when the rate of increase of the p.s.i. Starts to slow. You and I went to the same well-controlled school."

"We were taught right," Hammer affirmed. "I didn't like it."

"You didn't say anything," said Heavy Duty. "You just stood there."

"You know it wouldn't do any good."

Heavy Duty went silent. He rolled his eyes.

Hammer looked desperate. "I had words with him afterward."

"I don't remember you talking to him," said Blowfly.

Hammer scowled. "It was in private."

Gordon spoke up. "They were alone walking up to the crews' quarters."

"That's when I talked to him. Glad someone is not calling me a liar."

Bull wasn't intimidated. "Don't want a weak shoe. We take a kick deeper down and the kill mud we weigh up to will fracture it. Lose returns. Lose hydrostatic. Well, will come in. Could have a surface blowout, being this shallow."

Everyone's face turned ashen.

Hammer stood in the middle of the floor. "Been in a surface blowout out off Indonesia. Shut in the Hydril, made sure the Kelly was above the bushings, set the Kelly cock, and did all we were supposed to do when a well started belching. Then we saw bubbles in the water. The kick blew out at the weakest formation, just below the shoe. Didn't travel up the well bore to the surface, where we could deal with it. The rig started to list. Thought I'd K.M.A.G., kiss my ass good-bye."

"You tell Sunshine that?" asked Bull.

"Some of it, yeah." He went on to describe how the jack-up capsized and disappeared in "what looked like water boiling on a stove. Some fishermen came by opposite us 'n thought better of entering all that white water." He stopped, looked around, saw most were fascinated, and continued. "Been in blowouts before and since, but never been so scared. We were just lucky we got out of there when we did. When I looked back, I knew had we been a little slower the capsule would have sunk like a stone. Water was more air than anything else."

Blowfly scowled. "Sunshine had me write down the leak-off was fourteen pounds on the morning report. Them in the office will think it can hold thirty-five hundred pounds of pressure, which is what he wrote on his report."

It suddenly dawned on everyone. The impossible had happened. There was someone worse than Jim.

Jumping at his chance, Hammer emphatically claimed he was "gonna have some words with that drilling supervisor." He asked Heavy Duty if he was willing to testify for him.

"I guess I couldn't look at myself in the mirror if I didn't." Nobody made a wisecrack. Nor could I spot anyone holding back the urge to make a wisecrack. "I don't want to come back unless there's a good squeeze job to come back to."

Once the mudloggers came aboard the boat pulled away. The debate lost steam in direct relation to how far away from the rig we traveled. People appeared more interested in Kathy's and Penny's snuggling in a corner by the head. All were discreet about their voyeurism; the tryst was so touching. The crew was going home to race stock cars, hunt, fish, and get some of that "poon-tang". No one mentioned all the "honey-dos" they were looking at.

The ride home wasn't calming strictly because the seas were benign. It was calm because of the company I kept, or maybe my new perception of the company I kept. They probably were the same salt of the earth who had worked for Grandfather, the grandsons of those who more than once agreed to work without pay because they trusted him to make good when his finances improved. That spirit that Sid Richardson, Frank Phillip, and Henry Sinclair displayed during the oilfield's infancy and the Robert O. Andersons and T. Boone Pickens display today may be succumbing to the bureaucratic onslaught of petroleum engineers, rule and procedure followers whose purchasing power in giant corporations afforded them unassailable clout. But it is still the hands that make things work. Reports, faxes, and formal visits to the field cannot replace the people who did the drilling, twenty-four hours a day, seven days a week.

If not for this experience I'd be one of those who thought one made hole from an office, knowing the workers only from what was on their job applications and evaluations. I slunk into my chair, realizing how predictable I had been. Realizing how utterly predictable that was, I slunk even deeper into my chair.

CHAPTER 7

I must have dozed off because I awoke with a start when the engines shut down, started again, and we moved backward, stern first into the dock. Noticing the somber demeanor of the crew as they gathered their belongings, I only could ascribe it to their continued concern about the well. A feeling of pride swelled inside me. Maybe I was thrown to the wolves by divine providence. Maybe I'm destined to prove to the PIRG people that most in the oilfield are conscientious and reasonable, working folk and not out to rape mother nature. Maybe this Galatea was destined to become a Pygmalion.

Rather than charging onto the wharf, the crew disembarked orderly, with minimum shouting. Bull and Hammer didn't even swell up at the sight of salesmen. Both walked right by them and ignored their imprecations as they tagged along like ducklings. I noticed the cementer among the following. But he wasn't following. The most direct path to his car happened to coincide with the path the parade was taking. He was one of the first out of the lot. The toolpusher would have followed a short time later, had he had to pry himself from the salesmen. That he followed on his heels proved he ignored them altogether. Both he and Heavy Duty certainly acted like men on a mission.

The sight of Robert was a godsend, and it wasn't just because I found out my car wouldn't start. He was more than my sidekick, my Batman, my guide. He was my regent, someone who would see to my well-being, the only one who cared.

I kept an open mind about his new look. It wasn't too hard.
The cowboy boots and hat he wore were accessories. His big,
expansive face and expressive eyes would have kept him noble-looking
in a clown suit.

"Don't bother even trying to jump-start your car," he said after
we shook hands. "It's the starter. I saw the guy I bought it from had
kept it running the whole time we haggled. Probably worn out. Come
on, get in my new wheels. We'll deal with your heap later if we feel like
it."

He purposely had parked his truck at the far end of the dirt
parking lot. "Thought you'd enjoy walking in a straight line, on solid
ground, with no vibrations."

He had traded up to a four-wheel drive truck we had to climb
into. He also had traded his carousing for competition.

"Joined the Texas Mudslingers. Drove this baby at the Eagle
Speedway in Silsbee and already got her signed up at Speedway Ninety
in Beaumont. Once I learn the ropes, I'm going to buy a funny car, or
maybe a dragster."

On the way to the Shrimper's Lounge to meet up with Eddie, I
received an earful about the sport of racing vehicles through the mud.
In a matter of a few days, he had become an F.E. on the subject.

"The only race I lost was to a guy who thought he'd be cute
and slide across the trench with a high gear ratio and no mudguards."

"Let me guess. Karma has something to do with this," I said.

"His truck went airborne at the finish. Came down front first.
Totaled it."

That the prize money Robert won barely covered the cost of
minor repairs and towing led me to believe his career would be
abbreviated.

The Karma was equally unpromising inside the lounge,
prompting us to decide to leave as soon as we met up with our partner.

Not a bad idea, since the patrons were disgruntled Penrod
hands, temporarily laid off while their rig waited to be picked up for
work by an oil company.

"We had it made," said a dejected hand to an inquisitive barfly.
"Mobil wanted to sign us for a long-term contract at fifty grand a day
off California."

"Leave it to the Hunts," said another, sipping a drink. "Only
anyone who thought they could own all the silver in the world can

think they could get a better deal in the Gulf. Taking out a second mortgage." He shook his head.

I imagined what a dry haul on a heavy lift freighter across the Straits of Magellan cost.

The Johnny Paycheck song "Take this job and shove it" rumbled from the jukebox.

"Got that right," said the spokesman. Instead of scorning his self-pity, I found myself sympathetic toward him. It must be hard to be a pawn, especially one who knew the failings of his employers.

However, wary of my recent experiences, I didn't let my emotions corrupt my good sense. I watched what they ordered. Had it been beer I would have insisted we stand Eddie up and leave. But the solemn bunch ordered whiskey, the brooder's beverage.

Johnny Walker and Jim Beam weren't the only drinks the bartender served. He was adept at mixing tinkled pinks. At least that was what two women announced loud enough for everyone to hear. Announcing it for a second time succeeded in attracting the company. For a plethora of reasons the several who made moves toward them were winnowed down to two, who monopolized their attention.

That was two more than the number who harkened to another woman who walked in. Ravishing in leggy blue jeans and silken tresses she inexplicably was left alone.

"Hooker," whispered Robert. "No real man would admit he has to pay for it. And if she isn't, someone that hot would reject everyone who isn't an Adonis."

Not being an Adonis didn't deter Eddie, who made a beeline for her the moment he entered. Sitting regally in her chair she sniffed at his effrontery. In response, he just shrugged his narrow shoulders and marched off.

"It's her loss," he said, putting the defeat out of mind. His leathery face spouted a spider's web of cracks and fissures. "That capo I know, he said his under is interested in buying your old man's pipe yard, expand his business.

"Launder his money?"

"After me and my hypodermic needle made both of them a fortune on a long shot they started listening to me."

"You told him how wise it would be to vertically integrate his drilling operations?" I asked.

"I told him he could get it on the cheap. I didn't tell him I made sure the Feds took pictures while I was doing him a favor and saw to it they tested the horse."

"I hope you're careful," was all I could say. *He probably has forgotten more about the mob than I'll ever know,* I thought.

Robert reached out to shake his hand. "Got that right. I salute you, for putting one over on someone like him. You've got more guts than I'll ever have." He ordered a beer for him. The little guy leaned back in his chair, satisfied.

"Bet he'll run it better than the receivers ran it," I said, trying to change the subject. "What does a bank know about running a business?"

Eddie did not want to change the subject. After a mighty quaff, he remarked how good he now had it. "I'm his hot walker. Introduced me to some of his women. Weird how things work?"

If you have balls as big as Baltimore, I thought.

"Saw some of our fellow conscripts from the pipe yard," Robert informed us. "Interested in making good their threats to get back at those who cheated us."

"What do you mean expressed an interest?"

"You know, sue for back wages, testify, go to the papers."

"What will that underboss have to say about that?"

Robert looked at me incredulously. "What do you mean? He'll love it. Great publicity. Shows he's honest and cares for his people."

Our vibrancy attracted attention. Showing remarkable chutzpah, two professional types, in off-the-rack suits appeared above us, their body language kinetic with the urge to lavish us with attention. The one wearing expensive cuff links had to be a scout. They always were pretentious. I decided to pay more attention to his mannerisms than what he said. I know the spiel. How to plumb people for information was a skill they were particularly adept at. He leaned into my space to show interest, managed all the right inflections of voice, showed concern, and interest, and even laughed at my lame jokes. His partner watched. I didn't pay much attention to him, until I waited for a pause to extend my hand to the alpha male to say, "It's nice to have met you." The subordinate male's face turned ashen. His mentor was more sanguine. He forcefully shook my hand and started asking about me, hoping to get me to overturn my decision. But I didn't forget my decision and eventually worked up the nerve to turn my back on him.

Being as decorous as I expected, he thanked me and left. Even from behind I noticed he kept his composure. That he did not engage anyone else indicated we had that special something, and that it wasn't even worth trying to solicit information from anyone else.

The next "suit" to home in on us was a lawyer. He wasn't as discriminating as the scouts. We were the third group he talked to. Even so, he made the mistake of trying to flatter us. Flattery is as foreign in the oilfield as going to the opera, reading Kurt Vonnegut, or refraining from claiming you service the wives of the crew who is on the rig while you are ashore. Still, I found his request to be contacted whenever someone suffered an injury not altogether disgusting. Marble ought to be sued. Keeping hurt people on the rig to prevent LTAs is criminal. I referred him to Blowfly.

We finished our drinks during a medley of songs from the ex-cons of the country: Waylon Jennings, Merle Haggard, Johnny Cash, Willie Nelson, and David Allan Coe. The sounds of Bosephus escorted us out the door.

"A pale imitation of his old man," griped Robert, "Wish he'd gag on his silver spoon."

"Did you hate me for my silver spoon?" I asked.

"Never."

"Why not?"

"Because I knew you were destined to have it shoved down your throat."

Someone so brutally honest elicits confidence. I had no qualms about his returning to Silsbee after taking us into the city. I was sure he'd make out fine. With his pager, his survey company could reach him anywhere.

I'm sure Eddie will do fine too. We watched him "high-five" several employees at the gate of the Fairgrounds. We drove off as he was invited into a high-roller's limo.

I asked Robert to drop me off at Tulane, where I could regain my bearings. The sandstone buildings consoled me and centered me. They were the repositories of knowledge, factories of intellectual pursuit, uncontaminated by tripe and ephemera.

Near the science building, I passed a gaggle of belles in boleros and peplums paying homage to a wit wearing a half shirt. Joe Comedian delighted them with a joke only a little more refined than typical rig fare. Inside the building, the first person I saw was a student paying rapt attention to an elderly professor. From the elder's mellifluous tone of voice, he was patiently explaining a point the youth did not understand. That's what school should be, an island of knowledge and intellectual aspiration in a sea of arrogant ignorance and visceral pursuits. I wafted through the halls, not caring I wasn't wearing a disguise. I ogled profs and teaching assistants, peered into labs and lecture halls, and waited outside one classroom until it let out.

Leslie didn't see me. Cradling her textbooks, she exited in a fog of concentration, staring straight ahead. Nor did she notice me following her. I made sure of that.

It took ten minutes to compose a note to her, and two days to rewrite it. It wasn't half bad, explaining everything in an apologetic tone. I surprised myself, showing myself, I might have a career at Hallmark.

I purposely broke the law putting the letter directly into her mailbox. Any act of insurrection against a government that could shackle my industry with the Windfall Profits Tax and Byzantine regulations was all right by me. Time never dragged so slowly. It wasn't helped when Eddie started dating a stable girl half his age. Hearing them go at it through the thin walls of our apartment precipitated bouts of self-pity. Despite trying not to, I found myself jealous of their pillow talk, pining for romance and (I hated to admit it) to be understood.

I should be glad for my bro. He certainly knew how to make the best of a precarious situation. A mind is a funny thing. It can deduce what is the right way to act yet fail to make you act that way. Despite my self-awareness, each night I tossed and turned, awoke in fits of envy, and had to fight the urge to call Leslie at two, four, and six in the morning.

When I did call her, my voice must have sounded demonic, like Jack Nicholson's. Hers was soft, compelling, in a Miss Magnolia Sweetheart way. It's amazing how much Southern women hone their art. I swallowed hard when I took the plunge and identified myself.

"I knew who it was," she said.

"Why didn't you hang up?"

"Why should I?"

"You know what I did," I said.

"You know what I did."

"What do you mean?" I held my breath during a protracted pause.

"I asked for it. That's why I got so mad at you. I was as wrong as you."

"It hurt you more," I shouted.

She started to cry. "You can't imagine. But just because I was hurt doesn't mean I'm the only victim." Then she said something that stunned me. "Should I get sympathy for being hit by a car because I played in the street?"

"It wasn't your fault. You were feeling no pain."

"I hate that! I hate how everyone excuses their behavior because they are drunk. It's repulsive, hideous. I hate it!"

"Why the rebellion?" I asked her in the beer joint in the basement of the U.C. The dank atmosphere and dim lights provided the perfect ambiance for confessions.

"It wasn't right for me to blow up at you. I didn't mean to." She sucked the head off her beer. "I do those sorts of things, and it took a while for me to figure out why."

I let her take her time composing herself.

"I felt so bad after screaming at you. The last time I was so mad was when someone I knew received a scholarship I wanted, even though I had better grades and played piano better."

I did not want to know how she responded psychologically, though it wasn't hard to figure out.

"My first reaction was one of hate. What had happened wasn't fair and it wasn't just my opinion. I only pretended to agree it was time her kind got a chance. I smiled, hugged her, and bragged about her, all the while I hated her. She was so proud, so smug. Everyone was so happy for her." She knocked back a good slug. "I vowed I'd never be such a phony again. And there I was, doing it again, pretending everything was wonderful until I saw how they treated you, and not for what you did. They didn't care what you did. You could have killed me, and they wouldn't have cared. They wanted to hurt you because of what happened to you. And I was expected to stay a mannequin, with a smile painted on my face. That is my lot in life, to end up selecting another phony as my knight in shining armor."

From the ease she recited her speech I could tell she often had mulled it over, refined it, and was anxious to air it by the time I had called.

"I was your reality check?"

"It hurt to see you. You were everything that was loathsome, evil, monstrous. That's why I didn't recognize you. I had turned you into a caricature. To see you young, healthy, handsome was more than I could bear. You were supposed to be ugly, deformed, someone who deserved to be punished to do what you did to me. "She finished her beer and wiped her mouth with a napkin. "Anything that didn't fit my fake world had to be ugly and evil. It couldn't be that my fake world was ugly and evil."

"You recognized me even with the disguise I wore last time," I said.

She stared straight into my eyes. "What disguise?"

She calmed down over a Pina Colada. "Put me in a church and I'm a nun. Put me in a frat house and I'm whatever the actives want me to be."

"A chameleon?"

"I don't even exist. I am whatever I'm supposed to be." She stirred the swizzle stick in her drink. "I now know how people could let dictators' rule, like my political science teacher said."

She launched into a philippic about the sick dynamics of her home life. I didn't need to listen to affect the right facial expressions and body language. I knew the scenario, it being old and banal since I could remember. Social climbing mothers and workaholic fathers is the staple of American literature, and rife among the upper class. I should know. My real Mother can't put two sentences together without one of them including a criticism of Father. But that's not quite fair. I'm sure she's still hacked about her settlement. The oil boom took off long after the divorce.

The dysfunctional family is as American as apple pie, debouching upon the land a generation of neurotic hordes of psychiatrists feed upon.

"All I ever do is try to keep everything from blowing up, keep everybody happy." She squeezed my hand and looked as if she were about to cry. I fumbled through my pockets for notes I took while on the rig, hoping she'd appreciate them. I never expected they would thrill her.

Her face exploded with excitement. "This is totally fair. I'll make sure the Sierra Club sees the good with the bad." She ran an index finger over my diagram of the welder's modifications. "I'll show them this before I'll show them any of your complaints. Miss Geniality is no more. It doesn't matter who wants her to march in lockstep. She's not going to do it"

Her enthusiasm was infectious, something I needed to feed off. Like Emerson said, nothing of consequence is accomplished without enthusiasm. She had enough for the both of us. What had engendered it, I don't know, certainly more than just getting a "C" in math like last time. I only hope she's not manic depressive.

Her eyes blazed at my suggestion she conduct a scavenger hunt for the magazines Dennis requested.

Her expression obliterated the femininity her made-up face and coifed hair projected. "That'll fit into my plans perfectly."

Her plans blew me away. Starting with the Chi Sigma house, where I had seen back issues of "Foot Fetishes" and "Monster Jugs", she and several underage buddies were going to allow themselves to indulge in the frats' hospitality and take all evidence back to the Public Interest Research Group.

"It's payback time," snarled one voluptuous collaborator, Dorothy Goldstone. "They're going to drown in the alcohol they give us." I didn't know what had lit her fire. I didn't want to know.

Her two sisters-in-arms displayed equal venom. But without Dorothy's accouterments, they looked more like reformers should look like, androgynous, with close-cropped hair, and wearing slacks. Their peaches and cream complexions were their only concessions to pulchritude.

"We're going to get even, real even," Dorothy seethed.

"Somebody has to," said Mary, one of the short hairs.

I left when the experiences they started to compare began to sound like atrocities.

Considering how worked-up they got I expected to see four Joan-of-Arcs in full battle gear, ready to storm the parapets come next morning. I did not expect to see four giggly air-heads wearing tight skirts, chest hugging blouses, and, in two cases, thick long wigs. Nor did I expect to hear the nasally twang their voices affected. I had no idea women could be such actresses. From the bushes I marveled at how flippant they could be, acting like women frats hope women act like. I also marveled at how gullible the Greeks could be. They knew the girls, knew how they normally acted. Apparently, all intelligence and rationality disappear when it looks as if one of them might get lucky. It also is apparent the female avengers know it.

Maybe some of the injuries guys suffered when they were tackled during Derby Day or in coed football games weren't accidents.

The actives who invited them in were instantly smitten. The simpers which sprouted on their faces were so smug, I was thrilled Miss Payback preserved them on film. The only piece they were going to get was a piece of the Chancellor's mind.

For my benefit, the girls teased their would-be seducers with hugs and suggestive body language in front of the windows. Judging from the touchy-feely relationship they established, a lot of sexual innuendoes and plain trash were being aired.

The silhouettes became chummier with each window they passed. Flash bulbs lit up each toast. The entire show was delicious, including the departure. Like real troopers, the Rockettes danced offstage, kissing and hugging their suitors, leaving them dying for more.

"I hope I have made you as excited as you made me," Dorothy declared, holding her booty and her camera overhead.

"This has made my day," she claimed, stumbling on to the portico of a second frat house.

"Don't forget me!" wailed an active hanging out a window at a third house.

"Don't worry. I'll remember you." She drunkenly tripped over the curb.

We had to restrain her from visiting a fourth house. Luckily, she was so wasted she believed us when we told her we couldn't buy more film late at night.

Our hung-over Carrie Nation didn't call off the next day's siege until five citadels of sin were incriminated. My collection of porn magazines was nearly complete.

She was stone sober when she made good her pledge to remember the lovelorn suitor. She made a point to mention the third house to the *Times-Picayune.* The firebrand on the education beat ran with the story. She had it in for the boy's clubs and all things unrelated to higher learning.

Had Patty Green's articles appeared in the "Sports" section rather than the "Living" section, the brothers would have thrown up on effigies of her as they did of Roselyn Carter. If the truth is known, I had previously known of her only through her scathing diatribes of the football coach.

Armed and dangerous, she struck with so much virulence, that underage drinking became a *cause celebre*. Pictures of the would-be Lotharios looking drunk and pathetic appeared on the news. One of the authors depicted a no-nonsense reformer. Her steely eyes and military haircut advertised someone to reckon with.

A tragedy at an Ivy League fraternity party catapulted the event into a spotlight the frats couldn't hide from. From Sunday morning when the preppy died during a hazing incident to Friday evening, the major networks dwelled on the dangers of overindulgence. Mention of the Tulane scandal sparked a local outcry. All the guilty houses were put on notice.

"We kicked some ass," gloated Dorothy during an early morning debriefing at the University Center.

Leslie plopped her head on her hands. "It was all over drinking, not anything else they do," she sighed. "They still violate people."

"And cheat in school," said one of the two less demonstrative conspirators. "Have tests on file."

Leslie lifted her head. "What's the big deal about drinking anyway? It's the least of their sins if it's a sin at all. Half the world allows its young to drink. A teenager can get a drink in any bar in town."

"It's still better than nothing," I remarked. "The thing is, we've got them on the ropes with it, and unless I'm a terrible judge of character, Miss Green will keep the heat on until one of them loses a charter and she wins a journalism award. Look at what she did to Lindy Infante."

I stroked her hair, saying, "You're not alone in this. Don't forget that. I've got nothing to lose and have all the reason in the world to see this through."

She squeezed my hand. "I've got nothing to lose either. Father is a member of the Boston Club, so no matter what happens, I'll have all the status I can stand."

She was right. It didn't faze Father when a member he was doing business with went bankrupt. The club provided the ultimate safety net.

She took another sip, paused, then exploded.

"It's just the sex. Always the sex." Leslie's angelic face contorted with despair. "What are we? Receptacles?"

It turned out she just had returned from a visit to a girlfriend who had attempted suicide while I was away on the rig. She had attempted suicide after being fondled by an assemblyman. "She had to quit waitressing."

"No witnesses stood up for her?" I asked.

"If only they were that repulsive," her voice choked with emotion. "They accused her of lying."

"Did she protest to her union?" asked Dorothy with rising passion.

"She sure did and couldn't get another job. The doctors said if I hadn't rushed her to the hospital, she would have...have...died." The arm I put around her calmed her. "I was there when her stomach was pumped. Would that public official want her if he saw the mess, if he smelled it?"

"Men think we're just life support systems for our vaginas," said Dorothy, looking so alluring I could see how she became prejudiced. I couldn't bring myself to tell her what the oilfield thought. But I did conjure the most empathetic look I could muster.

"It's nice to know we have an ally," said Cathy, the fourth conspirator.

As if she knew what was coming Leslie put her hand on mine and pressed down when Dorothy began to speak.

"You know you can be a great help," the alpha female announced.

Before she went further, I feinted protest but found the hand that conveyed affection suddenly conveyed caution. How else could I explain its placement over my mouth? I quickly appreciated the gesture. If it wasn't there, I might have honestly answered her question about why I wanted the magazines...which would have led to further questions I could do without.

"He would have said it was my idea," Leslie explained. "It was his."

"Anyone who could think of such a great diversion is someone we need," continued Dorothy. "It showed you know how those spoiled rich kids think."

I hesitated to answer.

"Don't be modest. It's a talent as if you were one of them."

"They're not hard to figure out," I sheepishly said.

"Then you'll continue to help?"

I nodded and was completely taken off guard when Dorothy hugged me. So much for being able to determine character.

Leslie followed suit when we were alone. "You can do anything you put your mind to," she said emphatically.

"Why the confidence?" I asked.

"Because you don't quit."

It hadn't occurred to me that what I was doing was noble. I elicited their help for selfish reasons. It would be inexcusable for me not to lend a hand. Figuring out how to punish the frats might prove palliative. If I succeed, I might be emboldened enough to try loftier goals, such as enticing Russia to tear down the Berlin Wall, feed Ethiopia, or maybe convince Southerners Yankees aren't all that bad.

Nietzsche would be proud of me, for taking on several projects simultaneously. I have to admit, though, I wish I could just prove Father innocent. It's not because I miss my old life. I know if he's cleared, we'll again prosper. It'll be fun starting from scratch. If only he'd return my calls, tell me he'd like me to visit.

The cafeteria grew crowded. Conversations rose above the clanging of cutlery and flatware. Of those decipherable most piqued my interest.

Sitting close to me, a fresh-faced coed exclaimed to a friend how she was looking forward to working with the squatters of Mexico City. Her friend countered with an equally noble quest in San Salvador.

I felt good about that. And I felt good about not dismissing them as hopeless Major Barbaras. Maybe I can thank Dennis for my lack of cynicism. His being so odious.

It's much better not to view everything through dingy glasses or to wear earplugs. I want to see what I look at and hear what I listen to.

My companions joined me eavesdropping on an alumnus telling his former classmates, "Don't believe anything you hear. Forget journalism. Use your position on the "Hullabaloo" to get a job in advertising. Make ten times stretching the truth for a living than reporting." He went on to gloat about how his townhouse appeared on national TV during a presidential speech.

Then he made the mistake of asking me for the time.

"One a.m.," I replied.

The brat's face screwed up in perplexity.

"Hey, don't believe anything you hear," I said.

For a college-educated ad-man, his epithets were no more imaginative than those aired on the rig. Then again, the plaudits from my bunch weren't much better. Neither side improved after I remarked, "Now I know why ads are so banal."

"That was putting him in his place," Dorothy later asserted. "This school teaches greed and materialism."

"No, it doesn't," offered Cathy Landman, our youngest, shortest, and feistiest conspirator. "It refines it. Being greedy and materialistic is a prerequisite. Like high S.A.T. scores."

I asked for her compact.

"What do you see?" I asked, showing her her seraphic reflection in the mirror. "Appearances are not what they seem. Believe me!"

I could feel Leslie staring at me. Turning, I didn't expect to be consumed in the glow of an enchanting gaze. It was kind of embarrassing.

Her smile rendered me mute and stupid. I didn't know how to respond. I was afraid of responding. I couldn't say anything intelligent. She turned up the wattage of her smile and, when it was as intense as possible, she planted a kiss on my cheek.

CHAPTER 8

Late the next day I mounted my Rosinante (actually, Robert's pickup. He was laid-up, nursing injuries) and sallied forth. Instead of a naysayer to object to my third adventure like the niece who objected to Don Quixote's third adventure my Antonia had blessed me with all the encouragement in the world.

Leslie was the stuff of my daydreams en route to the dock. Thoughts of her mollified my disappointment we were to take a boat instead of a helicopter offshore. She also was the stuff of a real dream once I found a place to lie down on the boat. Visions of her were on my mind when Spud kicked the pillowcase full of magazines I was using as a headrest.

Although groggy, I couldn't mistake his not-so-subtle nod in the direction of a well-dressed professional. As my eyes adjusted to the dark, I thought I was still dreaming. The "dude" was Eugene Winetrob, a boarding school legend. Perpetually kicked out and reinstated, he had won kudos for mooning the admissions officer, for baptizing most of the local fountains with detergent, and for his gatoring. A card *nonpareil*, it was rumored he kept in his wallet the short hairs of a notorious Vassar coed and a frigid Jesus freak. As part of Pine Manor's lore, I recognized him from all the pictures taken of him and the likeness on the prize he inspired.

But that was then. This is now. Stiff and uncomfortable in his Brooks Brothers suit, he hardly looked like someone who'd be nominated for his eponymous award. A winner of the Eugene Winetrob sobriquet would be on top of the situation, cool, confident, not cowering in a corner, as subdued as Sambo. All inclination to introduce myself faded the longer I looked at him. His soft hands, manicured nails, shined shoes, and immaculate hair triggered a primal reaction in me, making me wonder if I wasn't becoming prejudiced.

A pencil popped up behind Spud's couch. "What's that stink?" he asked loud enough for most to hear. "Smells like a dead skunk."

"Chaps cologne," I said. It was what most at Pine Manor favored. "Perfume for men."

A few sniffs of approval I heard were tantamount to a high five by any of Eugene's circle, which was until recently, my circle. It was a sect it now occurred to me I no longer would want to return to. Not that I fit into my present environment. But I certainly was closer to it than Eugene's. His is one whose denizens never get their fingernails dirty and whose view of the world is distorted by the tinted office windows they hide behind. He is what I would have become had I become a Chi Sigma, a gatoring, mooning, business student craving to become a big shot. How far I had strayed from the superior example Grandfather had set scared me.

"I'd be ashamed to take home my paycheck if I did what he does," remarked Spud.

Eugene stood up and affected the persona of the wise-acre comic. "It's a tough job but somebody has to do it."

"What do you call a carload of lawyers at the bottom of a lake?" asked Turtle. "A start."

Returning to his seat did prove Eugene had the intelligence to know when to retire. Staying out of sight proved he could retain the presence of mind to withstand the verbal fusillade intended to goad him into popping up again. What he was doing here titillated everyone's curiosity. Why he hadn't taken a helicopter added to the mystery. Only when it was obvious we weren't going to find out did Mamou the Weenie Washer end the futility with a little levity.

The oversized elf stood up and announced he once had dealings with an attorney. "But it didn't do much good. They speak a different language than us working folks."

"He asked me if I had any grounds.

"'I say 'yes.' I have thirty acres.

"'No,' he says. 'What I mean, do you have a case?'

"'No sir,' I said. 'I got a John Deere, that's what I farm them thirty acres with.'

"'No, no,' he says. 'You're not understanding me. Do you want to bring a suit? Have you got a grudge?'

"'Well,' I says. 'I've got a suit hanging home in the closet, and the grudge, that's where I keep my John Deere.'

"He says, 'We're not communicating at all. Let's talk about your wife for a minute. Do you beat your wife up?'

"'Nope,' I say. 'She gets up about four-thirty, 'bout the same time I do.'

"'No, no,' he says. 'Is she a nagger?'

"'No,' I said. 'But that last kid of ours was. That's the reason I want the divorce.'"

"Doctors speak our language better," claimed Spud, adding to the gag. "My nephew asked our family doctor how long it takes for his wife to have a baby. 'First one, no telling. After that, count on nine months.'"

Eugene remained silent and I assumed still. I assumed because I had been told how hyper he used to be, always moving some part of his body, always making noise, and being the center of attention. And I didn't see any of that.

My memory (and new, low, assessment of him) didn't fail me. His coifed head popped right up when the motorman abruptly ended his uncharacteristic silence with a story rife with the possibilities of financial rewards. Popcorn's account of what his counterpart did on the opposite hitch almost got Eugene salivating.

The oil patch veteran erupted with the pent-up urge to talk. "He beat the hell out of Jim when that fat companyman replaced him with his kin."

The dressed-for-success frat brother glowed with dreams of a fat fee for prosecuting an assault and battery case.

"Don't even think about it," said the electrician to him. "I heard all about it. That chickenshit company man won't press charges, not after what the guy threatened to do to him once he got out of prison."

"That's extortion!" Eugene was livid.

That was nothing, as the crew soon let him know. They did so because they enjoyed seeing him stiffen with fear at what was to them ordinary behavior. I enjoyed watching him "lock up" as much as I enjoyed the stories almost everyone aired about what scofflaws their kind were. Rushing off to live in the woods when things got out of hand was nothing to them. It certainly didn't warrant bulging eyes and upraised hackles. I thought it was great. Finding out there were people not cowed by civilization was ambrosia to me. I never knew how much I craved to hear about it, proving how much being thoroughly socialized must have weighed upon me. The story Popcorn aired about the half-Indian, half-black Red Bones who lived on the Red River magnified our respective emotions, though mine weren't on display. Popcorn broke out laughing at Eugene's trembling lips when he said they never paid taxes or owned a social security number. But it was Eugene's babbling that precipitated laughter so loud it served to bring the hopelessly socialized intruder to his senses. Realizing he was making a spectacle out of himself he tried to redeem himself by insisting, "Those people need to be punished."

"People like them been known to kill folks who messed with their crab traps," said Spud.

Spouting some legal jargon Eugene redirected the conversation back to Jim.

"What I guess he means is there's still a case if witnesses come forward to testify," I translated in a sarcastic tone of voice.

Turtle popped up like a jack-in-the-box to convey the unlikelihood of that event. "We'd all like to knock Jim back to the bank," he said.

"But for my rodeo injury, I would have," claimed Tar Baby.

"How about a nice Hawaiian punch?" said the welder.

Eugene had no retort. Looking around at the sincere faces and probably assuming those he couldn't see were equally sincere he again sat down and shut up, this time for good, demonstrating a talent he could use reading juries.

Ruminating over the affair kept us quiet for a while. We took naps to pass away more time. But a couple of hours staying tied to the dock, swatting gnats and sweating like pigs started to grate on us, particularly when the boat skipper informed us, that we were waiting on the new mud engineer. "Was called hours ago. Only lives in Lafayette."

We were in no mood to be trifled with. And had we been trifled with; the perpetrator would have been in deep trouble. But we weren't trifled with. We were steamrolled.

"I'm here; you can go now," the out-of-shape provocateur announced upon arrival. He dropped his bags in the middle of the aisle slapped Dirty Dan's long legs and threatened to sit on them had the lanky derrick hand not pulled them down and slid over, relinquishing a couple of seats at the last second. His failure to protest was suspicious. Something was going on I wasn't privy to.

No one took him to task for bragging about the good night's sleep he got before hitting the road. "Can't sleep a wink on a boat." Nor did anyone reprove him for gloating about the misfortune that allowed him to replace Sunny. "Flew up to Chicago after his fourth margin call to find out what was going on. Found out what happens when you try to run with the big dogs, especially when they're all Yankees. They'll put it to one of us every chance they get." He eased into the seats Dirty Dan vacated.

"The other option holders got together to squeeze Sunny," I explained to Turtle.

"Like a bookie who makes sure all the odds add up in his favor," he responded.

"Something like that."

Why Eugene traveled with us rather than being flown out ASAP remained puzzling. Once we arrived at the rig, we knew he didn't represent Springer Oil. If he had Jim would have greeted him. Instead, he was bundled inside the rec. Room for a safety briefing like any new arrival. Nor did Jim greet him after he emerged to stow his gear in his room. Eugene had to initiate their meeting. By all reports he stayed in the office for the length of time it took to be subjected to the companyman's patent spiel about who was the boss and what was expected of third-party personnel. But it wasn't until he set about numbering and taking pictures of the steps on the starboard side of the crews' quarters was the mystery solved. Unfortunately for me, it was on Dennis' behalf. He had fallen them.

The B. and R. hand had refused to go in, be patched up, and then sent back to perform make-work, to avoid another Lost Time Accident charged against the rig. He had stayed ashore and hired a lawyer.

"Ain't going after Workman's Comp," Jim announced at dinner. "Said he'd sue for a million. I would."

"Can Springer Oil afford it?" asked Blowfly.

"Lloyds of London is the most prestigious insurance company in the world. Handles all of the big companies in the oilfield, those good enough to qualify." As usual, he punctuated his profundity with a bit of business. This time he blew the most voluptuous smoke rings I had ever seen, a dozen of them, each perfectly symmetrical.

My bemusement over Jim's stunt only temporarily suspended the funk I fell into upon not only finding out Dennis was gone but also the apparent failure of Hammer and Heavy Duty to follow through on the vow they made at the end of the last hitch. Neither they nor anyone else did anything. Call it childish but I couldn't resist taking my frustration out on Eugene.

Standing over him as he assayed his demeaning labors I asked if he enjoyed his job. He turned to look at me. "Who'd ever have thought a Eugene Winetrob would deign to perform such a pedestrian task," I said. His face screwed up into a question mark. "Had you known what passing the bar would require of you you'd probably have passed by a bar before the ink was dry on your license." I ducked inside the crew's quarters without seeing his reaction.

Out of curiosity, I checked out the LTA sign. The number "3" looked out of place. I was so used to seeing a three-digit number for the number of days since the last incident. The crew was only a few days shy of winning coveralls for avoiding the blemish for two years.

Come the next meal the topic ceased commanding everyone's attention, it being so frustrating. But, blind to the general sentiment, Jim edified us by stating how Dennis had a good case. "I told that toolpusher to lay down new strips." He inhaled a self-satisfied drag. "Once ran a contractor off when a floor hand threatened to sue after being slapped by a broken line. That toolpusher didn't change it like I said. That's why ya gotta nag, and check things out for yourself. The best boss is a hands-on boss.

"I checked the condition of my equipment each day I worked floors. That was in the days when the derricks were made of wood and the men made of iron. Had to be; there was no such thing as roustabouts then. We did it all, from the water table to the cellar. Didn't name those break-out and make-up tongs we worked with Pete and Maude after two famous mules for nothing." He stopped for another Herculean drag.

"Saw three-floor hands working chain tongs on our floor. I used to work them by myself like they were designed."

Mitch's peach-faced replacement innocently asked what an old-fashioned water table was. His quizzical look was utterly guileless. Rather than tell the novice it once cooled drill line from the top of the derrick and was now a synonym for the "crown", the "chickenshit" (as Jones called him) company man scowled and reproved the tyro for being so ignorant.

The fresh-faced recent graduate quivered as badly as Eugene before him, probably also wondering what he had gotten himself into.

Blowing smoke in Jim's face, Mister Fontenot launched into a story of his own. "I go back ways too; done some mighty impressive things."

Jim sniffed.

"Like when I entered the spinning chain contest they had in Midland." Imitating Jim, he too took a humongous drag. "Eased right up to the line, planted my feet just right, and let go. That chain wrapped around the pipe like it was magnetized. Six times below the tool joint. I can still hear the crowd; they hadn't seen--or heard of--someone wrapping that thing six times on one throw. The judges ended the contest right there and then, with maybe a dozen contestants to go. Nobody minded; they knew they'd never in a million years hope to do what I did. So, besides the usual seventeen-inch gold chain, I loaded a miniature derrick, Kelly and all, into my flatbed. Mayor said he'd rather see it on my lawn than in front of city hall." He winked at the mudlogger.

Jones piped up before Jim could respond (busy as he was chewing half a slice of pecan pie). "That's strange, 'cause that's what he said when he presented the city's miniature pumping jack to me for winning the next year." The electrician synchronized a big exhalation with the directional drillers to envelop Jim in smoke. "Comes in handy when I ask for loans; can play-act Billy Sol Estes with the bankers, let them think I've got oil on my property."

Unfazed, Jim blustered Oz-like from within the smoke, jumping from accolade to accolade he thought he received despite being ignored. When the other conversations finally ended he was exalting his talents at geology, claiming he told what lithology the bit drilled by the taste of the mud. "Knew them mudloggers missed the top of the Cotton Valley on the last Tuscaloosa Trend I worked. The limestone is tangy. Have trained my tongue like a wine taster trains his taste buds like a doctor trains his ears."

The phone rang. The moment he turned to get it we scattered like cockroaches caught in a sudden light. Only Dennis' replacement lingered and as we expected, he was caught in Jim's ambit when the ogre emerged from his office.

"Poor guy," I said, peeking out the rec. room.

"I don't trust that guy," said Dave, the mudlogger who took Mitch's place. "He reminds me of the druggies from school who burglarized dorms to pay for their habit."

"Playing peek-aboo?" asked the subject of our conversation, freed by another phone call Jim had to answer. I noticed pustules on the corner of his obscenely red lips. *Could he have Herpes?* I wondered. *If he's as debauched as Dennis maybe I can use him.*

I tentatively asked him how long he had been aboard. He straightened and looked directly at me. "Flew me right out. Marble knows who it needs." His beady eyes glowed.

"Finally, getting someone competent," I less tentatively said.

"I'm the best."

"All the better," I affirmed.

He put his arm around me. "I didn't expect anyone on the rig to know what they got." He looked at David.

"Sometimes you get surprised," said the novice, showing more savvy than I suspected.

Bob wrapped his free arm around David and motioned toward the exit. I nodded my approval and encouraged him to led us to his room, where we found out he just wanted someone to pay homage to his ego. Where I once stood in the sanctuary of an eccentric, I now stood in the midden of a slob. The detritus was a reflection of a mind consumed with himself, not some arcane metaphysics. The wastrel inundated David and I with a celebration of himself, from how he wooed the fair sex to how he impressed the hoi polloi (which he intimated included us).

Wrapping "a fifty around a roll of ones" and putting "all your money in the bank 'n make sure your lady sees your A.T.M. receipt" were two tips he boasted of. He stressed the importance of keeping one's shoes shine, claiming "it's the best way I know of showing you've got class." He tried to impress us with other ruses, but I wasn't listening. Neither apparently was David, as he soon excused himself, claiming he needed to attend to urgent business in his trailer. Terrified of being left alone, I insisted he had promised me a tour before we went back to work.

"Attitudes and money. They're the secret," Bob said in parting.

"Mind if I hide my wallet in your unit?" I asked David when we were safely away.

"Be my guest."

Maybe bouncing off one blocked door would lead me into an open door, I thought. The mudloggers did enjoy access to the sacred room when they turned in reports, faxed, and talked to the companyman.

The interior of the trailer above the shakers looked nothing like its exterior. The mud and rust belied the gleaming racks of the state-of-the-art technology. The minicomputers, printers, monitors, catalytic gas detectors, electronic panels, pneumatics, and their chromatograph were dazzling.

The Iranian didn't acknowledge me. He was busy looking at cuttings under a microscope in the third of the unit dedicated to investigating the pieces of rocks the drill bit cut and mud transported to the surface.

"Intimidated?" asked David as he entered behind me.

"No, impressed."

He was in his element. "This place energizes me. I don't agree with my coworkers who call it an outpatient clinic, built by tradesmen, and run by robots. It's a testimony to man's ingenuity to me."

The enthusiasm the mudlogger manifested during my visit was infectious.

"Computers are the way of the future," I said, adjusting the brightness of a monitor.

"That's for certain. All the readings from our sensors are beamed off a meristat satellite to Dallas and New Orleans."

"So we don't need Jim?" I asked.

"Maybe if the phones are down, or during an emergency."

"Glorified clerks?"

"More like airplane pilots."

"Until they accept that, they won't be screwing up the hole in power plays," I remarked as I fingered the ultraviolet box.

His shoulders sagged. "Yeah, I hoped I had seen the last of egomaniacs in school. I kind of guessed why he didn't want us to put sensors in the cement unit or in the hopper. The office has to trust Jim's word about how the cementing went." He reached for the changeover notes Mitch had left. "Says here we used Lost Circulation Material instead of cement on the third squeeze job we eventually did." He read the message verbatim. "'The carbide bomb we dropped proved the hole was half again washed out. But Jim insisted the turbulent flow around the collars caused it to come up late. He only added twenty-five percent more cement than calculated.' Standard safety measure," David informed me before continuing.

"'Surprise, surprise, the squeeze held for a fraction of a second when we pressured up.'"

"Wouldn't spend the money on Class 'H' cement," I said. "Using nut plug, walnut shells, and mica, is stuff that'll appear on the mud bill, not on the Halliburton ticket. He can look good saving a few thousand dollars."

He offered me a stick of gum. "Thought he'd have a stroke when he caught me copying the cementer's report. Now I know why. It's not 'top secret', you know. Need the information for the final well report Springer expects. It's part of the package our salesman sold them."

I informed him of other "Jimisms" and a few "Sunshineisms" I had witnessed.

He read more of the changeover notes. "'Sunshine said he'd wipe his ass before he'd sign our monthly job ticket. I told him he'd have to make sure his mark got through all three copies. He eventually signed."

"Sunshine and Jim must be birds of a feather."

An affirmative encouraged me to ask if he would be up for a little revenge.

The Iranian turned from the tests he was conducting to volunteer, "He had no right to speak to me the way he did when I asked him to fix the television set."

"You didn't!" I inadvertently exclaimed.

The little guy defiantly crossed his arms. "It is his responsibility to see the crew's emotional well being."

In a similar vein David confided how he had made the mistake of asking Jim what he thought pore pressure was. "He accused me of not knowing how to do my job and says so every time he sees me."

The sound of Jim demanding information over their phone postponed our talk. The service hand answered each question flawlessly. Jim slammed down the phone when he was through.

David chuckled. The Iranian seethed. "Maybe I should drop phenolthaline in his coffee."

"Him getting the runs is not worth the risk," I advised in a tone of voice that must have conveyed the familiarity and compassion I intended.

I surmised as much because David invited me to dinner. "I'll pay," he joked. All would be great except I forgot he was on the bottom of the rig's totem and it wouldn't look good if I displayed any empathy for him. Even sitting with him incurred disapproving glares. The solution I came up with I thought was brilliant. I discussed transducers, transformers, regulated and unregulated power, and whether it was more efficient divided into three phases...topics I must have picked up by osmosis, living in a world of males at home and in school. Satisfied I only was talking shop, the eavesdroppers returned to their meals.

I must have gotten careless when everyone but us finished because when we were alone David stiffened and eyed me contemptuously. "Why are you here?"

Trying to stay cool, I claimed I wanted to see the business inside out. "From the mud pumps to the kelly on the rig floor. My classmates are missing out by just studying finance."

He continued to stare at me. Trying another approach, I appealed to the environmentalist sympathies he must have nurtured in school by explaining how the rig could do a better job preventing pollution. He seemed to quit blinking altogether. Panicking, I flaunted my knowledge of the industry, impressing him with convincing evidence of the importance of contacts, barbecues, fishing camps, and duck hunts in the conduct of business. Had Eugene still been around he would have enjoyed hearing my story about how Grandfather had hired a lawyer to draw up a restraining order during a reorganization.

"Prevented his workers from being laid-off," I said. "As long as the action was tied up in the courts, the creditors had no say about them."

The sinister-looking night cook started chopping carrots very slowly. He looked away when I glanced at him.

Turning around, I noticed my table companion's lips were curled in a sneer. I sensed disbelief; worse, I sensed animosity. Maybe he thought I was deranged, maybe a congenital liar. I briefly thought about asking him to help me find my holy grail. But, by the way his body was tensed, aching to leave, I decided it only would further turn him off.

"Guess I ODed on Sunday School. Too idealistic," I said, feeling like the Hatter at the tart trail. No matter what I said I would be executed.

No good. He got up without making any excuses. I had blown my credibility. To him a duck out of water is no longer a duck; a hand is a hand.

"Well it's getting late," I bellowed. "Should get to bed; some people work hard for a living."

The night cook resumed chopping rhythmically. At least he'd spread word I was all right. Being spurned by the untouchables was no big deal. I had to reconcile myself to the fact there was nobody I could relate to.

On the way out, I noticed a new sign indicating the direction of the mess hall. "Gally", it read. Fitting.

The hell with it, I thought. *I'd brave the perils of burglary myself. Why do I need anyone? I just need some moxie.* The new six a.m. to six p.m. tour my team rotated to allowed me the opportunity to play Willie Sutton.

Come three a.m., when Blowfly was asleep, I took the chance, slipped into the office, and thumbed through the file cabinet, finding my hearing so acute I could hear my heart palpitate. One drawer contained a bonanza of paperwork: bills of lading, transfer sheets, invoices, manifests, hot sheets--all the red tape associated with renting, leasing, and buying a staggering array of equipment and supplies. Sunshine's signature appeared on the vast majority of the most recent. Jim's appeared on a few. The rest were signed by a man named June "M" something or other. The items the latter signed for really caught my eye. I don't remember seeing a new anchor chain, Davis Lynch shoe, or Earthquaker Jars on the rig. The few gallons of green paint on board were no where close to the dozens he had signed for on a shipping notice.

"Only the green monsters of Keydrill uses that much," said the mud engineer, startling me from behind. "Marketing. Like their claim they make faster hole with air conditioners on the drill floor."

"Just curious," I sheepishly said, anticipating the inevitable question. I picked up a field transfer sheet from the tray marked "incomming".

"How curious?" his sneer chilled me.

"Can't begrudge someone for learning more about his job." My voice cracked.

"If that's all you're doing." Toying with me, he pointed to the plaques on the wall. "See these?"

"They are impressive," I lied, while discreetly replacing papers where I found them.

"You bet they are. Jim's a genius."

The awards acknowledging his graduation from Well Control School and Pore Pressure School, as well as an Associate Degree in Petroleum Technology from Nichols State hardly indicated superior intelligence.

"Only a genius can get people to do so much for him. Bet he didn't do one homework assignment. I did all his math." Ronnie laughed a hollow laugh. "It's worth it. Paid for my room and keep. Gives me jobs too. Specifically asked for me to replace Sunny."

"He can be an 'In your eye' kind of guy," I said.

"In your eye? How precious. Now I can die and go to Heaven, I heard someone say 'In your Eye' out here. Jim would like to hear it. He's like that."

My face must have advertised the amazement that swept over me discovering Dennis' doppelganger. But, being like Dennis, he construed what I showed to be adoration. He couldn't possibly imagine he wasn't special, all of which gave me an edge. Swaggering, he held up an offset wire-line log. "Here's a stepout from the first well drilled in the block. Jim uses these electric logs to check the accuracy of them muddabber's log."

"Wouldn't think of working with them, would he?" I brazenly said, finding my little secret emboldened me.

The big goof unfolded the log and pretended to study it. "Like you want to?" He finally said. "Go ahead, make a copy of the resistivity and gamma ray squiggles. Get back in good with them Yankees."

I looked at him directly in the eye. "How did you know I was on a mission for them?"

He avoided eye contact. "Why else would you be here?"

"Why else?" I answered.

"Why else?" I asked myself an hour later, when I knew for a fact Ronnie was away, testing the mud in the mud pits.

Looking at the mud reports I could see why the agent provocateur patrolled the office. The number of chemicals increased by half whenever his signature appeared on the bottom. Ronnie must have made a killing on the extra Soltex, Drispac, lignite, barite, lime, and drill beads he used.

I wanted to photocopy the evidence after I had finished photocopying the log, but when the paper jammed, I had to give up on the idea. I got out of there before someone caught me.

David hesitantly thanked me for the logs. "That Ronnie has gotten us paranoid," he said, inviting me in.

Taking a seat, I spotted several marijuana seeds in an open drawer. No doubt they were left by Mitch.

"Ronnie was real nice to us at the start," he said, pouring a cup of coffee for me. "Before he started making demands on us. Wanted to put his laboratory equipment in our unit. Wouldn't accept the fact it wouldn't fit." He handed me the cup and leaned against the counter, letting the young sample catcher continue the story.

"Not an hour later, Jim was on my case, saying I wasn't doing my job right." He paused to reflect. "Why would he say I wasn't scrapping cuttings from the shakers with the smallest mesh screens? We didn't miss any fine sands. Mamou wouldn't rat on me."

I mentioned my encounter with Ronnie and joined in speculating how to deal with him. When I left I was pretty certain I had reestablished a relationship with them, once again proving how unifying a common enemy was.

As much things improved with the mudloggers things deteriorated with everyone else. Actually, things just got strange. Wallets started to disappear out of people's lockers. As they did wads of cash started to appear throughout the crews' quarters. No doubt they were traps Hammer planted to catch the thief. I could see him leaping from behind a door, ready to use his God-given talent in the service of truth and justice.

Then a Pumkin helicopter visited us. Favored by the USGS. (the police out here), the appearance of the Hunt brother's aircraft did not precipitate too much consternation. Only when dogs appeared did it attract attention.

Although on tour, I was able to get away, rush into the logging unit and warn the two workers.

"What are we to do?" pleaded the sample catcher as I held up a handful of seeds. "I'll never make logger if we get caught."

I looked at him as if he were nuts. "Logger! Hell, you'll be sent to Angola."

Then I remembered one of Dennis' stories and quickly sprinkled ammonia they used to make copies everywhere evidence might be found.

Just as I slammed shut a drawer Bull stuck his face in the door to order us to the galley.

Judging from the crowd only a skeleton crew remained to drill the well. Most were as subdued as us, bored by a lecture about what happens to thieves. Replete with all the condescension we've come to expect from Hammer and Jim, the diatribe managed to unite us as much as the mutual hatred of Ronnie united myself and the mudloggers.

Anticipating the next outrage, Turtle announced he had "killed one of the German Shepherds the M.P.s took to our hootch in Cam Ron Bay." The appearance of two handlers escorting two of their own German Shepards did not quiet him down. "Shot that bitch as it got off the helicopter."

"How'd you get away with that?" asked Mamou.

"Made it look like a sniper. Wasn't going to let no mutt land this ass in the stockade." The handlers pretended not to hear him as they positioned themselves.

In an orchestrated move Jim strode to the ice cream machine. "To make sure we have the safest workplace possible I decided we should look for people who might make it unsafe. I wouldn't be doing my job if I didn't do everything I could do, in that regard." He nodded to Hammer who, in turn, nodded to the handlers. Each politely asked a hand to accompany him out the galley.

Jut-jawed stereotypes were on hand when it was my turn to be shook down. While the dog sniffed my locker the Brown Shirts asked me to turn my pockets inside out, felt me up, and rubbed the bottom of my socks. They went through my locker and sneered when they didn't find anything.

In addition to the thugs, a conclave of twirps had set up shop in Bull's office to proctor a pee test. One chinless wonder watched as I urinated into a cup in the bathroom. Another sporting glasses so thick they'd start a fire in a snowstorm told me it was my right not to take the test if I didn't want, all while labeling a sample with the zeal of a research chemist. So did the buck-tooth nonentity who recorded the prominent event. Actually, they provided comic relief. Ronnie provided the horror. He conned the minor league urologists into allowing him to cart away the evidence.

"Done shook the last few drops on them," Tar Baby claimed during the post-mortem back in the galley.

"I'm gonna talk to a lawyer," snarled Dirty Dan, the derrick hand.

"I am glad all but one decided to cooperate," huffed Jim once everyone reassembled. "It's the kind of team spirit that will help sniff out the thief and ensure we have no more incidents. As for the individual who choosed to exercise his prerogative, I want him to know he didn't jeopardize his position. We don't live in Russia, you know."

"Shoulda done as he was told," commented Brother-in-law, sitting up in his chair. "That's the way I was raised up." I noticed no one chastised or even glowered at him.

I also noticed, later on (after our bosses finally admitted no drugs were found aboard and the thefts ended) who the hold-out was consumed everyone's attention, explaining why no one rebuked Brother-in-law. He had tapped into an ethos I might not have been aware of but had the sense not to question.

Only the failure of the mudloggers to hand out their alleged cache of baseball caps elicited comparable interest. I wish I had known. I could have scored points explaining what a mistake it was to circumvent the rig's rigid social structure by giving the floor hand one. David had to learn that lesson for himself. Those above roughneck on the pecking order demanded coveralls at the very least. Those below didn't want to be reminded they were below and so wanted a hat of their own. "Where's my hat?" was the plaint which caused his pleasant face to contort, which made him afraid to go out of his unit.

"I just wanted to make a good impression," he lamented when I visited. But so profound was his paranoia he suddenly welled up in terror. "You don't want a hat too?"

"Ronnie already gave me one, with a gold braid on the beak." I broke into a big smile. "And Kathy's already threatened to castrate him if I didn't give it to her."

"I bet she'd do it." He smiled.

"I bet she has experience." I told him about her and Penny and after I did all vestiges of remonstrance vanished. In its place was the friendship I had cultivated once the dogs had contracted a severe case of stuffed sinuses sniffing through their unit. The bond grew tighter as their alleged parsimony stood in contrast to Ronnie's largesse. I was the only one who defended them against the accusation one of them was the rebel who refused to pee. I did so by claiming they were too timid to attempt such an act. "You know how Yankees are," I'd say.

"Something some overeducated fool would do," grumped Penny's replacement, Fireball.

Jim also joined in the abuse. He did so by refusing to allow them to take Styrofoam containers of food to their unit when fast drilling prevented them from eating with the rest of us. He was constantly squawking at them over the intercom and, I was told, insisted they call their office at three a.m. to send out a spare gas trap. He listened in on the conversation to see if their boss took the order in an acceptable tone of voice.

The fact he did most of his bitching from Bull's seat in the galley wasn't ignored by the barge engineer. Unwilling (or unable) to figure out Jim just was taking out his frustrations at the world, not just Bull, the barge engineer got even by having us needle gun the paint outside Jim's room for two days straight.

Bull might also have been the one who called Jim to the drill floor for no reason. Everyone enjoyed watching him waddle down to the catwalk and struggle up the steps to the doghouse. Like Sunshine, he was more barnacle than human.

Even Dennis' replacement got in on the act, purposely burning Jim's after dinner popcorn.

Eventually people focused on Spud. Not sophisticated enough to hide his emotions, his nervousness gave him away. He was as jumpy as a squirrel, almost stabbing himself with a fork while eating, unable to focus on professional wrestling on TV, and becoming more demure than cocky, not sassing anyone for days. It was assumed only Ronnie could have ratted him out to Jim. Someone who had the gall to interrupt my phone conversation with Leslie in the wheelhouse by banging on the buttons of an extension in Jim's office proved he could be an insensitive blabbermouth.

Everyone I told what he did to me agreed he was culpable.

Spud was a marked man. Those who had congratulated him for being advanced to the floor when one hand failed to show up to go offshore now turned their backs on him. Seems rebellion was okay if you're going to be history, like Penny was, not if you're going to stay.

What had happened to me among the upper class happened to him among the lower class, like white chickens pecking a red one to death.

"Why does he think he's special?" Brother-in-law aired in the break room, to almost unanimous approbation.

"If that new B. and R. hand agreed to take it, so should he," added Hammer. "And how that drugged-up hippie ever passed, I'll never know."

It was no secret Spud's work suffered from the abuse, the snide remarks, and the ostracism. "He's not cut out to work floors," Fireball was reported to have said after the sinewy hand failed to pull his weight when they tripped pipe out of the hole. That it was Spud's first experience operating break-out tongs and tailing pipe into their slots didn't matter. He had a difficult time, not because he was drugged up, because he was taunted for having the guts to do what nobody else dared do.

As the story went, rather than put up with the abuse, Spud had complained, which irritated Fireball. "Don't need no rebellers up here. Only want team players," he was alleged to have said.

He couldn't be demoted. The opposite tour craneman had installed another relative in the position he vacated.

While laying down traction strips on the stairs leading to the drill floor, I came within earshot of the driller by the time he had finished the bit run and prepared to circulate on bottom. Throwing back the lever used to raise and lower the pipe, Fireball put a rope around it, leaned forward, and shouted in the direction of the standpipe manifold. "You've got to go."

Looking back from the sticky valve he had been fighting to open, the only man near the confusion of pipes responded with a look of sheer hatred.

"Oh, really?" said Spud. He marched to the rotary table. "If that's the case, then I guess I won't be needing this." He dropped his twenty-four-inch pipe wrench into the hole.

The sound the driller made will forever be emblazoned in my brain. I thought only animals were capable of such noises.

Like Penny before him, Spud had run himself off the rig. *Does everything these guys do have to be dramatic?* I wondered.

A few quick calculations on the paper I always carry, and I figured to within five seconds when the slowly rotating pipe torqued up. It quickly became stuck. The wrench must have wedged itself against the bit, somehow plugging the jets. You could hear the backpressure valves explode on the mud pumps. Unable to circulate or rotate the pipe, the only thing we could do was to move the pipe up and down a few feet. I say "we" because I was given a battlefield promotion, replacing the retreating hothead. I was in the right place at the right time.

Fortune also smiled for the rig. While working the pipe up and down all three jets in the bit became unplugged, allowing us to resume circulating.

We celebrated by breaking open a pouch of Red Man. "Take this chew and you'll fit right in," advised Mamou the Weenie Washer. "Be sure to spit out long strings. That's what we do up here."

So I not only said good-bye to Kathy and hello to Fireball. I had graduated from patrician dipping to proletarian chewing.

Instead of being introduced to a squeegee or another implement, I was introduced to the coffee pot in the doghouse. "To prove you can be useful," said my new boss, both teeth bared in a sinister grin.

The old coffee pot sat on top a rickety metal table inside the rickety shack. To get rid of the grinds caked on the filter, I shook the entire pot out the window. Out fell the metal insert. It dropped straight into the water and barely made a ripple when it hit.

"Got that perking yet?" barked Fireball.

Terror gripped me. What could I do? A confession was tantamount to a demotion. Brother-in-law would certainly take my place.

"That last crew buggered up the thing," I shouted in my most aggrieved voice.

Mister Fontenot and Fireball cursed. Hammer drop-kicked his helmet. My volunteering to fetch coffee from the galley soothed them somewhat, but not enough to quell another eruption which Jim instigated when he had arrived just as I was leaving. When I returned, I got to hear the toolpusher claim they might wreck the bit if they tried to shove the wrench into the formation. Jim insisted they had no choice, considering how much behind schedule they were.

"It don't look good on my record," the companyman snarled.

"It'll look worse if we have to fish for a cone," Hammer snarled back.

Jim asked the mud engineer if he could get linear flow around the bit if he kicked the pumps up to their max. Ronnie banged furiously on his calculator only to inform him it was impossible.

"I told you to put smaller jets in those cones," Jim declared. "Maybe another toolpusher would listen to me."

What Jim needed was another opinion, one from a superior, like the drilling supervisor who happened to arrive on a routine inspection.

Dennis' ex-benefactor couldn't resist taking charge of the situation. "Get some drill beads down the hole," the Douglas MacArthur look-alike said with Douglas MacArthur authority.

So the derrick hand, Dirty Dan, got to pour sack after sack of the tiny silica balls down the hopper in the bowels of the rig. Ronnie got to make a killing off his commission. And we all got to observe a murky plum of mud bloom on the water directly beneath the shale shakers.

The tiny beads traveled from the suction pit, up the hose to the drill floor, through the standpipe, the kelly hose, the kelly, down the drill pipe to the bit, around the impediment, up the annulus to the flowline, and into the possum belly, where they cascaded onto the vibrating shaker screens. They clogged them so badly the mud could not sift back into the circulating system. The hybrid polymer-gel mud fell into the Gulf, each barrel costing fifty dollars. The wrench did not budge.

Although I was the first to spot the spill, I did not immediately report it. I really didn't know it was unwanted, as we habitually dumped the previous batch of drilling mud as well as the salt water we used when we drilled out the drive pipe.

I absentmindedly hadn't moved from the same spot for five whole minutes.

"You got time to lean, you got time to clean," growled Hammer.

Mamou the Weenie Washer's brief, apocryphal story concerning two hands the toolpusher had run off convinced me to grab a brush and scrub with conviction. The hapless duo he told me about had committed the crime of concentrating on brushing the same grimy spot for half an hour, leading our enlightened leader to think they were goofing off.

I didn't just have to do as I was told. I had to hop to it, without question, as if I were an army grunt (which I'm sure most of my co-workers had been).

Told to clamber over the slick draw works, I clambered over the slick draw works, scrub brush in hand. Told to break loose a plug atop the casing manifold, I was helped into a grimy safety belt, and, with a sledgehammer, climbed the seven feet to break the plug loose. Told to tighten a pressure gauge I grabbed a thirty-six-inch pipe wrench, screwed its jaws around a hex nut, inserted a cheater bar on the end, and yanked so hard I was afraid I'd strip the grooves. I did this because I was expected to do it and was proud of it.

I also appreciated being hand-picked to grease the spinner on top of the kelly. It showed the gap tooth driller was willing to take a chance on me. To show my appreciation, I made sure he saw me insert a virulent new wad in my mouth.

"Remember!" warned Mamou the Weenie Washer as I prepared to ejaculate a sinewy, muscular thread.

With my tongue, I pried a well-chewed fragment free from my molars and worked it around until it activated a sheath of saliva. What exited the gap in my front teeth was amazingly smooth and accurate.

Fireball grinned, which was nice. So did Mamou, which was even better, as he was going to operate the air hoist for me. Rather than mock my ignorance, he patiently showed me how to put on the greasy riding belt and took extra care I saw how he threaded the hook through the eyelet.

"Don't want you worrying about anything but holding on to the kelly hose. I'll take care of you." He spat into a grating.

What I was supposed to hold on to until I reached the hose he didn't say, it being thirty feet in the air. A Peter Pan I wasn't. Then again, I doubt Mary Martin could have leapt very far encumbered with a heavy wrench, a grease gun, squeezed by webbing which cut off circulation, and the need to spit which exceeded any previous need to urinate.

Swung dangerously close to the kelly, I lurched for the bend in the thick rubber hose and held on like a drunken monkey when I reached it.

Like all else in the oilfield, ergonomics is unheard of when it comes to servicing the working parts atop the forty-three foot kelly. The greasy bolts did not provide the hand and footholds I needed as I scrambled over the slippery curves. My progress upwards inexplicably ended, even though I could feel increasing tension. Looking up, I saw the air hoist line tangled among the ten lines that suspended the massive traveling block.

Being in the shadows I couldn't see if Mamou was paying attention. It sure didn't feel like he was. Despite my shouts I could feel the line tighten.

The wind mangled the voices from below. I didn't know what to do. Horror stories about people being squeezed through the racking fingers, or whose feet became wedged and were pulled part raced through my mind, scaring me to death. Flesh and bones are no match against iron and one hundred twenty pounds of air pressure.

A jolt knocked me free and about knocked me out. I don't know how far I fell, nor did I care. Disoriented, seeing stars, and with the wind knocked out of me, I wanted down. Now!

"Grab it!" I heard Fireball shout over his speaker.

The hammer joint at the gooseneck, connecting the kelly hose with the kelly, provided a hand hold. Once I sensed a chance to stabilize myself, it provided a foothold too. Upon regaining my balance, I regained my senses, saw Mamou pulling the air hoist line free, and regrouped. Contorting myself I managed to position the wrench around the bolt that had to be unscrewed. Seeing and feeling it come out was a thrill equal to any I ever had experienced, a genuine achievement. I can't remember when I was happier than I was clamping on the head of the grease gun and shooting that sucker full of grease. Replacing the screw and returning to the deck filled me with more satisfaction than handing in a test I knew I had aced ever did.

I was wiping my hands when Fireball lifted up on the lever, the "break" Turtle informed me. He lowered half a joint into the hole. Instead of being sixty feet in the air, the spinner was forty feet up.

"Got the pipe free an hour ago," Turtle said, noticing my dumbfounded expression.

It should have occurred to me why all the big bosses had departed the drill floor. "Why couldn't you guys have done that before I worked on it?" I finally asked, spitting a mean looking chew into the trash can near the driller's console.

Fireball countered with a world-class projectile, accurate, clean, and of uniform consistency. "To find a chicken's snuff box you got to look up its ass," he cryptically said.

An oilfield Walt Whitman.

He wasn't the only one. On the bulletin board I checked after tour I noticed a bit of doggerel had replaced an instructional cartoon warning against loosening hammer joints until all pressure had been bled off.

"This is a story about people named Everybody, Somebody, Anybody, and Nobody," the poster read. "There was an important job to be done and Everybody was sure Somebody would do it. Anybody could have done it, but Nobody did it. Somebody got angry about that because it was Everybody's job. Everyone thought that Anybody could do it but realized that Everybody would not do it. It ended up that Everybody blamed Somebody when Nobody did what Anybody could have done."

The crowd that gathered while I read was of a like mind when they too finished. Jim had to be behind it, it being a not-too-subtle way of chastising us for not reporting the mud that had poured over the clogged shakers, into the Gulf before anyone stopped it.

"Thank God I'm out here," said Jim, surprising us from behind (no doubt unable to resist the urge to take credit for it). "Somebody has to look out for everybody, prepare for any contingency. Only I would have made sure we had more than enough barite on board. Would never have guessed why we'd need it but it is a sign of a good leadership to have it on hand." He paused to take in expected praise. When it didn't occur, he reared up and continued. "Woulda been in a world of hurt if we couldn't have added weight material to the mud." He looked directly at Fireball. "Wouldn't have needed it if everyone was doing his job." Instead of baring his teeth the big driller hid the few he possessed behind pursed lips and stormed off, obviously wanting to avoid a confrontation.

"Lost more mud than evaporation or hole fill would account for. Those drill beads scrapped off wall cake. Can't add mud fast enough. New mud has to be heavier than the old. To keep formation fluids from invading the well bore. Didn't have time to wait for the mud doctor build enough mud with right rheology to build a new cake."

He had more to say, but I left before he said it. Judging how Fireball and the mudloggers made themselves scarce they must have discredited themselves. I'd bet they failed to catch the loss of drilling mud. When they did reappear, they were demurer, (in Fireball's case, more restrained). The former didn't look anyone in the eye, the latter toned down his insults. As well they should. That's twice a driller and the mudloggers failed to detect a loss of mud in the pits.

Fireball became downright gentlemanly once all the lost mud had been replaced, its chemical properties restored, and a slick pill was pumped down hole while we were off tour. He didn't complain or offer his opinion whether Jim should have agreed to Hammer's assessment the wrench had to be fished out of the hole. Spud's stunt was going to cost Springer Oil at least a day of rig time plus the cost of a recovery operation.

Tripping pipe was one of those jobs I had put out of my mind. I knew it existed, and in all likelihood, I'd end up doing it, but I never really thought about it.

It's not an enterprise one should anticipate. It's too gruesome. Humans weren't designed to contend with ninety-three-foot stands of wrought iron.

Taking my cue from Turtle, I didn't try to lift the slips into place. Grabbing a handle, I helped him drag it to the rotary. The iron girdle was heavy, as one might expect of a device designed to hold up the drill string. We dropped it below the fat tool joint atop the fourth joint pulled up. It gripped the pipe as if it were magnetized. It was a good start, one which wasn't about to last. My lack of skill quickly threw off Turtle's and Mamou's coordination. The tongs I handled seemed to have a mind of its own, moving away from its guide wire whenever I tried to move it.   When I finally could aim it I was a hair off center. The right jaw banged off the pipe and snapped shut with the left. I needed all the muscle I had to pull back the lever that opened them. I needed all the dexterity I could command to wrestle the big wrench back into position for another go. This time the jaws hungrily grabbed the pipe where it belonged, below the female tool joint.

Turtle immediately slapped his break-out tongs snugly above the male tool joint. Fireball reeled in the catline. Dust flew off the chain as it jerked tight, torquing Turtle's tongs. The cathead it spooled into creaked. The pipe creaked. And I creaked, fearing a link would snap. The male, "pin" unscrewed with a groan. Fireball barked out an incomprehensible order.   Turtle motioned toward my oversized wrench. The bear-like boss wasn't going to use the air activated spinner like I expected. He was going to spin the rotary. After unlatching my tongs I backed well away from the rotary table, ensuring my foot didn't get caught as it spun around. I didn't stand far enough away to avoid the geyser of mud that spewed out once the joints were unscrewed. It was like taking a bath, only I wasn't allowed to clean off. "Forgot to tell you we didn't pump a slug," said Fireball. "Next time use the mud bucket."

"Afraid of U-tubing, with that weighted pill in the hole," explained Mamou. *Whatever that meant. I didn't even know what a "slug" was. Must be the same thing.* Rather than ask I lent a hand shoving the stand where it belonged.

Doing so we three resembled the flag raisers on Iwo Jima, tailing the ninety-foot metal pole onto a ten by twelve foot wooden square. I bet it wasn't half as hard for them to plant their pole as it was for us to plant ours. They didn't have to coordinate their efforts with a derrick hand on the monkey boards, racking his end into the fingers.

One.

Rather than yell at us Fireball yelled into his speaker: "What we need up there is a derrick hand, not a latch hand."

From a hundred feet up, Dirty Dan responded by yelling into his speaker: "What we need down there is a driller. Know of any?"

What we needed was someone to teach us how to work together. It was like trying to learn a dance number without a choreographer. We floundered in each other's way, pushed when we should have pulled, made easy tasks difficult, and difficult tasks nearly impossible. Fighting the tongs, the slips, the pipe, trying and failing to latch the mud bucket so no mud escaped, all in a confined space full of iron booby traps did not bode well for our continued good health. More than once I found myself hoping I'd get hurt. That way I'd have access to Jim's office, helping Blowfly shuffle papers. At least, that's what I told myself.

Each variant to the general task grated on me. Replacing worn tong dies, buckling the shields we positioned over pipe we were about to unscrew, keeping the mud bucket's hose connected to the drain, yanking the catline from the cathead, even hosing down the floor all broke our rhythm. Everything we handled was rusty and unyielding. The buckles seldom snapped shut; the hose constantly became disconnected; the catline constantly snagged; and we needed a wrench to turn the nozzle on the hose to the "open" position.

Only when we reached the fat collars and had to search for the bigger slips and the correct size lift sub did I look at my watch. I couldn't believe how much time had gone by. Looking at myself I couldn't believe how filthy I was. I was literally coated in mud. Getting back into the flow of things I also found myself amazed at how competent I had become, finding I could manhandle the heavy dog collar, the heavy slips, and the heavy tongs with surprising expertise.

Even Tiny remarked how adroit I was. His bulky frame may have consumed a lot of space, but it was space well taken. Squeaking at the top of his lungs, he offered encouragements, like a partisan spectator. Furthermore, he offered instruction we desperately needed. Without his hands-on teaching we'd have mimicked the three stooges, screwing lift subs on top of collars and tightening dog collars above the slips in order to "break" each stand. And we'd never have disassembled the rotary table to retrieve the rubber donuts above the wear bushing with any efficiency. I was proud to have inserted the hooks into the bushings after only once being told how. I was even prouder when I helped Mamou push them off to the side without any prompting at all. Tiny even helped scrap off the mud that had coated the blades of the stabilizer and helped dump the big pieces over the side. After a pep talk, he renewed his instructions, this time on how to lay down and pick up various subs and tools. We ignored Fireball's bellowing.

Everything required certain techniques and special hand-held tools. As for the chain tongs Jim said he used to operate by himself, we found that to be a bunch of bull. We three could have used a fourth using it to unscrew a stubborn five-foot orienting sub.

Under Tiny's continued tutelage I increased my marketability in remaining few hours, apprenticing on the air hoist, on the air tongs, and on the bit breaker box.

At the end of my tour, I was a different person than I was before my tour. I was dead tired. I looked like a clay man in a Flash Gordon serial. I was a valuable employee. And it felt good, so good I actually found myself slapping Mamou the Weenie Washer on the back on the way to the showers.

The bruise I found did not discolor me so much as provided me with an emblem: The Black and Blue Badge of Courage. I had worked before, had been exhausted before, but never to the present extent. As I shuffled off to dinner, I thought of Eugene and how he needed to perform twelve hours of real work. All his kind needed to, just like I did.

As I experienced during my previous foray to Tulane, I managed to hear more than I had previously heard, saw more than I had previously seen. Without Jim to brag about himself (he was busy learning how to use the new fax machine), the tired crew discussed the well--intelligently. I also noticed they possessed far more energy than I in the rec. room. Actually, it was kind of sad how successfully two-dimensional images rejuvenated them. Mayans needed cocaine and priests to do what they otherwise wouldn't do. Our home-grown natives needed Kari Fox and Amber Lynn.

They did go to bed earlier than me. Maybe the extra weight they packed massaged their muscles. All I know was that mine were in need of a lot of T.L.C.

My body wasn't much better come morning. I twitched and ached, unable to rise above the bad mood that befell me upon learning the opposite tour hadn't done a thing for twelve hours. They had waited for the arrival of a magnet Jim had ordered. All night they had mixed new mud in the pits. Contaminated by the pill and the additives Ronnie had injected, the old mud had turned to jello. Like "The Blob", the normally soupy liquid had oozed out the top grating, taking on the waffle pattern of the iron as it had grown.

It took dozens of sacks of expensive defoamer to restore the well's life's blood.

By correcting the problem, he primarily was responsible for, Ronnie must have made a grand or two. He made more on top of that once it was learned he was the one who had convinced Jim to spot a pill of expensive "Black Magic" to free the pipe.

I volunteered to throw chains during the trip in. Chain throwers on Fireball's floor didn't handle the slips or operate a tong. All a chain thrower had to do was wrap the catline around the lower pipe, and with a flip of the wrist, whip each curl to the upper pipe as it was lowered into place. Then came the fun part, pressing my hands on the chain as it pulled taut, screwing the upper pin into the lower box. One slip and I could kiss a fingertip good-bye. Over a decade after American ingenuity had landed men on the moon, I was performing a task developed back when the biplane ruled the skies.

Despite all the fulsome predictions of robots freeing mankind from drudgery, no robot was to be found helping us move the pipe from the wooden platform back to the hole. Except for periodically filling up the pipe with mud, everything we did tripping out we did in reverse tripping in. But with our movements more synchronized and no longer wearing a garment of congealed chemicals it was easier, not simple or fun, just easier.

How we pulled the kelly out of the rat hole after thirty stands in order to fill the pipe was comical, something cartoonists would enjoy depicting. With a twenty-foot aluminum replica of a shepherd's staff Turtle depressed a lever on the travelling block. Mamou and I pushed on the elevators the assembly was attached to in order to align the hook that had popped out with the eyelet on the kelly. Fireball jerked up on his brake just enough for the two to catch. Charlie Chaplin should have included the sight of the monster slipping out of the rat hole and swinging over the rotary. It'd have fit perfectly into the dehumanization "Modern Times" sought to depict.

It was only fitting the hex nut that opened the TIW valve on the kelly would be frozen. All the speed and efficiency the air spinner employed screwing the kelly into the protruding pipe went for naught. No mud was going to get pumped until I turned the nut on the TIW valve open. Then again, no mud was going to get pumped until Turtle opened the valve on the standpipe. Lucky for me, he took longer so I wasn't blamed for the delay.

It didn't take long to fill up the pipe. In no time we were back replacing the kelly into the rat hole just as clumsily as we had removed it.

A tremendous sense of relief accompanied the sight of the last stand being run into the hole. The roar of the mud pumps and squeal of the brake as Fireball raised and lowered the pipe was emancipating, suffusing me with the sense of a job if not all that well done, at least done and over with.

Or so I thought. The excited demeanor of the big shots who gathered around the driller unnerved me. I could sense something unpleasant afoot. For the first time I selfishly wished the well bad luck. But I needn't worry. My wishes carried as much weight as a flea's. Hearing we were to trip back out of the hole may have been as appealing as drinking Southern Comfort immediately after ralphing, but it was what we were going to do. The magnet apparently worked right off. How they could tell they've added thirty pounds to hundreds of thousands of pounds of pipe I don't know. But that's what they thought.

I know what I thought. I thought I couldn't do it, especially when I found out we again were to pull it wet. Too bad for us we again weren't going to slug it. This time Jim figured the heavy mud might dislodge the wrench, the "fish" as everyone called it.

I managed to avoid the first geyser of mud that accompanied the first stand we broke off, though I did slip on a puddle of the slippery goo.

I couldn't avoid the second geyser from the next stand we broke. We were ordered to use rags instead of the mud bucket to stanch the flow. It worked better than the iron girdle but not that much better. The hefty overseer made the mistake of making fun of us only once. By the time we had pulled all the "E" grade drill pipe we were adept enough with the rags to direct a particularly condensed stream his way, staining his bushy mustache grey.

Halfway into the "G" grade drill pipe, the mudloggers' sample catcher arrived to take our pictures. Given our foul mood, it wasn't the wisest of moves. His clean coveralls were like a red flag; his naiveté, an allurement. Floating around the edges of the floor with a simper on his face and a camera in hand he became a target, one that Dirty Dan couldn't resist. The stream of droplets raining on the tyro didn't originate from the heavens. It came from the monkey boards, with uncanny accuracy.

The victim continued taking our pictures unaware of his defilement. I initially wanted to make him aware of what was happening but gave up the idea. *Best he remains ignorant.* I thought.

He continued to grate on us. Both Mamou the Weenie Washer and Turtle sought revenge. Although I found myself empathizing with them and disdaining the tyro's total obliviousness of how he was affecting them, I couldn't condone any of their schemes. To me, the fool was just another irritant, along with the wind, cold, mud, and backbreaking labor.

Paradoxically, the job that stripped the two of their reticence prevented them from doing more than grumble. Consumed by work, dappled in mud and grease, we were mean and volatile. On our own turf, suffused with our own moral code, we were as dangerous as fraternity actives are away from the glare of authority. And we were rendered as impotent by our weariness as they are by the alcohol they consume.

"Five stands, three barrels," announced Brother-in-law from the trip tank, where the mud destined to fill the hole was held.

Five stands represented four hundred eighty-five feet of drill pipe. Four barrels of mud generally were needed to replace it, much like the water needed to replace bath water to its original level once a bather stepped out. The lost barrel was attributed to spillage on the floor.

The next five stands required only two and a half barrels to fill up. Fluids might have entered the well bore and were shoving the mud upwards, meaning the well was kicking.

Fireball spit into his trash can. "Somebody might have left a valve open." He ordered Mamou to go check, leaving Turtle and I to do the work of three, which we did with surprising alacrity, slinging the tongs and throwing our shoulders into the pipe like offensive linemen.

We stopped only when Mamou returned. Claiming none of the myriad of valves on the spaghetti bowl of pipes in the pit or pump rooms were out of position, and no mud was leaking elsewhere, he listened as acutely as we to the next fill-up.

"Five stands, two barrels," reported Brother-in-law over his squawk box.

Fireball's mustache curled. "I thought I was wrong once before. But it turned out I was mistaken." He reached for the rig phone. "Pick up companyman," he said in a worried tone of voice.

Jim then did something out of character. He issued a sensible order. "Wants us to circulate," explained Fireball.

"Bring the swabbed-in fluids to the surface and stop more from getting into the well bore," added Mamou.

Applying my college prep physics, I knew the coefficient of friction added by circulating made the weight of the mud heavier. Heavier mud would repress the further influx of formation fluids.

After unlatching the hook, I helped push the block over to the rat hole so it could engage the eyelit on the Kelly, which we then guided over the drillpipe, so Fireball could screw them together. While Turtle and I participated in a rematch with the valves on the standpipe and kelly cock respectively, Mamou descended to monitor the shakers. Dirty Dan hit the pits deep in the bowels of the rig. Fireball kicked the pumps on, slowly. After a few circulations we checked for flow. No drilling mud flowed out the flowline into the possum belly.

They say work makes men beasts. I say leisure reveals the beast in men. While cleaning the floor, Turtle grew madder and madder at the sample catcher. He seethed and spat, like a soul from the Seventh Bolgia, changed into a reptile, slimy and vile.

"Easy money," he hissed in front of several witnesses behind the draw works.

A dopey simper creased the kid's face.

Neither our Minos nor our Plutus could see the goings-on of this Contrived Comedy. The two portholes our fallen angels stared out of weren't high enough on the Wall of Dis the crew's quarters resembled for them to see over the big spool.

The worm was not bar-wise. Even I, with my meager experience, could sense impending danger.

"You like work, don't you?" asked Fireball, our Geryon.

Startled, the intruder responded hesitantly. "Who doesn't? I mean, we have to work. Don't we?"

"Yeah, I bet you can watch it for hours."

Blind and deaf to the not-so-subtle hints, the tyro didn't even attempt to bolt into the open. I would have. I think.

Turtle closed in. "You know, we don't let people watch us for free. You can't watch the Astros or Saints for free, and you can't watch us."

Appearing from nowhere, Tar Baby, the rig's only assistant driller, added his two cents. "We're professionals," he said. *Where was he when Turtle and I needed a hand?*   I wondered.

"We also got something all new fans of ours gotta go through," Turtle removed the applicator from a bucket of pipe dope.

The sample catcher looked terrified.

"We can do anything we want. And if you want to stay..." He twirled the stick in his hand and jabbed it forward. Several drops of the sticky substance oozed off the end like strands of snot. "You wear this."

Hemmed in between the metal wall and the draw works, with Tar Baby blocking one exit and Turtle blocking the other there was no place for the kid to go. Since Tiny was no longer around, I had to intervene.

"You're not going to do that," I heard myself say.

I recalled Robert's warning about getting into pissing contests. "Sucker punch'm," he had advised. And that's what I did, kind of.

Before he could react, I ripped the brush out of Turtle's arthritic hand and held it behind me. Adrenaline raced through my body and must have made me look convincing. The leprechaun actually cowered. The absent-when-there's-work-to-be-done assistant driller likewise held back.

"We're only kidding," I said to the kid. "Just trying to scare you. Actually, all we want you to do is fill out the "I", "D", "Ten", "T" papers in Hammer's office."

"Yeah, that's it," said Turtle. "That's what we want."

Tar Baby turned sideways, allowing passage. This time, the novice grabbed the opportunity and was out of hearing when Tar Baby added, "And bring back a left-handed screwdriver."

Turtle nervously chuckled. Tar Baby sniffed. I almost fainted. I knew the consequences of fighting. I had overheard conversations about the Coast Guard arresting guys who got into push fights. And I knew it didn't take much to get run off. My heart raced. I trembled. I had frightened off the saber-toothed tiger and my system needed time to get back to normal.

But rather than give it time to recover, I soon used the adrenalin that continued to course through my body to say something I'd normally never consider saying, but which needed to be said to ensure Turtle wouldn't have time to think. I asked Fireball not to stage out of the hole once we got the well under control. "We need to pull up that fish and get out of Dodge."

Turtle was aghast. He was looking forward to the periodic rests circulating every dozen or so stands provided. As Fireball reached for the phone to call Hammer I looked at Turtle while stating, "I want to earn my money."

Fireball grinned and patted me on the shoulder. "That's what I like to hear."

Turtle grumbled. He soon quit grumbling. Manhandling the big wrenches and fighting everything that refused to work the way they were designed didn't allow us the luxury of carrying a grudge. Although this time we enjoyed Tar Baby's help, come the end of the tour we still couldn't think at all. We certainly couldn't revel in the fact we brought the wrench to the surface. We were animals, capable of only grunts and groans; dumb, spent, and useless. Only in my bed, lying down before sleep was I human, smiling inwardly at what I had done, reveling so much in the courage I had displayed it became the stuff of my dreams, and when I awoke, the elixir which recharged me.

My newly discovered vigor drew suspicions. Bull gave me the evil eye. Hammer thought I was up to something. I could see why. Being enthusiastic in the middle of a two-week hitch was weird.

Knowing I was a marked man should have persuaded me to be discreet. But it didn't. It couldn't, not after my epiphany. Bob, Dennis' replacement chose the wrong man to be careless in front of. Spud, Pencil, or Fireball wouldn't have thought anything of the way he lingered in the materials closet. To them, he'd probably be just another stump-jumper doing something related to his job. To me, he was such a creep anything he did out of the ordinary made me suspicious. He needed to be watched.

One didn't have to be Sherlock Holmes to put significance on the fact the thefts of personal items coincided with the outpatient's arrival. Whether out of curiosity or genuine concern for the welfare of my co-workers I took a big chance rooting around in the closet once I found the lock was broken. To say I was startled to find a wallet in an empty can was an understatement.

It was Turtle's, with money and credit cards--platinum cards!

Now what? I replaced the evidence and bugged out, wondering what I should do, shocked...no, amused about the credit cards. It's so much bullshit. And to think I once thought that having them proved my family was special.

"Who stole your lollipop?" Fireball asked me during breakfast.

"I'm just ruing the fact I have licked all of them," I said, wishing I hadn't lapsed into my formal argot. Guess it was the best I could do, consumed as I was thinking about the platinum credit cards.

"By that look on your face, you're feeling bad about what you done to us," said Mamou the Weenie Washer.

"Good," said Tar Baby, the assistant driller (obviously pissed he had been forced to work).

They acted as if I made the decision to pull out rather than stage out.

Unable to contain myself, and wanting to direct suspicion to where it belonged, I complained about the new B. and R. hand.

"Worse than Dennis," Fireball concurred, wiping milk off his bushy mustache.

"Needs watching," Turtle said, not knowing how astute he was. I don't know why he hasn't checked his belongings. I check my stuff daily.

My return to the floor did not engender much trepidation. I knew what to expect. I actually looked forward to it, to prove I was competent.

My co-workers may not have shared my optimism but at least they quit griping. It was the higher ups who resembled Snow White's elves. Apparently, they liked the way things had returned to normal, with the mud weight in proving to be equal to the mud weight out when we circulated. Even the funnel viscosity was reasonable.

The new bit almost was back to bottom, the background gas was low, and we neither were gaining nor losing mud.

"It's the way I like it," said Fireball, stroking his mustache. "I don't get paid enough to fight the well." He checked the pipe tally on the metal table next to his consol. From a drawer he pulled out his Coon Ass calculator.

"You know how to operate one of those?" asked the directional driller, Mister Fontenot.

"Sure do. *Un, deux, trois,*" Fireball said, counting the fingers protruding through the holes cut in the miniature painter's palette. "We gots two more stands before we have to rotate through that tight spot," he concluded. "A little weight on the bit and we ought to get through it like nobody's business."

"Thank God for that calculator," said the directional driller. "Coulda never figured that out otherwise."

"Tools of the trade are important. "Certainly, more useful than that saw I used on the first day I went to work cutting logs for Boise Cascade."

"Bent teeth?" asked David, the mudlogger, as he copied the information in the driller's pipebook.

"Not that complicated, as it turned out. But before it turned out, I just sat there, scratching my head 'til the boss comes back to see how I'm doing.

"That man, he turns all shades of red when he finds I not done a thing. 'But, Mister Boudreaux,' I say. 'This machine here don't cut no ways I can see.'

"Mister Boudreaux, he reached over and takes the saw outta my hands and he yanks on that rope attached to it. 'What's that noise?' I axed."

All on the floor chuckled and probably would have stayed in a good mood had David not reappeared later on the floor. Sporting as stupid a simper as his sample catcher he reopened a wound that should have been left alone. By handing out company stickers he reminded everyone how they had been slighted when they didn't receive company hats. Such stupidity was dangerous. And I didn't care. Someone so out of touch with the society out here deserved what he got. The gospel Father preached decrying the need to learn the zeitgeist of people one deals with returned with thunderous relevance. I wanted to turn the hose I was operating on the ignoramus. Instead of fairy tales I was weaned on anecdotes about how Bechtel and McDermont learned all they could about Arabs before negotiating deals. I knew one didn't point the sole of his shoes at a devout Moslem before I knew the names of the three wise men. Hell, Father never would have closed the one deal he made with the ragheads had he not know about the interminable conferences they hold before making a decision.

The mudloggers isolated themselves from the iron and sweat of our world by their fiberglass walls and air conditioners, made no effort to learn about their environment. David deserved whatever deviltry the crew was going to commit when he fell for their sudden act of contrition.

"That's okay chaix," said Fireball. "I understand why you'd give us stickers instead of hats. We all get into a bind now and again."

Only someone not attuned to the thinking of the natives would be deaf to the sarcasm. It was as ominous as the drop in barometric pressure preceding a storm. Though I wasn't all that opposed to whatever my crew had in mind I didn't want to be part of it. Moreover, I wanted the victim to know I was in no way part of it.

"I'm going to clean the shale shakers," I announced. "It's still slicker than a cattle yard in a rainstorm."

So was David's coveralls after he was goaded into shinnying up one of the spare collars that were racked back. He didn't count on having to slide through a generous application of pipe dope when he came down. Nor did he count on being laughed off the floor. Judging from his slumped shoulders and hunched posture it must have affected him deeply. His stained coveralls and aggrieved spirit precipitated laughter wherever he went. Only in the galley did he cease being the brunt of the latest joke. It wasn't much of a consolation.

Harvey went crazy at the sight of him. "You had hats all the time. Dozens of hats, and you didn't give me one. Not one!" he wailed.

Doctor Jekyll turned into Mister Hyde. He threatened to poison the dupe's food if he didn't come across.

"What do you mean you're going to poison him?" asked Fireball. "Just serve him second helpings."

The cook ignored the insult, so focused was he on the primary object of derision. The personification of excess exceeded all decency and decorum. He embarrassed even the hard-core testosterone set, eclipsing Sunshine's most ferocious outburst by several magnitudes.

"Don't need no Jack Daniels to jump start him," said Popcorn.

"Got a ten year to life temper," Kathy remarked as she entered, diverting attention. Her capri pants quickly commanded everyone's full attention, leaving Harvey to rant in private.

I wasn't the only one who knew the significance of the tattooed numbers above her ankles. What Sam, Mister Above Average, the car thief from the pipe yard told me about how prisoners sometimes get permanently inked must be common knowledge.

"Do I hear the voice of experience?" Tar Baby, the assistant driller asked.

The craneperson plopped her foot on a vacant chair. "These numbers ain't no fashion statement."

The nausea fermented by the thought someone would pay her for sex surpassed the discomfort we suffered from Harvey's continued tirade. It was an insult to the exalted heights copulation enjoys out here, where men are men and all prostitutes are gorgeous.

"Let me tell you, if you ever write rubber checks make them as big as you can," she commented. "Doesn't make any difference, if it's over a hundred dollars. Could have written one for sixty thousand instead of six hundred. Got the same sentence."

The collective sigh was audible, and I swear louder than the hoarse grumbling the cook was reduced to. It also was so sincere no one laughed when Gordon asked why she just didn't write twelve fifty-dollar checks.

Returning to the service hands' conflict all were surprised how David's expressionless demeanor had sapped Harvey's fervor. The cook was drained, tired of saying the same thing over and over to no avail. Either the mudlogger had gone possum out of sheer fright or by cleverly figuring out how best to handle the insane. It didn't matter as, much to everyone's immense entertainment, the cook issued one last growl before lumbering ignominiously into the recesses of the kitchen, where he threw a few pots and pans on the floor in frustration. David's unaffected return to his meal was inspiring. He acted as if nothing had gone awry and when he was done, left without looking back. All catcalls and comments stayed stuck in people's throats, where they belonged.

For the first time I saw a mudlogger achieve respect. The respect he garnered spread to his colleagues. Not one comment was heard about the Ayatollah or his revolutionaries when the Iranian approached within shouting distance. Nor did anyone laugh about how juvenile it was to scoop samples from the shale shakers when the sample catcher neared. I wouldn't say they received respect. They just were left alone, which was a vast improvement from how they had been treated. It was a situation I didn't trust. No conviction is so easily overturned, especially by these salt-of- the-earth types.

Like I suspected, it wasn't to last. David was spotted wearing red bikini underwear to the shower, the kind Turtle claimed he lost in the laundry.

As if making up for the anomalous change of mind they reverted back to form with a vengeance. Scrutinizing him with an evil eye, they caused him to abbreviate his next shower. When he stepped out, he found his towel missing. He also found no one would let him take his turn at a sink. He was lucky to get out of the combination shower, restroom, and laundry room unscathed. All his colleagues were lucky they remained unscathed. Their mere presence evoked sinister looks and angry words.

David looked at me imploringly after his defense he brought wild underwear to distinguish them from other's laundry fell upon dead ears. I'm sure I contained my ambivalence about his situation, shrugging my shoulders and expressing a "what can you expect" look.

The geologist was just too geeky with his goofy glasses and clueless demeanor for the crew to buy his explanation.

"Only Turtle's retarded enough to wear queer's clothes," said Hammer. "Got to really be wrapped loose to want to get into his pants." He shuddered at the thought.

So did everyone else. The egghead was persecuted. He took to hiding in his unit. He avoided the drill floor, where a conscientious mudlogger needs to periodically be, to communicate with the driller and check his sensors. Accusations as ridiculous as those dreamed up by Harvey were hurled at him bereft of any rationality. I personally heard complaints about him for skipping a safety meeting, not wearing his helmet outside, and stealing Turtle's wallet.

"He has a bad attitude," said Jim at dinner.

I wonder why.

I stayed away from the rig's pariahs. Without alienating the crew, I diplomatically avoided helping them make the mudloggers miserable. It wasn't hard. All I had to do was privately agree with them. It may have bothered me when they accused David of stealing other items I subsequently found in the closet. But sometimes one can't avoid engaging in situational ethics. It wasn't a big deal. Throwing myself into my work and discreetly keeping track of the comings and goings of the traffic in the companyman's office kept my mind off David's plight. One last aborted attempt to get in and snoop around shoved the whole business out of my mind.

Only the advent of channel fever, intensified by the coming of squirrel and doe season, ended the persecution. It's amazing how forward-looking the crew becomes when the 'morrow is a harbinger of freedom.

"Gonna get me a doe ticket this go-round," said Fireball as we waited in the wheelhouse for the helicopter.

Bob, the B. and R. hand swaggered into our midst. "Not me, I'm after a trophy."

Tar Baby sneered at him.

Turtle leaned back against the sloping window and regarded him disparagingly. "What for? You couldn't get it out of the woods. You're so scrawny."

Weighing in at one hundred ten pounds, with a kit even lighter than most, it probably wouldn't be a problem to add him to the passenger list. But he didn't belong, not on the first flight, which his presence indicated he was about to join. Service hands caught clean-up flights. Nor did members of the lowest class mingle with those who were to depart earlier. To do so is a *faux pas,* and kind of stupid if you could grab a nap.

The sniffs and sneers his presence engendered cheered him. You'd have thought his name appeared on Reba McEntire's list of eligible bachelors by the way he flaunted the manifest.

"See, my name's on it, right with yours," he gloated. The smirk on the wastrel's face was noxious.

"What you might need is a dose of the prince," he said as we trooped out the control room to congregate at the base of the stairs to the helipad.

The helicopter that arrived looked odd. Usually by the time we could hear it, it looked like a big bird. This one looked like a bug. It rattled rather than "whooped" and acted as if it'd never get stable enough to land. Instead of a sixteen seat Sigorsky it was a four seat Pumkin special, a ratty orange crate that was chartered by federal agencies.

Oblivious to the changed miens of those behind him, the prince marched up the stairs, strode onto the pad, and into the waiting arms of two big plain clothes cops.

The ensuing pantomime was entertaining. The scrawny guy looked terrified.

"Like a deer in headlights," said Tar Baby.

"You should know," Turtle replied. "All the road hunting you do."

We all followed Hammer up the stairs.

"Hey, what gives?" His Majesty pleaded.

What "gave" was a shake down. The toolpusher relieved him of his tiny bag. Rummaging through it he proudly removed two wallets and held them up for all to see.

"This ain't legal! I got rights," the prince wailed, adding, "I was framed. Them mudloggers wanted me to get in trouble." He tried to wiggle free. The policemen each twisted an arm behind him, cuffed his wrist, and bundled him into a back seat.

"You can't get away with this." We heard him say as the door closed. He said something else once he was buckled up, but we couldn't hear.

"Probably something about seeing his lawyer," said Fireball. "Probably seen a lot of them in his time."

The tiny Bell helicopter lifted up, turned toward the wind, and struggled forward, its blades chomping out a chorus of "I think I can", and "I think I can" until it cleared the helipad and chugged away.

"Fly the friendly skies," said the welder.

Back in the wheelhouse, I watched it disappear into the horizon. As I did I gave in to an urge to look at Turtle, who I felt was staring at me. A Cheshire Cat's grin spread across his pudgy face, transforming him into the essence of wiliness.

I turned away but couldn't shake what it had forced me to admit. He knew how to divert attention and unearth the criminal. Worse, he knew I knew without knowing he knew. And he probably knew I thought he was too thick to know.

It was the last admission that plastered that grin in my mind. It was an albatross that festered no matter what I did, or who I talked to.

Believing it would go away by asking Jones, the electrician, why the name "Pumpkin Air" was misspelled on the craft only ended up curling the ends up into a more sinister crescent.

"Things seem to be a little off-center out here," I added.

"It's to be expected," the only clean-shaven crewmember said. "Throw a bunch of people together, every one of whom thinks he's smarter, luckier, or just better than the next and you're going to get a lot of things off-center." I must have looked at him imploringly because he elaborated. "Hunt's think a little luck is all they need to make it as big as their old man. Keep the names of all their companies down to six letters, Placid, Pumpkin, Portal, Pinter, Penrod."

"Same with the 'P'?"

He nodded, then let out a laugh. "There's not enough luck in the universe to save that bunch."

Turtle's big grin manifested itself in the clouds once I finally got airborne. It kept me humble. Under its glare I couldn't be smug about what I'd do with good luck. Look at my track record. I had mistaken what I was born into and got to enjoy for being more intelligent than my associates. Like Hammer, I had been a member of the Lucky Sperm Club. Unlike him, I never admitted it. His ability to jump was a physical gift, mine was economic.

John Wayne needed to dodge V.C. bullets to come to terms with his patriotism in the "Green Berets" and I needed my sojourn through the "The Looking Glass" to learn about myself.

My movie hadn't ended. I hadn't reached the denouement, when I can do what the Duke did, pontificate on an east coast beach under the glow of a setting sun.

The sun was rising in the east in my Gulf of Tonkin, shedding light on memories of Harvey crying, Harvey threatening David; over Hammer making a fool out of Bull, Hammer making a fool out of himself; over Bull's "hello" on the P.A., his animal noises; over Jim and all he did. It rose over memories of my guiding loads, operating a needle gun, working a pinch bar, my initiation to the air hoist, to servicing the kelly, tripping pipe, and to handling tag lines, shackles, tongs, and chains.

Then there was the hammerhead, the pigeon, the peppers, the card game, the boat ride and newspaper flight, all of which led me to believe I was lucky after all. It made me, if not appreciate the backhanded luck that had brought me aboard, at least understand the mess my family was in wasn't a complete calamity.

The edges of the ethereal grin turned down. It quit looking sinister and even began to look like a smile. It seemed to laud me for withstanding every challenge in what for the first time in my life a real adventure was not just another drunken weekend on the slopes or an outing on the beach.

As my ride reached cruising altitude, above the Salvador Dali canvas of clouds, I found myself worrying whether I had pulled my weight, or done a satisfactory job. Why was I a slower learner than my Brother-in-Law? Could I have done a better job if I again found myself a roustabout? As for roughnecking, I hoped my learning curve would steepen with time. Once I get to the house, I'm going to work on the muscles that ached the most, helping me perform better.

To me, Fireball wasn't a sand-blasted moolie, as Ronnie called all Cajuns. He was my boss. A professor of drillology whose respect I wanted to earn. I may know more about the Peloponnesian Wars, Marxism, and entomology, but he's the expert where drilling is concerned. And I bet those Ph. D.s who teach Petroleum Engineering at L.S.U. could learn from him too. Let them apply their chalkboard theories where it never rains.

The platforms and rigs exposed underneath gaps in the surreal clouds inspired further insights. For the first time in my life, I had performed not just to fit in, trying to impress those I considered my better, but for the sheer satisfaction of proving I had what it took. Bull, Hammer, Sunshine, and Jim could insult me from here to next year, and I wouldn't care as long as I knew I had done my job well. How did that ditty about the Klondike go? "Now I get me up to work,

I pray the Lord I shall not shirk. And if I should die before the night, I pray the Lord my work's all right." Somehow, it didn't sound so corny.

I almost regretted seeing the blue water turn brown. I'm sure Foreign Legionnaires were ambivalent about returning to France, the Lafayette Escadrille at trading their Spuds and Nieportes for single-wing mail planes, and Sir Edmund Hillary returning to base camp. Something is depressing about going where decisions were made on the information provided by the Jims of the world. The drilling superintendent was never told what a fiasco his drill beads were, according to Blowfly. It cost Springer Oil twenty grand to replace the lost mud and fifty grand in lost drilling time. Decisions were being made about the hole that does not take into account walnut shells and wood fiber preventing the formation from breaking down immediately below the casing.

On the other hand, I could see Eugene and the Chi Sigmas getting caught up in the boom long enough for them to lose whatever wealth they'd managed to accumulate. Someone who didn't know what goes on at a well-site, who never experienced Jim, and who was ignorant of what Sunshine got away with couldn't buy a profitable bottom-hole-letter, dry hole donation letter, back-in-rights, or make money entering blind pools and limited partnerships. The get-rich-quick schemes of these boom times will humble the "look at me, I'm an oilman" crowd come the inevitable bust.

The rig crew won't get caught up in the mania. They have their CDs and shares of Wal-Mart. If a future Zane Grey or Louis L'Amour portrays the Spuds and Turtles as later-day cowboys they'll airbrush their warts like their predecessors airbrushed the classic cowboys. I wouldn't mind. They knew how to survive Jim Duhon. And so did I.

CHAPTER 9

As we descended toward the linear brown beach and the marshland beyond, I came to realize what made the Acadians I worked with so different. There was no place to hide, no relief to protect them from the elements. If the Big Easy was the city that celebrated life between Hurricanes, Acadiana was the land that celebrated life during Hurricanes. It had to. It was so exposed.

The same feeling that compelled me to look at Turtle compelled me to take one look back. Despite the scratches in the window, I'm sure I saw the remnants of the smile fade into a frown before disappearing altogether. It left me wistful. I hadn't accomplished my mission. All I had gone through had been a diversion. Surviving Jim Duhon may have helped me feel better about myself, but it hasn't improved my situation or helped Father. There's no way I could take solace in anything I had done while he languished in Angola. How could I think sucking up to an autocrat was an achievement? Father probably is stuck in Angola instead of some country club because he refused to suck up to some demagogic politician. He probably was arrested in the first place because he wouldn't play their games.

The littoral landscape below was cut up by waterways. Just below the surface, deltas of tributaries could be seen debouching into the streams they fed. Grass grew in the shallows of what looked like stagnant feeders, but whose straight banks and "t" shaped estuaries hinted they were dredged and not natural. A drilling barge at the top of the "t" of one canal showed why it was formed. Tied to the rig were

two small crew boats. Several flat barges lined the ditch leading to it.
Hunting cabins dotted the landscape for a while, until giving way to an
occasional tank farm. With the appearance of a road, buildings started
to appear. As we banked right a river appeared, alive with commercial
boats and little motorboats cutting through their wakes. We followed it
until coming upon a port, crowded with docks and facilities on both
sides of the water and which increased exponentially in size as we
descended. Behind one of the pipe yards we slowed, aimed, and landed
on a grassy field hard by a big parking lot and two trailers.

Lugging our gear to the cars I overheard Turtle chew out
Mamou the moment the helicopter was far enough away to allow
conversation. "Why'd you hide Ronnie's Fann meter? I woulda throw
it overboard as I did with his pH papers and filter press."

Mamou shrugged, "I thought I'd made my point."

I chuckled and was thankful I was on the right side of these
guys. The movie "Southern Comfort" was more a documentary than a
work of fiction.

Spotting the prearranged spray-painted sign on a tree indicating
Robert had retrieved his truck I searched for a ride.

Fireball spotted me. "No floor hand walks." He pulled his
pickup beside me. Unfortunately, it already being packed with people
meant I had to accompany the baggage in the dog seat. The rear
window did not stifle Tar Baby's bray: "No one goes home sober,
either."

"Have no fear, the rotary specialists are here!" the big guy
bellowed upon entering the Shrimper's Lounge.

It took a while for my eyes to adjust to the darkness and my
ears to adjust to the music from the jukebox but once they did I could
see and hear what a commotion by the bar was all about.

From the sly looks and not all that subtle innuendo the barflies
were abuzz about a woman sitting in a far booth.

"A pro," whispered Turtle. The lust in his eyes was not
conveyed by his body language. He was stiff, immobile, as if afraid.

Tar Baby was more expressive. "She can whip me, beat me,
make me write bad checks," he said, without moving an inch toward
her.

Picking at her food, a dress-for-success businesswoman sat by herself. The presence of a leather briefcase did not elicit any reassessment of her status.

No Flatlander could identify a three-dimensional object, and no "Sound of the South" chorus member knew what to make of a career woman. I've seen them all the time, representing vendors, and insurance companies, functioning as corporate executives...performing jobs many men performed, and just as competently. I always was amazed at how seriously Father took them, given the type of women he married.

To everyone's amazement, I had no qualms walking up to her.

The prattle I emitted as I approached her started adagio pianissimo, rose to andante, mezzo forte when I introduced myself, and reached an allegretto crescendo when she motioned me to sit next to her.

"Was wondering when someone would hit on me," she stated. She ran her hand through her luxurious brown hair.

"You've got a lot to learn," I replied.

"What makes you think I'm not a snobby good ol' girl or a play for pay Patty?"

As one who had a hard time looking people in the eyes, I found it easy to look at hers. Framed by sensuously arched eyebrows and deeply set, they sparkled impishly.

"You haven't got a pinched mouth, and what would a working girl do with a briefcase?" I asked rhetorically, concentrating instead on her smooth skin and completely symmetric features.

We effortlessly segued into a breezy conversation the rowdy audience settled down to overhear and absorb. They must have concluded she wasn't a prostitute and deserved better than me.

At first one by one then two by two, admirers accosted her with a panoply of come-ons, some quite innovative.

"I had no idea they could be so creative," she remarked after the third effort.

"By now, nothing about them would surprise me," I shook my head in amusement. I looked up to see probably the only guy who hadn't yet tried to woo her. Listening carefully, I took a full measure of his shtick.

Who am I to say the rig mechanic hadn't invented the mouse hole? I thought. *After all, it doesn't take a genius to invent a hole.*

"I should be richer than Pete Rose for all the rig time I saved." The guy (Chester, someone said) looked at her, at first imploringly, then with discernment, misinterpreting her indifference for ignorance. He rambled on about how a joint placed in the hole he invented was easier to access than one lying on the "V" door. Her blank expression appeared enigmatic. He attracted everyone's attention. "A lawyer I know says that the contract I signed giving the company rights to everything I came up with wasn't legal."

Karen smiled politely. "That's nice."

Chester grew anxious. "I'm going to be rich."

"I'm happy for you." Her smile continued to restrained.

"I'm gonna be able to spoil anyone I want," he almost shouted.

"If that's what you want."

"You don't believe I'm gonna get the money." Becoming frantic, he started to take on the features of his namesake, Chester the Molester, the comic character featured in "Hustler". "I'll get it, don't worry about that."

"It's against the law to sign somethin' like that. I know I wouldn't have signed anything," proclaimed Blowfly, intensely following the conversation from a bar stool. I noticed a lot of signatures on his arm cast.

"He's right," added Pencil. "I got a cousin in law school who knows about things like that."

"Which school?" asked the object of their desires.

"Uh, Southern?" The driller tried to look calm.

"Isn't the school all black?"

"No, it's coed," his deep voice cracked with panic.

Karen maintained her expressionless look. The spectators snickered. Pencil swiveled his big head around in both directions. Out of respect, he was allowed to return to his drink with some dignity. Only Blowfly said anything.

"It serves you right," were the clerk's audible comments. He made other comments, but they weren't audible.

Chester retreated.

"You're pretty deft around these folks," I said softly.

"Hang them by their tongue. It's a standard negotiating practice," she replied matter-of-factly.

"Part of your job?"

"I'm a buyer for a national supermarket. Have to learn about these people. They are our future customers." She showed me her copious notes.

"'Moscie' is what Hispanics call Negroes," I pointed out.

"Wasn't sure about that one. Find anything else?"

I informed her that the B. R. 24 she had a question about was a riot stick and elaborated on the vaunted status enjoyed by tractor-trailer drivers.

"Am told they drive their rigs down the main drags to impress the women," I said. "Anyone who doesn't drive bulls is an animal hauler. They have horses in the engine, pigs or chickens in the trailer, and are jackasses behind the wheel." I finished by flippantly passing on personal opinions I've overheard, such disparate things as Jim's aversion to hands who tucked their coveralls into their boots, claiming they just were trying to come across as delinquents, and Sunshine's claiming salt dehydrates the skin.

"So now you know more about the compound than the fact the locals use it on everything," I commented.

"Seem to love it almost as much as pork rinds."

"Love anything fried."

On the second page, I penned the word "broken" next to the word "Gilflut".

"Didn't think it was a Hebraic derivative."

"Only thing Jewish down here is a fish."

A resumption of the debate about how to handle Chester's legal dilemma raised a cacophony of noise in the background. Egos clashed against egos like cymbals.

"Not exactly a Mensa convention," I said.

"Maybe I'm over-researching them," she looked up questioningly. "Might draw up a survey that's too difficult for them to take."

"Let me tell you something," I announced with conviction. "One week with them and their predictability will bore you to death. Several months with them and you'll never figure them out."

She smiled.

We continued our discussion, finding enough common ground for us to realize at the same time the crew's debate had turned into an argument and became ominous.

"What makes him so special?" I heard Heavy Duty say as Karen gathered her things and signaled for me to leave with her.

"Why would she want you?" asked Turtle.

"Why not?" asked the cementer. "I'm the right weight, just the wrong height."

"Woman ain't got no taste," snarled Tar Baby drunkenly.

"If I didn't have any taste, I would have left by myself," she whispered in my ear.

"Then you'll give me a ride?" I asked, trying not to sound too excited. "Riding with this bunch would be a death-defying act."

"Riding with me is a breadth-defining act."

"I need to expand my horizons."

"We all do." She bumped me as we exited.

Rather than bump her back or say anything I applied the family axiom about letting the other person make the defining move. I did open the car door for her and stored her purse in the trunk with my bag, but I didn't say a word.

Her silence was unnerving. She concentrated on the road, being as quiet as was the ride of the rented Lincoln Continental. Instead of arousing my libido, she started to arouse my curiosity. Her continued silence aroused worry. I wondered what I had done to irritate her. I wondered if she had something unpleasant in mind, whether the entire episode had been nothing more than a ruse.

"Saw a quaint restaurant further up the road. Want to go?" she finally said.

"Sure!"

We grew in familiarity, and even shared some jokes, by the time we reached the eatery up the bayou. Among the many topics we broached over a meal featuring turtle etouffee the one about the effects certain drinks had on her future customers interested her most. The anger beer encourages the violence of tequila, and even the contentment of aftershave captivated her.

"Think about it," I said while defoliating a burr artichoke. "Anyone desperate enough to drink Old Spice must appreciate anything he could get."

Rather than parry with a clever riposte she demurely said, "John Barleycorn is deceptive. He crept up on my Father one drink at a time until he killed him."

"My Father didn't succumb to the temptation," I replied. "Many of his peers had."

A homily on the wrath of the grape expanded into a discussion of other human foibles, mostly those of Father's peers. I went on and on about the hubris they displayed, how they overextended their business and acted like they had hit the jackpot. I ripped into them, and everyone else who lacked Father's character. I must have gotten worked up because I was shaking after I decried the fact that "they get to enjoy life and he doesn't."

I looked up to find her staring at me. Realizing I had said more than I intended and acted like a dork while saying it put a great big lump in my throat.

"Family loyalty. That's great," she said genially. "You don't see it much today."

Relieved she was decorous enough not to insist on what I meant, I launched into my background, emphasizing Grandfather's influence.

"I bet he had to deal with a lot of situations which seemed hopeless. That's just the way life is."

My back arched in anticipation of what she next was going to say.

"That he was so successful meant he had the character to deal with them."

Not hearing how lucky we've been was therapeutic. At one instance, I knew the main reason why I once had hated the great unwashed. I used to think all of them assumed someone more successful than they were just lucky.

"It's also probably why you clung to your kind," Karen added, proving she was as sagacious as she was stunning. "Only your bunch know the harder you work the luckier you become." She took a bite of her entree. "You just have to accept the fact most don't want to know why some people seem to get all the luck."

"Don't want to look at their reflection?"

"Do you?"

I quickly changed the subject. "What about bad luck?"

I waited for her to swallow. "What about it?"

"Why does it happen?"

"Bad luck isn't supposed to happen?" She took another bite.

I toyed with my food. "But for no reason?"

She snickered. "Excuse me, I don't mean to be rude. But do you think it's fair to put someone so high on a pedestal he doesn't have enough air to breath?"

"I do resent whenever someone puts too much pressure on me." I speared a piece of meat but hesitated to put it in my mouth. I brought up H.L. Hunt's sons and sounded wise by saying they were taking outrageous chances to measure up to their Father's success.

"The biggest shoes are the hardest to fill."

"So you resort to shortcuts?" I almost stabbed myself inserting my fork in my mouth.

"Depends on your moral fiber."

"Ours is the best."

She shook some Tony Chachere's seasoning on her etoufee. "My industry lacks the bumps yours does. It has a tiny return on investment, but everybody has to eat and will buy their food where it's the cheapest."

"But would your employees stay by you no matter what?"

"The few managers, yes. The rest are part-time help. That's one of the reasons our costs are so low."

"My family cared about all its employees. That's why they never sued or jumped to other companies. They even testified for us when others sued. Loyalty was our competitive edge."

"I'd like to meet your family. It sounds fascinating."

How fascinating, I didn't tell her until we had finished every sugary crumb of the pralines we had for dessert. I'm sure the confection helped sweeten her disposition enough to volunteer to visit Father as he rotted away in the maximum-security prison east of the Mississippi River.

She popped a stray pecan in her mouth. "In the meantime, I would like to pick your brain."

"That shouldn't take long."

"Don't ever underestimate yourself, even in jest. No successful person I ever met put himself down." She leveled a no-nonsense look at me.

"I only do it to disarm the competition," I rallied well enough to say.

"Well said. Maybe you are executive material after all."

The sophistication Karen radiated wrought a comfort I hadn't felt in a long time. She was a refuge of sanity in my insane world, a tether to the world I had come from, a world of familiar concepts and ways of doing things, devoid of sudden dangers.

I guess the rough weather that turned helicopters into eggbeaters and boats into corks must have flailed my nerves. I thought. Worrying Sunshine and Jim had crippled the well, making it incapable of withstanding another kick, didn't help. Nor did the fear of being runoff. Everything I had experienced contributed to a sense of insecurity. Karen counteracted the effect. Her maturity and sense of proportion soothed my ravaged breast.

It also was amazing how alluring and at the same time professional she could look in her K-Mart wardrobe and few baubles. She proved that a woman didn't need designer fashions, Estee Lauder make-up, and the latest Chignon hair-do to look classy. At least she did to me. A Henry James' <u>Real Thing</u> doesn't need accoutrements. Her natural radiance shamed all superficialities.

As I watched her drive, her hands firmly on the steering wheel, navigating flawlessly around curves that fell away precipitously to the water below, she inspired confidence. I was convinced she not only could help me with Father she also could help me with Leslie, help me to figuratively replace the black groom's broken arm, reestablish synchronicity, so I could prove unequivocally to my Dulcinea I'm her knight and shining armor.

Up the bayou, past a wealth of homes, a gas field, and a sugar mill on the right, winding around and through Bollinger shipyard (catching peeks of the Coast Guard patrol boats it was working on) to highway ninety, she remained relatively quiet. On the thoroughfare, through the budding oak gum forest, my Dorothea succumbed to my incessant questions about her background. I couldn't help myself. I never had met anyone like her.

Starting hesitantly, she revealed she had a traditional good ol' girl upbringing.

"If not for a house fire I'd have become another DeRidder statistic," she got around to admitting.

With her voice betraying emotion, she revealed how the unsightly skin grafts she had worn might as well have been I.U.D.s. They kept the local Pennys away from her throughout the first few breeding seasons. Her contemporaries were on their third husband and fourth child before her first divorce.

"Wouldn't have had a nice home, good job, or a college degree if I wasn't too deformed to attract a male. I always knew I was attractive, so I wasn't desperate like the girls who were convinced they were ugly."

She went on to tell me how she lived in her car after graduation and interviewed after preening herself in gas station washrooms.

"The gentleman who hired me thought it necessary to discuss the problems of home ownership. It didn't take me long to be promoted over him."

She opened up to me, grew more and more intimate with each mile. By the time we crossed the Huey P. Long Bridge, I knew I left Acadiana and my loneliness behind.

The closer we came to her house in Lakeview, by Lake Ponchartrain, the more anxious I became. What would happen? Would she think me a whimp if I don't come on to her? Would she come on to me? And if she did, could I perform? I wished the traffic on Clearview avenue was more congested. I wished there was an accident on I-10, on Causeway when we turned onto it. I wished we'd bust an axle on one of world-class pot holes in the subdivision. Pulling up to the townhouse was like receiving an exam paper, not knowing what to expect, worrying if there was information I didn't know as well as I thought.

What happened once the front door closed behind me was surreal. They say one registers impending doom in slow motion, absorbs every detail until one passes out. I must have gone into shock once I was led to the bedroom because, although I remembered everything that transpired while I was on the couch, I didn't remember a thing when I was in her bed. All I knew was that I enjoyed a feeling of well-being and contentment. It was similar to that which suffused me when we had talked and drank coffee in the living room. Both were *sui generis*.

A jumble of emotions and thoughts wracked me the next morning. I didn't feel compelled to check out Karen as she slept. It was enough to know she was beside me. Awarded a velvety "good morning" as she stirred was all the sensual arousal I could handle.

Because none of my frustrations were resolved I couldn't make the event out to be more than a delightful interlude. Maybe it was like pot. After a few tokes you still have the same problems. You just don't care.

A gentle hand over my mouth held back a torrent of inarticulate emotions I wanted to express.

"Don't say anything," she purred, her rich, thick hair falling down her face. "Nobody says anything intelligent when he first gets up."

I did watch her as she strode around the room in her nightie. She was amazing, a combination Catherine Deneuve, Katherine Hepburn and Lana Turner, savvy, saucy, and sensuous, a real gem.

I couldn't love her like I loved Leslie. Her maturity kept us spiritually apart. Something inside me sought an incomplete soul, someone who would grow as I grew. I wanted a companion who would travel the road to self-discovery with me. Only recently did I learn how much of it I had yet to traverse, with Karen acting as my Anne Sullivan.

Watching her dress, I couldn't bring myself to believe Oscar Wilde's witticism about not giving in to anything but temptation applied. Without her I might have wallowed in my inhibitions, become a cerebral know-it-all, hollow and boring. She didn't screw the shame out of me. She screwed humanity into me.

The intimacy of our proximity kept alive the sensations from last night. The smoothness of her skin, the aroma of her perfume, the sound of her voice, these were the attractions that kept me in her thrall. She had taken a worm and turned him into a hand.

Sure, Spud, Turtle, and even Robert wouldn't have let her lead. To do so would be unmanly. They'd rather tear the dress of a woman than let her charm them out of their pants.

It must be easy to read because she had no problem figuring me out as we sat around the kitchen table eating the breakfast she prepared. "Believe me, men who share themselves are more sensual than those who try to dominate you," she said between bites of her omelet.

"Why?" I asked, trying to look and act sophisticated. "My best friend has more women than a sheik."

"How many does he keep?"

"I never thought of that."

"How many of those he has would you want to keep?"

"I never thought of that either."

A brief aside about Father's turnover of wives introduced me to another side of her.

"Don't worry. Your Father can be salvaged. No one who has a son like you is irredeemable."

Keeping my head from swelling required all the character I could muster. It wasn't easy, since she wouldn't let me fall back on saying anything self-deprecating. I had to engage her in intelligent conversation. If I happened to voice an opinion, I had to back it up with proof. I never had such a conversation with a guy before, let alone a girl. Then again, I never experienced what I had last night before. I never, ever thought the two could occur together, with the same person, on the same occasion. When it was time to catch a cab home, I wasn't the same person I was when I went home with her.

For some reason it didn't surprise me Robert wasn't the same person he had been when I last saw him. It seemed whenever I changed, he changed, and vise versa.

Lounging in the overstuffed chair we found at a garage sale my former butler waved hello. "Hey, my man, I'm glad to see you." His smile spread over his face.

His sallow skin and emaciated body took me aback.

"My luck's holding out. Played some Cany-head football. Mudslingers against the pro fisherman who finished up a tournament." I must have looked curious because he took the time to explain the East Texas diversion. "Make up the rules as we go. A real test of skill and toughness. Bruised a kidney, bad. Doc says it might shut down."

"That's terrible."

"No, that's great. He decided to look at my liver and said it was in none too good shape and would degenerate badly if I continued pickling it. Need to eat better."

I noticed cans of tomato juice in the open liquor cabinet.

"Nothing like a real scare to steer you straight. Reminds me of a fellow dogger. Would have never met him if he hadn't been shot in the stomach. Trichinosis worms in his belly blocked the buckshot. Didn't know he had them."

Not one to beat a dead horse he set about debriefing me. Although I was frank about my experience, he could tell I left something out. He always could tell and rather than suffer an interrogation I told him all about Karen. I hyped her to the hilt. But instead of congratulating me on finding someone special he confirmed what I was aware of but wouldn't admit.

"You know she'd be better for your Father than for you."

I sagged. As it always does, the truth hurts.

He handed me a bottle of tomato juice, took a swig from his bottle, and said, "Let's face it, your Father's taste in women leaves a lot to be desired. It's a symptom of a cynicism that contaminates his entire outlook."

"Like yours?"

"Close. I'm pragmatic. Notice how I don't even try to latch on to them."

"I've noticed," I said, thinking of Dennis' rationalizations about women.

"They're all for fun. When I settle down it'll be with someone you wouldn't rate a five. 'To be happy for the rest of your life, never make a pretty woman your wife'."

"Not exactly the most profound lyrics in the world," I remarked.

"They're representative of a larger concept."

I told him how similar he sounded to the B. and R. hands.

"Sounds like he stands by his beliefs, and is not a hypocrite. There's no law saying eclectic logic doesn't work."

"Rube Goldberg logic."

"You engage in it. If you didn't, you'd have stormed the companyman's office and got that invoice, not come up with a back-assward, upside-down, inside-out plan to please everyone and his brother so they might help you."

I told him about my run-in with Ronnie.

"So why did you leave after the paper jammed in the Xerox machine?"

"Got me," I said aloud, although I think I knew why, but wouldn't dare admit it aloud. I barely could admit it to myself, it's so unbelievable. *I may have subconsciously forced myself to find an excuse to stay on the rig*

So I got on a pay phone by a neighborhood grocery story and dialed right up the number to Angola...after three aborted attempts. Again, I identified myself by using Grandfather's middle name.

Father's voice was tired, barely audible. He very grudgingly acknowledged me. Still, I pressed on, emphasizing the fact an attractive, college-educated *Fraulein* wanted to meet him.

"No woman would want to see me; not as I am," he mumbled in a chilling tone.

"This one would. Believe me, Father, she knows all about you."

"I doubt that."

"I told her everything."

"Everything you know."

I didn't ask him to elaborate. Instead, I insisted over and over she was unlike Kimberly or any of his previous wives.

Ultimately, he gave in, claiming, "I've got nothing to lose. I was spared for some reason."

What he was spared from I didn't know and wouldn't find out until I saw him. Which left me in a bind. I couldn't give myself up. Nor would I ever come up with an elaborate plan. *Nobody in history ever broke into Angola federal penitentiary*, I thought.

My silence must have been deafening. "Don't worry about being captured," Father advised. "I told everyone you had nothing to do with my troubles. My lawyers drew up legal documents stating as much."

Karen and I set out to visit as soon as she was free. The swamps insulating the city from the world mirrored my initial state of mind. The drooping moss and ghostly cypress were perfect projections of my mood. I couldn't get over how Father tried to hide behind me. That he hadn't dealt with his problems head-on was an insult to what our family stood for.

Maybe it was all the time I spent in the passenger's seat or the change of scenery, but I felt less vitriolic once we reached the pine-carpeted bluffs north of Baton Rouge. Where the air wasn't so stagnant and the sights so morose, I was able to think clearer, ponder facts, and ultimately conclude that Father's strange behavior before his arrest might have been because he knew he had broken the family covenant about sticking together. He sure broke one by letting the pipe yard deteriorate. Whether he also had broken the law was a question I'll defer until all the facts are in. After all, he was penitent.

I was glad I hadn't been rash. Sitting across from him in the stark visitor's room I had a harder time than usual looking him in the eye. What was merely a bad habit was exacerbated by his dead expression. I wouldn't have recognized Father had he walked by me on the street. Judging from his slumped shoulders and defeated demeanor I was not surprised when he admitted he had tried to hang himself.

"I was saved for some reason," he whispered. "Certainly, didn't deserve it." It turned out he was saved by a surprise inspection. A guard had rushed to his aid seconds before he would have succumbed. "If he hadn't known CPR I wouldn't be here. Heart stopped three times."

Trying to contain a welter of emotions, it was all I could do to keep the conversation formal, succinct, and general. I did not press him about his culpability. Judging from his disjointed responses to the soft balls I lobbed I doubt if he would have leveled with me if I asked anything pertinent. I had to surmise a lot, as to whether he again would attempt to do himself in. Satisfied he wouldn't, I genuinely felt happy to see him, and wished him well when my time was up.

I was even happier after Karen had spent her allotted time with him. He evinced in the last good-byes a guard granted me an optimism I hadn't heard from him for months. He looked invigorated. His voice was animated. Five minutes with Karen had done what no confessional ever could do. Priests advance to Bishops with far less talent at persuasion than those she must possess.

"Don't be a stranger," Father said to me in parting.

"You women can make or break a man," I said to her on the way out.

"It's our secret." She put her arm on my shoulder, buddy buddy-like.

CHAPTER 10

It was pure bad luck Karen wasn't around to impart her wisdom when Leslie barged into my apartment the next day. She would have known what to say to calm her. I didn't, being unable to remember all that had transpired before my hitch. What had happened on the water was too vivid. I still felt naked sticking my head out the door without a helmet on.

The emotions that had wracked me before going offshore had dissipated, creating a gulf between us. Hers had increased to near hysterics. Unable to either make out what she was upset about or inform her of my condition, I offered her tomato juice.

"I don't want any juice," she wailed. "I don't want anything." Her flaxen hair was gnarly and dirty. Her expressive eyes expressed inconsolable dread. "I called you all day yesterday. Where were you? You deserted me."

Trying to remain calm, I applied a little cognitive therapy, realizing she was acting out learned behavior. Explaining to her I needed a day to decompress from the alien environment and probably wouldn't wash.

"I am not going to talk to you until you control yourself," I said desensitizing her.

"I can't." She flailed her arms. "I can't."

"You must or, if you don't...." A wave of nausea swept through me. "You'll have to leave." Her body convulsed. She looked possessed. Her eyes blazed.

Not knowing how to deal with the hysterics (quickly thinking of things to do and just as quickly rejecting them) I assumed the most commanding presence I could; looked her straight in the eye; and, in the most resonant tone of voice I could command, ordered her quiet. She instantly went rigid.

I assumed a paternal tone of voice, explaining something I made up as I went along. It sounded so good I began to believe it myself. Each aspect emerged in revealing bits and pieces that could be assembled into coherent ideas after only a couple of repetitions. I told her her environment conspired to keep her down, dutiful and subservient. "It's based on the worry you somehow could expose it, damage it." I wasn't talking to her as much as I was admitting to myself what I knew but was afraid to express.

Leslie softened. She looked interested in what I might have to say.

"Your world is no different than my world on the rig," I said. "The workers are constantly reminded of their place. They are taunted and harassed until they move up the ranks. Those on top exercise their power arbitrarily. It's the only exercise they get. Both worlds are very stratified, with no room for dissent."

She shook as if afflicted with ague. I could see the rind of conventions crack and start to flake off.

"On a rig, given the nature of the work and the nature of the workers, it's the only possible system," I said, sounding too pedantic. "Except for the bosses, who would endanger everything just to show their ass."

She didn't flinch at the obscenity.

"Your people are worse than rig hands," I said. "Hands have to do something radical to get run off. Among your bunch, all you have to do is something different. Hands can be as weird as they want, so long as they don't steal anything or slow down work."

"There's a reason for the way we act, isn't there?"

"Fear."

"Of what?

"Like they say on the rig. It's the way they were raised."

She shook worse than ever.

I got frustrated beating around the bush. From nowhere I said "Your feelings are like the air. Can you color the air with paint? What anybody says or does to you cannot affect you if you don't let it. You had to be trained to let it. And so did I."

Her cocoon exploded into shards. Her demons suddenly evaporated. In front of me stood a butterfly where there was once a caterpillar, dumbfounded to find her prison had been self-imposed.

Looking at her I saw myself, finally facing a truth I hadn't been previously aware of. We inadvertently made eye contact. Doing so settled both of us down.

Having collected herself, she explained why she was so desperate to see me. While I was away the fraternities had quit squabbling among themselves and ceased calling each other "boys clubs", to unite in a concerted effort to smear the reputations of those responsible for their troubles. Being the most well-known, Leslie suffered the harshest criticism. Word was leaked she was a lush and a "pass-around-pack" who brought on her troubles.

Pictures of her at past soirees appeared to substantiate each claim. She showed me several photocopies of them. There she was, at one party after another, her arms wrapped around an active or a beer can, incriminating herself.

"I was ready to kill myself." She paused to reflect. "I mean, I was bad off. I needed to come to you."

"It might not have done any good if you came to me earlier," I admitted. "I was closer to being one of your detractors than you'd ever guess." I swallowed hard. "There was a time when I'd have been thrilled to believe anything bad about you."

She repressed a sudden fright. "Why?" she asked, her voice quavering.

"Because I knew I could never have you," I said after a moment's reflection.

"Have me?" she asked.

"Have you; own you, so you'd adore me."

"Really?" She accented each syllable. She sat in our overstuffed chair. I remained standing.

"I'd never admit it but that's how I felt; I'm sure how everyone felt. Want what we want when we want it."

"So, it's killing what you can't have?"

"Humiliate first."

"When did you become so smart?"

Robert appeared in the hallway. "Always had the seed of doubt in me. It just needed a little watering and an existential gardener." Robert grinned and moved on.

"Oh, Christ!" I exclaimed. "'A town without pity' was aired decades ago. No modern woman should ever get caught up in such trite morality plays, not today."

"It's not trite." Prepared, she pulled from her purse a recent copy of Tulane's school newspaper.

The future ad men who wrote for it took a leaf from the Chicagoan who had asked me for the time. Leslie's name appeared five times in the biased article. The rules of confidentiality, impartiality, as well as good taste, and competent writing, were given over to the type of reportage those with inquiring minds would enjoy.

"My parents want to send me to another school, Vassar or Smith."

Hearing proof of my suspicions of New Orleans plutocracy was so exciting I wallowed a little too long in my self-satisfaction. She began to eye me suspiciously.

"That's awful!" I exclaimed.

She hesitated, before adding, "They're worried what their clubs will say."

I gulped with the immensity of her claim. I didn't want to but I had to ask, "Even the Boston Club?" The mere thought of the last bastion of culture and civilized prerogatives being no better than any of the cabals of Babbitry was disconcerting. Without them, where could one revel in his personality protected from conformists as well as the envious and the demagogues who manipulated them? Nowhere.

"Even the Boston Club," she affirmed. My head felt like it was inside a clanging bell. I couldn't hear anything. I couldn't think. And I didn't have any idea how long I was unable to think because when I regained my senses, she was relaying proof of their culpability in a heroically controlled monotone.

"Me, a black sheep," she barely moved her lips. "Forget I was a Maid in Les Pierrettes and Harlequins, presented by Le Debut des Jeunes Filles de la Nouvelle Orleans, the Bachelor's Club, and the Pickwick club." Her voice deepened. "I also was presented to the Court of Rex, and a maid in the courts of Elves of Oberon, Achaeans, and Nereus. And forget my National Merit Scholarship, my years as a Candy Stripper."

"What about your sisters?" I asked. "Certainly, they know the score. Some of them must have run the same gauntlet."

She looked at me sternly. "Did any former Pine Manor classmate help you?"

"*Touché.*"

Leaping from the chair, she invested in a scream of all the horror and helplessness of gross injustice. "They say I pulled a train."

"They said that?"

"It's like blaming the Jews for the Holocaust. Saying I was like Janis Joplin."

Whose reputation probably was exaggerated, I thought. I put my arm around her and told her not to worry. "We have an advocate."

"Patty Green, the journalist?"

"If this doesn't win her an award, nothing will."

After I convinced her to take tomato juice, I managed to get her to sit down. Robert ambled in to engage us in light conversation. He soon had us calmed down, guzzling drinks and reflecting on our situation, being honest about ourselves.

"I can't quit worrying about what people think of me just like that. I've been doing it all my life." Leslie admitted.

"It's a whole different world once you burn your bridges," I said. "It simplifies things. Makes it easy to figure out what you need to do."

"What about my family? I just can't turn my back on my family."

"Why not? They turned their backs on you."

We let her think about it. "I guess I'm just used to doing what I'm told."

"It took me a hitch at a pipe yard and three on a rig to cure me of all loyalty to my bunch. Culture shock is a really good teacher."

"Frogs dropped into heated water will leap out. Those put in lukewarm water will stay until they are boiled," said Robert.

Leslie didn't blink. She didn't move. She just sat stone-faced until whispering (almost against her will) "Can I stay here for a short while?" She shook her mane of blonde hair. "To think things through?"

We had no problem reenlisting Miss Green's support for a counter-attack. The journalist loomed large, her horned-rim glasses steamed with anger. I pitied the frats.

From her command seat in her paper-cuttered war room, she announced how she was thrilled to find out how rabid the upper crust was. "I always suspected they're just white trash with money," she said. "I only was held back by my belief they were too pathetic to unite, like our blacks, too busy sniping at each other to unite into big gangs, as they have in Shreveport.

"The societies, the clubs, the Greeks they all have usurped power in this city," she hissed.

"Well," I said, a little breathless at the degree of her anger. "For good or bad, they have defined this town. Momus, Comus, there wouldn't be any Mardi Gras without them."

She didn't even blink. "They're a closed shop that has ruined this town. Operas used to open in New Orleans. We once were the most prosperous city in the country. Now we're another Peoria." She gulped bottled water, then shifted into fifth gear. "They're just a bunch of incompetent bankers. Only the Whitney survived the Depression. Yet they snubbed all oil money. They're as inbred as the Romanovs." She looked at me sternly. "You aren't a member of the New Orleans Country Club, are you?"

Taken off guard I did my best to deflect her accusation. "Oh, no. I didn't pick the right parents for that," I said, trying to be coy.

"So, you'd have joined if you could."

"Of course not," I affirmed. I wanted to add that they only have a twenty-five-meter pool. But thought I better not. If the devil's on your side, it's best not to provoke him (or her).

"You willing to divulge everything?" she asked Leslie, point blank. "Explain all the thoughts which went through your head when you were gang raped?"

Jesus, what a thing to say, I thought. I tried to maintain a poker face. Before I could add anything that would be more mindful of Leslie's sensibilities, my Dulcinea co-opted me, agreeing to be frank.

"Even to the point of naming names?"

"Even to the...." She squeezed my little finger. "Well, that's impossible, they were all new, not even pledges. I was pretty much out of it."

"How out of it?"

"Enough to know what was happening but not enough to do anything about it."

The wordsmith's eyes blazed with demonic possession. "We'll kill if you can prove it.

"People expect politicians to be corrupt and bureaucrats to be incompetent; it has a historical precedent. But let there be a whiff of moral turpitude against their women.... We just have to establish the fact you were a victim and not responsible for what happened."

Leslie's eyes squinted with confusion. She had told me she was partly responsible.

"It's the only way," Patty Green said, assessing the situation perfectly. "You don't deal with prejudices didactically. You fight brain-dead prejudices with brain-dead prejudices."

The verdict was in, I thought. *Her way was the only way.* By the calm that settled over Leslie's face, I could tell she also knew it was Miss Green's way or the highway.

Her resolve was severely tested when our advocate's article appeared. I was offshore, suffering two more weeks of frustration trying to get my hands on the "Client" copy of the invoice, mostly just to find out who signed for it, when I returned to find the Greeks and their supporters had spared no expense or effort skewering Leslie. It was them or her and they were determined it was going to be her. The gossip that swirled around her, the sniffs and smears were minor compared to the frigidity of her family, which itself attested to the pressures they were subjected to. But even those smears were nothing compared to what appeared in local periodicals. No matter what their circulation or ideological bent each printed something damning about her, not once bothering to identify its sources.

Through it all she grew more resolute, becoming ever more certain that retribution was the only possible course.

"You've been a rock," I said consolingly in Patty's break room (the U.C. being rife with eavesdroppers and naysayers). "A real heroine."

"Why is doing right so painful?" she said without a trace of the Kimberly-like whine that previously had inflicted her voice. She even looked more businesslike than desirable. I'm sure she's cut back on her *farding* and taught herself stress management. The girl was becoming a woman.

Seeing she has grown gave me the confidence to quit worrying whether she'd misunderstand something I'd say. I could plow ahead, concerned only about whether what I said made sense.

"A derivative of the maxim about the truth hurting I think is at work. You did more than just call attention to the fact your enemies weren't wearing any clothes, you made them realize it too."

"And Hell hath no fury worse than the snob shown he's just a bully?" She smiled at her assessment. "Want some coffee?" she asked.

"Always," I said. She popped out of her chair. "Hope I can get the amount of grounds right."

"If you err, err on the side of too much. There's no such thing as too much caffeine."

"We're like them. Know too much caffeine is bad for us but can't help ourselves." She fumbled with the filter and inserted as clumsily as I had on the rig.

"Human, all too human," I said, maybe worrying the subject. "And they keep showing they're bullies, make themselves conspicuous."

"Which makes them even madder," we said in unison, showing we not only were equally clumsy but now were thinking the same way.

Growing madder and madder, Dorothy Goldstone, our comely Miss Payback, got too mad about the smears Leslie suffered and was accosted by a group of Chi Sigmas she made the mistake of insulting in an alley.

"It was the dumbest thing they could do," she said from her hospital bed, wearing her bandages like a Purple Heart. "Now we've got the law on our side."

"They're dead meat!" agreed her companion, Cathy Landman, keeping a vigil by her bedside.

It was fun to watch our Amazons get torqued up. Tiny couldn't have gotten as excited over a championship game; nor did my ex-stepmother seethe as much over what she thought my previous ex-stepmother, Mona Lambert, did to dispossess her.

Miss Green's tracts were unsparingly frank. She mentioned Leslie, her parents, and their affiliations incessantly. And when Miss Goldstone was injured, offered it up as proof Leslie's detractors were no better than common criminals.   Patty's works gave off sparks, despite being buried deep in the "Metro" section.

The editorial she wrote in response to an alumnus who filed a libel suit sizzled off the "Op-Ed" page.

"How stupid of them to think they can deflect culpability. *De facto* powers are going to be *de jure* after all this is over," growled Dorothy, sounding more like a future lawyer of America than a beauty pageant contestant.

The radical chic emerged from the cardboard settlement erected to protest South African apartheid to turn rape into the cause *du jour*. Leslie used her antebellum porch as a soapbox, to rally the faithful,   For the public she traded her brave smile for an angry scowl, and when the school administration refused to investigate, shed all reticence and spouted declamations so inflammatory people listened just out of curiosity.

The chancellor, deans, provosts, and lower-level administrators stonewalled, covered up, and lied to the media--in general played right into the chic radicals' hands.

During a quorum in our new war room, I told Leslie she was being very brave.

Stirring her coffee, she ruefully remarked how "you don't appreciate how important the truth is until all you hear are lies."

"It's a lot healthier to face down the truth than hide from it," Miss Green stated. "Wait until my next piece hits the newsstands. I Iad to go right over my pusillanimous editor's head, all the way to the board. Thank God there's a few vertebrates on it."

For once, Miss Green underestimated her influence. The stir her article created convinced the alumnus to withdraw his suit. For, with the help of a mole, she had burrowed through the halls of ivy and dug up irrefutable dirt.   She reprinted incriminating memos and correspondence the prudent should have shredded. And she did it in a way that rearranged how people regarded Leslie. The powers that be became the villains. She became the victim. The heritage that had publicly ostracized Leslie sucked her back into the fold, protected her, and in one deep breath pretended they had been on her side all along.

The pedestal southern belles reside upon is unassailable. A girl from the Bronx can participate in a daisy chain or take a wicked leak. A daughter of the Confederacy maintains her virtue and powders her nose. To say anything different was heresy, tantamount to calling Jefferson Davis a fag or a carpetbagger a reformer.

The rape took on a life of its own, eclipsing the city council squabbles, daily murders, and a report on the Saints training camp one day; the legislative session, the indictments of Alexandria nursing home operators, and the effort to attract Boeing to Lake Charles the next day; and a commuter airline crash in Virginia, a forest fire in Idaho, and a drought in Texas the day after that. It grew beyond the school administration's and Greek organization's ability to handle. It became so big affiliates handed it over to their networks, generating national publicity.

Although public sentiment began favoring us, the tide did not completely turn. "Mother and Father are still beside themselves," Leslie informed me during another strategy meeting. "They don't like the publicity."

It may not be all that sensitive, but I felt safe enough in our relationship to remind her that five of the ten upper-class commandments require women to appear in the paper only when they're born, attend appropriate balls, are presented to society, marry, and die.

Unfazed, she remarked," Why am I not surprised they still want to banish me? I'm an embarrassment...shipping me off to our doctor like I was damaged goods, acting as if I was a criminal."

"Vance Packard's <u>The Status Seekers</u>."

"It's all so subtle, so they can claim with a straight face they are on my side. Their tone of voice; and their body language give them away. They might as well scream at the top of their lungs." She poured a copious amount of sugar into her coffee.

"I always thought family was more important than what people thought. Boy was I wrong. I overheard Daddy worry about what his colleagues would think."

I overheard the blood thrumming in my head, thinking how my fealty also had been strained to the breaking point.

Then she dropped the bombshell.

"May I move all my stuff in with you?"

My blood then throbbed. I asked if she considered it a good idea. "Won't look good," I said. "Impressions sometimes are more important than facts."

"The hell with that," she knocked back half the cup.

"Your parents pay your tuition."

"I'll take out a loan. Get a job."

"They'll miss you."

"Like they'll miss a valuable piece of furniture." She spilled coffee down her chin.

"People aren't always who you think they are," I remarked, thinking how I had underestimated the rig hands, mistaking their crudeness for lack of intelligence.

"I agree. I misunderstood my parents all my life."

I momentarily thought of saying they might change, offering up my theory Father felt so bad about trying to hide behind me that he had tried to commit suicide. But I didn't. I said no more.

I wanted to say "no more" when I helped her move out of the Sigma Sigma house. I quickly wished I hadn't glued the groom's appendage back. I needed a third hand. Why women need a wardrobe Grace Mirabella would be proud of to go to school was beyond me. Peering into her sisters' room, I noticed none were distinguished by their wall-to-wall shag carpet so much as they were by wall-to-wall clothing. They must have an outfit for every conceivable occasion, all openings, especially the opening of a wallet.

The place bred excess
reeked of privilege. The finery, plushness, and suffocating fragrance set up an ambiance that clogged my senses.

The last time I had visited, I feasted on the sight of so much feminine pulchritude my eyes, ears, and orifices lavishly ingested all available sensations. Now, with the goldfish in class, the odiousness of the place numbed me. It was a sumptuous prison, where luxury mixed with convention to atrophy the inhabitants. A Maggie, Amelia, a Babe, or a Golda this hollow hall could not mold.

"My place is more conducive to personal growth. You want to succeed so you can get out of it," I told Leslie as we left the storage facility where we deposited most of her stuff. "Let me warn you, prolonged exposure to my roomies would be dangerous to your life view," I said as we added to the few belongings already cluttering our inconspicuous apartment behind fraternity row.

"Close encounters of the third kind?"

"You'll experience a man from Mars overview of life, a real alien education."

"So long as I come in peace."

"They only prey upon the weak."

"Well, I guess they're out of luck. The only thing I'll do for them is clean up the place, and that's only because I cannot stand an unclean habitat."

I didn't say anything. I also made sure Robert and Eddie didn't say anything.

"You've been good so far. Keep it up," I told them as she was getting settled in my bedroom.

Robert nodded. Eddie winked before remarking, "Anyone who can corral a filly like her deserves to have his wishes obeyed."

He was right. Despite the whirlwind surrounding her, and all the prying eyes who strove to discredit her, she continued to hold up magnificently. She was a "mudder", undaunted by the condition of the track.

A victim who could milk her martyrdom on any touchy-feely talk show chose instead to milk the lap of human kindness. She changed all of us, converted our den of iniquity into a home, and turned my predatory roommates into gentlemen by the sheer force of her presence. Her ministrations of Robert's infirmity and the elegance of her bearing turned both satyrs into seraphs. Robert refrained from engaging in meaningless relationships despite the opportunities afforded him. Word of his misfortune must have been posted in every woman's washroom in the city, as record numbers came calling.

Eddie did not feast on Robert's rejected admirers. He remained monogamous with his girlfriend. And he kept remarkably calm about his involvement with the authorities uncovering graft at the racetrack. Every one of us respected his reticence to talk about it. I felt uneasy recounting my adventures as he asked. His were far more crucial and dangerous.

Saint Leslie had entered our midst and improved us, proving women still tamed men. And they don't have to look like Kathy, thank god.

CHAPTER 11

"All studs out, we're here," Eddie declared as he drove into the dock's parking lot so I could begin my fifth hitch offshore. The idle I was dreaming about ended when Leslie and I were hand in hand, departing together in the seldom-used workboat, her face having launched what a thousand others couldn't.

"It'll be my honor to take care of your young mare," Eddie continued. "Trust a former stable boy to look after a millionaire's thoroughbred."

I interrupted my gratitude to point at an amusing sight.

"Is that the guy you told me about?" Eddie asked, bemused.

We both referred to the flatbed truck that rolled onto the location. Behind the wheel sat the unmistakable figure of Sam from the pipe yard. Stenciled on the cab's door were the words, "Archelos Pipeyard".

"Let me ask you this, my friend," the former acquaintance said after we introduced ourselves. "Would it make sense to start all over at the bottom of another firm if I quit?"

"You were pretty set on leaving."

He pushed up the brim of his baseball cap. "Well, I did, for a while, when I came across an opportunity I couldn't pass up."

"You got yourself a Western Star?" I asked.

"No, I mean real talents," he looked anguished.

"You became a repo man?" (Remembering how he had bragged about stealing fifty cars)

"No, something at which I'm gifted, what makes me above average," he almost was in tears.

"I forgot. What makes you above average?"

"I was in a movie."

"As a grip?"

Pushing the brim down, he looked at me sternly. "An actor."

"The lead?"

Looking abashed, he mumbled, "Not quite the lead."

"A supporting actor?"

"Exactly," he beamed.

"Have speaking lines?"

"Not quite. I was in crowd scenes."

"Did your name appear in the credits?"

"No, not really. But I was in a lot of scenes. The best was cut, through."

Asking about the pipe yard took his mind off his fifteen nanoseconds of fame. He insisted the Mafia underboss had not bought it to merely launder money. He seemed to be making a real go of it. "Doing all the things I would have done." He pushed up the brim of his hat and I could swear spilled a drop of concern for someone else. "Except I wouldn't be as hard on people as he. Nobody dares do him wrong."

I wondered how the Wheel, the dispatcher, and those involved in the boomerang tag scheme fared. I didn't wonder enough to ask about them. Instead, I got into a discussion about what the contract with Exxon boded and parted agreeing it would be the mobster's undoing.

"No individual does him wrong. Wait until he sees what they'll do," I said.

"Gonna save every cent before those people run them into the ground, wanting freebies and stuff. Then Hollywood here I come."

"Break a leg," I said in parting.

"See you in the funny papers," the nondescript guy replied.

Moments later, Eddie inexplicably said the same thing as he too drove off, looking like he had the world by the tail. He "high-fived" me. Such expressive gestures were out of character for him.

More mysteries abounded. No crew boat was berthed next to the work boat on the quay. Springer Oil was going to spring for flights. Hands were streaming into the nearby trailers. Entering it, a sixth sense tipped me off to a change in attitude among my co-workers. Whether sprawled on the floor or curled up in a chair they slept sounder, snored louder than they ever had. Those engaged in conversation knew they did not have to keep their voices down. Those who bumped into a sprawled body didn't bother to excuse themselves. They didn't have to. A bomb wouldn't have made any difference.

The place had been transformed and energized. Could it be a hole in the ozone had fried their brains or a shift of the earth's axis?

Only once was my fragile psyche assaulted by a brain-dead exchange, where a raconteur asks a pundit, "How was your time off?" The stock reply, "Not long enough" and postscript "I hear that" would have been too boring to hear in profusion. Most who were conscious were more concerned with the well than with personal matters. They didn't even compare doe and squirrel kills and were raptly attentive to the information Bull and Hammer dispensed.

None of it was good. Jim's walnut and fiber casing shoe was breaking down, putting Springer, according to Turtle, "In a bind."

"Had to cut back the mud weight so much they can't drill," said Hammer, flicking his knife with authority. "Lost too much hydrostatic head."

By now knowledgeable about drilling, I knew anything less than thirteen plus pounds per gallon mud weight wouldn't hold back the fluid filling the pore space in the formation. Anything heavier would completely break down the weak shoe, thousands of feet above the bit.

"Haven't lost all returns, have they?" asked Pencil.

"Not yet. 'N doubt they will," Bull remarked.

I asked why not.

Flicking his knife with the abandon of a puppy wagging his tail, Hammer explained how he had words with Springer's head office. "June Melveaux is out there, now."

"The mad Coon Ass?" asked Turtle.

So that was it, the inexplicable ingredient, the intoxicant that transformed the morose Monday morning working stiffs into the spirited dwarfs whistling on their way to work.

"Jim did himself in," Hammer said.

"Accused me of stealing a bit. Called me personally," Bull interjected.

"A Hughes bit," interrupted Hammer.

I had seen the dire warnings printed on all boxes containing the company's products. Howard Senior had established a policy that has scared off generations of would-be thieves.

"One eight-and-a-half-inch insert bit had come up missing, 'n he decided it'd be better for him if I took it insteada him losin' it," Bull declared.

"I bet Jim stole it," added Mamou.

I remember how paranoid Father had been about keeping track of their rentals. It didn't make any difference if one stole it or lost it.

"Will put up with a lot of things, but lying ain't one of them," claimed Hammer. "Springer's used this rig for years knows all of us. Been out with their president more than I can count."

That the assignment was Jim's last chance (having screwed up whatever he was assigned) inspired Bull to snort, good and loud.

"Got his fat ass in a crack," the barge engineer remarked.

I glanced at the dock. The seldom-used workboat rocked gently atop the wake from a passing tug, making money for several people Dennis told me about.

Dennis was right, I thought. *Jim was too much an oaf to cut himself in on the graft*. The Yosarian I was after remained elusive.

Jim's removal accounted for some of the buoyancy. This Mister Melveaux, "the mad Coon Ass" accounted for the rest. He sported quite a reputation.

"Ever catch a dolphin with that caller he gave you?" Dirty Dan asked Pencil.

"Naw, blew on that whistle 'til I was blue; 'n only saw a few yellowtails and amberjacks."

"He knew who to give it to," Heavy Duty said.

"I'd fight you for saying that," Pencil said, "but my back goes out more than I do."

Exchanges erupted throughout the room, each more spirited and more intelligent than I'd have believed possible. The mere anticipation of working under June had unlocked hidden troves of wit. I was witnessing a phenomenon as improbable as a monkey typing Shakespeare. I wished I had a tape recorder, to preserve the brackish banter, maybe use it myself like the peasant songs Bartok used to construct his debatable classics, or the stories the local wit, Justin Wilson, fashioned into yarns.

A letter made its way around the room. Accompanied by a transparently fake admonition from Hammer, it further elevated morale.

"We got to accept the fact that herds of vultures are watching us like hawks, ready to sue if we don't fill out our paperwork exactly right," he said, handing out a safety memorandum. "Cross every 't', dot every 'I', and use grammar well."

He genuinely appreciated each smile the document precipitated. However, only I got him to feverishly work his knife. Only I laughed, with a resonance born of true appreciation, the kind that rattles my funny bone each time I watch the antics of the Pink Panther, Buster Keaton, the Three Stooges, and other artists eschewed by snobs.

It read, "I am writing in response to your request for additional information. In Block #3 of the accident form, I put a quote: 'Poor Planning' as the cause of my accident. You said in your letter that I should explain more fully, and I trust that the following details will be sufficient.

"I am a roughneck by trade. On the day of the accident, I was working alone on the crown of a drilling rig. When I completed my work, I discovered I had about 500 pounds of fittings left over. Rather than carry them down by hand, I decided to lower them to the rig floor in a barrel by using a pulley that, fortunately, was attached to the underside of the crown.

"Securing the rope at ground level, I then went back up to the crown. I swung the barrel out and loaded the fittings into it. Then I went back down to the rig floor and untied the rope, holding it tightly to ensure a slow descent of the 500 pounds of fittings. (You will note in Block #11 of the accident reporting form that I weight 135 pounds.)

"Due to my surprise at being jerked off the rig floor so suddenly, I lost my presence of mind and forgot to let go of the rope. Needless to say, I proceeded at a rather rapid rate up the side of the derrick.

"In the vicinity of the working board, I met the barrel coming down. This explains my fractured skull and broken collarbone.

"Slowed only slightly, I continued my rapid ascent, not stopping until the fingers of my right hand were two knuckles deep into the pulley.

"Fortunately, by this time, however, the barrel of fittings hit the floor, and the bottom fell out of the barrel. Devoid of weight, the barrel now weighed approximately 50 pounds.

"I refer you again to my weight in Block #11 of the Accident Reporting Form. As you might imagine, I began a rapid descent down the side of the derrick.

"In the vicinity of the working board, I met the barrel coming up. This accounts for the two fractured ankles and lacerations of my legs and lower body.

"The encounter with the barrel slowed me enough to lessen my injuries when I fell onto the pile of fittings, and fortunately, only three vertebrae were cracked.

"I am sorry to report, however, that as I lay there on the fittings, in pain and unable to move, watching the empty barrel under the crown, I again lost my presence of mind, and <u>I let go of the rope</u>."

What an anonymous Will Rogers had penned added its share of hope to the recent turn of events. From Leslie metamorphosing into a fighter, love saving Father, Jim receiving his just desserts, and the crew displaying a heretofore unsuspected level of sophistication (albeit still low brow), and now finding a pearl in the gumbo, it suddenly struck me that I might have used up all my karma. All my ying might have yanged before I had completed my primary mission. From now on I might be on my own, unable even to lament how, as I've heard said over and over, "If it weren't for bad luck, I'd have no luck at all."

"We're American Airlines, doing what we do best," the welder intoned as we loaded our gear aboard the sleek, sexy Sigorski 76.

Music piped through the headset neutralized the high pitch the engines reached attaining maximum rpm. A joke the captain related, concerning why a pound of pilots' brains cost researchers so much more than a pound of surgeon and dentist brains put us at ease, prepared us for the tedious safety orientation the FAA required him to recite. Mulling over the punchline eased the pain the recitation inflicted.

"You know how many pilots it takes to get a pound of brains?" he had said, contributing to the build-up of positive karma.

As before, the sprawling green and brown Holocene carpet below comforted me with its sense of continuity, a feeling of place in the march of time. Again, looking at the miniature bird's foot deltas it occurred to me how they mimicked the workings of the big one at the mouth of the Mississippi River, proving natural laws don't discriminate according to size.

Sunlight glinted off everything manmade and flashed broadly off expanses of water. Shadows from the few clouds mottled the landscape, all but one moving with glacial lassitude. That one moved so erratically it drew my attention to a flock of black skimmers, each synchronously cutting, weaving, diving toward a spit of dirt that passed for a beach.

Recalling the geology, the mudloggers taught me I noticed no long shore currents were visible to winnow out fine sediments, leaving sand.

A wave of calm swept over me. I couldn't help but imagine I was entering the Sea of Tranquility, where awaited adventure and discovery. Like a veteran astronaut, I not only looked forward to returning to the most salient experience of my life, I enjoyed the ride, seeing what few get to see, being privy to sights restricted to the fraternity of explorers. What the Apollo spacemen understood when they looked back on Spaceship Earth, I understood as we neared the rig.

It was so small, so fragile, a mote daring to exist in what appeared to be an infinite expanse. What inspired Earth Day and the need for better stewardship of the planet inspired me to recognize the need to nurture the marriage of science and business. The relationship needed counseling, compassion, and as much appreciation as any rain forest or wetland. It takes explorers with their geophones, drillers with their mobile rigs, mariners with their chronometers, refiners with their computers, and financiers with their calculators to find, extract, move, process, and market the oil. The taxes and royalties reaped by the government can be used to preserve nature and fund space missions which show us pictures of the little, exposed world we live in. Again, what goes around comes around.

In 1492 Columbus sailed the ocean blue, fat contracts in hand that let him live grand.

Of course, we had to find the oil first. So far all we found was trouble. Coupled with the horror stories the mudloggers had fed me about submarine slumps that sever legs, and fault slippage that sever casing, I did not need to see a boiling school of hardtails fighting over chum being thrown overboard. Where there are hardtails, there are sharks. Still, the vote of confidence given the new companyman maintained my high spirits. That he had an engaging personality was a plus. I'd take anyone who was merely competent, even if it was a Captain Bligh (who navigated a thousand miles in an open boat after being cast off by the mutineers. Jim and Sunshine couldn't navigate across a bathtub).

The good spirits the departing crew exhibited at the helipad was infectious, inoculating us against return-to-workitis with doses of "Junisms": practical jokes, bon mots, and examples of an aptitude not seen before on the rig.

"Him on the choke is like Roy Acuff on a guitar," said a departing roughneck.

On the choke? I thought, realizing they must have taken a serious kick. Images of Hammer's Indonesian blow out instantly swept over me, and just as quickly vanished. Jovial atmospheres do not nourish fear. The absence of any gallows humor further settled me. The kick had been contained. They had gone back to drilling, and not one departing hero had one deprecating thing to say about what had happened. Not one even wanted to "Get outta Dodge".

The cheery attitude continued unabated as I lumbered through the barge control room. Underlings assigned the second flight graciously moved out of the way. They moved away on the narrow stairwell as well.

Reminders about the boots several absentmindedly forgot to remove saved them from Bull's wrath. Only Turtle didn't pay attention. Only he made it all the way to the galley wearing the offensive apparel.

"That's okay," asserted a lanky individual. "My floors can handle boot traffic. If they can't, it's the cook who's not keeping the floors clean."

Swathed in room temperature comfort, I remained after the herd signed in to check out the log. Two pages deep, below dozens of tool hands who came and went there appeared the scrawl of "J" something, "M" something.

"But remember, Mister Harvey," said June. "I don't want to be able to eat off no floors, not here in the oilfield, where you measure everything with a micrometer, mark it with a crayon, and cut it with an ax." He gave we observers a wink. "And I want everyone to do his job exactly the same kinda way."

"Be all you can be," remarked the welder.

June tacked up a mock troubleshooting flow chart on the bulletin board. "Follow this and we have no problems whatsoever."

The crowd it attracted included the helicopter pilot, there to talk about taking on more fuel. But before he could utter one word the companyman accosted him with the claim, "What you doing here? Why can't we get you in the air? You fly boys are like seagulls. You eat all the time, shit all the time, squawk all the time, and have to kick you off the rig to get into the air."

That said, he pretended to ignore the delighted audience and continued tacking up the diagram.

The first of many arrows the sketch used to move the eye from block to block led to the one asking, "Does the damn thing work?" If the answer was "yes" it directed you to the block saying, "Don't fuck with it". If "no", it asked, "Did you fuck with it?" If the answer was "yes" it said, "You dumb shit", then asked, "Does anyone know you fucked with it?" If the answer was "yes" it said, "You are an even bigger dumb shit." It then asked, "Can it be fixed before your boss finds it?" If it could, it said, "You're in luck, hide it." If "no", it said, "You're in deep shit" then asked, "Will you quit?" If "no", it said: "You're fired." If "yes" it told you to "quit."

If the answer was "no" to the question "Did you fuck with it?" it asked, "Did anyone you are responsible for fuck with it?" If the answer was "no", it asked, "Will you catch hell for it?" If the answer was again "no", it told you to "Shit can it." If the answer was "yes" to the question, "Did anyone you are responsible for fuck with it?" it said, "Nail him", whereupon it again asked, "Can it be fixed before your boss finds it?" A "yes" led to the final injunction, "You're in luck, hide it."

Staccato chuckles coalesced into a wall of laughter as each eventually finished it. Only Brother-in-law didn't get it. He scratched his head and left.

"But June," asked Dirty Dan, the derrick hand. "If we follow this, who you gonna run off if something goes wrong?"

The tall guy made a face of mock reproach. "One thing goes wrong; ma la, all of you will go."

"But we're irreplaceable."

"What, there's no more tramps in Morgan City?"

"So how badly could we have screwed up to be stuck with you?" Turtle inquired.

June eased his athletic body into a chair. We followed suit. "I come out here to straighten you out. Somebody has to. Can't do it on your own. You're too excited by being here to think straight. Come on, admit it. It isn't your wives who make you come out here. No woman ever made a man go to work. All of them already gots all the money they ever wanted."

He let the snickers die down before continuing.

"You come out here 'cause you know this is where a pusher man wants you to trip all the time. Isn't that so, Mister Hammer?"

Our pusher man affected a contumacious pose and uttered a classic rejoinder. "Maybe on other rigs. Here they wouldn't dare smoke hemp." He flicked his knife for effect. "And I can safely say not one inch has been smoked on my rig."

The poker face the mudloggers maintained showed how well they had learned the ropes.

"Folks here earn their money," proclaimed Bull, getting his two cents in.

"I need to make more money than that," claimed Jones, a passable twin of our French-Canadian boss.

"All of us do," said June. "And let me tell you something you already know but might want to hear all over again. I know Marble gets the most out of people the first five years it works them. So does Springer. The higher up one goes the less he should get." Everyone looked at Hammer and Bull. But June continued before they could respond. "The suits don't do much of anything, and what they do sometimes hurts the company."

He straightened up and became serious. "Should the vice president have gotten a bonus last year after he left fifteen million on the table bidding for this lease? Fifteen million, when he could have bid a penny more to get the same thing. He watches our expense accounts like a hawk, saving nickels so we lose millions when our scouts couldn't find out what they needed to find out about the lease."

"Could have given the money to me," said Turtle. "I could have me a time with fifteen million."

"Got that right," Mamou the Weenie Washer affirmed.

"Could have put that stacked rig of Marble's busy drilling a deep hole," June continued. "The big shots are amazing. Know why we don't have jars in our drill string? That drilling superintendent says only incompetents need jars."

"Getting stuck is a fact of life out here. God can't prevent it," proclaimed Fireball.

"Wilson's been around forever, longer than Hughes, making money freeing stuck pipe that shouldn't have gotten stuck in the first place," Bull remarked.

"Tell that superintendent that."

"That's your job, June," stated Pencil.

"I might as well as yell at a passenger train. Wouldn't do no good. Mister Hammer and Heavy Duty only found trouble when they went to Springer. There's an umbilical cord between Marble and Springer that that supervisor, Roger Otis, is sucking on. If there wasn't, Springer would have done something. They wouldn't have been sassy to to our whistleblowers, asking them if they think they should drill the well."

Both the toolpusher and cementer must have gotten reamed so badly it kept their mouths shut about it.

"I too went round and round with him once, trying to put a backpressure float above the bit."

"What happened?" asked Hammer.

"A kick went right up inside the drill string."

"Them floats stop invading fluids like nobody's business."

"Taught him a lesson, didn't it?" asked Turtle.

"Sure did. Taught him to carry a grudge against me."

Business school pedagogues could learn a lot from June. They also could save bucks telling Wiley or McGraw Hill to keep their textbooks on motivation and follow June around, notebook in hand. Like Leslie, his influence molded mavericks into a herd, molded the nearly dysfunctional floor crew into a harmonious team. Fireball quit calling Dirty Dan a latch hand. Mamou the Weenie Washer, Turtle, and I began resembling Tinker, Chance, and Evers rather than Moe, Larry, and Curly.

June was able to do this by handling all situations adroitly. Appearing on the floor as if he could smell something afoot, he startled us all when he wrapped an arm around Tar Baby just as the assistant driller lifted to the floor a bucket full of beer bottles. He had lowered it to the boat participating in the fishing rodeo below with a note "put beer here" in it.

"What a great idea," June enthused. "These glass bottles are just what we need." He had us break off the kelly, break every bottle, and pour the shards down hole. There was not a dry eye to be found.

Through it all, our new companyman stood imposingly, with his hands on his hips. "It's rare to work with hands who are so imaginative. I bet there's no other bunch in the oil patch who would think to increase that rate of penetration with pieces of glass. Admit it, you got tired of not making hole."

We let Fireball speak for us. "Yeah it really upset us," he said.

Like clockwork, when the pieces reached the bit we began to drill faster.

The now alert mudloggers called Fireball on the phone, telling him there was a drill break--one sign of increased pressure. Less rock means more fluid-bearing porosity.

"What do we do with the cans?" asked Tar Baby.

"That's easy. We promise to give them to the fishermen who stay away from the flare boom. As many of them as there are, one is bound to stray too close."

"That's their problem," pronounced Turtle. "We got warning signs up."

"The warning signs we had up in East Cameron didn't stop a boat from tying up right underneath our boom. Fried the guide and two fishermen."

"Springer get sued?"

"They sure did," June answered.

"How much?"

"Millions."

"That's why you're careful?" asked Fireball.

"Money doesn't mean much to the dead."

"It does to the living," said Turtle.

"You can't put a figure on a body's worth," interjected Heavy Duty (who somehow sneaked up to the floor).

"Your body would be worth three times as much as ours," joked Pencil.

"It's not folks," complained June. "It's lawyers and others who cheat the system."

"Crime in the suites, not the streets," I said.

"You're partly right. It's worse, 'cause they get folks to thinking only suckers work for their money. Turns people into little mobsters, 'wiseguys,' always looking for easy money."

"Everybody puts in an honest day's work on my rig," affirmed Hammer.

"What about them mudloggers?" asked Tar Baby. "Their shack is like a break room, with that big radio and couch."

"They'll earn their keep," the toolpusher affirmed.

As if on cue, the mudloggers again called Fireball, telling him the shards had reached the surface five minutes later than calculated. The bad news ended all other considerations and precipitated a debate whether the washout occurred at the bit or at the shoe and what it meant.

The controversy carried over into the shower. It might have made it to the galley but the sight of June in Bull's seat, merrily blowing cigarette smoke across the table at the barge engineer, preempted it. We were thankful he was on top of the situation well enough to not be neurotic about it. On the contrary, he animated us by browbeating Bull about the importance of providing employees with pleasant working conditions.

"Don't you agree?" June asked.

The barge engineer mumbled something that sounded like he agreed.

"That's great. I like to see everyone on the same page."

The ploy proved effective. Bull replaced the ratty TV in the recreation room with the one in his stateroom. The temperature on all floors became exactly the same seventy-two degrees. He did try to force the services to pay into an entertainment fund. But he was forced to give the money back.

"Admit it, won't you feel good about returning that money?" asked June when he found out about it.

Bull didn't dare dispute him.

Evidence of June's Cultural Revolution was ubiquitous. Instead of "Hustler" and "Penthouse" copies of "Field and Stream" and "Southern Outdoors" graced the coffee tables in front of the couches. Throughout the staterooms, "American Cooner", "Guns and Ammo", "Fishing Facts", and "Mississippi Game and Fish" replaced "Velvet", "Cherry", "Oui", and "High Society". Rather than reading about the amorous adventures of Edy Williams or Kitten Natividad on the commode, I learned how to track deer and turkey in various terrains and conditions. Jimmy Houston, not Jamie Gillis was the male star of the tapes we played. The only female stars were does.

It turned out June was more than a savior; he was an entertainer who would clear out the lounge whenever he performed. Why should we be satisfied by passively watching lightweight schmaltz when we could participate in heavyweight schmaltz?

"This is a whoopie stick," June informed us in the galley, "This propeller nailed here at the end, see it goes round when I stroke the stick with this pencil."

"It's them notches what sets up the vibrations," said Popcorn, the motorman, divulging the obvious.

"That's true; but the magic comes from you say 'whoopie'", which June said as he abruptly stroked the rod in the opposite direction. The plastic propeller momentarily paused before whirling counterclock-

wise. "It's all in the saying the magic word."

"Hell of a deal," said Brother-in-law to Hammer.

The toolpusher sniffed (which I attributed to professional jealousy).

"Here, Mister Hammer. You try." The companyman handed him the two implements. "Just remember the magic words."

Knowing this might be his last chance to regain his status as top critter, Hammer furrowed his brow and scratched and scrapped, epitomizing ineptitude as much as a metronome epitomizes precision. The propeller stubbornly refused to turn. Struggling to find a rhythm, he cursed with the demeanor of a frustrated infant.

"No, no, Mister Hammer. Those aren't the magic words. You're scaring it."

Hammer finally accomplished what every taskmaster sets out to do. He had broken we lowly workers...with laughter.

After letting it subside June decided I should be the next victim. Remembering Dennis' injunction against novices trying to master games that experts made look easy, I did not try to emulate June. I rubbed the sticks together with all the rhythm my honky soul would allow and took satisfaction in turning the propeller once. The notches had to be stroked with the touch of a virtuoso. Only a genius like Houdini or Doctor J. could make it spin the opposite direction on their first try.

The same was true with the rope tricks he showed us. Superior to Bull's, they would have taxed dexterity of a pickpocket or magician. After watching them, I went to bed puzzled why June would want to hone his parlor room talents and why he seemed so indifferent about the washout. Then again, Mister Guidry, the crew boat captain, acted the same and he was competent. Still, I couldn't help but rue the fact June was more chief jester than a paragon of leadership. Maybe it is all one could hope for out here; all this place could beget. Abe Lincolns are born in log cabins, not creole cottages.

The appearance of the mudengineer the next morning at breakfast eased my worry about his competence. Disheveled and filthy, Ronnie looked as if he had been up all night earning his money, trying to keep the mud properties where they belonged. The way he bore his infirmities with dignity not only proved he had some measure of success but also proved he was under June's spell. How else could his transformation be explained? Literally overnight the jerk had become admirable.

Proving how much he willingly subjected himself to June's sorcery he readily harkened to June's side and almost as readily acceded to a truly bizarre request. "Come on, I want you to meet my pet. I told old Jewels about how good you are and what a good job you did last night fixing the well. His tail started wagging. And let me tell you there's nothing which wags faster than a happy muskrat's tail."

"You're full of it," the mud engineer replied playfully.

"Better watch what you say. Jewels is enough Cajun to misinterpret everything."

"Like them coaches of the Southeast Conference who are saying 'Bama is washed up," sneered Tiny, suffering from the recent spat of bad press his alma mater's team was suffering.

June led us to a cardboard box in his office. Ronnie leaned down to see if there was an animal inside.

"Can't you see her eyes?"

Room light reflected off two orbs peering out from the darkness.

"She's in there waitin' for you to say somethin'. She's not good at patience, so you'd better say your hellos now."

Hunkering down, Ronnie said, "I don't see anything." He then let out a scream and leaped backwards, trying to escape the dark blur that jumped at him.

All of us held our collective breath and released it with a gush of amusement once we figured out what had happened. On the floor lay a mop of hair with shiny button eyes. Jewels was a wig.

"The old girl can stir a man faster than the prettiest gal in town," June claimed. "Fastest hairpiece in the South." He placed it on Ronnie's bald pate. "Maybe you'll like her better if you wear her."

He advised the mud engineer to keep it on. "We can't afford for you to catch cold. Don't want none of your brain power evaporating out all that skin you got up there."

After collecting himself Ronnie affected a sheepish grin. He was allowed to depart in peace, with no stigma attached. After all, any one of us could have been the brunt of the joke.

June kept the work environment pleasant. Very little seemed to bother him. The only thing that got his goat was a phone call from the drilling superintendent, Roger Otis. As we all later agreed, the super was a fool to deny his request to run either a Cement Bond log (to see how weak the shoe was) or a porosity sensitive tool.

"That shale density of the mudloggers is useful, but not that useful," June affirmed to his peanut gallery. "Better to make decisions on what a high-tech wireline tool says, than where pieces of shale rock fragments settle out in a column of special liquids.

"Their dxc and overlays only use surface sensors. It says nothing of what is going on downhole, in the rocks. "

"S.W.A.G.," said Bull, in full sycophantic capitulation.

"Scientific Wild Ass Guess," confirmed our companyman. "American Petroleum Institute allows for one hundred percent error."

"Save a nickel, lose a dollar," said Hammer to the full approbation of all present.

"Spend a dollar, lose ten dollars," I said to June, hours later in his office. A phone call had awakened him before I could compare his signature with the scrawls on the incriminating evidence in the files. *Figures,* I thought. *I knew his sending Blowfly home to recuperate and ordering Gordon to work only twelve hours a day was too good to be true.* Still, I didn't mind. Being caught in his office was no big deal, not with his open-door policy. By removing company news items from the hall to a cork board inside he encouraged people to come in.

I actually was glad I was interrupted. If I wasn't, I wouldn't have been privy to an incident which someday would be consecrated by the preamble "Now this ain't no shit". After fielding the call, June was so dumbstruck he didn't care to ask exactly why I was there. He was glad to have a witness.

"He can vouch for it," he oft repeated to the incredulous.

If I hadn't been there, listening to his responses I'd have been among the doubters, thinking he was trying to put something over on us. Any rational person would. One cannot believe anybody--let alone a drilling supervisor--would order a drastic change in direction we were drilling because he had a dream we were encroaching into another lease. A dream!

Our directional driller's determined refusal to do so cost him his job.

"It was all I could do to make up for Jim's and Sunshine's meddling," griped Mister Fontenot. "Getting that hole back on target, after correcting for the stabilizers they had me put in the Bottom Hole Assembly. That took the fight out of me. I'm out a gas, and scared. Neither circulated long enough to clean the hole. Short trips were out of the question. Cuttings accumulated, kept grabbing the pipe since we kicked off."

But that wasn't the reason he was running himself off. The drilling superintendent had told him he didn't want us to plug back and kick off. He wanted us to change direction where we were.

"Such short radius drilling can't be done with today's technology. Maybe he can dream up a way, but until he does, I'm not going to take the fall," he remarked.

His replacement echoed the same sentiment after arriving on a late evening helicopter. He went about putting together and dropping his multishot tool into the hole with all the verve of a mortician. So did all who helped him, so shocked were we that Roger Otis was, as June put it, "As serious as a heart attack" about doing the impossible.

Our morale plunged, negating much of the ground gained by June's presence. We all had pride in our work and did not want to see the well ruined.

"Couldn't ya at least have gotten him to let us run casing?" implored Mitch, the mudlogger over dinner. "We're only a few hundred feet from casing point. There's no reason not to set it high. We're through the sand we have to worry about. It's all shale, so what's the difference?"

"Yeah, kick off a sidetrack here. OCS-G-1559 Number One, Sidetrack Number One," suggested Fireball.

"I wish I could," June lamented. "He wouldn't even go for the idea of calling it a geological realignment or a bypass."

"As curved as that hole's going to be, we're never going to slide that iron wall cake down there," said Hammer.

"Prognosis says that string is to be run at eight thousand feet true vertical depth, period. Doesn't matter if measured depth is a cork screw."

"He didn't let the prognosis get in the way of his dream," remarked Hammer.

"I tried to talk him out of it. But you can't argue with someone who's two stands off bottom." June looked to me for support.

"He's right," I enthused. "Solomon couldn't have done better."

June smiled at me. Without even trying, without compromising my ethics or good taste I won his approbation. I guess it's what happens when someone knows his *dharma* (if what I gleaned from Robert's impromptu guidance was correct).

The establishment of a common enemy also helped our mood, affecting people in different, positive ways. It affected Harvey in a way that nighttime or a full moon affected creatures of lore. Like a vampire or a werewolf, it altered his morphology. It gave him a backbone.

Bull barely finished proclaiming how often he had been on "Those companymen's asses to quit messing with nature" before he spoke up, saying, to our astonishment, "I've been behind this counter months now and I haven't heard you tell nobody nothing."

The barge engineer was dumbstruck. "I can't believe you said that."

"I can't believe I took so long. Guess I learned too well to keep my mouth shut in the joint."

"You're in trouble."

"Good." The cook knocked over several pots retreating into the recesses of the kitchen.

"Better get someone to taste your food for you," Turtle advised.

Bull was so stunned his clichés failed him. He withdrew, tongue-tied, only to later reappear collected, articulate, and ready to "Come down hard on Harvey".

Harvey co-opted his thunder. "I've been thinking, Mister Bull. Whatever you do, I want you to do knowing this. I once fell in with a bunch who stole watermelons. The farmer put up a sign saying he had poisoned one. Well, I want to tell you, I put up a sign of my own. The next day that farmer woke up to a sign that said there were two poisoned watermelons in his patch."

It took a while, but Bull eventually got the message. Harvey had something on Bull and wasn't above using it, rattling the skeleton in the barge engineer's closet. All Bull could do to save face was tell the cook to return several bottles of salad dressing to the cooler.

Rumor control later on passed the word Harvey's trump card reeked of stale beer. It was concluded that Bull's unusual number of surprise inspections of the storeroom might have something to do with the number of confiscated beer cans Hammer said were missing.

Had we merrily been making hole, we would have thoroughly investigated the matter. We would have made it priority number one, made it the diversion which would keep us from becoming too fixated on doing a good job at what we were hired to do.

Escalating problems with the well redirected our attention. We didn't brook distractions. We listened attentively to the amount of gas the mudloggers called out as well as the mud weight and funnel viscosity the shaker hands and derrick hands periodically announced. The situation was getting dangerous. Fearing the pipe might get stuck against the wall or caught by cuttings that accumulated in a depression, the directional driller tried to cautiously redirect the bit from a northwest to a southwest quadrant. Tried, because whenever he put weight on the bit he'd stall the mud motor. When that happened, he had to pick up and ease the bit back to bottom. Over and over he worked the pipe, making very little hole.

Two days of fighting to make hole left the new directional driller weary and pessimistic. I don't know how he did it. The only sleep he got was when he nodded off in the chair in the doghouse. Food was brought to him in styrofoam containers. He must have the patience of Job. I know I'd go nuts working so hard with so little to show for it.

None of our bosses shed tears for him. They didn't chastise him. They did everything reasonable to help but showed an almost callous indifference to his ordeal. June even offered up some deprecating jokes, which Jeff took good-naturedly.

"That's why he gets his big salary," Brother-in-law informed me after I said I felt sorry for the guy. That I did not confront his callousness went to show I must be beginning to understand the ethos out here. *It may seem cruel, but it at least simplifies things,* I thought. *Maybe having everyone know the score promotes efficiency.*

The situation remained in doubt. But whatever the outcome, we did not fret because "We're doing all we can do" (to again quote the doughty roustabout).

The survey Jeff took on the morning of the third day indicated we were at last headed in the correct direction. As if God was on our side, drilling immediately became easier, in fact too easy. Keeping the rotary still while maintaining a small amount of weight on the bit (in order to shove the bit in the direction the bend in the mud motor was pointing) should have slowed the rate of penetration. Instead, we "slid" as fast as we had drilled three days ago, when we turned the rotary at seventy rpms and kept much more weight on the bit.

Mitch appeared on the floor with what looked like log paper and a transparent overlay. Watching he and June pour over them in the doghouse piqued my curiosity so much I had to ask the mudlogger to explain it to me the minute June left to receive a phone call. I must have looked puzzled at his explanation because he quickly got to his point.

"What all this means is that we're drilling in pressure. Maybe more we can handle. All we have to do is get out of this impermeable shale and into some permeable sand, where fluids can overwhelm borehole pressure." As if to verify his claim, the sample catcher announced a vast increase in gas, meaning we were reaching an under balanced condition.

That startled us. What June said upon his reappearance on the floor shocked us.

Judging from his stunned look, the call must have been from Roger Otis, the drilling supervisor.

"He ordered us to cut back the mud weight." Was all he could bring himself to say. He didn't elaborate. He didn't have to elaborate. It was all we could do to swallow the order. Only when we had partially digested it were we interested to find out the origin of the incredible order.

"The genius read an article about induced pore pressure," June later said in the galley. He was calm enough to light up a cigarette. "Decided it would be would make him look good if he is right."

"What happens if he's wrong?" asked Turtle.

"Which he is," added Fireball. He is thinking of ballooning. If that is the case, we need to spot a non-compressive pill downhole."

June blew a nervous puff and expounded on the variation of the theory the guru insisted upon. "The friggin' expert said there are certain cases when increasing the mud weight can cause the well to mimic underbalanced conditions, causing gas to increase and the well to kick.

"So, all of a sudden increased background gas doesn't mean what it's always meant," said Jones.

. "Only way to tell for sure is to get on the choke. No casing pressure would confirm ballooning," said Fireball.

"Well, if we decrease the mud weight and don't gain mud or gas, then he's got something. If we raised the mud weight like it makes sense to do we might blow that shoe, lose so much mud we can't hold back formation fluids and take a kick at that shallow shoe," June responded. "We can see if we are ballooning if we lose mud while we pump with the lighter mud and see if we gain it back when we shut the pumps down."

"What if we get back a lot more than we lose?"

"Then the hole is plastic like a credit card. What you end up paying is going to be a lot more than it's worth."

It looked as if we'd start paying the entire balance five minutes into my next tour. We had decreased the mud weight two points when the alarms on Fireball's console went off while we were drilling, effectively proving Mister Otis' theory was not applicable to our situation. We were gaining mud in the pits. The mudloggers called out one thousand units of gas, meaning the mud was twenty percent saturated with hydrocarbons.

"A kick, that's it," June stated. "I'm going to shut her in."

"A few hours working that choke gonna rob you of your good humor," said Ronnie, as he furiously figured up what the mud weight needed to be raised to contain the unwanted influx.

"Ma la, let me tell you, only a Cajun can sit on that panel in the rain, snow, in anything for hours and still crack jokes," June proclaimed as he rushed toward the choke manifold.

The drill floor reverberated with the Koomy unit kicking in on the Texas deck. No longer did the sound of the brake squealing and mud pulsing through the pipes and hoses dominate. The symphony had segued into an andantino mezzo forte movement, punctuated (if you were close) by June's story telling. His b.s. fostered confidence the Hydril's annular would hold and the kill mud would throttle the kick. Which probably was why he talked, because all of us left on the floor were alarmed when he stopped. We worried when we saw him rush to the crew's quarters, and it wasn't because he left Hammer to monitor the pressures and ensure Fireball pumped at the correct speed.

Although the flow of mud down the kill line and contaminated mud out the choke line continued unabated all our hearts palpitated when he returned.

"So where are the jokes?" asked Ronnie.

"I said I can tell stories when I'm working the choke, not when I got to be in two places at the same time. Only when my body is in the ground and my soul is in heaven can I do that." He didn't need to mention who had phoned him.

To prevent a reoccurrence of him having to abandon his post Tiny volunteered to relay the next inevitable call from the drilling supervisor. It made sense. And we all foolishly felt confident with the arrangement. We forgot whom we were dealing with. The land-based sage refused to talk to the safetyman.

That hacked everyone off, but not as much what he had to say.

June maintained his composure as best he could. "Sonnavabitch wants us to open up the choke, see if it's really flowing."

The hundred years of experience present concurred that would be an incredibly moronic thing to do. We were taking a kick, with pressure on the shut in drill pipe pressure and casing pressure gauge. Nobody minded me looking at the gadgets. We already had decreased the pressure on the casing manifold from three hundred to one hundred fifty pounds per square inch. It looked as if we might get it zero if we were left alone.

"You're not going to do it, are you?" asked Hammer, betraying fear in his voice.

"You want to lie about it on your report?"

Ever expressive, our toolpusher's eyes bulged with the thought of the consequences of being caught. I noticed he also kept his butterfly knife sheathed.

"He's got the stroke," June replied resignedly.

"And we get the shaft," replied Hammer. "Can't you go over his head?"

"You want Sunshine here on the next helicopter?"

Looking around I could tell everyone was thinking the same thing as I, that if the big dogs didn't bark about Mister Otis having us change direction because of a dream they certainly wouldn't object to swapping out companymen. I also could tell everyone had so much respect for June it was unthinkable to question his knowledge on how the game of office politics is played.

"So let's go make one hellava goal line stand," asserted Tiny, the super fan. He punched the air with his right fist.

The imposing leader huddled with Ronnie to figure how best to go about opening the choke. "He didn't say we had to be in a big hurry," June said.

Knowing we're about to do something idiotic as intelligently as possible energized us. Some of us volunteered to work into the next tour. I started out asking to give Ronnie a hand pouring chemicals into the suction pit. The minute I did I noticed Tar Baby writing in Fireball's tally book. Knowing the assistant driller also needed to help Pencil during the next tour I asked our driller if I could take the place of Tar Baby helping him with the IADC report in Hammer's office.

"Fireball wants me to give him a hand," I told the opposite tour derrick hand in explanation why I had to renege on my offer to help in the pit room. As I hoped he yielded to the driller's higher status.

Once inside the office Fireball hovered over me until satisfied I could transcribe what was in his pipe tally book onto the big pad. There wasn't much he could do anyway. As I suspected by watching how Tar Baby did most of his writing for him, he was nearly illiterate. Once done, I wandered into June's office, expecting to find Gordon. He wasn't at his station, proving (I guess) office people don't care about operations as much as those at the fount.

Jumping on the opportunity being alone afforded I went through the office like a dervish, comparing the signature I traced from the log book with those on the paperwork June recently signed. Once

I familiarized myself with all the variations of it on recent field transfers, bills of lading, order tickets, and whatnot, I "tore into" the rear of the file cabinet. Behind the records for nonexistent blue paint Sunshine signed for on this well, were the transfers sheets, weigh papers, and pink sheets June signed for on the previous well.

I didn't have to look long to find evidence of his culpability. A spare anchor I never saw aboard was the first I spotted. Digging deeper, others appeared in rapid succession, leading to the holy grail. Wrinkled and creased, wedged in the back was a green "Client" copy of invoice 41552, delivery ticket number BE 13137.

Except for the legible final two numbers it was an exact duplicate of the gossamer thin "Shipping" copy in my wallet. The figure $175,000 appeared on the last line, just as it did on the last line of the "Shipping" copy. June's unmistakable signature appeared on an upper line, next to the date. On August fifth, 1980, the most engaging man in the Gulf engaged in a most unaugust act. On that date he cut himself in on a fifty-five-thousand-dollar kickback that cut me off from Father, and Father from everybody else. The "Double nickels" Robert said he was accused of bilking Uncle Sugar out of had gone into June's pocket.

If Father turned down the bribe he wouldn't have gotten the contract. I thought. If he didn't do it somebody else would. If he hadn't "played ball" to get the contracts the yard might not have been able to hire new workers, hire me. Sam might have had to be above average someplace else and the Wheel would have had to ply his idiosyncrasies in a more appreciative venue, like a gulag.

Looking closer at the "Client" copy, I noticed a crease on the bottom third of the form, as if it had been folded back. I also noticed all pertinent information and signatures on the top two thirds were darker than those on the "Shipping" copy. Which was odd. They should have been almost illegible (it being the third of three forms). A pen could have traced them onto a carbon and another copy slipped underneath, where the number "120,000" could have been written on the bottom line. I don't know what good a doctored "Client" copy would do; but it certainly looked like one could exist. Maybe both the fake and the real copy were faxed to an accomplice who saw to it the wrong copies got into the right hands in Springer's office.

It was then I realized the initials "R." "M." (the shipper), stood for Richard Marks, Dick, the trucker who refused to acknowledge me at the pipe yard. He had to be getting a cut of the action. That's why he pretended not to know me.

June had corrupted him too. Like Professor Moriarity, he had used his talents to get away with breaking the law. *Being competent and a born leader carries with it the onus of integrity,* I thought. *It was like Abraham Lincoln cheating on Mary Todd or George Washington lying.* It shattered my faith in men. For that, there was no pardon. The more I thought about it, the more galled I became. If you couldn't trust the Junes of the world whom could you trust? He was execrable.

I couldn't stand looking at him during the next tour. I enjoyed seeing him get splashed by mud as he peered into the flowline. I wished he'd fall all the way in. Unable to wait for divine retribution, I thought of expediting the process, conjuring all sorts of temporal agonies to give him a taste of the punishments his soul was going to suffer in the hereafter. It certainly wasn't going to hover above his remains upon his death. It was going to writhe underneath it with all the other frauds and thieves.

All through Tiny's impromptu safety briefing behind the drawworks, I envisioned him neck deep in boiling pitch and tormented by black devils, suffering with all the other grafters in the Fifth Bolgia. It was his future hell I cheered at the conclusion of the meeting, not the super fan's "Do it for the Gipper" encouragements.

The cheer proved to be more akin to the rebel yell heard on Cemetery Hill, than the Roughriders' charge up San Juan Hill. Like Pickett before us, we probably had made an irrevocable blunder.

I glanced at the flowline to the right of the drill floor. The mud flowed as rapidly as it would have had the pumps been turned half way on. Except, from the lack of vibrations underfoot, I knew the pumps were off. By the driller's console, I noticed Fireball's weight indicator read three hundred thousand pounds when he picked up, over one hundred seventy thousand pounds more than it should have. It read two hundred thousand pounds when he slacked off

"That block, it don't weigh but fifty thousand. The drill string, around two hundred thousand," June informed us. "It's losing its buoyancy."

"We're in a heap of trouble," asserted Tar Baby.

"Trouble, your ass. I know trouble, and this ain't it," countered Hammer. We looked at him incredulously. "Not yet, anyways."

The brake jerked upward, taking Fireball's hand with it. He turned on the pumps. Mud roared down the flowline. Gas increased.

"That's enough of that," said June as he raced to the choke manifold. He again closed the Hydril. The rubber inside the inverted cone-like apparatus atop the Blow Out Preventers fit snugly around the pipe, shutting the well in. The casing pressure increased to nine hundred p.s.i.

"How about you Ronnie?" June announced over the intercom.

All but me grinned great big grins when he told the mudengineer to start weighing up, countering the drilling supervisors order.

"Aren't you worried about getting stuck?" asked Fireball mock seriously. "More weight could shove that pipe against the wall. Got enough crooks in it."

"What about breaking down the shoe?" asked Hammer, joining in.

"I found myself more than once trusting my life to a jalopy held together with baling wire. Wish I had bailing wire instead of barite to add to the mud."

"It's still not good to play with the mud weight," said Fireball. "Jacking it up and down."

Not getting the little morality play all the devil's advocates were playing, Tar Baby ran out of patience. "That main spring they got broke a gear telling us to water down the mud." Seeing we all smiled, he continued. "Blew an engine telling us to open her up."

After the hell we went through wrestling the TIW valve on the kelly closed we were thrilled to see the casing pressure drop and gas fall with the addition of the weight material. We ended our tour on a hopeful note.

And we began our next tour on a more hopeful note. The shut-in casing pressure had declined and gas fell to seven hundred units. We decided to pull up so all the kelly was above the rotary. Tar Baby released the annular's rubber, freeing the pipe.

The hookload decreased, at first dramatically, then tapered off. For awhile. We almost made it. Fireball pulled up forty feet before the hexagonal extension of the kelly came screeching down five feet. The brake squealed as he again raised it to as far as it would go, where it paused before coming screeching down. We were stuck and, without jars in the B.H.A. to work us free, we were going to stay stuck.

Several repeats prompted the future denizen of Hades to remark: "Looks like we gotta make our stand where we are. Let's shut her in all over again."

So while we again wrestled the TIW valve closed our bosses repaired to the Totco panel where, with one pull on the lever, they attempted to seal off the annulus.

The Koomey unit (which charged the annular and the rams) started acting up. Its cylinders hissed and coughed. Rushing down to the Texas Deck, between the drill floor and the rig floor, Hammer and Bull fought with the row of rusted levers and frozen valves, showing the grit and gristle responsible for their rising to the top of their profession. We laborers fared no better when offered turns at the reluctant device. The preventive maintenance pulled on the machine had been as good as the planning which had gone into Pickett's charge up Cemetery Ridge.

"The hell with it," shouted June. "Gotta crank it shut."

We workers were to be lowered below the drill floor to play with the grimy Blow Out Preventers. Like that, all the muscles we had developed in the course of our work we put to use on the blind rams, the topmost of the three sets of rams that either closed around the drill string or cut it. There was no such thing as turning the wheel that activated the rubber seals too tightly. Once the next kick reaches the surface a pin-sized gap could be deadly.

The safety belt did not provide much of a sense of security. I played great ape, perched on a greasy bolt above an angry sea, yanking on a slimy, recalcitrant wheel. In the shade, the floodlights offered only oblique lighting.

"I'll lick all the mud off these B.O.P.s if it leaks," swore Turtle as he helped me pull on an eight-foot cheater bar.

The casing pressure gauge held steady at few hunred p.s.i. With the pumps turned off, the shut in drillpipe pressure gauge was not as close to it as it should be, which set off a debate just how inconsistent the mud weight was. The two should be equal.

"Casing pressure should increase if gas is migrating up the hole," said June. "It expands."

Whether true or not, it was obvious the kill mud hadn't broken down the shoe. As long as both the shoe and the rams held, the kick would be contained. With Popcorn and Jones and whoever else they could enlist working on the Koomey unit it looked as if Pickett might be able to withdraw to fight another day.

Why the casing shoe and rams held was a mystery. According to the mudlogger's and Ronnie's calculations, even using Jim's bogus leak-off test results, the shoe should have fractured, and the Blow Out Preventers, they hadn't been tested since I hired on. Cameron Iron works may be a topnotch manufacturer, but even God periodically tests his products.

Our state of bliss wasn't to last.

"Would screw up a wet dream," said Turtle the next day, when word came down we were to open the well again.

"To see if we're still taking a kick," explained June. "That wheel said we couldn't have hand closed the blind rams if there was much pressure was on them."

June must have been curious too because he deferred to this new decree even though it was as bad as those which preceded it. "Sometimes you get more than what you expect to get by going with the flow," he explained. He ignored the mudlogger's insistence they could tell exactly how powerful the kick was from the SIDPP reading.

All I could do was offer the reticent guy a sympathetic affirmation. I knew grandfather wouldn't dismiss him because of his lowly status. That June could only aggravate my new low opinion of him.

Like rubberneckers, we who were not to question why but were to do and die lined up along the railing to watch the opposite crew open the ram Turtle and I had sacrificed our backs to close. As had happened the last time, mud rushed down the flowline as if the pumps, not nature, were pushing it.

"If we weren't taking much of a kick before, we are now," said Hammer.

"Only good thing 'bout dying is that you're the last to know about it," Pencil commented.

The flow picked up, spewing forward in violent spasms.

"Remember, women and children first," said Kathy.

"So when do you go?" asked Turtle.

"Nobody is going anywhere," June announced, confident the bladder Jones and Popcorn et al finally installed in the Koomey unit was ready to go.

For a minute, it did. But like God's experiment with Jesus, it didn't solve the problem. The months of inattention had crippled it.

"I can kill the well blindfolded," June insisted.

"Maybe blindfolded you can," said Hammer. "But not looking at it. Can't kill the well slow and steady if you're fighting the equipment."

June reluctantly agreed.

As expected, with the extra pressure supplied by the kick, the blind rams failed to close, regardless how much Turtle and I again threw our backs into closing them. The wheel exhausted us, far too much to perform an encore on the five-inch pipe rams immediately below.

"Come on up," ordered June, after we exerted our last ounce of strength fighting the equally rusty blind rams. "You no good to me now."

Asked about equipping our replacements with sledgehammers, June became apoplectic. "Would rather stumble over them than pick one up. Crew wreckers, that's what they are. Drains you worse than a woman."

Nevertheless, Dirty Dan and Mamou employed them on the pipe rams, the set designed to fit snugly around the five-inch diameter drill pipe we were using. That the rubbers wouldn't fit around the various diameters of the tools that made up the B.H.A. was a problem we'd deal with later. We were happy no mud leaked. We were secure, for the time being.

All agreed we should install gauges between the casing hangers in the wellhead. We needed to check for seepage between casing strings, in case one ruptured.

Bull's suggestion we replace the bad blind rams with the spare set we kept on board spawned the laughs he was seeking. Doing it at our convenience, under no duress was dangerous enough. Doing it atop thousands of pounds of pressure courted disaster.

To none of our surprise, the next phone call to draw June off the floor was one that ordered him to do exactly that. The madman on the bank wanted them swapped out "ASAP."

"Whaddya say?" several tremulous Indians asked their chief.

"What do you think I said? I told him if he wants them changed, he can do it from his office."

"What he say to that?" asked Mamou.

"Said he's gonna come out here and make sure it's done and done right."

"We're saved!" Turtle exclaimed. "Thank the Lord."

"Hope he gets here soon," remarked Dirty Dan.

"Didn't know you thought so much of him," said Fireball.

"Him? The hell with him. I want a window seat."

"I don't think it's right to cut down our boss," Brother-in-law complained. "He wouldn't have gotten where he was if he didn't have the answers."

"Oh, he had the answers all right," Turtle responded. "It's just that they were to the wrong questions."

Posterity would forever be denied the others' ripostes. A rumbling underfoot interrupted their *bon mots* in mid-delivery.

"She's coming up the drill pipe," Bull shouted.

"It wouldn't of, had we a back-pressure float above that bit," Hammer snarled.

"Maybe that supervisor knows how to get one down there now, being such a genius," said Tar Baby.

"Maybe his big butt can cork the hole," grumbled Turtle.

The standpipe manifold started to hum. We gasped as the pipes turned white with frost, at first wafer thin, then thicker with each passing moment. The supervisor was not going to rescue us in time. The entire floor shook. The pipes started to vibrate. Someone activated the flare boom. Like a big lighter, it spat into flames.

June ordered us off the floor and asked Tiny "To assemble the troops." Turning to Hammer, he remarked, "It's time we prove we're underpaid."

"Us hosses gonna shine," the toolpusher claimed.

Spurning glory, Bull left with the safety man.

"Chickenshit," snarled Fireball.

"He'll be a lot more useful being where he's supposed to be," Hammer stated, matter-of-factly. "We'll all be."

I stood in awe of Hammer's and Fireball's grace under pressure. A gibbon breaking into an aria couldn't have amazed me more.

"You'd best dag along after him," Hammer told me. "No need to risk your ass."

That ass got a boost downstairs. I didn't pay attention to what was going on around me when I paused to look at the foam in the flowfline. Before I could figure out how it got there, Mamou blundered into me, knocked me into the railing. I didn't regain my equilibrium until two steps down. The sense he failed to knock out of me a blast of mud from the shakers succeeded in knocking out of me further down. I might have fallen to the main deck had Mitch not grabbed me. He was gone before I could regain enough faculty to thank him.

Everybody was in a hurry, pushing, shoving, rushing toward the capsule. Those emerging from the crews' quarters had on layers of clothes. We from the rig floor did not change out of our greasy tatters but at least we wore boots and helmets.

Arguments about which escape capsule to go to broke out.

"That current's gonna smash us into the legs if we don't go the backup one," claimed Pencil.

Dirty Dan concurred, saying "The engines can't fight them waves." He led the rush to port side of the rig.

The intercom crackled with excited voices. The flare swathed us in heat, and when the flames really spat, almost scorched us. The entire rig vibrated. Missing from all the rattle and noise was the sound of the alarm, or of Tiny's little voice orchestrating the event. We were on our own.

That being the case, when it dawned on me I had left my keys and wallet in the logging unit. I turned to leave.

"You can't go," decreed Bull. "Don't want people scattered all over creation."

Scanning the assemblage, I noticed a cohort wasn't among them.

"Gotta look for Turtle," I said in mock panic.

"I'll organize a party."

"Let me join it. I know where he might be."

In the heat of the moment, the barge engineer agreed to someone else's idea.

Dirty Dan, Red, and I headed out. Only the derrick hand and the roustabout returned with the stray. I had faked a little dizziness from the smell and "recuperated" inside the mudlogger's trailer, gathering the essentials of life. The idea of being stranded without an I.D., cash, or keys scared me. I couldn't do it. I'd be like going naked, becoming a displaced person. And a d.p. in the banana republic down here is like an immigrant being stranded on Ellis Island without his papers.

The documents that would reestablish my place in the world, which might exonerate Father, weren't paramount. Had they not been in the wallet, I honestly don't know if I would have sought them. Triage is brutal. But I guess you first must have a stomach in order to stomach a situation.

Heavy Duty certainly needed his. It acted like an umpire's chest protector, cushioning his falls as he stumbled toward the craft Bull finally told us to enter.

"Hey, quit shoving," he cried as a wave of evacuees pushed him through the hatch. "I'm moving."

"Not fast enough," growled Tar Baby.

Like in a scrum, the impatient bunch hoved into the mass of flesh, knocking him forward. He tumbled down the rickety stairs and crumpled on the floor, blocking passage. No one wearing a life vest could get by. For a moment I considered returning my vest to the nearby bin where I got it. Instead, I barreled forward, knocking him down as I did. The world stopped as he blundered near the lever that would jettison us into the water. By sheer luck his center of gravity shifted away from it. Ensuring it stayed away, everyone behind me swarmed over him, pushing him further away, leaving him bloody and crying like a baby. Only when we threatened to bloody more of him did he drag himself to a couple adjacent seats and buckled up.

We did a good job of filling in the back seats first and unscrambling which seat belt was paired with which seat.

Then we waited. The increasing heat catalyzed the smell of gas with that of the musty interior to assault our senses. On the lower level, wedged between two bodies, with my head between Mamou's knees, I took several deep breaths and calmed down and reconnoitered the situation. So did others.

"I was asleep when I was woken up," said Popcorn. "Was in the middle of some kind of dream...."

"I was asleep too," interrupted Sambo.

"Not me, I heard it all," remarked someone I didn't recognize in the dim light. "Had to change my shorts it scared me so much."

Taking the bull by the tail, our barge engineer faced the situation. He saw to it the drains on the exhaust and engine air pipes were closed, the ventilation covers and air intakes were opened, and was in the process of giving the greasers on the stuffing box a good turn when in stepped Fireball.

"I'll take charge," he announced.

"I'm in charge of the secondary boat," Bull countered.

"The secondary boat becomes the primary boat when we have to use it."

"That's right," Tiny confirmed, at last making an appearance.

The barge engineer grunted and resumed his preparations.

"Two turns. That stern gear has to be turned twice," Fireball insisted.

"I do 'n it'll break," Bull objected. "One's enough."

"Try it."

Bull's immediate acquiescence impressed upon everyone how serious the situation was.

Tiny quickly turned our attention away from the barge engineer. And, for once, it wasn't because of the anomalousness of his miniscule head perched on his huge body or the squeaky voice that emanated from it. This time it was because he had trouble when he called out people's surnames. Not that he couldn't pronounce them. It was just that no one responded.

"Mouton, Pitre, Chiasson, Trahan," he said. "Ah, come on, I know you are here. The capsule wouldn't be full if you weren't."

"Never hear it said the way you say it," explained Popcorn, guessing he was the "Mouton" Tiny referred to. "Don't hear it much at all. Only see it on bills and I try not to look at them."

"What about your paychecks?"

"Wife sees them before I do."

Tiny resorted to spelling out the names.

Fireball pumped several times on the starter. The engine wouldn't turn over.

"Check the accumulator," advised Bull. "Gotta read three thousand."

"I know. I know." Fireball knocked the safetyman backwards as he climbed over to the machine. He also pushed Turtle backwards as he got up to help. "Don't need no boy's help," he muttered.

"See a boy here and you can kiss his ass." The words sizzled and snapped.

Before Turtle could do whatever angry amphibians do, white gas thundered out the shaker house. The stampede to see it bowled over both antagonists.

"June musta diverted the flow," said Kathy.

"Don't know if that's a good idea. That Poor Boy Degasser ain't designed to take that much pressure," remarked Dirty Dan. "That's why we flared it in the first place."

The gas drifted over us.

"Nobody make a spark," Tiny ordered.

"Lucky no H2S alarm went off," said Pencil. "Be graveyard dead."

Bull turned to Mitch. "Hope you turned off everything in your unit. Don't need that agitator motor banging around in your gas trap. Friction could cause a spark."

Mitch looked panicked.

Fireball chuckled. "Don't make no difference. That mud stirrer blown out of the possum belly with the gas trap and everything else."

The gas abruptly ceased blowing.

"Maybe it's trying to bridge over," stated Jones, the electrician.

As if in response, grey mud belched out the shaker house.

"Maybe not."

"Hole's gonna empty of mud," Mamou claimed. "Then what?"

Tiny resumed calling names. The smell of gas was becoming overpowering.

"What about the shackles keeping us up here where we really don't need to be?" asked Popcorn. "We gotta release both of them."

"So go ahead," stated Popsicle, the opposite tour motorman.

"I will." He did, pulling out both the bow and stern pins. "I'm always doing what you could do but don't want to do."

"Gotta put in that plug," added Tar Baby.

"Only need it if we have to put into the water," said Dirty Dan.

"What are we doing packed like peas in a pod if we're not going into the water?" asked Turtle.

"So I can take a group photo," remarked Tiny, sarcastically.

If he did, it'd show us smiling, cheering both the charge Fireball finally sent to the throttle, and Tar Baby's successful search for the hidden drain. It would also show us grinning at the driller as he comically fumbled with the controls. He couldn't find the correct gear.

"Want to hit the ground running," Fireball remarked.

"Yeah," said Bull. "But not backwards."

"It ain't in reverse."

Tiny confirmed it was.

"Don't make no difference, forward, backwards, long as we get outta here."

Hammer chose that moment to leap inside.

"Ain't nobody gonna see my tracks. I flew across that messy drill floor."

The derrick rattled and rumbled, tempting us to again storm the hatch to take a look.

"Don't even think of it," barked the toolpusher wasting no time to exercise his authority.

With a boom, the derrick flared like a torch.

"That's it, we're going!" Hammer shouted.

"What about June?" asked Fireball.

"Yeah, what about him?" asked several others.

"Might be fricasseed. I told him not to divert the kick back through the degasser. I told him not to play Davy Crocket, not to fight to the last."

I wanted to see June fry. *He might as well get used to it.* I thought. *He's going to be charbroiled for eternity.*

Flames spat horizontally as well as vertically.

"Close them hatches," ordered Bull.

"Vents too," added Tiny.

"Lower this thing," Hammer ordered. Ronnie reached for the descending rope.

The heat grew uncomfortable. We began to sweat.

"My chest! My chest!" complained Heavy Duty. "It's happening again."

Tiny dropped his clipboard and rushed to the cementer's aid. The air became suffocating.

"Open the stop valves on them air flasks," said Hammer.

The craft shook on its way down. Hammer pushed Ronnie aside and grabbed the lowering rope.

"Adjust that reduction valve," the toolpusher barked.

"This man is having a heart attack," said Tiny.

"So take care of him. It's your job," Popcorn remarked.

"I need help," Heavy Duty whined.

"I ain't gonna blow into that mouth, might be swallowed," said Turtle.

"Got that right," agreed others.

Smoke seeped inside. The engine began to fail.

"Open the manometer valve. Get that aft air flask on line," ordered Fireball.

"I'll give the orders," Hammer growled.

"So what are they?" asked someone.

"Uh, do as Fireball said."

A rush of pure oxygen sent us soaring. The engine churned back to life.

"Gonna need that second bottle for my patient," said Tiny, as he came up for air.

"Like hell, we might need it," Turtle objected.

"Us first," affirmed Bull.

Smoke obscured all sights, a second roar obscured all sounds. A blast knocked us back in our seats and singed our faces.

Ronnie let the rope slide faster, tipping the craft. Tiny tumbled into Bull, knocked him backwards, toward the red lever. The presence of mind the barge engineer displayed avoiding it proved remarkable. Hammer couldn't have been more agile.

"Let that fat boy alone," he mumbled, extricating himself.

"He's a sick man," Tiny decried in Heavy Duty's behalf.

"He'll be a lot sicker after I get through with him."

A wave suddenly battered us. Others smashed into us in rapid succession.

I thought Hammer was a hair early telling Fireball to open the bottom valve on the suction side of the pump and to pull the governor handle, turning on the seawater spray. But I'd have sworn he was on the money when he told Bull to pull the infamous red lever. After the violent jerk, I expected to feel the sensation of floating on the surface, not dangling in the air. Luckily the mud engineer hadn't let go of the rope. Instead of flopping into the water, we hung suspended long enough for Bull and the driller to open the fore and aft hatches. Ronnie held on tightly as they uncoupled the blocks. When he resumed the descent the gripe wire snagged on the bow, upsetting whoever kept his seatbelt on, and throwing whomever didn't into the stern.

A wave rammed us amidships. We almost capsized. It was all Bull and Fireball could do to close the hatches. More waves continued the assault, hitting us at various angles, some breaking into whitecaps, others hitting us with their full force, banging us around as we dangled at a forty-five-degree angle.

Dante's Purgatorio had nothing on us. What exquisite drama. With Tiny ministering Heavy Duty, and the rest of us carefully trying to resuscitate ourselves, I dared any Francis Ford Coppola wannabe to capture the moment. I dared Francis Ford Coppola to do it. And if he did it, would he have embellished it the way we embellished it? Would he have me ignore Mamou the Weenie Washer when he tapped my shoulder, then my head? Maybe Alfred Hitchcock would have had me ignore the danger signs, like Tippi Hedron had in "The Birds".

I doubt either would stoop to drenching people with vomit. That's something Stephen King would do. Finding how thoroughly disgusting it was, he'd have everyone do it. The ribbon of slime that arched out the shaker hand's mouth after he pushed me out of the way smelled as awful as it looked. It triggered a barrage of equally vile projectiles from others, coating the recumbent cementer and the medic, and precipitating a pandemonium no amount of training could have prevented.

Those scrambling away from the deluge tipped us to starboard, unsnagging the gripe line. The bow plopped into the water, throwing whoever wasn't buckled up against the bulkhead. We capsized.

"Grab the railing!" yelled Tiny.

"This thing ain't gonna cork if you don't!" shouted Hammer.

"I can't see anything!" someone cried.

"Keep your seatbelts on!" shouted Bull.

"I can't reach them bars," an anonymous voice complained.

People tumbled over each other, splashing around in the puke and water. Several scrambled too close the cupola. A savage wave knocked them back.

"Right itself, my ass," howled Turtle.

A monster wave lifted us up, exposing the hatches.

"I'm not going down in this bucket!" Turtle shouted.

"I hear that!" someone seconded.

A crowd set upon the doors, unlatching and folding them up. Only a few made it out, when the crush of bodies behind exceeded the force of the water pouring in. With fewer people pushing from behind those in front couldn't overcome the surge.

I stumbled over Heavy Duty. My foot slipped out from under me, depositing me headfirst in the ooze.

Water rushed inside.

"We're going down!"

"Close them doors," Hammer commanded.

"You close'm," several said in tandem.

The air grew stifling hot. We were being broiled.

"There's bubbles on the water!" Came the dreaded shout. The shallow casing shoe had at last completely given way, draining mud from the annulus, allowing a new influx from that depth. We were experiencing a surface blowout.

Cries and curses wrought a chaos that fed upon itself, transforming us into fiends. I know I felt a distinct pleasure stepping on Heavy Duty's fat face as I scrambled to the exit. I certainly wasn't penitent when I finally reached it. My only concerns were timing a wave crest and how much of the hot air I should suck in before I jumped out.

The shock of being in the water didn't terrify me. Nor did the fact I quickly submerged.

Calm, I said to myself. *Think things through.*

I could feel myself sinking.

Come on, I thought. *Grace under pressure. See which way your bubbles float. Open your eyes; look for light.*

Conserving my air, I made sure not to thrash around trying to find out what was the matter with my life vest. I didn't need to attract sharks. Let them attack those who didn't have the presence of mind to compose themselves. I wasn't going to go stupidly. Should I go, I didn't want to go to Heaven. If I died, I want to go to Valhalla. I want to prove I'm worthy, not by devotion, but by character.

If waiting until I was certain the lighter colored water was "up" before making my move and refraining from gulping air when I did break the surface showed character, then I showed character. Wotan wouldn't admit someone who drowned diving for the bottom when he thought he was ascending. Nor could anyone dumb enough to swallow hot oil make it into Elysian Fields. Heaven might take them. And Heaven can wait.

I continued showing valor, moving across the current, through the debris, swimming underwater whenever possible, and finding just enough buoyancy to stay afloat.

Entering heavier, cleaner water I rolled onto my back and let my defective life vest do whatever work it was capable. Swimming the backstroke allowed me to observe the scene. The crimson flames shooting out the derrick, melting the monkey boards and turning the wrought iron red, lorded over the conflagration in the shakers as well as the lesser fires burning across the rig. The boom extending over the side no longer flared. Smoke hid the sign warning fishermen to keep their distance.

The entire scene reflected off the water. The waves scrambled the primary colors into a kaleidoscope of shades and hues. The bubbles lent a dappling effect, each pop being rife with peril.

Angling toward the standby boat, assured of rescue, I could relax, compose myself, and regale in the fact I was safe. *For those who hadn't made it out, too bad,* I thought. Darwinism prevails in emergencies, where the fittest, not the fattest survive. Athleticism and ingenuity is paramount when one is thrown on his own resources, when natural selection holds sway.

A floating object attracted my attention. My twenty-thirty vision couldn't focus well enough to precisely identify it. But my intuition led me to believe it was human. That extra sense also led me to believe I had time to play hero, show the fearlessness that would guarantee entrance into a manly afterlife should I fail.

I slipped into a cauldron of bubbles. I did not panic when I felt myself drop lower in the water. I quickly found I only had to arch my back and kick like hell to draw abreast. Throwing my arm around the man, I drew him in, scissor kicked, and paddled with my free arm until we entered water dense enough for the standby boat to float on.

Treading water, I blew the whistle on my vest and flashed my emergency light. And I kept blowing and flashing until the workboat finally drew near. But rather than accept the proffered hands which were eager to hoist me aboard once whomever it was I rescued was safe, I swam away. The sound of their protests dissipated too quickly for me to figure out what they were saying. I didn't know if they were warning or encouraging me. Didn't matter. No one seemed to be making a move to help me as I went after what looked like a body floating face up.

Maybe no one saw him. Maybe they knew it wasn't a body. Maybe none of them was stupid enough, dense enough, or just pissed off enough to risk his butt to enter the maelstrom.

Conditions had worsened. The water was more aerated, the waves more cruel. They smacked me with debris and churned the burning oil slicks into conflagrations that seemed to ignite the air. Stretching my neck as far out the water as I could to grab a breath, I saw people swarming on the gunwale, watching. *They're too chicken to help,* I thought. *They probably think they are too important, too special. They're too unimaginative to help, to do something, anything.* By staying afloat, I proved the bubbles that kept the boat away probably might still support two people. But, by dint of already being in the water, despite their hollow protests, it fell to me to go the extra mile, to do what none of them would do.

The main current had shifted, forcing me to fight it. The fatigue that tore through my muscles, that ruined my form and slowed progress, that was my problem. *Why don't I just circle the rig, check for more evacuees, hold off my own rescue until all were accounted for?* I thought. *The cowards probably expect that of me.*

A sharp pain in my leg reduced my already slow pace. Undeterred by flashes of light barracuda or mackerel reflected, I picked up the pace.

Caught in an eddy by a leg, bobbing on cross currents, the victim was easy to grab. Extracting him wasn't as easy. Those same currents acted like a suction to keep him where he was. I had to reach in and yank him out by the collar. When he was out, I could not ride the current I had fought to get there. I couldn't find it. But, overwhelming all other problems was the almost insurmountable one of motivation. Unlike the last victim, I was able to identify this one. And when I did I wanted to drown him. Well over six feet tall, with short brown hair I could tell it was June. I should let him go with the flow, like he had said it's sometimes best to do. I should let him be, show him I too know how to play the game. I could say I did my best. Nobody would dispute my intentions. Nobody could see what I'm doing. *The world would be a better place without him,* I thought. *It doesn't need more thieves.* I'd be doing the world a favor if I let him be.

He was lucky. If the currents hadn't slackened or had it been harder for me to summon a second wind I would have left him behind. Had he slipped out of my grip I know I wouldn't have risked retrieving him. But had he regained consciousness he'd really be in trouble. The impulse to ensure my face was the last he'd see before seeing the devil's might overwhelm me.

I towed the albatross to a burning ribbon of oil I couldn't avoid. Alternating handholds on June, I managed to pull my t-shirt out from under my coveralls and wrap it around his face. I then quit treading water, sank as deep as I dared, and arrowed forward, moving fast enough to keep the under garment from slipping and exposing his skin.

Kicking furiously, I felt as if I was swimming in boiling pitch. My entire body burned. I had to keep my eyes closed and my teeth clenched. As for my outstretched arm, it cried for surcease. When I could feel myself succumbing to the pain I bowed upward and, with one final effort, kicked as hard as I could, up to the one spot which didn't feel as hot as those around it.

My hair crackled as I broke surface. My face felt as if it had been thrust into an oven. Still I held onto June. The sight of all his clothing above water engulfed in flames tightened my grip, for the third time wrung from my muscles an effort no conscious command could have. I pulled him into clear water and dunked him all the way under. A rim of third-degree burns framed his ruddy face when I let him up. With all his hair burned off it looked like a skull.

Out of the corner of my eye I could see the invoices and paper money burning on the other side of the tongue of flames. I checked my back pocket. It was empty. My wallet was not in it. Soaked in oil, it was alighted like a flambé. For a moment I considered going after it and the invoices. I'm sure I would have, had my legs not started to hurt. I thought they were cramping, but several stabbing pangs told me otherwise. Then I felt a pain that doubled me up. Something bumped me as I grabbed my ankle. Keeping my eyes shut, I didn't know what it was. Realizing I had let go of June, I started to reach out for him. A rifle report preceded the zing of a bullet entering the water a few feet from me. Others followed. I tried to open my eyes but they stung from the oil. I only managed to squint. Blood mushroomed around me and appeared in profusion near June as he floated away. A shadow draped me in darkness. I reached out for the companyman, but as I did something hit me on the head. It was a life saver buoy. A volley of bullets ended my inept attempt to use it to paddle over to June. A chorus of voices encouraged me to take care of myself. I draped my right arm over the donut and allowed myself to be dragged toward the boat where I was grappled and hauled aboard by a forest of hands.

The same dozen hands that hauled me up restrained me from going back down.

"Ma la, dem kingfish won't chew much on him no ways," the skipper told me. "Him, I know him. He's from Abbeville. Fish don't eat nobody south of Lafayette. Too briny."

Someone started to attend to my bleeding legs. "But he'll drown!" I protested.

"Law of physics keep that from happening. That Melveaux he too full of hot air."

He stayed afloat and the fish, they were nowhere to be seen.

"See what I says 't'?"

I did, and I could also see why he said it. Mister Guidry was capable of saying anything.

"Spectacles, testicles, watch, wallet," he muttered as he crossed himself. "Good Lord please get that companyman out of the water before he scares all the fish so far away we never can catch them."

While his sons were busy rescuing June, the distaff side of the family took care of me, staunching the flow of blood from my wounds and the flow of venom from my mouth.

"We know you don't mean to harm him," said Mrs. Guidry. "We saw what you done for him."

I reiterated how I wanted him to be fully aware of what was happening when he received his just desserts.

"Of course you do," said her cousin.

"No. I'm serious."

"Of course you are," said Mrs. Guidry.

I paid them only as much attention as a patient needed to pay and focused on the rig.

"It's like the Fourth of July," said Mister Guidry from the steering console behind the pilothouse.

It's what incompetence looks like, I thought. *No, it's what letting incompetence go unchecked looks like.*

The derrick glowed red hot.

"Like a Roman Candle," the captain remarked.

Not having seen a Roman Candle, I did not dispute him. But if he was right, I could see why they were so popular. The tower of flames, the roar, and the acrid smell were overwhelming. We stared in awe of the vengeance nature meted out. At least those of us who had witnessed the folly leading up to the disaster did. For every Gordon cowering in the cabin, Pencil staring at the wrapping around his hands, or Sambo crying like an infant, there will soon be a horde of armchair heroes excited by the film taken by the "Channel Eight" helicopter that would be edited to resemble war footage. The opportunity to pander to vicarious thrill-seekers had launched the media into the air before one boat with a water cannon showed up. The need to find out what happened sent the USGS. airborne. As for the Coast Guard, they had scrambled to offer aid and assistance. Yellow P.H.I. helicopters filled the skies. I only could surmise who rode in the blue Air Logistic chopper. But I'd probably have a good shot at being right if I guessed the drilling superintendent occupied the passenger's seat.

I could see him driving the pilot crazy, barking orders into his headset. Whereas the other crafts moved in predictable patterns, his bolted all over the sky, diving so low the blades churned the water, and coming so close to the flames I'm sure they felt the heat. Flying through the spray from the water cannon the tug that finally arrived spewed might have cooled him down. But I doubt it. He must really be pissed. June was lucky he was out of his reach. He also was lucky he was unconscious as rescuers laid him next to me. If he wasn't, he might have been better off taking the full fury of his boss' wrath than what I'd say to him.

"Did everyone make it okay?" he unrepentantly said from the cocoon of blankets and bandages he was wrapped in.

I did not, could not, immediately reply. And it wasn't because I didn't know the answer.

"Damn it, June," I eventually barked. "Why can't you be a pure bastard?" I propped his head up so he could see look out the window from the table he lay upon. The crewboats and workboats testing the edges of the boiling water, the water from the tug's cannon spewing so ferociously it bent a stairwell, the precipitous list of the entire rig, as well as all the flotsam and fires lent one to disbelieve what one saw.

But rather than comment on it, he repeated his question, and seemed to take solace in Mister Guidry's assertion "If all the chatter over the radio mean anything, we got everybody."

"What about the cementer?" I asked.

"Don't worry about him, t. He was what most of the chatter was about. Moby Dick was not so much trouble."

The heart attack June must have learned about telepathically had been nothing more than nerves.

I tilted June's head further back, so he could see the activity in the air.

"That wheel up there must be madder than an oilfield wife that run out of gin...good," he whispered.

The flotilla headed in piecemeal. From what we heard over the radio Tiny tried to keep it together, his squeaky voice shrill with emotion. But Bull and Hammer overrode him with their own orders. Several captains just ignored them all and did what they thought best. Mister Guidry did.

"No shrimper ever filled his hold by following the fleet," he explained as we wheeled about, away from the scene. "These shrimp we got need to go to the dock before they spoil."

The scene at the dock was reminiscent of that which previously had greeted the toolpusher and barge engineer times three. The crowd surged upon us as we either hobbled or were carried ashore. The reporters and their cameramen were as obnoxious as the salesmen had been. I don't know which is worse, the sycophants or them. I do know no sycophant knocked me into a davit, hurting me. The media types were so bad, paramedics had to push them out of the way to take care of the injured.

They're no more than maggots on carrion, I thought. *No wonder journalism and communication are popular majors among frats. It suits their personalities.*

So does studying law. Eugene proved that. Hiding, like viruses, inside the crowd, lawyers began to afflict us. One such varmint slipped his card in June's pocket as he was being carted toward an ambulance. Another, a company stooge, called me aside to advise me to sign a waiver.

"Just a formality," he claimed.

"Then there's no need to sign it," I heard myself say.

"It's best you do."

"You mean it's not voluntary?" I asked in mock astonishment.

"It depends upon whether you like your job."

Growing braver, I remarked, "That's not being particularly fair, talking that way to an invalid."

"I don't want you to think I'm pressuring you."

"Pressuring is not the proper word. Threatening is, as in blackballing."

"You misunderstood me."

"I understood you all right." I elbowed him out of my way.

For now, I didn't have to worry about not having my wallet. For the time being I was going to be a V.I.P.

The reception at Our Lady of the Sea in Galliano was the exact antithesis of my experience at rush. Hours into my stay I was treated as well as I was at the beginning. Others filled out paperwork for us, medical personnel doted on us, newsmen interviewed us, and when things quieted down lawyers swarmed over us. The place was infested with helicopter chasers. I bet they monitored ship to shore transmissions.

"You lawyer types keep your ear as close to the microwave as tow truck operators do to their police scanners," I told the first vulture to accost me as I lay in bed.

"I am a professional," the smarmy guy replied in high dudgeon.

"Yeah, that's why your advertisements are sandwiched between credit for bankrupts and dating services at one a.m. on TV."

Watching him contain himself was a treat.

"Hey, I thought you guys were on my side," I said as he retreated in silence after throwing his card on my covers. I did thank him for it. *I can use it as mulch; it being so full of bullshit.* I thought.

A Deke was next up. He was a new hire--a junior associate, assigned duties the partners felt beneath them. Immaculately attired, freshly shaven, his pin prominently located on his lapel, and reeking of cologne, he was Eugene's twin. Which wasn't surprising, given what conformists both were.

"I can fix you up for life," the clone promised.

"Why, will I constantly be breaking down?" Watching his face screw up in perplexity, I added, "With your broad mindedness and imagination, you too could work offshore."

"I'm here to protect your rights." Judging how expressionless he was he could have recited anything, from a Maoist slogan to Reggie Jackson's slugging average.

"I rest my case."

Exasperated, he quoted a six-figure number he could win for me. "If you let me represent you."

"It's illegal for you to solicit business," I bellowed. "So go, and bring back a partner. I'd like to waste the time of someone who bills twice as much as you."

I was having fun. Why was crystal clear. I had no intention of making a small fortune on my misfortune. Workmen's Compensation was good enough if the fish bites did any long-term damage. I knew how onerous the tax is for a business. I didn't consider Springer a trough the disabled and their lawyers should wallow in. More than one of Father's competitors had to endure suits generated by soft tissue injuries--the disease only lawyers can diagnose.

Besides being well treated by the staff as I lay in bed I also appreciated how well they kept me informed. The fact no one but June was seriously injured was a great relief. No innocent was going to suffer because of Jim's, Sunshine's, and the superintendent's bungling. Realizing this put me in a good mood, an ornery mood, where I couldn't resist one last dig.

The third solicitor was too irresistible. Midas didn't promise as much as he promised me. His pledges leaped out his mouth after I expressed my desire to sue (if not for pain, then suffering) every contractor and manufacturer who had anything to do with the rig. His beady eyes shined like cat's eyes. He drooled, and was nearing a state of orgasm, promising me the moon when I shut him down.

"Naw," I said. "On second thought, I won't."

His joy turned into desperation. His padded shoulders didn't just sag, they collapsed.

As if on cue, Father and Karen walked into my room, diverting my attention. She was stunning in her fashionable outfit and subdued makeup. Her symmetric face and overall projection of health commanded so much attention she almost obscured Father (whose big smile went a long way to offset his somewhat haggard appearance). I was thrilled to see his arm around her.

"She paid my bail," Father enthused, and why not? A woman spending money on him was like a concubine spending money on a sheik. I sat up to throw my arms around him when he came close. He initially recoiled, but slowly reciprocated, until he was squeezing me harder than I was squeezing him.

"I like close families," Karen remarked.

"One I hope will becomes extended," I replied as she took her turn hugging me. "One where I'll be your Orestes and you my Electra." The dapper barrister looked perplexed. "Brother and sister," I said, with attitude. He shifted his weight toward the door. I stared daggers at him. He took a tentative step. "Don't even think about giving me your card," I said. He picked up the pace until he was almost running.

The door hadn't even closed behind him before Father and I began sharing memories and, with Karen, entered into a conversation we never had before with a woman. She was genuinely intelligent and witty. I don't recall ever having heard a girlfriend or wife of Father's put together three related sentences, let alone surpass his considerable gift for gab. Rather than be put off, he took pride in her elocution, and encouraged her, letting her both initiate and elaborate upon the topics discussed. He didn't utter a peep when she broached the particularly sensitive one he and I tip-toed around.

"You are accusing him of making bribes?" I asked, defending Father.

"She's right," Father admitted. "I did."

"But you had to, to get contracts," I insisted.

"Not really." He drew Karen near. "Thanks to the mirror to my soul here, I confessed I did it to get better jobs than I would have if I played by the rules." He suddenly became demure. "I did more." He looked at Karen. "I sold items to an offshore company I had set up, so I didn't have to pay taxes when I resold them at a higher price."

"But you sometimes have to go with the flow!" I exclaimed, paraphrasing June.

"Doesn't mean I have to be. Your Grandfather didn't."

"And look what it got him. His name is mud," I said, referring to the way politicians smeared him.

"Not inside the industry, where it matters."

"So you're not going to defend yourself?"

"*Nolo Contendere.*"

"I'll wait," Karen remarked. "He's worth it. Besides, it'll be fun starting from scratch when he gets out. With my looks and Roger's brains, how can we miss?"

Not one cynical comment came to mind, meaning the smart-ass in me might have been replaced by a new maturity.

My stepmother-to-be number five and Father stayed until the end of visiting hours, offering support. They also were as curious as I was to find out how everyone was doing. The several people we continued to call for information corroborated what I first heard. Except for June, all had been fished out of the water suffering little more than mild shock. Heavy Duty had floated away like a jellyfish, but so well insulated was he with fat, he could have floated to Padre Island before falling prey to hypothermia. Tiny and Turtle also ended up equally waterlogged. June paid dearly for staying until the end. He needed skin grafts and infusions of blood. Even the soles of his boots had melted onto his feet.

My experiences with the mackerels and barracudas weren't unique. Only Ronnie had been severely bitten. All his wounds were on his rear.

My wounds certainly did not warrant the week I spent in the hospital. It wouldn't surprise me that my delayed release was directly related to the time it took Marble Drilling and Springer Oil to marshal its legal defense. None of their lawyers proved brighter than the goof who wanted me to sign a waiver. Had I heard more than five minutes of their condescending blather, I might have sued out of spite.

Why Robert hadn't shown up until late proved entertaining, although not particularly revealing.

"Was booked for attempted murder," he stated, looking as unrepentant as ever slouched in a chair next to me. "All bogus. The boyfriend of a chick I picked up went ballistic. Jumped on the hood of my truck then told the cops I tried to run him down."

"What about the girl?"

"She was hysterical the whole time, said he wanted to beat her up. That's why she got in with me."

"So why didn't she testify?" I was beginning to feel like a straight man in a comedy routine.

"She was long gone by the time the boys in blue arrived."

"You tell them about her?"

"Yeah, and the dude said I was trying to kidnap her. He said he was trying to rescue her."

"So you're out on bail, parole, what?"

"I'm free." He sat up. "The dude didn't really have that good a look at me. He was knocked really woosie."

"You're pretty easy to identify."

"Not if I'm smiling."

"You don't smile."

"Exactly. I kept a big ol' grin on my face when their Mathew Brady took my portrait. Took four of them, each time telling me to wipe it off."

"And they couldn't force you to look solemn?"

"You got it. Looked like a clown. The guy didn't recognize me at all."

"What about your truck?"

"No blood, no dent, no proof. His word against mine."

The narrative set the tone for the rest of the visit, one that left me energized and optimistic. His approbation of all I've tried to do and what I intended not to do (such as make a big deal of my injuries) was a balm.

"You'll be rewarded for each scar, mark my words," he assured me. "If worse comes to worse, you can always go back into the oilfield. Maybe you can become a mudlogger. That's the last thing someone who sued is going to get to do. The Employees Information Service knows they're the best educated and best informed on the rig. Stay on rigs for forever, always learn the skinny."

Leslie's late appearance did not bode well. I knew she had been away testifying against Chi Sigma. But that was days ago. She should have seen me sooner.

To say I was apprehensive as she entered the room was an understatement. Perhaps her campaign had soured. In the heat of the moment, she might have rescinded the pardon she had granted me. *Maybe I'm no more than the loathsome monster I once was, as guilty as sin*, I thought.

The stern look she leveled at me terrified me; it transformed her angelic appearance. To lose her was to lose everything.

"I'm sorry to be one to tell you this," she ruefully said as she shuffled forward, holding back a torrent of emotion. She handed me an article from the "Living" section of the *Times Picayune*..

"He was called Eddie," it began. "That's all, Eddie. A private man, he never revealed his real name or where he came from. He kept to himself, yet he was a fixture around the local racetracks."

It went on to relate in a respectful (even envious) tone his unusual calling. "Few other stoopers were as successful, making a living off other people's impatience, free from bosses or clients."

The author used the last sentence to shock the reader. It shocked me.

"What a tragedy then, that this independent spirit should become another depressing statistic of our increasingly violent society."

He had been shot.

"I'm sorry. I know what he meant to you. It's so senseless, so sad." She sat down on my bed and held my hand.

Stunned, I didn't know what to say. I couldn't say anything. I didn't want to say anything. Leslie tried to console me, but I was inconsolable, remembering the good friend. She stayed by my side, offering comfort and compassion and when she had to leave gave me the biggest hug and longest lasting kiss I've ever experienced.

Not long after she left, the few facts the *Times-Picayune* mentioned combined with particulars Eddie had related to me to fashion an ending more sensational than the paper had reported. A parolee let out because of prison overcrowding or a deranged street person hadn't sent him into his next life for a few dollars. The mob had done it.

He must have told the wrong person what he knew about the track. Or maybe he decided to play with so much fire he knew he'd never survive, such as ratting out a wise guy to his underboss.

"I cannot die young," I remember he once said.

Sharing my secret with Leslie the next day at our apartment helped a lot.

"Even the dog races are fixed," I cried as she led me to the couch.

She placed a reassuring hand on my shoulder.

"I don't care what Robert says," I wailed. "The bad guys always win."

"No, they don't. If I thought they did, would I have done what I did?"

Her statement almost knocked me out. It made me realize exactly what she had done. After months of witnessing almost comic bluster and having experienced a lifetime of posturing, I had to be told when I had witnessed true heroism. The defilement and shame she must have suffered would have immobilized me. She didn't have to go public or push her cause until something was done. She could have swallowed it and become a neurotic housewife, smug in the knowledge her past hurt her more than the past of other neurotic housewives.

I gingerly held her hand and interlocked our fingers.

"You're right," I murmured. "It can't be all bad if people like you exist."

"Or you."

"Me? What did I do except try to get back what I lost?"

"You saved both the company man, and, what do you call him, a crane man called Satellite?"

"Someone had to do it."

"See!"

"But with June, I just wanted him around to see he gets what's coming to him, what I'm going to do to him. Besides, you can't compare something done in a matter of minutes to something that takes months, that'll hound you for years. How many Congressional Medal of Honor winners went on to live lives like Ralph Nader or other social icons?"

"Did anyone else rescue someone?"

"They probably didn't have the opportunity."

"Maybe they weren't prepared mentally and emotionally to do it. You were the only one capable of saving those two."

"I don't think I would have done it before I went into the oilfield. See, I still needed a catalyst. You did what you did on your own."

She kissed me on the cheek. "The oilfield brought you out. You had potential before you were excommunicated."

"There was Grandfather," I said.

"I had my Grandfather, so to speak. I needed you to plant doubts in my mind. I knew something was wrong when the Chi Sigmas mistreated you when you were selling hotdogs."

"That's why you ran away?"

"I was so confused. I just knew I had to get away, from all of you, to sort out my feelings."

"And you sorted them out in my favor?"

"I let you find out my name."

"At the Sierra Club booth?"

"I was genuinely interested. Reading also helped, not just Chaucer or Milton. Faulkner wrote about a woman who refused to change her circumstances although it made her miserable. It was the way I was raised," they say offshore.

In utter awe of her, I held off making my overt displays of affection. Regardless of what she said, I knew I couldn't have risen above the pain that must have afflicted her. I was only hurt externally. She

was burned to the very core.

I remained emotionless until it occurred to me that not expressing my true feelings would disrespect her. She had taken up the cudgel to make the world a better place, not just for women, but all of us, to create a better environment for the expression of all that was genuine.

I put my arm around her and held her close. She purred with delight and continued purring as she turned around to melt into me. With our lips together, we explored and petted each other, and reassured each other. The threat of someone walking in on us heightened each sensation, shattered every reservation, and ultimately gave us the courage to put an end to the worry by repairing to the bedroom where we consummated our relationship. No one saw how clumsy and reserved we were and if someone did he'd see how each misstep helped drive us closer and closer until we were one.

CHAPTER 12

We became inseparable. Much to her parents' consternation we became engaged and I proceeded to set myself up as a gadfly.

Caving to Springer's insistence, I cashed the weekly Workmen's Compensation checks they set up for me, learning how powerful the addiction to receiving free money was. It enabled me to help establish a rape crisis center; author articles about the oil industry; and, when Leslie's parents quit paying her tuition, orchestrated investigations with the Public Interest Research Group on whether Tulane students were charged too much for their education. I just had to make sure not to be too physically active, lest an insurance detective was taking pictures.

That my literary efforts were rejected only fired my resolve. Nobody seemed interested in my take on the oil industry, now that I'm a friggin' expert about it. I wanted to change people's perception of it, how remarkable the technology was, what credit to human intelligence it was, and how susceptible it was to human foibles. Editors who either did not read them, or included in my self-addressed envelopes the excuse they did not fit their current needs proved they wanted people to remain ignorant. Nobody, not even "Reader's Digest" was interested--and I sent them the most arousing account about the blow-out possible.

The "Morale Equivalent of War" had gone the way of Billy Beer. It was amazing how quickly people had forgotten about gas lines and fuel shortages.

The dreary rejection of the masterpieces tailored for local readers (those who had at least seen rigs) could only be explained by the fear publishers harbored toward local and state officials. A state where ex-governors didn't have to present winning bids to be awarded lease rights to drill in state waters is a state with an ethos that doesn't take kindly to reformers. Stories about government agents being shot during crackdowns on state employees working on the private properties of their bosses appeared in the back pages. Still, there had to be one publisher who wasn't scared, who wanted to make a difference.

Only against the Greeks did my efforts make an impact. The speeches I wrote for Leslie received rave reviews. The "Hullabaloo" and *Times-Picayune* printed snippets of them. Channel Six once ran a sound bite of her reading one of my most purple passages.

As for my mates, I visited Mamou the Weenie Washer, Spud, and Turtle before ennui set in, when I'd call and write instead. They proved to be genial hosts, thrilled to see me. The shaker hand-treated me to the chicken fights in Maurice, where we got to see Popcorn's one-eyed Popeye in action. Spud drove me to Penny's "World Renown Taxidermy Emporium (We Mount Everything)" near Columbia, Mississippi, where I got to eat a meal prepared by his new wife, Kathy. And I got blind drunk on Budweiser with Turtle. He was a "Bud Man and Saints fan."

I ran into Dennis when I passed up Houma's Carriage House for a night of local color at the run-down Pilgrim's Hotel.

"Got it made," he smiled a crooked smile. His bloodshot eyes remained weary. "Run an elevator for ten a day on top of room and board. Had me a time with my settlement check."

"Like a limp dick, can't beat it," I replied.

"Save your shibboleths for the rig."

"As insightful as you are it's a mystery why you haven't become a companyman," I said, scratching his itch in middle-class English.

"Life isn't fair."

Wrong, Dennis, I reflected. *You reap what you sow.* At least, he did, as he showed me his one-room efficiency. I did notice he spent more time showing me his microwave oven than his eclectic library. We parted with him condescendingly draping his arm on my shoulder and wishing me well. I noticed he did not ask me to see him again.

You reap what you sow, I recalled as Karen told me what kind of sentence Father was looking at.

"Ten years for pleading guilty," Karen blurted out in my apartment after trying to be more decorous. "Ten years, not counting what the Feds are going to pile on. What he did was wrong, but it wasn't that wrong."

It dawned on me she was ignorant of the Louisiana way of doing business. It had been steeped in my bones since I could remember. That my family refused to go along with it is what made me proud of them.

"Father is paying dearly not for what he had done but for being out of the loop," I said, calmly helping her sit on the couch "One has to do more than make a profit here. One has to establish a network of people who owe you favors." She concentrated on what I was saying. "The policy he had of not sucking up to police juries, commissioners, prosecutors, and judges is going to be his downfall. Those he hacked off by not offering bribes are going to show the public how wrong it is to offer bribes."

"My company encountered the same thing in Mexico."

"Yeah, business is a lot more than giving out customer satisfaction surveys." I then told her about Walt Disney, and how he once considered building Disney World in New Orleans East. "One dose of the way we do things here and he was gone."

"Unless you're prepared for martyrdom or have an army on your side you've got to deal with the world as it is," Robert advised. "I used to get all worked up over the difference between reality and appearances until I found Immanuel Kant."

"Who said it was okay to be confused," I said.

He looked at both of us. "Let's get a beer. I'm buying."

Pints of foreign lager and ale at Cooter Brown's might have numbed Karen and I but they made Robert voluble. And when he got voluble he sometimes made sense, or at least was interesting.

After a great deal of bantering Robert affixed a compassionate look at me. I braced for anything and was glad we were in a poorly lit booth.

"You've been dutifully following your *dharma*," he said sincerely. "You fulfilled your duty to your family, yourself, and God, who's probably enjoying the show. You have made your *Vaisyas* caste proud." He knocked back a big slug. "You proved respect for all living things, your *ahimsa*. Even did the Gandhi thing, used your *moksa*, the state of liberation you reached, for political reasons. And still, nothing seems to be going right." He leaned back, reflectively. "So we have to change tact."

I couldn't wait to hear what that tact was. Karen smirked with amusement.

"I know all about your John Locke and Adam Smith beliefs. But maybe something can go awry if you overemphasize individuality. Even the Scottish economist warned about too much of it."

"Be Buddhist? I do yoga," Karen said.

"Why not? Give up personal desires to be part of a suffering reality which we can rise above."

I never heard Robert repeat anything by rote. It gave me pause. But I decided to humor him.

"Think of the self as an illusion?" Karen rhetorically asked, beating me to it.

"I know it's a stretch, but just try the Buddha's path, free yourself from the world and its cravings. Maybe that way you can reach enlightenment."

"You mean fake it until I make it?" I asked.

"Except you don't care if you make it."

"Hey, even the gods suffer."

So with nothing to lose I wrote down the steps of the "Eightfold Path" the "Awakened One" claimed would free one from one's self and one's cravings in order to reach enlightenment (where we might find out how to help Father and put the powers-that-be in their place).

"Promise you'll check them off as you go," Robert said as we slid out of the booth. It may be sacrilege, the gods may be displeased, but I promised. Who knows, maybe a new way of thinking will help me think of new things.

"Insanity is doing the same thing over and over even though it doesn't work," I said.

"There's a reason Buddhism stood the test of time," our Doctor Pangloss said, getting into the car.

All four of us employed the eight-step program. We needed to. We needed the right effort to find new lawyers to handle our case once the firm we started with realized we probably wouldn't have much to pay even if Father was acquitted. Then, when we found them, we needed the right mindset to deal with them. They weren't top-drawer, to say the least. We certainly engaged in the right lifestyle, not by choice but by necessity (though we wouldn't have been extravagant if we could).

Life soon forced us to engage in the right thinking. Soon after Christmas my workmen's comp ran out, just in time to catch the most incredible collapse in drilling in history. By spring only two thousand rigs were under contract compared to four thousand five hundred a few months before. Hopes to return to work were nil. Robert lost his job and was lucky to apprentice himself to a subcontractor, learning how to lay tile and put up a dry wall. When Karen's company pulled out of the territory, she joined Leslie's waiting tables at the Red Rose on Tchoupitoulas. Proving we were right acting, we moved to a cheap apartment on Magazine, right in front of a bus stop and close to the flat Lee Harvey Oswald had rented. I hired on at various local businesses, pushing pizzas and waiting tables. The harassments weren't half as vexing as roughnecking. I didn't have to terminate my employment at New York Pizza and Que Sera. The managers wanted me to stay. They said I handled all the pranks the frats pulled very well, such as refusing to take a call-out order for twenty large pizzas and denying service to a table of rowdies. I also engaged in right speaking by fending off those I couldn't avoid with clever retorts or by not saying anything at all. But the incidents kept adding up, interfering with business, and I didn't want to be a burden.

The Greeks did me a favor by pursuing me across the metropolitan area, pretending to be interested in the cars I hawked at Benson Ford and the supplies I sold at Stat Office World. Miss Green was thrilled to include anecdotes of their harassment in her articles.

We all engaged in the right meditation by letting Karen teach us yoga.

The only time I veered from the path was when I manned the crisis phone line. I'm sure my frustration at honoring Eddie's courage in such a minor way was part of the reason I snapped at the first Wiseacre male caller.

"You try to bite my ear off you might end up with a mouthful of skin that used to be on my backside," said a vaguely recognizable voice. "Grafted my hinney on to places that show so I don't scare nobody."

I quickly returned to the path and practiced the eighth step, the one about right seeing (or hearing, to be accurate) "June Melveaux?" I asked.

"That's the guy."

"Why would I want to talk to you?" I wanted to ensure he was being serious.

"Why? It's not often you get to talk to a crustacean, man to crawfish."

"Crawfish?" I asked although I knew what he meant.

"A fellow who says one thing and later crawls sideways on that what he says."

He elaborated in the break room of the small office a half-hour later, looking gaunt, and a little deformed. His ruggedly handsome face was just rugged. He wore a wig.

"I look like I am, for the first time in my life," he conceded. "I'm not all that pretty inside."

"Rotten to the core?"

He admitted how he had known who I was, and what I was doing all along. "A mud bug got senses all over himself. He knows when something is scratching to get him."

"Why didn't you run me off then?"

"What, and let you get to thinking you could get the information you want sweet talking the secretaries in the office. They gots photocopies of everything."

"Are there copies floating around?"

"All the evidence a blind Columbo needs is in the files some real pretty women keep in good order. Wining and dining with them would have been more fun than working offshore. They're better lookin' than rig hands. And smell a whole lot better, I guarantee."

I mentioned how easily Robert would have accomplished the mission.

"You underestimate yourself. Lack confidence. Anyways, are you good with computers, a golfer?"

"You mean a hacker?"

"That's it. If you are you could have gotten what you wanted without having to touch a tong, throw a chain, or break any hearts. Springer just started using them two years ago. Still swapping over."

Again, remembering Father's injunction about this particular point in a negotiation, I sealed my lips. "Whoever speaks next loses" was the operative phrase that directed my actions.

"So you wondered why I called?" June asked after a full thirty seconds of silence.

"It did cross my mind."

"As they say, cross a Coon Ass and you got an enemy for life. Make a friend of him and he'll give you his traps, his wife, his lugger, whatever you want," he said. "I guess the point is I went ahead and done something you're going to like." He spoke in a quiet voice.

"Don't be too sure."

"I did something that might get me into a bind."

"Good."

"The big shots in the government got more good on me than just the money I took from Springer."

"Am I supposed to be worried?" I asked. I'm sure I was as transparent as the Invisible Man.

"I knew you cared. If you didn't you wouldn't have done what you did for me."

"I'd have saved Ronnie or Hammer."

"But you didn't."

"I didn't have to. Besides, I was only being fair. You risked your life for us on the rig floor, staying as long as you did."

"Doing my job."

"What good are you going to be to Father, anyway? No matter what you think you can get away with with the Feds, Springer is going to make an example of you. I'm sure that superintendent has got the red ass."

"I bet I'm going to do a lot of good. I got my father's brains and my mother's charm, and with the two, struck a deal with all the main springs I talked to. You see, I agreed to spill the beans on folks who got a lot more beans than me if they let me and Roger off easy."

"They agreed?"

"Of course, they agreed. When I say I know where a lot of beans are, I mean a lot."

"You in a witness protection program?"

"Who, I leave my ranch and stable?"

"Quarter horses?"

"Women."

"You don't quit," I said.

"That's why I'm staying. More stubborn than moss. Can't help it. It's in my blood. Being run off once was enough for my people. Our feet are firmly planted in the swamps."

"Up to your necks."

"That way no one will notice us."

"Make sure nobody kicks you accidentally. I risked my butt for your hide," I said.

"I keep my eyes just out of the water, like a big ol' gator."

Accepting the fact I lacked his wit I didn't try to match it. Instead, I remarked how I'd prefer to remain in the dark about his machinations.

"I'm a lousy liar," I explained.

He put his hand on my shoulder. "This world would be a lot better place if everybody was a lousy liar. The trouble with the world is there too many who are good at it."

"So you going to keep doing it?"

"Not me, not anymore. The trouble with good liars is they keep lying when they get caught. They only have one talent."

"Or maybe they're so talented they believe their lies."

He put both hands on my shoulder. "Not doing that is the biggest talent of them all." I suddenly became capable of looking at his alien, featureless, face. "It's not for only you I want to do right. I want to see if I can do it, see if I'm not too far gone."

"You just proved your honesty." I wanted to embrace him but rejected it in favor of a handshake even my wrestling coach would have said was unnecessarily strong. I didn't want to intimidate. I wanted to convey a lifetime of welled-up sensibilities. And he reciprocated. But he needed both hands to do it.

June did a good job proving to himself he could be honest. After months of frustration, Father's appeal finally was ruled in our favor. We all were thankful for the suspended sentence he received. And we did a little gloating about the police jurors, commissioners, and officers of large independent oil and service companies who were indicted on an average of nine charges each.

"They would have been accused of more, but who would the prosecutors hunt and fish with if they went up the river for more than a year or two?" Robert explained.

Nothing happened to June. He was the "source" mentioned in the articles about "Sources led investigators...."

Leslie and I married in a double ceremony with Father and Karen. We set up housekeeping together on the second floor of a Victorian mansion the landlady had allowed to become entered into the National Registry.

Leslie graduated in biology and took a job at the local Department of Agriculture Research Center near City Park. I followed suit in Petroleum Engineering at the University of New Orleans. In Eddie's honor, I threw myself into the crisis center as it grew to include services besides rape counseling. The entire mood of Tulane and all of local society was shifting. Sure, it had tried to diminish what had proved to be an embarrassing incident, but it was becoming caring and concerned, if not all that reflective and regretful. It was fun to be in the vanguard of a movement, with Leslie sitting in on committees that reviewed the fraternities' behavior, me writing articles people read, and both of us spending our free time together, reveling in the fact we were contributing.

We weren't the only ones. Karen became a buyer for Wal-Mart. With her steady income and Robert successfully doing contract work on mansions, Father and I felt confident enough to start a consulting business (like everyone else out of a real job). We instructed companies on how to be more efficient. Just in case, we also leased equipment and ran a hotshot company to transport it. As we figured, as times got tighter and company inventories of tools shrank, well-by-well contracts proliferated. Long-term planning became a pipe dream. Managers would demand the special equipment we provided ASAP, which was fine with us, as they inevitably figured the best way to cut costs was to do without our expensive advice. Unlike many others, we survived the vagaries of the industry, at times employing over fifty, other times, a mere half dozen.

And we didn't have much trouble with our employees, as I took what I learned from June, Jim, Sunshine, Bull, and Hammer to be a consistent, fair, honest boss they knew not to pull any nonsense on. At least I hoped I was.

Then in 1986 Sheik Yamani became fed up with supporting the price of oil and released into the market millions more barrels a day. When Saudi Arabia reached its OPEC quota all the hopes and dreams of our already crippled industry crashed into the despair of ten dollars a barrel crude. The oil-producing states tumbled into a depression.

But lest I dismiss Robert's belief in karma as juvenile he brought word of an event that restored my faith.

"Sam, that master thespian, was above average," Robert said as he burst into our place while the rest of our extended family ate dinner. "He knew the pipe yard was in heap big trouble when they put a tiger in their tank."

Being a gentleman, Robert let me translate to the women what he meant. In addition to explaining that he was referring to the arrogant reputation of Exxon, I added how every major had its defining personality. "For instance, Chevron's white-bread yuppies and Texaco's a bunch of good ol' boys," I said.

"That lob who had Eddie wasted, he got him," Robert continued. "Don or no Don, it didn't matter to those who make more than the GNP of most countries. Bled your pipe yard dry wanting free services and not letting it take on other customers.

"That mafioso got tired of pumping money from his real businesses to keep that laundry open. So what does he do? He does some creative accounting so he can pay off more jocks to fix races. The trouble was, that some of them didn't want to fix more races and ratted on him.

"The D.A. indicted him the same day Exxon found out he had cooked the books. He found out an oil company can be as hard-ass as any compare'. They not only dumped him then and there they sicced their lawyers on him so no one who had anything to do with him could buy the yard."

"Did Eddie have anything to do with this?" Leslie asked.

"What do you think got the D.A. interested in the first place, and gave those jocks the cajonnas to squeal?"

That none of this appeared in the paper said volumes about what a coup it was.

We all clanked glasses in honor of our little stooper.

In the ensuing months of more and more failing businesses and economic despair no one else bought it, even for back taxes (which encouraged Father and I to plan to do just that whenever we scrapped together the money and sweet-talked enough bankers).

Visiting it was cathartic for me, like returning to boot camp would be for a veteran. The dilapidated buildings and weeds were like the ruins of a lost civilization. Saying it was the end of my innocence wasn't quite right. The end of my ignorance was better. It was where I fell out of my sedan chair and mucked around with the natives, where my prissy outlook and soft hands had hardened under relentless pressure. It was where I had met real people, became a Captain Courageous, and became a damn good worker, too.

I made a point to stop at a greasy spoon on the way back. Sometimes I'd find folks interested in working for us. And sometimes, I'd pick up hints on how to make money, such as driving someone's car to Atlanta and towing an empty U-haul back with a vehicle someone needed to drive to New Orleans. Every available U-haul had been driven out of town; none were being driven into town.

Sometimes it netted serendipitous rewards. The eatery I stopped at on General DeGaulle in Gretna offered one such memorable encounter. It was there I spotted Kimberly, my dear ex-stepmother, tending the counter. Her diligence was commendable, scuttling from customer to customer with a concern on her face that was positively professional. Her demeanor camouflaged her looks. One had to stare at her to see the curves her uniform concealed. Call me impressionable, but I found her more alluring now, with no décolleté, and grease stains where strings of pearls once hung. The dime-store baubles that replaced the expensive jewelry Father had insisted she festoons on herself gave her a more wholesome look.

Still, it was the athleticism she displayed performing the precise movements of her trade that attracted me most. I didn't know she had it in her. She probably didn't know she had it in her. And she kept up her fevered pace all the while holding several conversations with much less nasal vacuousness than I remembered.

No doubt the collapse of the oil, real estate, and savings and loan industries had dried up the pool of sugar daddies, forcing the local Kimberly's to go to work.

"That girl works her buns off," my waitress said when I mentioned her. "Works graveyard shift at Denny's when she gets off here."

"Good worker?" I asked.

"One of the best. Must of learned all the right habits, had good parents, real conscientious, if you know what I mean."

I certainly did, I thought.

Getting up to pay my bill, I couldn't help but run into her. As I did, Heavy Duty's twin made an oblique proposition to her.

"I deserve better than you," she scolded, shrugging him off.

"You know you do," I told her.

"We all do," she insisted.

The conviction in her voice was so compelling I hugged her. Realizing who I was, she hugged me back.

"I missed you," she said.

"And I missed you," I responded.

"Let's not let that happen again," we said simultaneously.

Laughing, I knew a miracle had taken place. I respected her and realized she respected me. Unbelievable.

ABOUT THE AUTHOR

I'm a Yankee who became a damn Yankee when I wouldn't leave the South. When I did leave, it was overseas, where I comfortably acquired the moniker of "Yank". I have two bachelor's degrees. The one in geology I used to support myself, the one in history showed I am curious about human nature. This curiosity culminated in *Thunder in the Wind* after I found out about a Cree named Almighty Voice while I was engaged in geologic fieldwork in Montana. His revolt almost united the tribes, as had Pontiac's and Tecumseh's before him. I was predisposed to write about Indians as, being from Northwest Indiana, I grew up on their lore and history. I even achieved the rank of Eagle Boy Scout, where my advancement mirrored the age societies of most tribes. I defended Kansas from the communists as a 1st Lieutenant in the Army and was a junior golf champion who got to play with the University of Houston golf team. I've been a journalist and wrote copious op-eds, dozens of short stories, and at least 10 books, mostly fiction. I've put four up for sale. *Thunder in the Wind* won a Best Western award. I am a member of the Writers Guild of America Divorced, I supported myself as an oilfield geologist, often overseas.